THE FACE OF AIR

Something flickered at the edge of the overman's vision. Garth whirled and saw a blurry redness hanging in mid-air and glowing faintly. As he watched, the thing suddenly resolved itself into the image of a face—a not quite human face, twisted and sneering, with curving fangs protruding from its upper lip.

"Aghad!" Garth recognized the face of the god of hatred and vengeance he had seen carved on the small idols in the Dûsarran markets.

The thing grinned. "Greetings, Garth. Would you care to guess whom we plan to kill next? Will it be another of your wives? One of your children? Or perhaps we'll kill one of your friends here in Skelleth. Will you guess—or just wait and see?"

Garth hacked at the thing with his sword, splitting it.

The face grinned again and vanished completely, with a sound of fading laughter.

The
BOOK
of
SILENCE

Book Four of *The Lord of Dûs*

Lawrence Watt-Evans

A Del Rey Book

BALLANTINE BOOKS • NEW YORK

A Del Rey Book
Published by Ballantine Books

Copyright © 1984 by Lawrence Watt-Evans

Library of Congress Catalog Card Number: 83-91130

ISBN 0-345-30880-4

Manufactured in the United States of America

First Edition: January 1984

Cover art by Darrell K. Sweet

Dedicated to
Mary Ellen Curtin,
even though her suggestions
have been modified
beyond recognition.

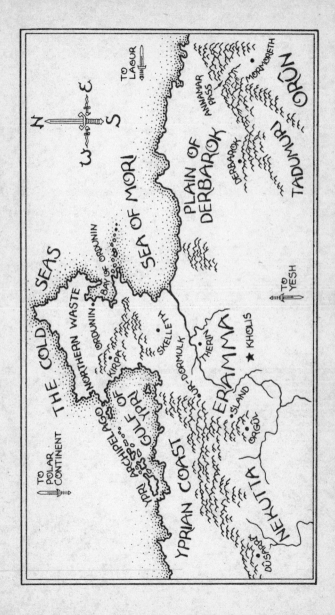

CHAPTER ONE

The last caravan had departed ten days before, and the next was not expected for at least a fortnight. Skelleth's market lay still and almost empty in the watery sunlight of early spring. No merchants or farmers disturbed its silence, though a few loafers and strolling pedestrians were in sight. On the east side of the square, the door of the new Baron's house was closed, indicating that its occupants were not to be disturbed. Garth, one of only two overmen still in Skelleth, sat in the King's Inn, staring out the window at the lifeless market, with nothing to distract him from his own sour mood and gloomy thoughts.

No news had come down from the Northern Waste since the last snows had melted. That meant that Garth had received no word of his family, nor a report about his latest petition to the City Council of Ordunin, asking that his sentence of banishment from the Waste be revoked. He was still an exile from his homeland, stranded in Skelleth for lack of anywhere better to go.

From the overman's point of view, Skelleth was not a particularly pleasant place to dwell, but it did have certain advantages. First, it was on the border, the closest human habitation to his native city of Ordunin; therefore, his family could visit him more easily here than elsewhere, and his petitions and letters to the Council could be delivered more quickly.

1

Second, he was on good terms with the local rulers. Saram, Baron of Skelleth, before being elevated to his present position, had been the closest thing Garth had to a human friend. The Baroness Frima was the only other person who might possibly be considered for that title; Garth had brought her to Skelleth himself, after rescuing her from a sacrificial altar in her native city of Dûsarra. It was he who had introduced Frima to her husband.

Furthermore, the treasurer and Minister of Trade was the former master trader, Galt of Ordunin, the only other overman still in Skelleth. Garth had brought him down from the Waste to aid in opening trade between Skelleth and Ordunin. That trade was flourishing now, despite the fact that Galt, like Garth, was under sentence of exile.

Third, although the local populace did not, in general, like or trust Garth, it had learned to accept his presence. The people of other human towns might not be so accommodating. Three centuries had passed since the Racial Wars between human and overman had dwindled away to nothing, but hatred, Garth knew, could linger long after its cause was forgotten.

Fourth, at least at the moment, Skelleth was at peace—and that was an increasingly rare distinction. Although the news from the lands to the south and east and west tended to be muddled and sometimes contradictory, Garth knew well that most of the world was at war. No one, including the Eramman barons themselves, seemed to have a clear idea which side any given baron was on in any given war; yet by all accounts, that uncertainty had not impeded the fighting one whit. The greater wars provided the excuse for settling old border squabbles or for simple raiding and looting. The civil war in Eramma, begun almost three years earlier when the Baron of Sland rebelled against the High King at Kholis and declared him to be a false king and foul usurper, had settled down into an apathetic lack of cooperation after Sland had been defeated in a long and messy battle. The war between Eramma and Orûn, which had been launched by the opportunistic King of Orûn in hopes of taking advantage of Eramma's seeming dissolution, appeared to have reached a bloody stalemate along a front somewhere to the southeast of Skelleth. Despite the justification of an ancient border dispute, the war was not popular in Orûn and had created such discontent that there were now rumors of impending civil war in that land as well.

Vague reports came in of wars in the western realm of Nekutta, though no one seemed to know who was fighting whom, and no word at all reached Skelleth from Mara, Amag, Tadumuri, Yesh, or the other lands of the far south.

A possible fifth reason for Garth to stay was a result of the fact that Skelleth was peaceful and in a far happier state under Saram than it had ever been under his predecessor. With so many of the world's trade routes disrupted by war and insurrection, Skelleth's very worthlessness had helped to make it a center of commerce. No conqueror in his right mind would bother with so desolate a piece of land, so far from all the traditional caravan roads; that left Saram and his patchwork government free to pursue untraditional trade wholeheartedly and unhindered. The merchants of Skelleth, with their lord's active encouragement, dealt impartially with the men of Eramma, the overmen of the Northern Waste, and the mixed society of the Yprian Coast. With no assets but peace, a willingness to trade, and a manageable location, the town had grown prosperous for the first time in mortal memory.

It had also, in Garth's opinion, grown placid and boring.

No one else seemed to share his feeling. Galt was too busy buying and selling, planning new routes and new methods, or setting prices and taxes and tariffs to be bored. He had become far wealthier than any other overman since the Racial Wars, yet he appeared interested only in expanding trade, enriching the treasury, and acquiring still greater wealth.

Saram seemed content to enjoy the rewards of his new position as Baron while others did the work. He held elaborate feasts to greet every new envoy or caravan master, dressing himself in fine furs and embroidery—overman work, imported from Ordunin—and growing steadily plumper, thus losing the trim fighting form he had had when he served as a lieutenant in the guard under the last hereditary Baron of Skelleth.

Frima didn't appear to mind her husband's added weight. She had arrived in Skelleth with nothing; even the clothes on her back had been borrowed from Garth. She had been no one of importance, a tinker's daughter who worshipped the night-goddess Tema and was kidnapped by the rival cult of Sai, goddess of pain. Garth had rescued her and brought her to Skelleth against her will, leaving Dûsarra, long the greatest city of Nekutta, devastated by fire and plague. He had not wanted the inconvenience of caring for her and had turned her over to Saram. That had led to their marriage, and thus to her present position as Baroness. She seemed far more grateful to Saram, who had taken her in, than to Garth, who had saved her life. Though she still treated Garth as a friend, her primary interests in life now were pleasing Saram and enjoying their sudden wealth. Despite certain disappointments—her only child so far, a son, had been born dead—she was happy. She did not find her new station at all tedious or boring.

The other humans of the village might have been bored, but Garth ignored them entirely. They, in turn, avoided him for the most part. They could not forget that it was Garth who had murdered the old Baron some thirty months earlier, Garth who had led a company of overmen in the sacking and burning of the village. Men, women, and children had died. All the Baron's guardsmen had perished except the disgraced Saram, who had been removed from the guard for refusing to kill Garth in a previous confrontation. It had been this elimination of all other candidates, rather than any real qualifications for the job, that had made Saram the new Baron of Skelleth.

Galt had gradually been accepted and forgiven; his part in the battle had been small, and his trader's expertise had so benefited the village since its reconstruction that he was now something of a hero. Garth, however, remained an outcast.

At first there had been others among the surviving overmen who had chosen to stay in Skelleth after its destruction, and even after the rebuilding had been completed, but they had gradually drifted away with the passing months. Some had returned home to the Northern Waste and been pardoned for their part in the attack, though the Council steadfastly refused to pardon Galt and Garth, the two supposed leaders. A few had gone to explore the Yprian Coast and had not returned. One had been sent a special envoy to the court of the High King at Kholis, whom Skelleth's government still recognized as the rightful lord of all Eramma.

At one point there had been talk of using the overmen as the nucleus of a new company of guardsmen, but nothing had come of it; Skelleth had no military at all at present, save for the handful of warbeasts that the overmen had brought. The great animals were now tended by a special contingent of the Baron's staff, an entirely human contingent. Garth believed this to be the first time in history that warbeasts had been under human care.

He had considered demanding that he be put in charge of the creatures, on the grounds that it was not fitting for warbeasts to be tended by mere men and women, but he had never actually done so. He had feared that he would be turned down, as he had been turned down for every other duty in Skelleth. To be refused a position as a keeper of beasts would be too much for his pride; he preferred not to risk it. There had been enough blows to his self-esteem already.

The aversion to his presence that the townspeople displayed did not bother him; he was accustomed to it, could understand it, and furthermore cared very little for the opinions of most humans. There were, however, other matters.

His three wives, one by one, had come to Skelleth to see him, once the City Council had revoked his chief wife Kyrith's house arrest, imposed for her part in the sacking of Skelleth. Each had come, but each had refused to give up her home in Ordunin to join him in exile.

His children had visited as well, accompanying trading caravans, but he had not even troubled himself to ask them to stay; they were old enough to fend for themselves and make their own homes without his meddling.

Overmen did not have the strong family ties that humans had, but the triple rejection by his wives, and the failure of any of his five offspring to volunteer to settle in Skelleth, still hurt.

The City Council had refused petition after petition, so that he could not rejoin his wives in Ordunin. The councillors had, in truth, not even taken the time to consider his requests; they were too busy trying to deal with the worsening depredations of human pirates along their coasts and could spare no time from that obsession to discuss clemency for a troublesome renegade prince. Garth had tried to argue, by proxy, that he had fought pirates before and could be of sufficient value in fighting them again to make his pardon a real public benefit, but the Council had continued to ignore him nonetheless.

Things had started to go wrong when he found the so-called Sword of Bheleu in Dûsarra. Until then, his word had been good and his actions his own—but at his first sight of the weapon, he had begun to lose control. He had taken it from the altar of Bheleu, god of destruction, without any conscious decision to do so, and thereafter had been seized every so often by fits of what appeared to be a form of bloodthirsty madness. He had gradually come to realize, though, that some external power was possessing him, using the sword as a conduit. Even knowing that, he had been unable to free himself.

As the power had gained in influence and clarity, it had declared itself to him, claiming to be Bheleu himself, come to assert his dominance over the dawning Fourteenth Age, the Age of Destruction, through his chosen mortal host.

Garth had declined to serve willingly as host to the god, if god it truly was. His refusal had done little good; the god had controlled him anyway, and he had been unable to put down the sword.

While under the sway of the god and his sword, Garth had slain the previous Baron of Skelleth and destroyed much of the village.

In the days that had followed, as he became more aware of the sword's nature and seemingly limitless magical power, his companions had grown to trust him less and less. That had been the period when Skelleth's new government had taken shape, and Garth had been excluded on the basis of the madness the weapon had induced. He had not argued with that decision; he had been conscious of his own erratic behavior and therefore had been far more concerned with freeing himself of Bheleu's control than with village politics.

The sword was a magnificent weapon, a great two-handed broadsword with an immense red gem in its pommel. It was supernaturally indestructible, able to cut through stone or metal with ease, and could control the elements, summon or disperse storms, even shake the very earth. It gloried in fire and could burn in a hundred strange ways without being consumed. Had it not been under the evil aegis of Bheleu, dedicated to wanton destruction, Garth would have been proud to be the chosen wielder of such a thing.

As it was, though, he had wanted nothing but to free himself and he had at last done so. He no longer had the sword. The sword alone had been responsible for his madness, so that with its loss he was himself again; for these two years and several months past, he had been as sane and trustworthy as ever in his life, yet he was still not allowed to hold any post in Skelleth's little bureaucracy for fear he would again turn berserk. He resented this exclusion.

Perhaps the deepest hurt to his pride and self-esteem, however, was a personal matter, one closely tied to the malevolent power of the Sword of Bheleu and to his freedom from that power. The voice of the professed god of destruction had told him that he, Garth, had been born to serve Bheleu; indeed, he alone had been able to wield the sword, and on his own he had been utterly unable to resist its hold.

He had not freed himself alone.

Just to the north of its market square, Skelleth had an ancient tavern called the King's Inn, and in this tavern dwelt an old man who called himself the Forgotten King. It was the presence of this individual that, more then anything else, made Skelleth a center for important events.

Garth was not entirely sure whether, on balance, the King's presence was good or bad.

He had originally come to Skelleth seeking the King, because an oracle had told him that only the Forgotten King could grant him the eternal fame he had, at that time, thought he wanted. He had returned to Skelleth a second time, after getting over that particular aberration of desire, because the King had pointed out the possibility of trade. He had gone to Dûsarra at the behest of the mysterious old man and had brought back Frima, now the Baroness, as well as the Sword of Bheleu and the knowledge of trading prospects on the Yprian Coast. His life, and the influence he had upon Skelleth, seemed to have been inextricably linked to the old man since Garth first left Ordunin.

In Dûsarra he had learned something of the King's history; the old man was apparently the one true high priest of the god of death, the chosen of The God Whose Name Is Not Spoken, just as Garth was the chosen of Bheleu. As such, the King could not die; he had lived through several ages and now desired nothing but the death that was denied him.

In pursuit of his own destruction, the Forgotten King had sent Garth on several errands. He sought to perform some great suicidal magic; from various clues, Garth had tentatively decided that the old man hoped to manifest the Death-God himself in the mortal world, so that the King might renounce the bargain made so long ago. The problem was that the proposed magic, whether Garth had correctly determined its nature or not, would involve many deaths, by the King's own admission. Garth did not care to contribute to unnecessary deaths and had therefore refused to aid the King further.

Then, though, the Sword of Bheleu had possessed him, and there was no power Garth could find that could free him from it, save the power of the strange old man. Of all the Lords of Dûs, the dark gods, only the god of death was more powerful than the god of destruction; thus only the chosen of the Final God, in his own right perhaps the most powerful wizard who had ever lived, could break the link between Bheleu and his chosen one.

To free himself, therefore, Garth had sworn to aid the Forgotten King. He had promised to fetch for him the final item needed to complete his magic, an object of great arcane power that he called the Book of Silence. Garth had sworn that oath knowing he had no intention of keeping it, and the suppressed knowledge that he was an oathbreaker, a being devoid of honor, in thought if not yet in deed, had gnawed upon him ever since.

As an injured man would probe at an open wound, fascinated by the pain, Garth found himself haunting the King's Inn and watching the Forgotten King for hours on end. The King had told him, when first he swore his oath, that he was free to roam, as long as he checked back every so often. The old man had not yet told him where the mysterious Book of Silence might be found; he said that he had left it somewhere, centuries ago, and was trying to recall where. When he did remember, Garth would be sent to retrieve it. Until the memory returned, Garth could do as he pleased.

There was nothing else, however, that he felt any need to do, and so he stayed in Skelleth, alternately wandering aimlessly through the streets and sitting silently somewhere, glowering at the village, as he now sat in the King's Inn and glowered at the quiet marketplace.

The Forgotten King was there as well, seated at his usual table. His presence there, at almost any time the tavern was open for business, was so reliable that he was thought of by the villagers not so much as a regular patron, but as a permanent fixture, like the dark wooden paneling of the walls or the heavy oaken tables. Day after day the old man sat alone, unmoving and silent, in the back corner beneath the stairs, wrapped in his ragged yellow mantle, his face hidden by his tattered cowl.

As he had a hundred times before, Garth turned away from the window and its view of the square and stared instead at the ancient human.

The King gave no sign that he was aware of the overman's scrutiny, but Garth had no doubt that he knew he was being watched.

Half a dozen more ordinary humans were in the tavern and they had all certainly noticed the overman's presence. Most had seen him turn away from the window as well. Overmen were unmistakable, and highly distinctive in Skelleth. Garth's size, quite aside from any other details, marked him as something different from the common run of humanity; he stood almost seven feet in height, but was so heavily muscled as to look almost squat. He dwarfed the chair he sat upon and seemed out of proportion with the entire taproom, though in truth he was of only average size among his own species. His eyes were large and red, the oversized irises bright blood-red, though his pupils were as round and black as any human's. Unlike human eyes, no white showed, only black pupil and red iris.

His hair was dead straight, dead black, coarse, and thick; it reached his shoulders and no farther, though he had never cut it. Sparse black fur covered his entire body, save his hands and feet and face. Where no hair or fur hid it, his skin was leathery brown hide, like that of no other species that ever existed and certainly unlike anything human.

His face was as beardless as a woman's; overmen grew no facial hair, and his body fur stopped well short of his chin. His cheeks were sunken by human standards, normal to his own kind. He had no nose, but two close-set slit nostrils. To human

eyes, a healthy overman bore an unsettling resemblance to a
human skull; the hollow cheeks, missing nose, great red eyes,
high forehead, and hairless jaw all contributed.

Garth's hands, too, were unlike a human's. Rather than
having a single thumb at one side, his hands had both the first
and fifth fingers opposable, making possible acts of manipulation that humans had trouble even imagining.

It was hardly surprising that men and women feared overmen, as they feared anything that seemed monstrous and strange.
Nor was it startling, therefore, that the other patrons of the
King's Inn should glance occasionally in Garth's direction,
wary of what he might do. Garth in particular, of all overmen,
they feared; the possibility of a new berserk rage such as those
brought on by the Sword of Bheleu was always at the back of
the villagers' minds.

When he turned away from the window, therefore, to look
across the taproom at the yellow-clad figure at the back table,
what little conversation there had been faded and died. The
townspeople watched, to be sure that the overman was not
looking at any of them.

Garth rose, and even the rustling of clothes and the bumping
of chairs ceased.

His gaze wandered for a moment from the old man to the
great barrels of beer and ale along the western wall. His mug
was empty; he picked it up, made his way through the tables
and chairs, and drew himself a fresh pint. The innkeeper, a
plump, middle-aged man, stood nearby and silently accepted
a coin with a polite nod.

Garth sipped off the top layer of foam, then let his gaze
wander back toward the Forgotten King's table, where it settled
once more on the silent old man. Without quite knowing why,
he moved in that direction.

When he reached the table, he thumped his mug of ale down
and seated himself across from the King, as he had done so
very many times in the past three years.

"Greetings, O King," he said.

The old man said nothing.

Garth looked him over, as he also often had done. He noted
again that the old man's eyes were invisible, lost in the shadows
of his ragged yellow hood. No one, as far as Garth knew, had

ever seen the Forgotten King's eyes. A thin wisp of white beard trickled from his bony chin well down his yellow-wrapped breast. His hands lay motionless on the tabletop, things of bone and wrinkled skin more like those of a mummy than the hands of a living man. The scalloped tatters of his robe hid the rest of him from sight, so that little else could be said of his appearance with any assurance, save that he was thin and seemed tall for so aged a human, though still shorter than any grown overman.

Garth wondered, once again, why the old man wore rags and why they were always yellow. Garth had heard him referred to as the King in Yellow, so it was scarcely a temporary or recent habit, yet there seemed no reason for it. The old man had money, the overman knew, and power, yet he spent his days in this ancient inn and wore only tatters. When Garth had first sought eternal fame, the Wise Women of Ordunin had described the yellow rags to identify the Forgotten King.

Garth had long ago lost interest in the pursuit of undying glory that had originally brought him to the King; the price had been too high and the rewards, upon consideration, too intangible. He no longer had a single goal he was consciously pursuing. In fact, he did not know any more what he wanted from his life, though he was sure of certain elements. He wanted to go home. He wanted the respect of his fellows, and to be rid of the stigma he now bore of being known as subject to fits of madness. Beyond that, he was unsure.

He did know, however, that he wanted nothing from the old man, unless it was the spontaneous renunciation of his oath. The King's gifts and bargains always seemed to have unwanted strings attached; Garth's dealings with him had been full of unspoken words and hidden meanings.

Still, Garth found himself at this back-corner table more and more often.

It was, he told himself, a natural curiosity in the face of the old man's enigma that drew him, that and the lack of anything better to do. He was without family or friends and had no job to occupy his time; why should he not take an interest in such a mystery? He could speak to the old man without making bargains, without being sucked into his plotting and planning.

If the thought had ever occurred to Garth that he sought out the King because the old man, alone in all of Skelleth, had absolutely no fear of Garth or the Sword of Bheleu, he had dismissed the idea as absurd and irrelevent.

He gulped ale, then said, "Greetings, I said."

The King moved a hand, as if to wave the overman away.

Garth was not willing to be turned aside that easily. He knew something of the King's background and had some idea of his immense power, but he was not frightened. Very little could frighten Garth; he would not allow himself such weaknesses as unnecessary fears. He shrugged at the old man's gesture and drank ale.

The King sat unmoving, watching with hidden eyes.

Garth finished the contents of his mug, motioned to the tavernkeeper for more, and stared back.

The King was old, Garth knew, older than anything else that lived in the world. He had survived for more than a thousand years at the very least, perhaps for several thousand. He had been in Skelleth since its founding three centuries earlier. He could not die in the natural way of things. It was hardly surprising that his behavior should be strange.

As Garth had pieced together the story, the King, in the dim and ancient past, had made a bargain with The God Whose Name Is Not Spoken, Death himself. The King had then been a monarch in more than name, the wizard-king of the long-lost and forgotten empire of Carcosa. He had sought immortality and agreed to serve as the Final God's high priest in exchange for eternal life. In time he had come to regret his bargain and had forsaken the god's service, only to find that he was unable to die. Blades could not cut him, blows could not harm him; the petrifying gaze of a basilisk had left him untouched. He still possessed knowledge and magical power far beyond anything known since the fall of Carcosa, but he had no call to use it, for it could not get him the one thing he wanted.

One great magic could attain his death, a mighty spell requiring both the Sword of Bheleu and the Book of Silence. He had the sword, but lacked the book. Garth had sworn to fetch the book in order to be free of the sword, but he did not intend to fulfill his vow.

As far as Garth was concerned, that put an end to the matter, save for one detail. He had not been called upon to carry out his promise; he was not yet truly forsworn. He was able to maintain a pretense of honor—a pretense he knew to be false—as long as the King did not demand that he fetch the book.

The King had not made that demand yet only because he had not recalled where, several centuries earlier, he had left the book. Garth hoped that the memory was lost forever; then he might never be forced to break his sworn word.

At the same time, though, he found himself wishing that the affair were over with, that the oath were broken and done, rather than still hanging over him.

He leaned back, his chair creaking a protest beneath his inhuman weight, and could not resist asking, "Have you remembered yet, O King?" His voice was expressionless, for overmen's emotions were displayed differently from humans'. The mixture of bitterness over his false oath and anticipation of its final ruination that had prompted the question was so well hidden that Garth was not really aware of it himself.

The King said nothing; his head moved very slightly, almost imperceptibly, to one side and then back.

"You must tell me where it is, old man, if you want me to fetch it."

The King did not reply and moved not at all. Garth felt a surge of anger at this silence.

"Speak, old man," he said.

No answer came. Garth's annoyance increased.

"Has your tongue shriveled in your head, then, O throneless King? Are you trying to imitate the corpses you resemble, since you cannot rightly join them? Have you now forsaken speech, the better to serve your foul black god?" He did not shout; his voice was flat and deadly, a dangerous sign among his kind.

The Forgotten King moved slightly, as if emitting a faint sigh, but still said nothing. Garth drew breath for another question, but was distracted by the arrival of the innkeeper with a fresh mug of ale. The overman snatched it from him, swallowed half its contents at a gulp, and then ordered, "Be off, man!"

The taverner risked a glance at Garth's baleful red eyes and inhuman face, then hurried away, wondering if it would be safe to cut the overman's next serving of ale with water. He knew the signs of Garth's anger; rudeness to underlings like himself was one such indication. He did not want to worry about dealing with an overman in a drunken fury—but an overman enraged at being cheated might be equally bad. He looked at Garth's mail-covered back and decided, at least for the moment, that his reputation for honest measure and good drink was worth preserving. He could only hope that the old man would calm the overman down.

Garth was in no mood to be calmed down. When the innkeeper had moved away, he asked, "Why do you not speak? Is it perhaps that I am unfit to address you, O King of an empire long since dust, monarch of a dying memory, lord of a realm unknown? Is the Prince of Ordunin, a lord of the overmen of the Northern Waste, suited only to serve your whims, but not to speak with you? Does the master of ashes and woe, wearing rags and tatters and dwelling in a single dim room of an ancient inn, not deign to answer the exiled killer, the disgraced berserker? Will the servant of Death not choose to acknowledge the pawn of destruction?" His voice was calm, as still as water pooled on black ice, and laden with far more threat than any shout as he said, "Answer me, old man."

The old man answered. "Garth," he said in a voice like ice breaking, "why do you disturb me? You know I prefer not to waste words in idle chatter."

The overman was wrenched momentarily from his anger by the sound of the old man's voice, a sound unlike any other, dry and brittle and harsh, so unpleasant to hear that it could not fully be remembered. He regained his composure quickly, however, and replied, "Is everything I say idle chatter? Have I not the right to an answer when I ask a polite question?"

"Hardly polite," the old man demurred. "I will answer, however. No, I have not yet recalled where I left the Book of Silence in those ancient days when last I held it."

"So I must linger here, still waiting?"

"Garth," the old man replied, "you are bored, frustrated by inactivity. You are a warrior, given to violent action, not to sitting about a peaceful village. I have told you from the first that you are free to leave Skelleth and that your oath does not hold you here, as long as you return at intervals to learn whether or not I have recalled where the Book of Silence lies. Why, then, do you not find yourself some task to occupy your time, rather than remain here disturbing my contemplation?"

So long a speech was unusual for the King, and Garth knew it well. He realized that he must have seriously annoyed the old man. His own anger, however, had not faded.

"And what task shall I pursue, then? Where am I to go? I am forbidden the Northern Waste and therefore cannot aid my homeland against the human pirates who assail it. What other task awaits me? I have little taste for roaming aimlessly, particularly when the world is strewn about with wars and battles that do not concern me. I have no reason to side with any human faction and no desire to kill merely for my own amusement, so I will not join in these wars. I am welcome no place outside Skelleth. I have seen Mormoreth and left it in the hands of men who comrades I killed in self-defense; will they greet, me as an old friend? I have visited Dûsarra and left it aflame and plague-ridden, its every citizen my enemy. The other lands and cities of the south are unknown to me, and overmen are unwanted strangers throughout. Where, then, shall I go?"

"What of the Yprian Coast?"

"And what might I do there, but find another tavern wherein I might sit and be bored? I am no trader, I know that now; I have no desire to seek out new markets and new routes."

"Think you that is all that may be found there?"

"What else might there be? Farms and villages, markets and men and overmen. The caravans have told us what may be found there, and it does not interest me. Others have gone before me as well; where might I explore that they could not have preceded me?"

"Must you be first, then, as you were first in coming to Skelleth, first to think that overmen might trade here?"

"For all the good that did me, yes. What point is there in doing what has been done before?"

"I think, Garth, that you resent the ingratitude of those who have benefited from the trade you began."

"Perhaps I do, old man; what of it? Does it matter to either of us that I am scorned by those I have made wealthy? Or that my old companions allow me no responsibilities in the village I gave them? They are no concern of ours. I am sworn to aid you in your death-magic, O King; that is what concerns us. I am waiting for you to tell me how I may fulfill my oath."

"I have told you that I have not yet remembered."

"Then I must wait until you do."

"And plague me with angry questions?"

"Should I so choose, yes."

The King did not reply immediately; during the pause, Garth drank the rest of his ale and decided against ordering another.

"Garth, I would have you leave me in peace," the old man said at last, "so that I might be able to think more clearly and recall more easily what I wish to recall."

The overman shrugged. "I care little what you would have, old man. I am not sworn to heed your every whim, only to fetch your book and aid you in your magics."

"You are bored. What if I gave you a task that could harm no one, but would result in great benefit for many innocent people?"

Garth stared into the depths of his empty mug, then looked up, gazing across the table into the shadows that hid the old man's face.

"What sort of a task?"

"Slaying a dragon that has laid waste the valley of Orgûl."

Garth considered. His anger was fading, but his mind was slightly hazed with liquor. "A dragon?"

The old man nodded, once.

Garth thought it over. He *was* bored. He was irritable from inaction. It would be good to travel again, to see new places, to spend each night somewhere different from the night before. It would be good to get out of Skelleth, away from so many unpleasant memories. It would be good to accomplish something useful, and there could be little doubt that killing a dragon was useful. He had never seen a dragon, but he was familiar with the stories and legends about them. All agreed that the creatures were huge, dangerous, and phenomenally destructive. He himself had been a destroyer far too often in the past, he felt; here, then, he might find a chance to make up for some of that by destroying a menace worse than he had ever been.

In a way, it might be a step toward avenging himself on Bheleu. The god of destruction had used Garth as a puppet, and the overman resented that. He felt that it might be a small sort of retaliation to kill a creature that could be considered one of Bheleu's pets.

He nodded. The more he thought about the proposed adventure, the more it appealed to him. "I think I'd like that," he said.

The Forgotten King's mouth curved into a faint smile.

Far to the west, in a windowless chamber draped in black and dark red, a man stared at the image in his scrying glass and smiled as well. The image had been exceptionally clear and detailed, and he had been able to read the overman's lips. He had only the tail end of one side of the conversation, but it was obvious that Garth was being sent on an errand of some sort. That should provide an excellent opportunity for actions long delayed. Nearly three years had passed since the overman had defied the cult of Aghad, smashed the god's altar, and slain his high priest; much had happened during that period, but the cult had not sought vengeance. Haggat, the present high priest of Aghad, was a patient man, and had taken his time in gathering power and planning his actions. He had wanted to be sure that nothing would interfere with the proposed revenge. Now, at last, everything was ready.

He put down the glass, blew out the single candle that lighted the chamber, and went to give the order that would set the prepared machinery in motion.

CHAPTER TWO

Garth was unsure just where, amid the hills and mountains, he had crossed the border between the Eramman Barony of Sland and the independent region of Orgûl; if there were any signposts or markers, he had missed them in the dark. Shortly after dawn arrived, however, he topped the crest of the final encircling ridge to see the valley of Orgûl spread out before him, its fields and forests a thousand shades of green, its rivers gleaming blue and silver in the morning sun. He saw no traces of the draconic ravages he had been led to expect.

In fact, he thought as he looked out across the countryside, Orgûl appeared far richer and more peaceful than the lands he had traversed to reach it.

For the first three days after leaving Skelleth, he had ridden at a leisurely pace across flat plains brown with mud, traveling openly by day and stopping freely at the very few inns and taverns along the way. He had been turned away once, simply because he was an overman, but had met no other serious inconvenience or opposition until the third evening, when, amid the smoldering ruins of a farm that chanced to lie between disputing baronies, a human soldier took a shot at him with a crossbow. The quarrel missed its target, and the man fled when Koros, Garth's warbeast, bared its fangs and roared; Garth himself did not even have to draw his sword. Still, he knew he had been lucky that the bolt had missed; he had not seen the man crouching behind a broken wall.

After that he had traveled by night, sleeping by day in whatever cover he could find. The land had grown ever richer as he moved south; though he could see no color by night, at sunset and dawn the earth was lush and green—where it hadn't been burned black.

That first burned-out farm had not been unique; as he continued on to the south, he found many others, usually in clusters along the invisible lines between baronies. Nor were farms the only things destroyed; he passed an inn that was reduced to charred timbers, and a gallows nearby held three rotting corpses. On one piece of prime land the blackened crops were still smoldering. Some fields had been destroyed not by fire, but by marching feet, and one had apparently been the site of a recent battle; it had been churned into a muddy waste, strewn with broken links of mail and scraps of cloth spattered with dark blood. Everything of value, every weapon that might be reforged or melted down, had been removed, though Garth suspected that had been the work of looters rather than the contending armies.

He rode by still more farms, some abandoned, some where families cowered behind barricaded doors, and others where the doors were wide open in welcome, on the assumption that resistance to the whims of soldiers would be fatal. Garth avoided villages and towns and castles, giving them all wide berths, and dodged any armed men he spotted in time. No unarmed humans were to be found abroad after dark.

Those few patrols and sentries that he could not avoid, for whatever reason, invariably let him pass unhindered after the warbeast clearly indicated that it was ready to defend its master. Only rarely did Garth feel it necessary to draw a blade or speak a serious threat. He considered himself fortunate that he had not encountered any company larger than a patrol squad, nor any other sniping bowman with a grudge against overmen.

Eramma, in the throes of internal war, he had seen as a patchwork of the land's natural wealth and the barren leavings of battle.

The last portion of his journey had been the worst. The fighting had begun when the Baron of Sland had attacked the

High King at Kholis, and although the High King had never managed to restore his full authority, several barons had helped him make sure that Sland would no longer be a threat. The troublesome Baron had been assassinated after his defeat on the field of battle, and his successor had made peace with his Eramman neighbors—though Garth had heard rumors that the new Baron had designs on the lands beyond his western border, outside Eramma's limits. Unfortunately, by the time this peace had been established, much of Sland was a burned-out desert. The land showed some signs of recovery after a year of peace, but was still largely desolate and empty. Garth had been relieved to get up into the hills, into the forests where he was not surrounded by mud and ash.

And now, as he emerged into the valley of Orgûl, the warm, green vista before him was a staggering contrast.

It was very odd. He had spoken with people along the way, wherever it had seemed safe to do so, and those who had heard of Orgûl at all had also heard of the dragon; they had described the valley as a scorched wasteland. Even in Sland, the survivors, racked by hunger and disease, had considered themselves more fortunate than the people of Orgûl. They had spoken of burned crops, seared fields, empty, ruined villages, and whole populaces devoured or destroyed.

That description did not accord with what Garth now saw. He wondered briefly if somehow he could have gotten turned about in the forest's darkness and wound up in the wrong valley. The sun was where he had expected it to be, and he had noticed no other trails as he had ridden, but he resolved to ask the first person he found.

If he was lost, he had no idea where he might be or how to get to the real Orgûl. He had little choice but to assume that he had indeed reached his destination and that the stories of the dragon's depredations had been exaggerated. He wondered whether the Forgotten King had known more of the situation than he had said; Garth hoped that he was not once again becoming entangled in some labyrinthine scheme the old man had concocted.

With an almost imperceptible shrug, he urged the warbeast forward. The spire of a small temple gleamed golden above the trees before him, not more than two or three leagues away at most; he was sure that he would find a village there, and someone from whom he could ask directions. If there were no one in the temple or village, then it was a safe assumption that he was in Orgûl and that the dragon was real and terrible.

The ride down the hillside was pleasant; the highway wound down from the promontory through a final patch of forest before opening out into farmland, and the morning sun poured through the leaves in a spatter of honeyed light. Birds sang on either side. A deer wandered across the narrow road, then turned and fled at the sight of the warbeast. Off to the left, Garth heard the splashing of a rocky stream, its cheerful burble accompanying him down the slope. He glimpsed a hawk overhead, soaring in graceful, wide circles.

It seemed utterly incredible that this peaceful valley could harbor a dragon. Dragons were said to be the most formidable and destructive creatures in all the world, and the dragon of Orgûl, Garth had been told along the way, was the most ferocious dragon ever known. Something here was not as it seemed, and his mistrust of the King's motive for proposing the mission steadily increased. Having come this far, however, he was not inclined to turn back.

The road he followed was little more than a narrow trail at this point, but it was not seriously overgrown; Garth wondered what traffic it bore that kept down the weeds and grasses. He had been told that no outsiders dared venture into Orgûl and he decided that the Orgûlians themselves must be responsible. This implied that they still conducted a minimum of trade with the outside world, which did not quite accord with the stories Garth had heard. The people of Orgûl had been described to him as a dwindling handful of humans who lived constantly in hiding and in perpetual fear of the monster that ruled their land.

Obviously, if this valley was Orgûl, all the stories were greatly exaggerated.

The exact details were immaterial, however. He had come to dispose of the dragon once and for all, regardless of the extent of the damage it caused. A single unnecessary death was enough to justify his task.

It struck him as odd that the Forgotten King should allow him to risk his life in such an altruistic venture—if altruistic it actually were. He grew more certain that the old man had some ulterior motive, some subtle and selfish reason for sending Garth off on this journey.

His thoughts were interrupted by a growl from his beast; he glanced down at the creature's flattened ears, then at the road ahead.

A figure was emerging from one side of the forest and waving desperately at him. Whoever this person was, he evidently wanted the overman to stop. Garth spoke a word to his mount, and the warbeast came to a smooth halt a pace or two away from the man.

The overman glared down at the human. He was aware that his appearance, particularly when mounted upon Koros, was impressive and even intimidating; he made good use of that fact at times.

The man hesitated, gazing up at the huge, dark form of the overman. He had heard of overmen, but had never seen one before. Descriptions had not done them justice, and he was certain of Garth's species only because he knew of no other large humanoid beings.

Koros he could not place at all; he simply stared.

Two pairs of inhuman eyes stared back, one set golden and catlike, one red as blood and whiteless, but otherwise *almost* human.

He himself stood a little over five feet tall and was thin; the overman, he judged, was nearly seven feet in height, were he to stand on his own booted feet. He was not standing, of course, but was seated atop an immense and frightening animal, black as the heart of a cave and resembling an oddly proportioned, long-legged panther.

The man had never seen, nor heard of, a panther eighteen feet long and five feet high at the shoulder. The warbeast looked *down* at him, and he was not accustomed to having animals look down at him. Its rider, noseless, dark-skinned, black-haired, and beardless, towered above him as if he were no more than a crawling infant. Still, he finally managed to gather himself together sufficiently to stammer out his message in the face of these awesome intruders.

"Turn back, my lord! Do not venture further, I beseech you!"

Garth stared down a moment longer; then, without moving, he demanded, "Why not?"

Momentarily cowed still further by Garth's bass rumble of a voice, the man had some difficulty in continuing, but at last got out, "The dragon, my lord! The dragon has once more awakened, after a month's sleep, and is very hungry! I fear that this time the entire valley is doomed!"

After a brief pause, intended for dramatic effect, Garth asked, "This is Orgûl, then?" He wondered about the mention of a month's sleep; could that account for the valley's green richness? No, he decided, it could not. He had ridden through parts of Eramma that were not yet recovered from mere human battles after a year's respite; how, then, could the devastation caused by a dragon vanish in a mere month?

"Yes, my lord," the man said, "this is the accursed valley of Orgûl, home of the great dragon."

"I have come to kill this troublesome beast," Garth remarked casually.

"Oh, my lord, it cannot be done! His hide is like steel, his fangs like swords, his talons like scythes! He can outfly a hawk, and his breath is flame hotter than any forge!"

Garth saw that the man was almost trembling, but could not guess at the reason. He supposed that it might be fear of the dragon, or fear of Koros, or fear of himself, or some other emotion entirely. Even after living among them for three years, he still did not fully understand humans and knew that he did not.

"You think to frighten me, little man," he replied. "Know, though, that I am Garth, Prince of Ordunin, Lord of the Overmen of the Northern Waste. No beast lives that might defeat me." This was not exactly true, he knew; he would not care to tackle a hungry warbeast, and a dragon might also prove too much for him. Still, a little boasting was expected from a warrior. His statement was not quite an outright lie; had he kept the Sword of Bheleu and allowed himself to become the pawn of the god of destruction, he could easily have butchered any dragon that might exist.

He did not have the magic sword, but only an ordinary broadsword of good steel; even so, he thought he would be able to deal with the monster.

The man tried again, saying, "Please, my lord, turn back; the dragon is no ordinary beast!"

He was clearly desperate, and Garth hid some small surprise. Why, he wondered, was this fellow so concerned? Even if he was completely convinced that the dragon would kill both overman and warbeast, why should that upset him so? He had given his warning, done what he could to prevent a catastrophe; why should he be so distressed at Garth's determination? In Garth's experience, humans did not worry much about what befell overmen.

"Do you fear that I shall enrage the dragon?" he asked. "Is that why you seek to turn me aside?"

"No, no, my lord, I am concerned only for your own safety! Other heroes have come, and all have died beneath the dragon's flames and claws."

Garth shook his head slightly, mentally dismissing the man's actions as incomprehensible. "Stand aside, little man," he said, "lest Koros trample you." He signaled to the warbeast and rode on, ignoring the continuing protests and warnings that the man shouted after him.

It was not much later, and the sun was still low in the east, when Garth rode into the village that clustered about the temple spire he had seen from the slope. The shrine itself was an open pavilion, ringed with pillars that supported its spiraling cone of a roof; it faced onto a small plaza, from which five roads led off in various directions. A handful of small, tidy, thatch-roofed cottages stood on each of the roads, and a larger structure that might have been an inn, with a roof of red tile, occupied one corner.

The plaza was paved with tessellated stone, and a small fountain played in its center. As Garth's warbeast neared the pavement, a breeze tinkled its way through miniature bells that hung from the eaves of the temple, joining the hiss and splash of the fountain and the soft steps of sandaled feet.

The villagers stopped and stared at Garth's approach, and the footsteps ceased. Then someone turned and ran for the inn, and the streets cleared almost instantly.

Garth found himself alone in the center of the square, looking about at the five roads with no idea which one he should take. It was time, he decided, to ask for directions. Getting himself and his beast a meal wouldn't be a mistake, either, he thought. Koros was already drinking from the fountain, which reminded Garth that he, too, was thirsty.

He dismounted and stepped up to the fountain, where he filled his hands with water and drank.

A sound behind him caught his attention; he let the rest of the water drop and whirled, his hand falling automatically to the hilt of his sword.

The door of the inn had opened again, and several people were emerging. A white-haired man stepped forward from the group and addressed him.

"Greetings, my lord overman!"

"Greetings, man." This human, Garth thought, unlike the one he had met on the road to the village, at least had the grace to speak politely.

"My I ask, my lord, what brings you to our humble village?" The man's manner was almost fawning.

"I have come to slay your dragon, to save you from its depredations," Garth replied, making an effort to sound casual.

The spokesman hesitated, then said, "My lord, do not think us ungrateful, but we ask that you turn back. We do not wish to see another great man . . . ah, I mean, another great warrior such as yourself die fighting the monster. Too many have perished already."

"I have no intention of dying, man."

"Do you suppose that any of the dragon's victims did? Please, my lord, turn back. You can do nothing for us. You would only throw your life away."

Garth was becoming annoyed by this manifest lack of faith in his prowess. "My life is my own, to throw away should it please me to do so," he said. "I have come to fight your dragon and I am not to be turned aside so readily, frightened by mere words."

The spokesman bowed in acknowledgment of Garth's words, but said, "We do not seek to frighten you, my lord, only to advise you. It would be foolish to waste your life in battling the monster."

Garth's temper, already frayed, gave way. "You are the fools," he called, "to refuse a chance of freedom from this menace! I am Garth, Prince of Ordunin, Lord of the Overmen of the Northern Waste, who brought the White Death to the black city of Dûsarra, who stole the sword of a god, who has fought the beasts of Death himself! I have come here to slay the dragon and I will have no one tell me that I must not!" He realized, as he finished his speech, that without consciously intending to, he had drawn his sword and was flourishing it about.

The little group of humans had clustered together and backed away from him a step or two, toward the inn. The spokesman looked back at his companions for support and, finding little, said nothing further.

His anger spent, Garth returned his sword to its scabbard and added, "But first, I have not eaten recently and would prefer not to face death on an empty stomach. Is this building whence you all came an inn, where an overman can break his fast?"

The spokesman reluctantly admitted that it was.

The inn was called the Sword and Chalice, though its signboard had fallen years ago and never been replaced. Garth had a goat sent out to his warbeast while he himself consumed a hearty meal of roast beef, carrots, and ale. He ate surrounded by a ring of wary villagers, silently watching his every move. He steadfastly ignored their presence and made a point of paying no attention to their comings and goings.

He paused in the midst of his meal at the sound of women screaming in the plaza, but a quick glance out the door reassured him. The screams were in response to the warbeast's eating habits. Koros had killed the goat with a single blow of its paw and immediately devoured it, hair, hooves, and all, though the warbeast spat out the horns and larger bones. Those villagers who happened to be watching had been horrified to see a living animal reduced so quickly to a spatter of blood and a few scraps.

When Garth had eaten his fill, he rose, tossed a gold coin on the table, and walked back out into the plaza. The circle of villagers parted before him, then coalesced into a single mass and followed him out—all save the innkeeper. He had not expected to be paid, and took a moment to hide the coin before joining his fellows.

Half a dozen villagers were watching in fascinated revulsion as Koros licked the blood from its paws. They were maintaining a safe distance, Garth noted; he was pleased by that. It showed that they respected the beast's power.

"Whose goat was it?" he demanded loudly.

A woman timidly raised a hand in an affirmative gesture. He tossed her another of his gold coins, which she caught deftly and quickly pocketed.

A boy at her side whispered something and was hushed. Garth noticed men and women staring at him, at the warbeast, and at the broadsword on his hip and the battle-axe slung on the saddle. He looked around, but the spokesman was nowhere in sight. Choosing a man at random, he remarked, "I take it you see few warriors around here and fewer overmen."

The man gaped at him, then gathered enough wit to reply. "Yes, my lord. Very few. The dragon keeps them away. No overmen, ever."

"I would think that many would come to try their skill at dragon-slaying."

His unhappy respondent glanced to either side, but saw no sign that any of his townspeople were willing to take over the burden of the conversation.

"No, my lord," he replied, "not anymore. Long ago there were some, but the dragon killed them all, and after a time they stopped coming. There were never overmen, though; only the men of the Baron of Sland, or roving mercenaries and adventurers."

"They stopped coming?" Garth said, encouraging him to continue.

"Yes, my lord. After all, there is no reward offered, no great prize to be won."

"Nothing but a chance for fame and glory, and the risk of death, more easily found elsewhere, to be sure." Garth nodded, then swung himself up into the saddle.

"Forgive me, my lord," the man said, gathering his courage, "but why . . . ah, why have you come here? Why do you bother with our accursed and wretched valley?"

"Your valley does not seem wretched to me, man. I have come here out of boredom, people of Orgûl; I grew weary of a life of quiet and decided, on a whim, to come here and aid those the dragon oppressed. I have lived for more than a century and adventured in many lands, but never before have those I came to aid tried so hard to turn me away."

"But, my lord," someone protested, "we seek only to prevent the loss of another brave—"

"Enough, human," Garth interrupted. "Tell me, now, which road is most likely to lead me to this vile monster?"

Reluctantly, the man pointed to the western road, and with a word in the warbeast's triangular ear, Garth rode on.

Chapter Three

The road he took from the plaza appeared to run through the village's commercial area; the houses on either side held small shops, displaying fine rugs and fabrics in their many-paned windows, or delicate carvings, or gleaming pots and kettles, or other goods. A blacksmith's forge trailed smoke into the blue of the sky, but the smith was not at work as the overman passed.

Even though the people he encountered shied away from him, averting their eyes and hurrying out of sight, he enjoyed the ride. This village, it seemed to him, was more the sort of place he might have liked to live in, if he were to live among humans, than the wastelands of the north. Skelleth might be flourishing, but it was still cold and dirty and gray, huddled on a barren plain against the long harsh winters; this village was bright and cheerful, trailing off without a border into the surrounding green of field and forest, rather than being chopped off short by a ruined city wall. The sunlight was warm on his back, the breeze fresh with the smells of abundant greenery.

Garth found it quite impossible to believe that this was the home ground of a dragon as terrible as the one he had heard described. He puzzled anew at the Orgûlians' insistence that he turn back.

Looking about, he wondered idly whether overmen had ever

29

lived in this delightful valley, back in those long-lost legendary days before the Racial Wars, before his people were driven into the barren Northern Waste. For centuries the overmen of the Waste had believed themselves to be the only ones to have survived those bitter wars, but recently Garth himself had discovered that others still lived on the Yprian Coast, a region nearly as desolate as the Waste itself. Could there be more, scattered about the world? Might some still linger in the hills around Orgûl? Garth found that an appealing fancy; this country was one he would have enjoyed calling his home, and it pleased him to imagine that it might not wholly be wasted on humans.

His musings were interrupted when his eye caught a sudden movement in one of the village shops; he turned to see what had drawn his attention.

The last of the buildings that lined the street was a strange little shop on the left, its mismatched windows full of whirling, whirring clockwork toys. Fascinated, Garth stopped his mount, swung himself to the ground, and went over for a closer look. He was in no real hurry, he told himself; the dragon had reportedly gone its way for decades, and another few moments would surely make no difference.

The shop's display held dozens of intricate toys, full of gears and springs, which did amazing and delightful tricks. An armored warrior, with head and hands of china, swung a miniature sword in long, swooping strokes, narrowly missing the bent-over back of a mechanical smith striking sparks from a half-formed steel rake with a stone hammer—the head of which, Garth realized, must be flint, a clever method of creating the sparks that so resembled those of a real blacksmith at work. Nearby, a toy dog wagged its tail, its tongue moving as if panting, and a plaster witch stirred a tiny copper cauldron. Elsewhere, dancers whirled, acrobats leaped, and animals paced, in a glittering festival of copper and brass and silver and ceramics. A few devices had no recognizable form, but were unabashed machines, tossing arms and gears about in complex and fascinating patterns.

Garth had never seen so fine a display of machinery; northerners, either the humans of Skelleth or the overmen of Ordunin, had little time for such inessentials. Clockwork was used for clocks on ships, which needed accurate timekeeping for navigation, but was seldom used elsewhere.

He could not resist a broad grin as he studied the things; he hoped that no one noticed it, lest it destroy the image he had been cultivating of the implacable inhuman warrior. Anyone who saw it, though, might not recognize it for what it was; humans were not always able to identify the expressions of overmen, being distracted from the fundamental similarities by the hollow cheeks, thin lips, and noseless slit nostrils. The two species reacted somewhat differently to various situations and emotions, furthering the confusion. To the uninitiated man or woman, Garth's happy smile might appear to be a ghastly grimace; his delight in the clever toys and machines to be bitter disgust.

The shop window was not lighted, and Garth's own shadow blocked out a measure of the morning sun; he peered in, trying to make out the shapes that flopped and fluttered in the dimness at the back of the display. A brass rooster crowed, with a flapping of wings, and he marveled anew.

"Would you like to buy one, my lord?"

Startled, Garth whirled to face the owner of the pleasant little voice that had interrupted his studies. A small, white-haired man stood in the door of the shop, squinting and blinking in the bright light of day; he smiled, revealing a jawful of randomly assorted gold and white teeth.

The overman stared at the man for a moment, then back at the window, where the swordsman's blade continued to miss the smith's broad back and swinging hammer by the breadth of a few hairs; where the yapping dog bounced merrily along and the plaster witch grinned gruesomely.

"I think I might, yes," Garth said at last. "Are they expensive?"

"Oh, no," the little man replied. "I don't need much to live on. I have a pension of sorts—I suppose you could call it a pension. Enough to make do, at any rate. But it does get so dull! So I keep making these toys, to amuse myself. The children seem to like them. Have you any children, my lord?"

"Five; two sons. They're grown, though, old enough for families of their own."

"Grandchildren, then?"

"Not that I know of; I haven't been home lately." He smiled wryly to himself at that.

"A pity, a pity." The old man shook his head, looking downcast, as if it were the greatest tragedy of his life that this fine overman should have no grandchildren and should be so long away from home.

Garth's smile became a little less bitter; the man was amusing. "Did you say that you find this village dull? What of the dragon, then? Does it not provide enough excitement for you?"

"Oh, the dragon . . ." The man shrugged, as if the legendary monster were beneath his notice. "I meant that doing nothing for myself was dull, not that there had been no excitement in my life. I like to keep my hands busy when the dragon is not about, my hands and my mind." He gestured, wiggling his fingers to show that they were still agile.

Garth decided that he liked this fellow. "Have you children yourself?" he asked.

"Oh, all long since grown, like your own, my lord; even my grandchildren are married now, some of them." He glanced at the shop window. "Tell me," he said, "which do you like the best?"

Garth turned back and studied the collection; his gaze wandered over ships and horses, men and castles, women and machines. The swordsman had run down, frozen in midstroke with his sword thrust out before him.

"I cannot say," Garth replied. "I have not seen them all run. Some are not displayed to their best advantage here."

"Come inside, then, and I will show you more closely any that interest you." The toymaker grinned and beckoned, and Garth followed him.

The building's interior was dim and smelled strongly of metal and oil and herbs. A narrow passage led between two great tables that held the two window displays; beyond, a fair-sized room contained a fireplace and oven, a table, a few chairs, and a workbench. The last was cluttered with gears and wheels and snippets of copper, chisels and scissors and knives, powders and pastes, jars and vials, a potter's wheel, and a pedal-driven lathe. At the rear, another door stood slightly ajar.

Garth looked over the two tables; dozens of toys were displayed, perhaps a hundred or more. The toymaker wound up a spider that danced in circles as the cauldron-stirring witch ground to a halt.

Everything was a maze of arms and legs and wheels, plaster faces staring in the waxed-paper windows of wooden castles, and Garth could not imagine picking a single favorite from the muddle. He let his eyes roam, and found himself staring at a glistening copper shape that gleamed in one corner.

"What's that?" he asked, pointing. The object stood out because of its smooth, curving surface, unbroken by flailing arms or whirling gears.

The old man followed his pointing finger and fetched the object in question out into the light that poured through the window. It was a copper sea gull; two eyes of smoky quartz stared unseeingly from its tapered metal head, and its wings were polished to mirror brightness. "Ah, my lord," the old man said, "you have excellent taste."

"What does it do?" Garth asked.

"Why, what else would a bird do but fly?" He pulled a silver key from somewhere, inserted it in an opening in the mechanical gull's back, then gestured for Garth to follow him back outside. "Let me show you."

The overman followed and watched as the toymaker turned the key. With a small click, the key stopped; the old man pulled it out and, with a proud smile, cast the gull away.

Garth instinctively reached out to catch it, to keep its graceful curves from being scarred or broken by its fall, but it did not drop into his waiting hands. Instead, its metal wings caught the breeze and flapped once, twice, lazily, with the languid grace of a living sea gull, and it swooped away. Riding the wind, it glided upward, then looped back and circled slowly overhead. Garth gaped in astonishment.

For several long minutes the gull soared overhead, flapping smoothly now and then, gleaming golden in the morning sun; then, gradually, it settled lower and lower, until at last, with a rueful smile, the toymaker reached up and plucked it out of the sky.

Garth heard a click and a final soft whirr, and the gull was still.

Garth stared at the man with deep respect. "It is very beautiful," he said. "I was not aware that such things could be built of mere metal."

The toymaker looked down, obviously embarrassed. "Well, actually," he admitted, "they can't. I cheat. It's not just clock-work."

"It's not?"

"No. I use magic."

"Oh," Garth said knowingly. He had seen magic before, more of it than he liked. At least, he thought, this magic was harmless.

"I didn't originally—at least, I don't think I did. I started off using just clockwork when I was an apprentice, but I found right from the first that I could make machines that no one else could understand, things that worked when by all rights they should not have. Even when I built my clocks and toys in the usual ways, mine would run far longer and more smoothly than any of the others. I got better and better at it, too, until I was doing things that were plainly impossible to do with just clock-work. I had no idea how I did what I did back then; it simply came to me, as naturally as breathing, without my ever thinking about it. When I realized what was happening, I studied sorcery briefly; even though my teacher said I had a real talent, I didn't care for it. It seemed too dangerous, too uncertain. I went back to clockwork, but now I know a bit more about what I'm doing. I even use spells intentionally now, though I still make them up, rather than follow the old formulae. As I said, I have the knack for it. A fellow who came through here last year, fleeing from Sland, a wizard by the name of Karag, told me that it wasn't anything to be concerned about. He said that there are a lot of minor magical talents like mine scattered about; prob-ably one of my ancestors back in the Twelfth Age, when magic was widespread, was a wizard of some sort, and I inherited a bit of his lingering power without knowing it."

"I had no idea it could work that way," Garth said.

"Neither did I when I was young, but it seems that's just how it *does* work. That gull wouldn't fly if anyone else had made it. I've shown other tinkers and craftsmen how to make flying toys, and they've done them just as I do, but theirs don't fly at all, they just fall."

Garth reached out, took the gull from the toymaker's hands,

and turned it over, studying it. "Magic or not, it's a beautiful thing," he said.

"Yes, it is," the toymaker agreed.

"Do you wish to sell it?"

"Of course; I have no use for it. Besides, I have others and I can always make more. Would you like it?"

"Yes, I think I would; it's a wondrous device, whether clockwork or magic. What is your price?"

The man named a figure; Garth declined politely. After a brief and mild bout of bargaining, a price was settled upon as fair to both parties.

"Will you take it with you now, then?" the toymaker asked.

"No," Garth answered, handing it back, "I think not. I am seeking after the dragon at present; were I to take the gull, I fear that it might be broken in the fight. I will stop here and buy it on my way back, at the price agreed upon, if that will suit you." After a second's pause, he added, "Assuming, of course, that I come back; the stories I have heard of the dragon imply that I may not."

"The dragon?" Surprise and concern were plain in the toymaker's face. "You've come to slay the dragon? Oh, dear. That's most unfortunate."

"Is it?" Garth asked as he moved to mount his warbeast. "It may prove unfortunate for the dragon; it has never faced an overman before."

"Well, that's true," the old man admitted, "but still..." He fell into a confused silence and stood watching, the metal bird in his hands, as Garth rode on past him and out of the village.

CHAPTER FOUR

Garth rode for an hour through peaceful groves and flourishing farmland; on all sides, blossoms were giving way to budding fruit and grain, and it was obvious that, barring some disaster, there would be an abundant harvest at summer's end. He could still see no sign anywhere of a dragon or a dragon's depredations. He did see, to his surprise, recent footprints, all human, on the road he followed; they were wide-spaced, as if the men who made them had been hurrying. They all seemed to run westward, the same direction in which Garth was bound. He wondered if the makers of the marks had been fleeing from the dragon. The villagers had seemed quite certain that it was awake and active and somewhere west of the town; perhaps they had seen it pursuing some of their countrymen along this highway.

There was no trace of the dragon itself, however. Garth scanned the horizon.

To the north and east, he saw nothing but trees. To the south, a few clouds hung in the sky above green fields. To the west, the hills reared up before him; the valley was narrow at this, its northern end, and he had already crossed half its width.

To the southwest, a thin trail of smoke was curling upward, blue smoke almost invisible against the blue of the sky.

He signaled Koros to stop, to allow him a better view; the warbeast obeyed, and Garth stared at the faint wisp. It seemed to be growing thicker as he watched.

Dragons, it was said, breathed fire. Garth had never taken that aspect of the monster's description very seriously; legends tended to be distorted in the retelling. Still, there was general agreement that much of a dragon's destructiveness resulted from fires. Garth had assumed heretofore that the creatures might produce some sort of highly combustible substance, a venom or vapor, perhaps.

If they actually did produce flame, however, then the smoke he now saw might be coming from the monster.

Of course, it could also be coming from village cook fires and hearths, but he saw no sign of a town in that direction— no temple spires or roofs above the treetops. If there were a village, though, perhaps the people would be able to direct him to the monster's current location.

He pointed toward the smoke and called a command to his mount. With a growl, the warbeast turned off the road and began running cross-country toward the thickening column.

Koros' normal pace was almost unnaturally smooth and silent, far more comfortable for its rider than that of any other mount Garth had ever ridden; but when running, even though it was loping along well below its full top speed, Koros bounded up and down in such a manner that Garth was forced to cling precariously to its harness, rather than risk being thrown.

The beast's long strides ate up the distance, carrying the overman over farmland and meadow with phenomenal speed. Animal and rider passed through an orchard, then a patch of pine forest, then out into a new stretch of meadow. Beneath them, the ground began to slope upward, and Garth saw that the smoke was rising from just beyond the crest of a grassy hillock.

If he were to ride on directly over that rise, he realized, he might find himself face to face with the dragon without any time to prepare; the monster could easily be lurking in ambush.

He called a command, and Koros came to a sudden stop. Garth gathered himself together and looked at what lay before him.

He was on an open expanse of grassland, unfarmed and

apparently wild; ahead, the land rose into a sort of mound, and the smoke behind it streamed upward in a single thick column. It did not look like the dispersed traces of smoke from a village or the thin mark from a farmhouse chimney. Some farmer might be burning debris, or a cremation might be under way, but Garth thought that caution was called for in any further approach.

Beyond the rise, the ground sloped downward again, into a riverbank; he could not see the stream itself, but the broad cut into the earth that extended in either direction beyond the hillock could be nothing else.

The nearest cover was a patch of forest that he had passed through on his approach; it lay a hundred yards behind him.

He had, he judged, four choices. He could head on directly over the mound, he could circle it to the northwest, he could circle to the southeast, or he could retreat into the woods.

He glanced down at the warbeast's harness, making sure it hadn't been loosened by the fast ride he had just finished, and considered. Remaining where he was did not seem prudent; he was out in the open, an ideal target. If he advanced, he did not know what he might be facing. If he retreated, the dragon might depart—assuming it was there at all.

He would have to face the unknown eventually; he decided to advance. If he looped to the northwest, his shadow would be away from whatever awaited him, but the sun would be in his eyes when he turned south again on the far side of the mound. If he went southeast, his shadow might signal his approach.

He had just resolved to head on directly over the mound, slowly and cautiously, when Koros let out a growl that he recognized as indicating surprise. He looked up from the harness and found himself staring straight at an immense red-gold dragon that was sailing down at him on huge, batlike wings.

It had made no sound, no bellow of challenge, no great flapping; but now that he was alerted, he noticed a faint hissing that he had not heard over the breeze rustling the grass.

The creature was at least a hundred feet long, with a slender, graceful tail winding out behind it and a long, arching neck. Its wingspan was even greater than its length, easily fifty yards, perhaps sixty or more. Its hide was covered with glittering scales that flashed like golden coins in the sun.

Its head was a thing of horror; its gaping jaws were black, and long, curving teeth lined both top and bottom like rows of knives. The great heavy-lidded eyes were faceted ovals, as red as Garth's own but without white or pupil. Smoke billowed from its flared nostrils and streamed back behind it.

Seeing it, Garth realized for the first time that perhaps he might not defeat the creature. It was much bigger than he had expected and had the advantage of flight and was armored as well. It really did breathe flame, apparently. He understood now why the villagers had despaired of ever killing such a monster; it moved with sure grace and calm power, a truly awesome sight as it swooped down, gleaming in the sun.

He drew his sword and waited for its attack.

It swept past him, out of reach overhead, enveloping him in a cloud of black smoke; he fought down the need to cough, but blinked frantically to clear his eyes. The hissing grew, crescendoed, then faded as the monster drew away. The smoke stank; it was greasy and vile, and the smell of it filled his nostrils.

When he could see again, he looked up; the dragon was looping about in the eastern sky, coming back for another pass. It had not actually attacked him, he realized, but merely spewed forth its smoke as if it meant to blind or frighten him.

He watched it, his face immobile and calm. It would soon learn that overmen, or at least Garth of Ordunin, could not be frightened easily.

He signaled for Koros to turn, so as to face the dragon's next pass, then stood in the stirrups and swung his sword as it rushed down at him.

He did not strike squarely, but the blade dragged along the side of one great, curved talon, making a harsh scraping sound. Again the monster did not actually attempt to hit him, but merely swooped by, leaving a trail of thick smoke behind.

He whirled when it was past and saw it swinging around toward him again. Its mouth gaped wider, and it roared, belching forth an immense cloud of smoke and fire.

Garth watched the monster spout yellow flame and black smoke and realized that he might do well to retreat, at least temporarily. The thing had been easy on him; it could have fried him on its first pass, yet it had not.

He wondered why. Perhaps it wasn't hungry, and merely wanted to drive him away without a fight. Or perhaps it *was* hungry and did not want to destroy its dinner. It probably preferred its food raw, not roasted.

Koros roared an answer to the dragon's bellow and turned to face it; the warbeast, at least, was still ready to fight. Garth decided against retreating; he had come to kill the thing and he would never kill it by fleeing.

The creature finished a long, slow turn in mid-air and came at him again, screaming this time like a maddened demon, its cry like nothing the overman had ever heard before. It tore past him, inches above his lowered head; he thrust his weapon upward, where it glanced ringingly off the creature's forelegs without seeming even to scratch them. Garth doubted the dragon had felt the blow through its scaly armor.

The monster wheeled about again, and again it rushed down the sky at him, even lower than before; he leaned sideways in the saddle, ducking out of its path, and struck upward again. The point of his sword bounced and scratched along the creature's belly, then rang metallically from a hind leg and was knocked aside. There was still no sign that the dragon had felt a thing.

If it came in any lower on its next pass, Garth knew, he would be unable to duck under it where he was. As it looped about with another roar, he prodded Koros' flank with his heel and shouted a command.

The startled warbeast broke into a run, moving forward under the dragon's next howling lunge. This time the monster spat forth a jet of flame that seared the grass where the warbeast had stood a moment earlier, and Garth congratulated himself on his decision to dodge.

He watched intently as the creature turned again; it moved smoothly and gracefully, but was not actually very fast in maneuvering. It seemed unable to bank more than a few degrees; Garth guessed that, perhaps due to its size, it was not as stable in flight as a bird. A sufficient tilt might bring it down. He wondered if there were any way to use that against it, then forgot about aerodynamics as it swept down toward him again.

He sent Koros sideways this time, turning the warbeast out of its path. He misjudged slightly, or perhaps the dragon had allowed for his motion, and he felt the heat of its fiery breath at his back. Koros roared in pain; the fur of its tail had been singed.

Garth patted the warbeast, apologizing, as he considered the situation. The traditional method of dragon-slaying, according to legend, was to find some minute chink in the creature's armor and strike at it. He had seen no sign of any flaw in this dragon's defenses—but then, he had been too busy dodging to study it very closely. Still, the armor on this monster seemed almost unnaturally perfect—countless rows of fine golden scales in flawless, gleaming array.

The dragon was not making another attack, he realized; instead, it was circling, far out of reach. It appeared almost to be waiting for something, as if to see if the overman still intended to fight. Garth considered retreating, then dismissed the idea. When diving, the dragon moved with the speed of a falling stone, and it could probably catch him from behind before he could reach the forest. It might, he thought, be trying to coax him into just such a foolhardy maneuver.

He watched it wheel about, and an idea struck him. The thing was gigantic, and as it made the far part of its turn, he glimpsed its broad, smooth back, as wide and solid as the deck of a ship. If he could get atop it, he could hack at it at his leisure; with its limited aerodynamic ability, it might be unable to dislodge him. He had used a similar technique against a monster once before, the great worm that lived beneath Dûsarra, though that particular creature had not had the benefits of flight, flame, and armor.

The difficulty lay in getting onto the thing, but even that might not be impossible. He looked down at Koros' black-furred back, shoulder muscles rippling under its hide as it shifted its stance. He had seen the warbeast leap to and from low rooftops, and bound over crowds of humans. It could almost certainly manage the jump he wanted.

Of course, he was not at all certain that he himself could manage his part of the feat he planned, but if he did not, it would probably mean nothing worse than a long fall. He could take a fall. He could see little to be lost by trying; the dragon could slay him just as easily if he did not make the attempt.

The dragon still circled smoothly in the sky above the mound; he turned the warbeast toward it and gave the command to charge.

Koros roared, so loudly that Garth's ears rang, and began bounding up the slope. Seeing this, the dragon turned and came to meet the overman and warbeast, bellowing and screaming and smoking like a burning city. As they drew nearer to one another, Garth gauged the distance carefully and, when he judged the moment to be right, shouted the command to leap.

Koros leaped, jaws wide and claws out, to attack the dragon; the warbeast was roaring with bloodlust. Garth felt the leap as a great surge upward; so smooth was the movement that he hardly realized when Koros left the ground. As the dragon loomed up before him, a gleaming coppery wall, he leaped himself, flinging himself upward from the saddle to grab at the monster's neck.

He struck hard against a shining red-gold flank and clung desperately, digging fingernails into the overlapping of the scales and scrambling upward with his feet.

His faithful mount, thrown off course by his own jump, hit the dragon full in the chest, then fell away, yowling with pain and anger, as its fangs and claws failed to penetrate and grip the gleaming armor.

Garth watched, concerned, as the warbeast fell. When Koros landed, catlike, on all fours and rose, apparently unhurt, Garth turned his attention back to his own situation with great relief.

He had a precarious purchase on the monster's shoulder, the wind whipping about him as the dragon sped through the skies. With all his superhuman strength, he forced himself upward against the hard scales and, with muscles straining, managed to haul himself up atop its back.

When he felt that he was reasonably secure between the mighty shoulders, he looked the beast over. He was surprised to discover that the scales felt fully as metallic as they looked.

The dragon seemed to be searching for something, looping back and forth across the mound and the meadow below, and Garth realized that it was unaware of his presence on its back.

It could feel nothing through its armor and thought that he, too, like Koros, had fallen.

He smiled, brushed aside a lock of black hair that had fallen into one eye, and drew his dagger. He had lost his sword in his leap, releasing it without conscious thought when he had to find a fingerhold, but his axe was slung across his back, and the dagger's sheath was secure on his belt. He set about prying at the scales on the back of the dragon's neck, wedging the point of the knife beneath their overlapped edges and working upward.

The scales tore loose and fell, tinkling down past the dragon's wings into space. To Garth's surprise, the monster did not react. He leaned forward to look at the spot of hide thus uncovered, as the wind of a high-speed turn lashed at him.

Beneath the scaly armor was a fine wire mesh, and beneath that, Garth could faintly make out a myriad of gears, chains, springs, and sprockets, ticking quietly.

He sat motionless for a moment, absorbing this discovery of the dragon's true nature. Quickly, he reached a decision; he could not kill this thing, obviously, and now he decided that he did not want to destroy it. He sat back and waited.

It was almost pleasant, crouching atop the broad metal back of the dragon as it swooped through the air. Garth had never flown before and found what little he could see from where he sat to be intriguing indeed. The wind was fresh and exhilarating when the monster was not in one of its sudden turns or dives, and the view was amazing.

He did not have to wait long; after a few more passes across the hillock and meadow, the dragon looped back up across the riverbank, then soared gracefully down into the gaping mouth of a cave on the eastern shore, at the base of the hillock. It braked by cupping its wings forward.

Inside the opening, it folded its wings and settled neatly to the ground, landing with a heavy thud and a mild bump. Then, in a scant second, it froze into total immobility, losing completely its incredible semblance of life and becoming a mere metal construct.

Garth glanced up and about and saw that the entire inside of the mound was hollow. Nor was it a natural cave; stone arches braced the ceiling, and niches were occupied by flaring oil lamps. Three young men stood off to one side, well away from the dragon; they had not yet noticed its unwanted passenger.

The smoke that still streamed from the creature's nostrils suddenly thickened, and a loud hissing came from somewhere beneath the overman; then the smoke stopped entirely, leaving a thinning cloud to obscure the chamber's sooty upper reaches.

Garth leaned over the dragon's shoulder and watched as a door in its belly swung open, just barely visible to him beyond the curve of chest and foreleg. Three men crawled out, then two more, and finally two more still.

Garth lifted the axe off his back with his right hand, keeping his drawn dagger in his left, and vaulted down to the cave floor. He landed in front of the party of seven that had emerged from the dragon, with the other three humans to his right. The jump was longer than he had realized in the poor light, but he managed to catch himself and keep from sprawling, though it was not the dignified and dramatic entrance that he had hoped for.

The men froze, staring at him in astonishment. He stared back.

After a moment of stunned silence, Garth demanded, "So it was all a fraud?"

The faces of the men were blackened with some sort of gritty dust, but Garth thought he recognized one of them as a person he had seen in the village where he had eaten that morning. It was this man who answered. "No, no . . . I mean, not originally. There was a real dragon once, really there was."

"But he died," another man said.

"We fed him poisoned sheep," a third added. "It was really very simple. My grandfather told me all about it."

"And you built a new one, so that no one would know it was dead. Why?"

The men looked at one another; it was plain to Garth that they were terrified of him, overawed by this huge inhuman warrior they faced, and none wanted to be the first to give an answer he might not like.

"Why?" Garth demanded again, brandishing his axe.

There was a sudden babble of response as they all decided simultaneously that not answering might be even more dangerous than speaking unpleasant truths. "To frighten off outsiders and keep away invaders," one replied.

Garth lowered his weapons; everything was suddenly clear. Orgûl was a peaceful valley; any warriors it might once have had to defend it must have died fighting the dragon. Yet it was surrounded by avaricious warlords who would gladly turn it into a battlefield—the Baron of Sland, for example, would undoubtedly be delighted to have an undefended target for conquest that was not a part of the Kingdom of Eramma and thus not covered by the terms of his predecessor's surrender. While the dreaded dragon had lived, though, no one had dared to attack; the tales had kept potential invaders away, assuring them that the monster could destroy an army.

The Orgûlians had not meant to harm anyone, but merely to protect their homes. They had not slain Garth with their toy even when they had a chance. They could have burned him to death three times over, yet had not. He could not hold against them their desire to defend themselves and to frighten away a menace to their security.

It was impressive indeed, this device of theirs, and obviously a needed precaution; stories alone would not have staved off adventurers forever, but the sight of a dragon flying overhead, perhaps snorting fire and smoke, would deter all but a dedicated lunatic such as Garth.

He looked at the great machine and asked, "How does it work?"

The change in the human faces was dramatic as the tension suddenly dissipated. "Oh, it's most complex!" a young man, perhaps only a boy, exclaimed. "Come and see! There is a furnace for the smoke and flame, and one man works that, and there's one to each wing, while another serves to guide them. I control the tail, and Deg, here, controls the claws, and then there's a man in the neck. It's all most intricate, and all clockwork, all mechanical, machinery like no other. It takes all ten of us all day to wind it."

Garth nodded in response to the youth's enthusiasm, and a tentative smile appeared here and there among the humans. "Who made it?" he asked, though he thought he knew the answer.

"Why, old Petter, the toymaker, did most of it, designing

and building most of the machinery. The smith built the frame-work, and the tinker and three apprentices made the scales. Gerrith the jeweler made the eyes, and the whole village worked on it where we could. Every town in Orgûl helps in mining coal for the furnace now..."

Another man interrupted, asking desperately, "You won't tell anyone, will you? It's all that keeps the Baron of Sland away!"

Garth's grin faded. "I should tell the old man who sent me here—but no, I need not do that; I can tell him, truthfully, that the dragon is dead. I will say nothing to any other, and I think that you need not worry about the old man; he speaks little and will keep silent about it."

"That's all right, then," someone said. Relief was evident on several coal-darkened faces.

"Would you like to see inside?" the young man asked.

Garth nodded. "Yes, I would. But I must not stay too long; my warbeast must be found and its injuries tended."

"I don't think he's hurt much," one of the dragon's crew volunteered.

A roar from the mouth of the cave confirmed his opinion; Koros had had little trouble in tracking down the dragon. It stalked silently into the chamber to greet its master.

Garth made it welcome, then remarked to the man who had last spoken, "*It*, not *he*; only the neuters ever grow large enough to be ridden." He told the warbeast to behave, then followed the youth into the dragon's belly to study the workings of the great machine.

CHAPTER FIVE

Garth spent the night in a room at the Sword and Chalice, but the inn had no stable adequate to house Koros, so the warbeast stayed out on the plaza. There was little danger that anyone would try to steal it or any of Garth's belongings still on its back; the beast knew well who its master was, and would not accompany a stranger without Garth's orders, or permit anyone but the overman to disturb the supplies it guarded. No one in his right mind would argue with a warbeast. No one mad enough to try would survive the argument.

The overman arose late, a good hour after sunrise, and took his time in preparing for his departure. The afternoon, he knew, would be more than enough for him to find his way out of Orgûl; once he was in Eramma again, he intended to travel by night, as he had done before.

When he had finished his packing, eaten a hearty breakfast, and made sure that Koros had been tended to, he swung himself into the saddle, ready to leave. Before Koros had taken more than a single step, however, he changed his mind and ordered the warbeast to turn west rather than northeast. He had no reason to hurry; no urgent tasks needed to be undertaken, no one eagerly awaited his return to Skelleth. It could do no harm if he lingered for a visit to the toymaker; after all, he had a purchase to make.

Koros had no objection; it strode silently down the western street and halted obediently at the door of the last shop.

The door was closed, and the curtains were drawn across the display windows; Garth saw no sign of the old man. He dismounted and rapped lightly, twice, on the wooden panels.

A muffled call answered him, and a moment later the toymaker emerged, blinking in the bright sunlight. He stared up at the overman.

"Oh, it's you," he said with an uncertain smile.

"Greetings," Garth said. "I hope I did not wake you."

"What? Oh, no; I was just eating my breakfast. Hadn't had time to open the shop yet." He blinked again and then said anxiously, "I heard about your fight with the dragon. I hope you didn't hurt it too much; I'm not sure whether I could fix any serious damage. It's mostly magic, you know, and magic is tricky stuff. I'm no wizard; I don't usually know how what I do works. I just build things and they work—or sometimes they don't. Did you do it much harm?"

"No," Garth replied. "I pried a few scales from its back and I might have scratched the belly a little. I think that hurt my sword more than it hurt the dragon—or maybe the blade was dulled when I dropped it." He had retrieved the weapon before returning to the village; it had not been bent, fortunately, but part of one edge, from the tip halfway to the hilt, had been ruined.

"What about yourself? Were you hurt?"

"No. My warbeast's tail was singed, I'm afraid, and it seems to have been bruised here and there."

"Oh, I am sorry!" The man stared past the overman at the beast, his face radiating sympathy.

Garth decided that it was time he got to the point. "I came for the gull," he said.

"Oh, of course!" the toymaker exclaimed. "Just a moment!" He vanished back into the shop, then emerged a few seconds later holding the metal bird. Garth accepted it, paid out the agreed-upon price of half a dozen silver coins, and placed it delicately on the saddle.

"You'll need the key," the old man reminded him.

Garth turned back and held out his hand; the toymaker

dropped the silver key onto his palm, and he closed both thumbs over it. "Thank you," he said as he dropped it in his purse.

"Take good care of it," the man said. "It's one of my finer pieces."

"It is indeed," Garth agreed, gazing at the gleaming clockwork gull. "But not your finest," he added, with a nod to the west.

The toymaker smiled. "No, it's not my finest, but my very best is not for sale." He watched as Garth seated himself in the saddle, the copper bird perched before him, and gave a command to his mount.

Koros turned and headed back through the village, its smooth, silent progress carrying it and its master quickly northward out of Orgûl.

That steady stride seemed effortless, and the warbeast could keep it up for hours on end, perhaps days on end; Garth was continually impressed by the creature's incredible power and stamina.

It took them the remainder of that day and the following night to reach the northern edge of the Barony of Sland, moving along the foothills east of the mountains that formed Eramma's western border. Garth made camp atop a ridge overlooking the desolate site of a moderately recent battle.

His brief stay in Orgûl had put him in a state of mild euphoria. He had not fought and slain a monster, but instead had found that his real task, that of freeing people from the menace that beset them, had been accomplished long before by the threatened people themselves. That was heartening; only rarely in his long life had he seen much evidence of human competence. Even among his own species, it often seemed that the average mortal had no more ambition or wit than a lower animal had. Too many people were willing to suffer under various forms of oppression, rather than make the effort necessary to improve their lot.

No one among the overmen of the Northern Waste had attempted to come south overland for any purpose during the three centuries of relative peace that had followed the Racial Wars; they had been told that the border with Eramma was guarded night and day by ferocious human warriors and they had believed it until Garth made the journey to Skelleth himself, for reasons of his own, and discovered the pitiful state of the human defenses.

No overman had troubled himself to explore other kingdoms until Garth, on an errand for the Forgotten King, ventured into Nekutta and learned that there were other overmen still in the world, living on the Yprian Coast. And no attempt had been made to establish trade until Garth began it.

Among humans, the people of Skelleth had tolerated an insane baron without serious complaint, ignoring his bizarre behavior and occasional arbitrary executions, until Garth murdered him. In the Nekuttan city of Dûsarra, the populace had made no protest against the domination of the cults of the dark gods, nor had it tried to halt the kidnappings and human sacrifices of the more vicious cults.

In Orgûl, though, when heroes had failed to kill the dragon, ordinary farmers had managed to poison it, and common village craftsmen had built and maintained a replacement to ward off other predators, more human but no less vicious.

That fact cheered Garth considerably.

His own behavior pleased him as well. For the first time, he had ventured out into human lands beyond Skelleth, accomplished as much of his purpose as he saw fit, and headed homeward without killing a single person.

He was, he had been told, the chosen avatar of Bheleu, doomed to symbolize the Fourteenth Age, the Age of Destruction. Heretofore it had seemed that he was destined to bring chaos and disaster wherever he went; he had led the sacking of Skelleth, been responsible for bringing the White Death to Dûsarra, been involved in the death of the wizard who had ruled Mormoreth and killed its population, and, he suspected, somehow contributed to the collapse of the Kingdom of Eramma.

On this particular journey, however, he had not destroyed anything, nor killed anything more important than goats, and those only for food for his mount.

This raised his spirits so much that even the battlefields and soldiers he passed on his way north did not dissipate his good cheer. He moved on past Sland and along the mountains until he came within sight of the towers of Ur-Dormulk, where he turned east and circled around the city. He had traveled this far by night, but from here on, the population was thin and the land inhospitable; the war would therefore not be much in evidence. Furthermore, beyond Ur-Dormulk, overmen were no longer totally unknown; the Yprian caravans had been crossing these lands occasionally for most of the past three years, and the people were accustomed to them. Householders would not attack Garth on sight simply because of his species.

He could, if he chose, travel by day and use the highway to Skelleth openly.

Switching his schedule all at once, however, was not particularly convenient; instead, he lengthened each leg of it, riding on into the morning until he was too weary to want to go farther, then sleeping on past sunset until he awoke naturally and fully rested. He did, however, follow the high road; the plains were still muddy from melted snow and spring rain.

He finally came within sight of Skelleth around noon, but he had been awake since midnight, so that as far as he was concerned, it was late in the day and he was ready to rest. He had bought a goat for Koros the previous morning and eaten well himself, at a small farm he had passed, but he had had nothing since, save for a handful of dried fruit and salted beef; his provisions were beginning to run low. He was tired and hungry and looking forward to cold ale and hot food at the King's Inn, followed by a soft bed in the house he had rebuilt for himself from the ruins at the edge of town.

The prospect of a good rest, and his lingering good mood, put a smile on his face. He glanced down at the clockwork gull he kept on the saddle before him; he had not cared to pack it away where it might be damaged by bumping against his other belongings. It gleamed golden in the thin, dreary light that seeped through the thick clouds overhead. The weather had been good throughout his trip, but he knew that could not last much longer; indeed, the sky looked very much as if there would be rain before nightfall.

When he glanced up from the metal bird, Garth noticed that something or someone stood outside the town wall, beside the highway he rode upon. His smile faded. The last time he had ridden up this highway, someone had been waiting upon it, an overman named Thord; he had been posted there as part of an inept siege laid by Garth's chief wife Kyrith, and it had been that siege which had led to the sacking of Skelleth. Garth did not much care to be reminded of that.

He wondered whom or what he was seeing; the distance was such that he could not yet make the figure out. He hoped that, whatever it was, it was not the harbinger of more trouble.

The thing stood about the height of an overman, Garth judged, or perhaps an unusually tall human, but the shape seemed slightly wrong. He rode on.

When he had drawn somewhat nearer, he saw that it was, indeed, an overman, or something very much like one, but slumped forward, and with something projecting upward at the back of its neck.

Another of the warbeast's long strides allowed Garth to determine that the overman—if such it truly was—was hanging from a post or stake, apparently lifeless.

Garth was confused; he had no idea what this thing could signify, what overman could be there, or why. He did not like it. The figure was utterly lifeless, and Garth wondered whether perhaps it was an effigy of himself, put there by some enemy, a townsman, perhaps, who had never forgiven him his part in Skelleth's destruction.

The other possibility, that it was a real overman's corpse hung up as a warning of some kind, was much less appealing.

He rode closer and began to perceive details. Black hair hung down limply, hiding the face; the hands were pulled back, out of sight, presumably tied to the pole or to each other. The figure faced directly toward him. A blue tunic covered the torso, and brown leather riding breeches the legs, with mud-spattered boots on its feet. There was a disturbing familiarity to it.

The possibility that it was just an effigy grew dimmer with each step and vanished long before he reached the corpse's side.

The sensation of familiarity increased, and with it Garth's concern. By the time he told Koros to stop, he was seriously worried, convinced that he had come upon the body of someone he knew well.

He dismounted, and as he turned toward the suspended corpse he realized for the first time that it was female. Over-women were not as clearly differentiated from overmen as women were from men; there was no difference in height, and both sexes were equally flat-chested, though males tended to be broader at the shoulder and narrower at the hip. The primary sexual distinction was in the odor.

With the realization of the sex of the corpse, he was suddenly sure of its identity; he ran to it, hoping that he was wrong, and lifted the drooping head.

He had not been wrong. It was Kyrith. Her red eyes were open, blank, and staring, and her leathery brown skin was cold and clammy; Garth could have no doubt that she was dead.

He was so horrified, so caught by her dead gaze, that he did not at first consciously notice the marks on her forehead. Like all their people, she had a broad, high forehead, the skin drawn tight across the bone; now her brow was caked with dried blood, and blood had congealed in rivulets down either side of her face.

When Garth was able to turn his eyes from hers, he saw the blood and followed the dried streams to their source.

There were cuts in her forehead, many of them, but not mere random slashes; Garth did not immediately see the pattern, for the blood had blurred it, and shock had dulled his wits. As he continued to stare, however, he made out the nature of the marks. On her right side was a horizontal curl, and a diagonal, and then a long downstroke—the rune for A. Next was the upward curve, hooked downstroke, and downward curve of GH, then another A, and finally the short upright and long double curve of a D—except that here the curve was broken and awkward, more like a series of short slashes. Runes were meant to be drawn with ink on paper, not cut into flesh.

AGHAD.

Garth knew that name well. Humans swore by it, sometimes, and used it in jesting reference to liars or unfaithful spouses, but Garth knew it to be no joke. It was the name of the god of hatred and treachery, and of a cult he had defied and defiled when he robbed their temple and slew their high priest in Dûsarra about three years before.

The cult had made a habit of casual and gruesome murders, and had sworn vengeance upon him, but he had long since dismissed it from his thoughts. He had believed the cultists to be limited to their own city, far to the west, and had considered their threats merely human boastfulness.

He had, he saw now, been wrong.

No trace remained of his earlier euphoria, nor of the boredom and purposelessness that had driven him to undertake his errand to Orgûl. A cold, hard determination burned in his breast; he would destroy the cult of Aghad, and if the means could be found, he would kill the filthy god himself. Garth was an oathbreaker, forsworn, so he made no spoken vow, but his unvoiced commitment was none the less certain for that.

The initial astonished horror was fading, driven out by rage, and he looked over his wife's corpse.

A cord was wrapped around her throat, then looped back and tied around the stake. Wire bound her wrists behind the post so tightly that it had drawn blood, gouging deeply into the flesh. A third strand, this one of hideously inappropriate gold braid, passed across her chest, under her arms, and up to a spike driven into the back of the stake; it was this last that actually supported most of her weight and held her upright.

Garth drew his dagger and cut away the braid with a single short slash, then caught the corpse with his left arm as it started to slump. Another cut severed the line around the neck, allowing a small pouch he had not previously noticed to fall to the ground.

He ignored the little bag for the moment as, holding his dead wife with his left hand and body, he tried to pry apart the wire at her wrists. It resisted; although it had the appearance of cheap iron, the wire notched the blade of his knife when he worked the point underneath. Nor could he find any loose end whereby he might untangle it.

He lowered the body into a sitting position, the hands resting on the ground behind the stake, and considered. The followers of Aghad, he recalled, took a perverse delight in doing everything they could to infuriate their victims. They were also fond of mutilation. They probably intended to frustrate and annoy Garth with some manner of trickery, until he became sufficiently maddened that he would sever Kyrith's hand to free her from the post.

The wire, he decided, must be ensorcelled in some way.

There was no point in struggling with it—yet he had no desire to gratify the Aghadites by dismembering his wife.

The problem could be handled in another way. He fetched his battle-axe from the warbeast's saddle and, with three blows, cut through the foot-thick stake just above Kyrith's sagging head. Having eliminated the spike that had held the braid, Garth was able to lift her easily, so that her hands slid up over the broken end and came free.

That done, he remembered the pouch that had fallen from the neck cord. He laid the corpse gently on the ground and looked for it.

The little bag lay where it had fallen, at the foot of the stake. He picked it up, opened it cautiously, and drew out the roll of parchment it contained.

He had heard of spells that worked through runes, of messages that could bind an unsuspecting victim to the writer's will, but he did not seriously consider it likely that this parchment was anything of that kind. He thought, rather, that it would be a threat or a boast, or perhaps both; the Aghadites had seemed to him the sort of vicious creatures who would not be satisfied with the mere fact of murder, or with the crude attribution carved on the corpse's brow.

He unrolled the parchment and read the following: "Greetings to Garth of Skelleth, once Prince of Ordunin. The righteous vengeance of Aghad has begun, and you will suffer a thousandfold for the affronts you have committed. For the desecration of the god's shrine and the murder of his chosen high priest, you will pay with everything you value. All those you care for will die horribly. Your sons will die slowly as you watch. That which you have built will be cast down and destroyed. That which you have opposed will be exalted. That which you own shall be taken from you. As your pain grows, know always that Aghad will take joy in it, and his worshippers will laugh at your agony."

There was no signature.

Garth crumpled the parchment in his fist and thrust it into a pouch on his belt. Before he could withdraw his hand, he felt a sudden warmth, and the smell of smoke reached his slit nostrils. Startled, he withdrew his hand and dumped the pouch onto a patch of bare earth.

Nothing remained of the note but smoldering ash.

He snorted. If the indestructible wire had not been proof enough, this little demonstration left no doubt that the cult was using magic against him. He looked up, glanced quickly around, but saw nothing. He had fought magic before, several times, and knew it to be a real and sometimes deadly force; he would need to keep a careful watch.

Someone, he realized, might be watching him even now, and he could no longer resist speaking. "Your god will not save you, filth," he said, his voice flat. "Your cult will die, to the last man or woman. My wife's forehead bears your death warrant." He picked up the axe he had dropped and, in a sudden display of fury, splintered the stump of the stake with a single blow.

In Dûsarra, in his inner chamber, Haggat watched the overman's actions and permitted himself a small, silent chuckle. Events were proceeding almost exactly as he had envisioned—though the failure of the wired wrists was slightly disappointing. It was still much as he had wanted. The stolen magics were working perfectly.

This might, he thought, be worth the long wait.

CHAPTER SIX

His anger under control once more, Garth returned the axe to its place on the warbeast's saddle. He looked around at the scattered shards of the stake, then gathered up everything of possible value. That done, he picked up Kyrith's body and ordered Koros to follow him. Carrying his dead wife in his arms, he marched into Skelleth.

The manner of expressing certain emotions differed between human and overman. Overmen made no show of grief or anger on their faces, but instead displayed at such times an expression that in humans would appear to be one of utter disinterest. This was not a result of training in stoicism or any other cultural influence, but a difference in genetic makeup. An overman who seemed bored might be in a murderous rage.

A human guard was posted at the southwestern gate—not a professional soldier, but a volunteer, put there not so much for defense as to run ahead of an arriving caravan to inform Galt and the town's merchants of its approach. The man assigned to this job carried a crossbow and a short sword, more or less as a formality.

The individual who was on duty at the time of Garth's return from Orgûl had not heard the overman's approach, having dozed off in the shelter of a ruined wall. He had stirred slightly

57

at the sound of the axe smashing the post, but did not come fully awake until Garth's footsteps had drawn quite near.

Startled, he got to his feet, his hand on the hilt of his sword, and prepared to call a challenge.

Garth's face was calm and still, but had the guard spoken, Garth would have taken delight in killing him, probably using only his bare hands. He was in no mood to deal with strangers, particularly human strangers; the cult of Aghad was comprised mostly of humans. Few overmen took an interest in anything so ethereal as religion.

Only the fact that the guard recognized both Garth and Kyrith saved his life; he was so shocked at the sight of the corpse that he could not speak at first, and when he had recovered something of his composure, a glance at Garth's blood-red eyes discouraged any questions he might have had. He stood back respectfully and let the burdened overman and riderless warbeast pass unhindered.

When they had moved on up the road, he debated briefly with himself. He was supposed to run ahead of new arrivals and give warning of their approach; Garth, however, was a resident of Skelleth, however unwelcome his presence there might be to some of the villagers. Furthermore, the overman did not look as if he would appreciate a welcoming committee.

The guard decided, with a glance at Garth's armored back, that he would prefer facing a charge of dereliction of duty to risking the overman's annoyance. He stayed where he was.

Most of the outer portion of Skelleth was a ring of uninhabited ruins, a reminder of the town's long decline; only the central area, around the market, was populated. As a result of this, Garth walked some distance on empty streets, between fallen stones and broken beams, before he was again seen by human eyes.

Like the guard at the gate, the villagers who saw his approach recognized him. Remembering the sacking of Skelleth and seeing the warbeast at his heels, they hung well back and let him pass without hindrance or comment. The traditional fear of overmen had been largely dissipated by three years of trade, but Garth's berserker reputation, the sight of the corpse, and the presence of the warbeast were enough to send even the boldest scurrying out of his path without concern for their dignity.

He reached the market unmolested, not having spoken a word since he entered the walls. There he lowered Kyrith's body to the ground, turned toward the new house on the east side of the square, and bellowed, *"Saram!"*

Windows opened instantly, and faces peered out. Saram's was not among them, but Garth recognized one that appeared on the upper floor of the Baron's house. He pointed at the girl and shouted, "You, there! You get Lord Saram out here!"

The girl, Saram's housekeeper, vanished inside.

A moment later the front door opened, and one of the Baron's clerks thrust her head out. "My lord Saram is occupied at present, my lord Garth," she said. "How may I help you?"

Garth's hand fell to the hilt of his sword. He replied, slowly and clearly, without shouting, "You will inform Lord Saram that if he is not out here within the count of twenty, he will not live to see the sun set today, and this stinking village will not see tomorrow's dawn."

The clerk's politely noncommittal expression vanished instantly, to be replaced with a gape of terrified astonishment. She disappeared back inside, leaving the door open.

Garth did not bother to count; as he had expected, Saram appeared on the doorstep within a few seconds, a napkin in his hand.

The Baron of Skelleth did not trouble to look about, but simply stared directly at the overman. "What is it, Garth?" he asked, a trace of annoyance in his voice.

Garth's reply was toneless and deadly. "Come here, human," he said.

Saram knew better than to argue. He came; halfway to where Garth waited, he suddenly noticed Kyrith's body and stopped dead. After a moment's hesitation, he continued on and stood a few feet away, staring down at the corpse in surprise.

"What happened?" he asked.

"*You* will tell *me* that, man, or I'll burn this town to the ground. How could this happen?"

"I don't know, Garth, I swear by all the gods! She came into town two days ago, looking for you; she said you had sent an urgent message asking her to come to Skelleth. We told her it must have been a mistake, that you'd been gone for days, and that was the last we saw of her—until now. I thought she'd gone back north again, gone home?"

"She was last seen alive two days ago."

"About that; 'twas midafternoon of the day before yesterday."

"She has been dead only a few hours at most, Saram. Where was she in between?"

"I don't know, I swear it." The Baron met the overman's gaze for a moment, then turned back to the corpse.

Garth reached out and grabbed the front of Saram's elaborately embroidered tunic. "What do you know about the cult of Aghad?" he demanded.

Startled, Saram looked up again. "What cult of Aghad?" he asked. "There isn't any, is there? I never heard of anyone outside Dûsarra who worshipped him or any of the other dark gods, and the White Death has destroyed Dûsarra."

"Look at her forehead, human." Garth released Saram's tunic and grabbed his neatly trimmed back hair, pulling his head down close to Kyrith's face. Saram looked as Garth added, "There was a note as well, a magical one that destroyed itself after I read it. A cult of Aghad still exists, and his followers have killed my wife."

"I don't know anything about them," Saram insisted after Garth allowed him to straighten up. "Perhaps 'tis some other enemy of yours, trying to avoid the blame."

"What enemy?"

"How should I know? Maybe 'tis that bunch of wizards that tried to kill you three years ago."

"No; why should they kill Kyrith? Why would they not attack me directly? I am no longer defended by the power of the Sword of Bheleu; the wizards would surely know that. If they sought revenge they would simply slay me, attacking directly, as they attacked me before. No, Saram, this is cruelty for its own sake; this is the work of evil people, to kill an innocent like this just to get at me. It must be one of the cults I angered. The followers of Bheleu are all dead; the priest of Death is a harmless old man. I did nothing to anger the cult of P'hul. That leaves four: Tema, Andhur Regvos, Sai, or Aghad. Only Aghad takes pride in treachery; had one of the others slain Kyrith, that cult would have proclaimed itself openly. The followers of Aghad might have lied and blamed others, but no one would falsely accuse *them*. It is in truth the Aghadites who have done this, I am certain."

"Then what do you want of *me*?" Saram asked. "I am no Aghadite."

"You are the Baron of Skelleth. Whatever happens in this town and the territory surrounding it is your responsibility."

"I accept no blame for this murder, Garth."

"You have allowed the cult of Aghad to exist, to take action in your domain."

"I have not! I told you, I thought the cult was extinct."

"The cult is not extinct, Saram, but if you value your life, you will do what you can to see that it *becomes* extinct."

"Of course I will! Do you think I want more murders? Do you think I do not regret this one? Kyrith was my friend, Garth, and you are my friend as well. What has hurt you has hurt me. I wish that there were something I could do to undo what has happened, but I am as mortal as you; I cannot turn back time."

Garth did not reply; the phrasing of Saram's defense reminded him that he had other business to attend to. As Saram had said, he was merely mortal and could do nothing to restore Kyrith to life, any more than Garth could—but there was one person in Skelleth who was something other than mortal. The Forgotten King was the chosen of the god of death; he had lived for centuries, perhaps for millennia, and had powers and abilities greater than any ordinary priest or wizard.

He was also a treacherous old schemer. Garth did not say so to Saram, but he suspected that if anywhere in the world there was anyone other than the cultists of Aghad who was implicated in Kyrith's murder, it was the Forgotten King. His part in it, if he was involved, might have been anything from the most indirect sort of encouragement to planning and carrying out the whole scheme himself and falsely accusing the Aghadites. The old man could, of course, be innocent, but Garth would not take that for granted; the King had been entangled in Garth's life too often for the overman to dismiss the possibility of his complicity. It was the old man who had suggested that Garth should go adventuring and who had proposed his destination and thereby ensured a certain minimum travel time.

Perhaps the old man had planned the whole ghastly murder for some perverse reason of his own; perhaps it had been calculated to goad Garth into some action he would otherwise have avoided.

It was just as likely, though, that the cult of Aghad had simply seized upon the opportunity Garth's absence had presented and that the old man had had no part in it.

Garth had mulled this over while carrying Kyrith's body through the village to the market; the possibility of the King's involvement had been immediately obvious as soon as Garth had gotten over his initial shock.

It bore looking into, but he had wanted to acquaint himself with the available facts about Kyrith's return from Ordunin and whatever was generally known of her death. The Forgotten King, with his reluctance to speak, would have been of little help there. Nor had Garth wanted to waste any time in alerting Saram to the murder, the probable presence of the cult of Aghad, and Garth's anger.

He had done that; now he could turn his attention to the King.

Saram's words had also suggested a faint possibility Garth had not previously considered. The King, no mere mortal, had an undeniable connection with The God Whose Name Is Not Spoken; if there was anyone in all the world who might be capable of restoring Kyrith to life, it was he.

With that in mind, Garth turned, leaving Kyrith's body on the packed earth of the marketplace, and marched toward the King's Inn. "See that she is not disturbed," he called back over his shoulder to the Baron, "and that the cult of Aghad is driven from Skelleth."

Saram stood in openmouthed astonishment at this sudden change. Garth seemed to have abandoned the conversation in midstream and had simply walked off after dragging him, Saram, Baron of Skelleth, out of his home. Koros, too, was apparently caught by surprise; the warbeast gave a low, questioning growl, which the departing overman answered with an order that meant "stand and guard." Saram looked at the beast, noticed the gleaming metal bird on its back, and grew still more confused.

What, he wondered, was that thing? He looked again at Garth, then back at Kyrith's body, and decided to stay where he was until he could get everything straight in his mind.

Garth stalked across the wooden weighing platforms that occupied what was once the site of the old Baron's mansion, across the narrow strip that used to be a back alley cut off from the square by the mansion, and through the open door of the King's Inn.

The tavern looked very much as it always had; there was no indication that anything within was not as it should be. The heavy, worn tables were in their accustomed places, the great brass-bound barrels still lined the west wall, and the vast stone hearth still took up most of the east. At the rear, stairs led to the upper floor, and the Forgotten King's table stood in the corner beneath. Everything was clean, with the soft sheen that could only result from centuries of use and care.

The tavernkeeper stood by one of his barrels, a mug and a polishing cloth in his hands; two customers were conversing over wine. The Forgotten King sat motionless at his table.

Garth marched across the room. He did not bother to seat himself, but stood beside the King's table and demanded, "What did you have to do with it?"

The old man croaked, "Nothing."

"Is that all you have to say? Am I to trust you so readily?"

"I swear by my heart and all the gods, by the true name of The God Whose Name Is Not Spoken, that I had no part in your wife's murder."

Some portion of Garth's mind was aware that the old man was taking this seriously indeed, to make so long an answer so quickly, but his anger would not permit him to consider that. "And what good is your vow? How can it bind you? Death holds no terror for you, old man; you have little to lose in that regard. Nor have you shown any thought for your honor; what need have you of honor or trust, you who have incomprehensible power and no desire but death? You have abandoned the service of your god; can I know that his name still holds you?"

"You cannot be certain. Take my word or not, as you please." The old man's ghastly voice was as dead as ever.

Garth was by no means so calm; with a wordless bellow, he reached out and grabbed the King's throat in one huge hand.

"Lying scum!" he cried. "Deathless monster! Do you dare to mock me at such a time?" In his rage, he cared little for accuracy or fairness and ignored the fact that, if any mockery had been spoken, it was he who had mocked the King and not the reverse. He squeezed.

His hand went limp and dead, falling with a heavy thud on the table.

"Your pardon, Garth. I lived for several years with a broken neck once, long ago, and I have no desire to repeat the experience."

Garth stared down at his hand. Sensation returned in a sudden rush of pain. He had bruised several knuckles on the oaken tabletop.

The discomfort quickly faded to insignificance, but served to distract him from his anger long enough for his rationality to reassert control. As the incident had demonstrated, the King had power. Garth could not harm him, but he might be able to use him. After a moment's hesitation, he moved around the table and sat down opposite the old man.

"It is I, rather, who should ask for pardon, O King," he said. "Forgive me; I let my grief get the better of me. I came here not to challenge you, but to ask a favor. I do not know the limits of your power, O King; perhaps what I ask cannot be done. Still, I must make the attempt. Can you restore Kyrith to life?"

The King paused before he moved his head once from side to side. "No, Garth. I am sorry."

"It is not possible?"

"I cannot do it."

"Why not? You are the high priest of Death; have you no power over him?"

"You ask me to undo the god's work. Could you create with the Sword of Bheleu, restore what you had destroyed?"

Garth had to acknowledge that he could not have done such a thing; the very essence of the sword's power was destruction. He was not willing to give up completely, however. "What of your own spells? You were a mighty wizard in your own right, were you not? Knew you no magic to restore the dead?"

"If ever I did, it is centuries forgotten."

"Is there no talisman that can serve? Bheleu has his sword, and the Death-God his book; has the god of life no totem?"

"The totems of the Lords of Eir lost their virtue at the center of time, in the Eighth Age, when the balance first shifted against them. They have no power now, if they still exist at all."

"Is there no way to shift this balance again?"

The old man shrugged almost imperceptibly. "There may be; if so, it would be in the Book of Silence. That is not the totem of The God Whose Name Is Not Spoken, but of Dagha, god of time, the creator of both Eir and Dûs." He stopped suddenly, as if he had meant to say more and then thought better of it.

Garth, listening intently, noticed the peculiarly abrupt stop, but could read no meaning into it. He ignored it and considered instead the words that had preceded it.

He had taken it for granted that the Book of Silence was the totem of The God Whose Name Is Not Spoken; after all, the Forgotten King had obviously expected, three years ago, that Garth would find it on the Final God's altar in Dûsarra, as he had found the Sword of Bheleu on Bheleu's altar, and the Stone of Tema on Tema's altar, and the Stone of Andhur Regvos on the altar of Andhur Regvos. Furthermore, the book was needed for the King's great final magic, and Garth was fairly sure that that somehow involved conjuring the Death-God into the mortal world. That, too, seemed to imply a link with the Final God. Garth knew relatively little of human theology, and most of what he did know he had learned on his trip to Dûsarra, but he had had the definite impression that Dagha had few dealings with mortals. He had never heard of any cult of Dagha, nor any temple dedicated to Dagha. Why, then, should so powerful a talisman be linked with this obscure deity?

It did not seem reasonable. He decided that the King was lying, hoping to trick Garth into keeping his oath and fetching the Book of Silence on the basis of a false hope that it might aid in the resurrection of his dead wife.

If he could expose this trickery, he might find himself in a better position from which to deal with the old man.

He reached this conclusion in barely three seconds; the pause in the conversation was scarcely noticeable before Garth said,

"Indeed. Then what is the Death-God's totem? Surely you must have it, as his high priest and chosen vessel."

"I left it in Hastur, in my chapel." The King's voice was softer than usual, barely audible, a grinding, scratching whisper. He seemed not to be looking at Garth, though how Garth knew that, when the old man's eyes were as invisible as ever, he could not have said.

"Hastur?"

"Hastur, capital of Carcosa."

"Where was this place? Surely the chapel must be long gone; I have never heard of Hastur, and Carcosa has been forgotten for centuries by all save yourself."

"The barbarians took the city and it became Hastur-dar-Mallek, Hastur-of-the-Barbarians, but they could not have destroyed it, even had they tried. They buried it instead, Hastur below, Hastur-dar-Mallek above." There was a strange animation in the old man's tone.

"I have never heard of Hastur-dar-Mallek, O King."

"That was long ago, before overmen were first created; the name has been shortened to Ur-Dormulk."

"Ur-Dormulk? That was your capital?" Garth was astonished. He had heard the Forgotten King speak of his long-lost kingdom of Carcosa once or twice before, but he had not paid very much attention to the stories. He had never doubted that the old man had once been a true king, yet he had not seriously supposed that this vanished empire had had any connection at all with the world as it was in this, the Fourteenth Age.

Now, suddenly, he was told that Ur-Dormulk, the most ancient and independent of Eramma's cities and Skelleth's trading partner, which he had seen from afar on his trips to Dûsarra and Orgûl, was once the King's capital. This revelation provided a new and more definite link between his own era and the old man's vague past. Somehow Garth had always thought of them as two separate worlds, unconnected save by certain magical objects and by the King himself; it required a major readjustment of those thoughts for him to realize that it was all one, divided only by time.

There were a few seconds of silence as the overman absorbed this news. Then he thrust it aside; it was not relevant.

"You have not said what it was that you left in your chapel."

"I left them both there, the Pallid Mask and the Book of Silence, and I sealed the chamber with the Yellow Sign. I knew that the invaders could not pass that, and that they could not use the book or the mask if they did, but I posted a guard as a matter of form. I was still concerned with form then, and with my reputation as a great wizard."

"You remember, then? The Book of Silence is there? How very convenient that you should recall that just now!" Garth did not try to keep the scorn out of his voice; he was quite sure that it was no coincidence that the King's memory had returned just as he had suggested how the Book of Silence might be of use to Garth.

The old man seemed to be almost lost in reverie, quite oblivious of Garth's tone; he made no answer.

"Do you think, then, that I should fetch the book immediately, so that Kyrith might be revived?" Garth's tone was still sarcastic, but there was a sincere thread of hope in it.

The Forgotten King shifted suddenly, and the tattered edge of his hood flapped. "No," he said.

"No?" Garth's surprise was genuine.

"Your wife is dead, Garth," the King said, "and I know of no way she can be restored to you. Even were the cosmic balance shifted again, and the totem of the god of life found and used by its rightful master—for I promise you, we who are bound to destruction and death could not touch it—I doubt that it could turn the corpse into anything better than a halfrotted vegetable. Too much time has passed already."

"Is time, then, the crucial point? Could not the god of time be coerced, with the Book of Silence, into undoing what has happened?"

"No. I doubt that the book wastes space on anything so trivial."

"The reversal of time, the resurrection of the dead, are trivial? Why, then, have you recalled where it lies? What good can it do me now?"

"There was no deception in my sudden memory, Garth; your mention of the Death-God's totem, the Pallid Mask, reminded me. I had brought the book from Dûsarra so that I might have both my great devices in a single safe place."

"In three years, you did not recall so simple a fact?"

"In three centuries, three millennia, I did not. Perhaps I was not intended to; though I do not currently wield the mask directly, no greater power has freed me of my patron as I freed you of Bheleu. The Age of Death is not yet come, but Death holds sway in every era."

This presented Garth with another new concept. It had never occurred to him that the Forgotten King might himself be the victim of the machinations of the gods beyond the fact of his immortality. Garth had assumed that the old man had had no contact with the gods since he left the service of The God Whose Name Is Not Spoken, that he dealt with no being more powerful than himself. The suggestion that his patron deity was still affecting him, perhaps involving him against his will in some divine scheme, was unsettling.

The entire conversation was becoming unsettling; it was getting out of hand, Garth decided. He had come with the intent of asking a few simple questions and receiving a few simple answers. He had wanted to know what part the King had played in Kyrith's death and whether she might be brought back to life somehow. He had not wanted to listen to details of the King's past, or to anything about the Book of Silence that might remind him of his own false oath. The King was being more loquacious than ever before in the three years Garth had known him, but everything he said related to his own concerns, rather than to Garth's. In mixed anger and desperation, Garth declared, "I care nothing for that. Answer me my questions."

The King said nothing.

"Is there any way known to you, no matter how fantastical or difficult, in which Kyrith might be restored to life?"

"No." The old man chopped the single syllable off short, but it was unmistakable and definite.

"Have you any reason, however slight, to believe that there might be some way *not* known to you?" Garth was reluctant to give up until he had exhausted every possibility.

Again, the King said, "No."

That seemed final; Garth could think of no other approach. The old man might be lying, but if he were, Garth had no way of coaxing the truth out of him.

"You had no part in her death?"

"No. I am no oathbreaker."

The added phrase hurt, and Garth wondered whether the old man knew of his intended infidelity. It was only after a few seconds of silence that he realized that the King had had no need to mention his oath, for the King did not like to speak unnecessarily. Garth had no choice but to conclude that the King knew very well that the overman had sworn falsely when he agreed to fetch the Book of Silence and was reminding him of it as delicately as possible.

He was not at all sure why the old man should do so. Perhaps, Garth thought, the King meant to shame him into fulfilling his false oath. The overman leaned back, his chair creaking beneath his shifting weight, and thought in silence for a moment.

In Dûsarra, watching his scrying glass, Haggat decided that this was an ideal opportunity for his next planned event. He gestured to his waiting acolyte, who hurried off to tell a priest, especially trained for this coming performance, that it was time to begin.

A moment later, in the King's Inn, something flickered at the edge of the overman's vision. He whirled, startled, his hand already on the hilt of his dagger, since the table's presence would have made it difficult for him to draw his sword.

The glinting had not been, as he had first thought, the gleam of firelight on metal. There was no one behind him. The flash of light had come from something he could not identify, a blurry redness hanging in mid-air and glowing faintly.

It hovered at the level of his eyes, perhaps a foot wide and a foot and a half in height, a blot of color against the dark background of the taproom.

This, obviously, was magic at work. He kept his hand on his dagger, though he knew ordinary weapons would probably be useless against whatever it was. Various possible origins for the thing passed through his mind. It might be a manifestation of Bheleu, come to reclaim him with or without the sword. It might be a sending of the council of wizards that had sought to destroy him, as a menace to the peace of Eramma, three years earlier. It could be something the Forgotten King had contrived, for reasons of his own, or it might have been sent by the cult of Aghad as part of its revenge upon him.

He had, he thought, made altogether too many enemies in his life, and too many of them possessed of supernatural power.

The blot was changing as he watched; it swirled and roiled about, not like smoke or even liquid, but as if it were made of flowing light. It grew, and shadows appeared within it.

Red was Bheleu's preferred color, but that was the bright red of fire or fresh blood; this thing was of a duller, browner shade, like blood that had dried. The King was the King in Yellow, but could, of course, use any color he chose; the council wizards had employed a wide variety of spells. Still, Garth found that he associated the unhealthy hue of the thing with Aghad.

As he realized that, the thing suddenly resolved itself into an image. It was a face, a not-quite-human face, twisted and sneering, with curving fangs protruding from its upper lip. Garth stared; he knew he had seen it, or one like it, somewhere before.

He glanced around; the Forgotten King was paying no attention to this manifestation, nor to anything else for that matter, but the tavernkeeper was staring in horror. The other customers had departed.

Garth turned back; the apparition was still there, hanging motionless, as if waiting.

"What are you? Why are you here?" Garth demanded. "Speak, O vision, and explain yourself!"

The face grinned and replied, "Greetings, Garth. It is good to see you so untroubled that you can share a drink and pass the time with this doddering old fraud." The voice was a low rumble, lower than any human voice and not easy to understand; it spoke with an accent unlike that of Skelleth, but one that Garth had heard before.

"Who are you?" Garth asked.

"Do you not recognize me? Have you never seen my likeness?"

"You are familiar, but I cannot place you."

"Ah, so feeble a memory, and in an overman! It is scarce three years since you invaded my home and destroyed my altar."

"Aghad!" Garth remembered now where he had seen that face; it had appeared on the small, carved idols sold in the Dûsarran market. The accent, too, was Dûsarran.

"You do remember! I am flattered!"

"Filth!" Garth spat. He did not give any serious consideration to the possibility that this might be the god himself; he was quite sure that it was some sort of trickery contrived by the cultists. He shifted, so that the table would not impede him, drew his sword, and rose to his feet.

"I had feared that you would be displeased by my paltry attempt to return the favor you did me, but I suppose you must have tired of your bitch years ago. Perhaps you would like to thank me for freeing you of her?" The thing grinned again.

Garth's sword came up and slashed through the image in a single smooth motion. It cut a narrow swath through the ethereal substance of the thing, but the speaker did not seem perturbed. In fact, it did not seem to notice his action at all. Garth had hoped for some sort of magical feedback.

"I notice that you haven't troubled to bury her; were you planning to feed her to your warbeast? You need not fear for its health; we used no poison. Nothing that could harm a warbeast, at any rate; we did not want to hurry her death. She took quite a long time to die; we found it very enjoyable. Would you care to guess whom we plan to kill next?"

Garth growled low in his throat and slashed at the image again, striking vertically this time. The sword passed through without resistance, leaving the floating image divided into quarters, but still unconcerned.

"You're not guessing, overman," the voice rumbled. "Will it be another of your wives? One of your children? Your cousins, or your uncle? Your friends on Ordunin's City Council? Perhaps the next won't be an overman at all; maybe we'll kill one of your friends here in Skelleth. The old man might do for a start. Or perhaps we might take the best of both worlds and kill your traitorous comrade, Galt the swindler. Will you guess, overman? Will you guess, or will you just wait and see?"

Garth hacked at the thing again, splitting it further and leaving six fragments. The face was no longer clearly visible; the edges of each segment were blurred, and the whole image seemed to be distorted.

It grinned and vanished completely, with a sound of fading laughter.

Garth stared at the empty air, then looked about, seeing no sign of any further supernatural manifestation. The sword still in his hand, he announced, "Hear me, Aghadite scum! I have had my fill of you. You owe me a life for my wife's death, and a hundred more for the manner of it. I swear that I will find you and destroy you, wherever you may hide. I will return to Dûsarra, smash your temple, and grind it into the dust. Your magic will not protect you; your god will not save you. I swear this, by everything I hold dear."

There was no answer but the silence of the almost-empty tavern.

CHAPTER SEVEN

After a long, wary moment, Garth finally admitted to himself that he could do nothing more immediately. He sheathed his sword, flexed the bruised knuckles of his right hand, and sat down again.

The apparition's words rankled, particularly the remarks about leaving Kyrith's corpse untended. One didn't bring a cadaver into a taproom, however, and he had hoped that the Forgotten King might resurrect her; that had seemed more important than providing the body with an appropriate rest.

He glanced at the Forgotten King. The old man wasn't going anywhere; Garth could come back here later if he decided he had to speak with him further. Without any more conversation, he rose and marched out the door. The King said nothing and made no move to stop him.

A crowd had gathered in the market, clustered about Kyrith's body. Garth was tall enough to see over their heads and noted that they were maintaining a respectful distance. A young boy had clambered up on the base of the statue that stood near the center of the market, a statue that had once been a young thief who had been petrified by a basilisk by the order of the previous Baron of Skelleth.

The crowd's presence irked Garth; it did not seem fitting that these members of an inferior species should cluster around

Kyrith's remains like a pack of wolves around a dead warbeast. "Get away!" he bellowed. "Go home, all of you!"

Startled, the townspeople's faces turned toward him, but no one moved to depart until he picked up two women on the northern fringe, one in each hand, grasped by the shoulder, and placed them off to either side. They backed away, rubbing where his hands had gripped, and the rest of the villagers backed away as well.

"Go home!" Garth bellowed again; he drew his sword for emphasis, and people began vanishing into houses and down streets. A moment later no one remained in the square but himself and Saram, both standing over Kyrith's body. Koros stood nearby, as it had stood since its arrival in the market, the copper gull gleaming dully on its back.

Saram watched Garth closely, waiting for him to speak.

The overman spent a few seconds staring down at his dead wife's face. It was sinking in that she was really dead, gone forever. She had always been his closest companion in Ordunin, much more so than his two remaining wives; he regretted, now, that he had spent so much of the last few years away from her.

Word would have to be sent to Ordunin. She had kin there, not just her sister and co-wife Myrith, or her other co-wife Lurith, but two brothers and a few nephews and nieces. At last report, her mother was still alive. Kyrith alone, of Garth's wives, had no children; Garth had regretted that before, but now it seemed almost comforting somehow. Fewer people would grieve over her loss.

The overmen of the Northern Waste were not much given to elaborate ceremony and did not bother with funerals after the human fashion; since most had no belief in an afterlife of any sort, there was no religious necessity for them. The custom was, rather, to combine the disposal of the body with the division of property, whether by the reading of a will or by adjudication. The body itself was ordinarily sunk in Ordunin's ocean or buried in more inland regions, without fanfare, once the property settlement was announced and no doubt remained of the subject's identity and death.

That would not be appropriate here, Garth decided. Shipping the body home would be difficult and unpleasant, and the people of Ordunin would think it wasteful and eccentric, at the very least. Holding the reading of the will in Skelleth would seem equally bizarre to all concerned, since, save for himself, none of her heirs were present or likely to turn up; to the religious and sentimental humans, it might well seem callous and disrespectful.

There was certainly precedent for separating the ceremony from the burial; overmen who died at sea were simply tossed overboard, and the ritual of legacy was performed later on shore. A death in a foreign land, it seemed to Garth, would follow the same pattern. He would see the body interred in Skelleth, and Kyrith's other family would hold the ceremony in Ordunin, without either Garth or the corpse.

To keep up the dignity of his species among the humans of Skelleth, Garth knew that some sort of ceremony, though perhaps not a real funeral, would be in order. He would have to devise something.

For the present, however, there was no hurry. He knew that humans waited as much as two or three days before burning or burying their dead. He wanted to use that time to consider how best Kyrith's memory might be honored. He recalled what he had heard of human customs and broke the silence by saying, "She must lie in state."

Saram had been waiting for some such indication of Garth's plans. "I will have a bier prepared immediately, in my audience chamber," Saram said.

Garth nodded, and the Baron hurried away.

Once in his house, Saram summoned the nearest courtiers he could find and sent them to locate an appropriate platform and fine cloths to cover it.

He knew that running errands for the overman would not help his image as an authority figure, but he didn't much care. Garth was, after a fashion, a friend, and he had just received a terrible blow; one had to forgive him for failings of etiquette under the circumstances. Saram did not resent being manhandled and ordered about. He knew that he would behave no more politely or rationally if his own wife had been murdered.

The very thought of Frima's death gave him a moment's discomfort; he shook it off and began planning what he could do to eliminate the cult of Aghad from Skelleth.

In the square, Garth knelt and studied Kyrith's body. It was not immediately obvious what had killed her; the wounds on her forehead and bound wrists were quite minor, really. He felt her throat, and although it was bruised and lacerated, she did not appear to have been strangled.

He moved a hand to her chest and felt broken ribs.

He stopped, withdrew his fingers, and stepped back. He had decided that he didn't really want to know the extent of what the Aghadites had done to her; it was enough to know that she was dead and that they were responsible.

The marks on her forehead would have to be covered, he thought, while she lay on display in the Baron's house. The blood would need to be cleaned off her face. If he was going to subject his wife's remains to human ritual, he would do everything he could to ensure that the ceremony remained as dignified as possible.

Koros growled, and a shadow encroached at the edge of Garth's vision. He looked up to see a human, covered by a loose, heavy, red robe, face hidden by an overhanging hood, standing nearby. The overman could not tell if the figure was man or woman.

The people of Skelleth did not ordinarily wear robes or cloaks; the people of Dûsarra did, and this robe was the color of dried blood. Garth's hand fell to the hilt of his sword.

"What do you want here, human?" he demanded.

"Greetings, Garth," the creature said. Its taunting voice was male, Garth decided, and the man spoke in the guttural manner of the Dûsarrans. "I came to bring you a message."

"What message? From whom?" The overman wrapped his hand around the sword's hilt.

"We heard your oath just now, and your offer to come and visit us in Dûsarra."

Garth drew his sword, but did not attack; he was wary of unseen menaces.

"You will be welcome, of course. We would be delighted to have you stay with us; on your last trip you rushed off so quickly! This time you really must stay to dinner."

Garth saw no sign of any hidden threat, yet the Aghadite messenger simply stood, speaking calmly, ignoring the overman's bare steel.

He was probably armored, Garth reflected. He thought that

padding and metal would protect him. The heavy robe was to conceal the helmet and gauntlets that would have been exposed by the sort of tunic normally worn in Skelleth.

"We have a request, though," the Aghadite said as he extended a long, bare finger and pointed it at Kyrith's body. "You bring the meat."

With a wordless bellow, Garth swung the sword.

The blade struck the man's robe and instantly exploded in a burst of red flame and splintered steel, leaving the overman clutching the useless hilt. The Aghadite laughed, but even in his state of unreasoning fury, Garth could detect the nervousness in that laugh, its forced quality. The man was not as sure of himself as he wished to appear.

Garth tossed the broken sword aside and reached for the Aghadite with his bare hands.

A wisp of red smoke swirled up from empty air between them; Garth ignored it as the man backed away hurriedly. The Aghadite was not yet running, merely stepping back, away from Garth's outstretched hands. Garth knew that he could catch the man; no human could outrun an overman. He grinned and advanced; the Aghadite continued to retreat.

The red smoke thickened and grew, gathering about the human, and Garth belatedly remembered seeing a similar mist once before. With a growl, he lunged forward, wasting no more time. His fingers closed on the edge of the red cloak, then passed through, holding nothing but air. The Aghadite had vanished.

Furious, Garth whirled, looking for other enemies, and with a cry of anguish saw Kyrith's body disappear in a red cloud.

He ran, but in the second or so that it took to reach it the corpse had vanished as completely as the Aghadite or the image that had spoken in the King's Inn.

He staggered to a halt in the center of the market, staring about wildly. Several of the people of Skelleth stood watching him, clustered in small groups in the streets that led out of the square. They muttered among themselves. Garth realized that they had seen the entire affair, had seen him humiliated, had seen Kyrith's body stolen. They had done nothing; no one had moved to aid him.

But then, he thought, why should they? He was not their

kind, and the Aghadites were. At least none had joined in taunting him.

"Leave me!" he bellowed. "Get away from here!"

A few of the villagers obeyed, retreating out of sight; more did not. Garth glared at them, and a few more backed away; others met his gaze without flinching.

Seeing no practical alternative, he resolved to ignore them. He turned and stooped to pick up the stump of his sword. As he did, Saram came running from the door of his house. The entire altercation had lasted only moments, and he had not at first realized that the noises outside were of any real concern.

"What happened?" he called.

"Shut up," Garth replied.

Frima's head appeared in the doorway, but she said nothing. Saram came to a stop, looking about the market, his eyes returning regularly to the spot where Kyrith's body had lain. He glanced at Garth, but did not care to venture a question.

Garth stood, glaring at the hilt and the jagged shard that projected from it. Somehow the Aghadites had acquired a powerful magic. They had apparently possessed some sorcerous devices or methods at the time of his previous encounter, in Dûsarra, but it had been his clear impression that they had relied primarily on trickery and simple machinery. Now, though, they seemed to be using real wizardry. The red mist that caused people to vanish had been used by the council of wizards he had fought, but never before by the priests of Aghad. The protective spell that had shattered his sword was nothing he had ever seen them demonstrate before, and the floating image that had spoken to him in the tavern was also new.

He knew that ordinary weapons were not enough against magicians. He had defeated the wizards only by wielding the Sword of Bheleu, and it had been the sword that he used to slay the high priest of Aghad.

He had given the Sword of Bheleu to the Forgotten King to free himself of its power, but now, he decided, the time had come to take it back. He would use it to destroy the cult, and then, he told himself, he would return it to the King's keeping. He knew that Bheleu would try to reassert his authority, try to take over Garth's body and possess him utterly, but he believed that he would be able to resist, to direct Bheleu's destructiveness, long enough to do what he had to do. The Aghadites had angered the chosen of the god of destruction, and they would be destroyed in consequence. Garth would use any means needful to make sure of that.

He obviously no longer needed to waste time on Kyrith's funeral arrangements, with her body stolen; he marched north across the market and into the King's Inn.

Behind him, Saram, Frima, and several other people watched him go. When he had vanished through the tavern door most of them went on about their business, but Saram and Frima followed him.

At his table in the rear, the Forgotten King sat exactly as he had sat when Garth left the inn. The overman made his way across the deserted taproom and seated himself, as if he, too, had never departed the place. Saram and Frima found seats at a nearby table, but did not intrude or do anything to draw Garth's attention.

The room was silent for a moment. Garth was aware of the two humans behind him, but did not care to acknowledge their presence. The King acknowledged nothing, merely stared at the table, as he usually did, his eyes fixed on the little spot of mismatched wood near the center. The Baron and Baroness watched, making no attempt to hide their concern for Garth; they watched, but said nothing.

Finally, Garth spoke, addressing the yellow-robed old man.

"Greetings, O King," he said.

The King said nothing.

"I have come," Garth continued, "to ask that you free me from my oath, given three winters back. Return to me the Sword of Bheleu and release me from my commitment to aid you, and all will be as it was."

The old man gave no sign of replying, but Saram burst out, "Garth, have you gone mad?"

"Silence, human," Garth said without turning. "This is not your affair."

"Garth, that thing will possess you again and drive you mad! You might destroy Skelleth again, and that means it *is* my affair. I cannot allow you to take back the sword!"

"Silence!" Garth bellowed. "Saram, I need that sword to take my vengeance upon Kyrith's murderers; their magic protects them from ordinary weapons, and I have no other magic available."

"I cannot allow it," Saram insisted. "Not in my village, not while I am Baron."

Garth turned to face him and said, "I have no intention of staying in Skelleth with the sword. Once I have slain whatever Aghadites I may find here, I will go to Dûsarra to destroy their temple, as I have sworn to do. I may not return. If I do return, I will try my best not to bring the sword back with me. If I do bring it, rest assured, I will be doing everything I can to keep myself free of its control. I do not like the sword, but I need its power. Now, be quiet!"

Saram had half-risen as he protested, and would have stood and argued, but Frima was pulling at his embroidered sleeve, urging him to sit down again and listen. Reluctantly he yielded and sank back into his chair.

Garth glared at him for a second, to be sure he was done arguing for the present, and then turned back to the Forgotten King.

"Your pardon, O King. I ask again, let us abandon our agreement, and return to me the Sword of Bheleu."

The old man spoke, without looking at the overman. "No. You must being me the Book of Silence."

Garth hesitated. He could no longer agree and simply hope that he would not be asked to deliver; the King had remembered, just minutes earlier, where he had left the book, where it might be found and recovered. Garth had hoped that by taking back the sword, he might avoid the problem and retain his pretense of honor; it now appeared that he was not going to be allowed that luxury.

Now that he took the time to think about it, even through the haze of his righteous rage, he realized that he had been ridiculously optimistic. The King had no reason to free him of his vow. He cared nothing about whether he had the Sword of Bheleu or not; he wanted only to have the Book of Silence.

No, Garth corrected himself, that was not quite right. The old man's greater magic required both the book *and* the sword, if the overman had understood him correctly. That made him even less likely to agree to give up both.

"Let us forget my oath for the present, then," Garth said.

"I will not ask you to renounce it, but rather will ask simply that you return to me, only temporarily if you would prefer it so, the Sword of Bheleu."

"If you do not renounce your oath, then when will you fulfill it? I have told you that I know now where the Book of Silence is."

Garth struggled to keep his anger under control, not to lash out uselessly against the old man. His face was so slack and expressionless with rage that he appeared almost half-witted, like a drunkard or one under the influence of narcotic potions. He still held the fragment of his sword; to dispel some of the tension in his body, he rammed it down against the table. The jagged, broken edge bit into the oaken tabletop, scarring it, but did not embed itself as a real blade would. Instead, it turned and skidded across the surface, gouging up curls of wood. Garth's wrist was twisted painfully, and his sore knuckles scraped as well.

The pain added to his fury, and he lost control, blurting out the truth. "I have no intention of fulfilling my oath, foul deceiver. You extorted my agreement, knowing I had no choice. I would rather die in disgrace than aid you."

Behind him, he heard Frima gasp, and Saram draw breath.

The King lifted his head slightly and murmured, "Your word is not good? Your sworn vow means nothing?"

Feeling cornered, his fury subsiding as he realized his mistake, Garth replied, "No."

"The vow you swore in this place not an hour ago is meaningless?" The old man's voice was a low grating that tore at Garth's nerves.

Rage flowered anew, and Garth said, "I did not say that! I *will* destroy the cult of Aghad."

"Can one oath be binding and another meaningless, sworn by the same tongue?"

Garth, trapped, said nothing, and a moment of tense silence ensued. Saram and Frima dared not speak.

"Garth," the old man said at last, his voice more nearly normal, but with a trace of either sorrow or sarcasm in it, "I regret to hear this. If you are not bound by your oath, then I must propose a new bargain. You want the Sword of Bheleu so that you may destroy the followers of the god of hatred and those responsible for the death of your wife. I want the Book of Silence so that I may perform a certain magic that will cause many deaths, my own among them. I will not give you the Sword of Bheleu at present, but we both may yet have what we want. You want the Aghadites dead. I want to complete a spell that will kill them."

He paused, and Garth said, "What?"

The King lowered his head again and said nothing.

"Do you mean that your magic will destroy the cult?"

The old man nodded.

"Are you sure?"

The King shrugged.

Garth tried to think; it was difficult, for his mind was full of anger and confusion.

It had never occurred to him that the King's final magic might be guided, that the King might have some control over who died when it was performed. Garth had assumed that the spell would involve conjuring The God Whose Name Is Not Spoken into the mortal world and that, thus freed, the god would kill all those in the immediate area.

Perhaps this was not the case at all. Perhaps the god would demand a certain number of deaths, but this summoner could choose who would be sacrificed in order to banish him again. That seemed to be what the King was implying. There was no reason to assume that a god would be limited by distance or even by time; weren't gods supposed to be everywhere and nowhere all at once?

He did not trust the King, however.

Furthermore, there seemed to be something unsatisfying about the solution the King proposed. Garth wanted to kill the Aghadites *himself*, to see the color of their blood, to watch them die.

"I . . ." he began, then stopped. "I am not sure."

"Another bargain, then. Bring me the Book of Silence, and I will loan you the Sword of Bheleu. I must require it back from you eventually, but I am sure you will not object to being freed of the god's control."

Garth turned that proposal over in his mind and, awash in fury as he was, could see nothing wrong with it at first. He would have the Sword of Bheleu, and with it he could destroy the cult of Aghad. He dismissed without thought the fact that he would be giving himself over to the god of destruction rather than simply wielding a weapon; it did not occur to him that Bheleu might not be satisfied with killing only Aghadites.

He did, however, realize that he would be delivering the Book of Silence to the Forgotten King, and after planning for three years to avoid that, he was reluctant to give in so quickly simply because the King now claimed that the other victims of his magic would be Aghadites.

The old man might be telling the truth; it might be that delivering the Book of Silence to him would do no harm to innocents. Although Garth had been fooled in the past by partial truths and things left unsaid, the King had never, so far as he knew, told an outright lie.

This was a matter that deserved more than a moment's thought, but there was no time to waste, he felt, in his pursuit of his wife's murderers.

That pursuit would go nowhere, however, without the Sword of Bheleu.

If he accepted the King's offer, he would be in possession, at least temporarily, of either the sword or the book, and it was his belief that both were required for the final magic. If he remained unconvinced of the King's intentions, he could always withhold whichever totem he had at the time; after all, he was already forsworn, in his heart, and had no more honor to lose by such treachery. It would, he thought, be a just repayment for the King's own deceptions and manipulations.

"Yes," he said at last, "I agree. Tell me where I may find the Book of Silence, and I will bring it to you."

"I left it in the royal chapel of my palace in Hastur. That palace is now a part of the crypts beneath Ur-Dormulk. Signs and portents will be sufficient to lead you to it." Something like glee was in the old man's tone.

"Will you provide me no further guidance?"

"You need none."

Garth found himself growing wary. He was beginning to realize that he was again trusting himself to the Forgotten King, again agreeing to perform an errand for the old man. Always before, such errands had had unwanted and unpleasant results.

Even his journey to Orgûl, just completed that day, had ended in Kyrith's death.

An idea occurred to him, a strange idea. Always before he had set out alone, while the King stayed in Skelleth and awaited his return. Garth had been a messenger, a servant. What if the King were to accompany him this time? The old man's magic could protect them both from whatever difficulties they might encounter; they would travel as equals, rather than Garth's assuming the inferior's role again.

"O King," he said, "will you come with me?"

Behind him, Saram and Frima stared. The King was silent for a moment before replying, "No."

"Why not?" Garth demanded. "Why must I act on your behalf?"

"I cannot venture far from Skelleth. My power is centered here."

The old man's tone was final, but Garth was in no mood to be put off. "Why?" he persisted. "Because you have lived here for so long? Is it possible that you do not wish to discomfit yourself?"

"No," the King said, with perhaps a trace of anger in his voice.

"Then why? Why did you come to Skelleth in the first place? How did you become trapped here? Explain yourself!"

"This place is the center of power in this time, as Hastur was of old; the world's energies have shifted with the ages. I had no choice in my dwelling place once I had given up the book and the mask, but was compelled to live wherever the power's heart might be. Had I the book once more, I could go where I pleased."

"You left the village once, when I gave you the sword."

"Only a few leagues, and yet that was near my limit."

"What would happen to you, then, if you were to leave?"

"Garth, this is not your concern."

"What would happen?" the overman insisted.

"I cannot leave."

"What if I were to carry you?"

With apparent reluctance, the King admitted, "I would lose my strength, both physical and metaphysical. I would have no more power than a corpse, yet I would still live."

"You mean that you would be unable to work magic?"

"I would be unable to move or speak or see or breathe; I would be in appearance as ancient as I am in truth."

That explained, of course, why so powerful a being dwelt in this miserable border town and needed an ordinary overman to run his errands. For that reason, if for no other, Garth was willing to accept the King's explanation, at least for the present. He still hoped, however, to have some sort of further aid.

"Then can you give me no protection against the cult's magic?" he asked.

"No."

"You might loan me the sword now." That, of course, would be ideal; he could then simply renege on his agreement.

The King did not bother to answer. Garth knew that, quite aside from his own present trustworthiness, once he was beyond the King's power it might not be Garth but Bheleu who occupied Garth's body; no oath or power would be able to restrain the god or bring him back to Skelleth against his will, if the King's power were in truth limited to the immediate area.

"They have powerful magic," he said, as a last resort.

The King shifted slightly, but said nothing.

"The image of the god, for example. What am I to do if they attack me with such things?"

"That was a simple messenger image; it could not even speak until ordered to."

"What of the spell that shattered my sword?"

"A warding spell against metal, useless for any other purpose."

"The red mist that caused the Aghadite and Kyrith's body to vanish, then."

"A teleportation device taken from a dead wizard; they have few more and will not waste them."

"Surely, though, they have other magic and will not hesitate to use it against me. Can you do nothing to protect me?"

"Have you turned coward, then?" The King lifted his head, and though his eyes were still hidden in shadow Garth thought he saw a glint of light. The springtime warmth seemed to fade from the air of the tavern, replaced with a clammy chill. "Regardless of what magic they may possess, did they not say that you would see all those you care for die before your own time came to perish? They will not harm you directly, then, until they have carried out their threat. Now go! Fetch me the Book of Silence, and trouble me no more until you have it!"

Disconcerted by the King's sudden coldness, Garth nodded and rose to depart. Saram and Frima rose as well. The Baron began to speak, to make one more attempt at dissuading the overman, but Garth ignored him and stalked out into the marketplace, where a thin rain had begun to fall.

CHAPTER EIGHT

The eastern gate of the ancient walled city of Ur-Dormulk stood between two massive stone towers, set in a gap in the ridge that supported the eastern ramparts; the great valves themselves were carved from two immense sheets of ebony, bound in the brown-black hide of some extinct monster. There was no shining metal or bright paint anywhere on the gate or the somber gray walls to either side. The tower walls, Garth saw, were carven from roadbed to battlement with spidery runes of a tongue that he had never seen before.

Some of the runes seemed to have an odd familiarity about them that Garth could not explain to himself; he wondered idly what language they represented, and what they said. Perhaps they gave a history of the city's founding, he thought, or were protective incantations of some kind.

He was quite sure from the very first that they were not Eramman or anything like it. As a child, he had come across other, older languages, all dead, and this strange script was none of them.

Of course, he told himself, Ur-Dormulk was very old. It had stood, much as it was now, before Eramma became a nation half a millennium ago. There had been plenty of time for the builders' native tongue to die out.

The whole matter was irrelevant, he told himself. He had

an errand to perform. Despite the protests of the Baron and Baroness, and the arguments Galt had made when he had been informed of the situation, Garth intended to find the Book of Silence and return to Skelleth with it.

He was not completely certain as to exactly what he would do then, save that he would somehow pursue his vengeance against Aghad's followers. He was not sure whether he would give the Forgotten King the book or whether he would take the Sword of Bheleu, but he had not cared to say anything that might cause anyone to doubt his intention of honoring his agreement with the King.

Saram had gone so far in his concern for the overman as to offer to accompany him on his journey; Frima had protested, and Garth had turned him down. Saram had a barony to run, and could not go haring off on adventures without warning. Garth had no commitments, save his vows to fetch the Book of Silence and to destroy the cult and temple of Aghad. He did not want to involve anyone else in either of these.

As a compromise of sorts, he had accepted a letter of introduction to the overlord of Ur-Dormulk, signed by both Saram and Galt. That had been his only concession, and it was a practical one. If he was going to search the city looking for signs and portents, he would very much prefer not to have to worry about explaining himself to guardsmen or homeowners while doing so.

His only other delays had been to make a few basic preparations. He had left the copper gull at his house, borrowed a sword, and bought a few supplies, but had been in Skelleth so briefly that this new journey seemed almost a continuation of his trip to Orgûl. The mood, however, was very different; this was a task of real personal consequence, not the casual lark his attempt at dragon-slaying had been.

Since he intended to introduce himself to the overlord or at least to his representatives, he had no need for stealth in entering the city. That was just as well, as he saw no easy way to pass the fortifications unseen. Unlike Skelleth's ruinous outer wall, these were intact and well maintained, extending quite some distance along the ridge top and then turning back westward out of sight.

Seeing no other entrance, he had ridden directly up to the

huge gate, and now sat for a moment looking up at the black portal and rune-covered towers.

This was the sort of fortress the legends of Ordunin had described Skelleth to be, until he had ventured down and discovered for himself how greatly the stories had exaggerated. He wondered why he had heard no tales describing Ur-Dormulk.

It didn't matter, he told himself. He was stalling, putting off the necessity of announcing himself and having to deal with unfamiliar humans.

"Ho, the gate!" he bellowed, refusing to delay any longer.

An answering shout came, much more loudly than he had expected.

"State your business, overman!"

He looked, but could not see any face above the parapet, and the echo from the towers made it impossible to judge just where the sound had originated.

That, he decided, was probably intentional; the builders of this city had done their work well.

"I come from Skelleth on a personal errand; I bear a message, as well, from the Baron of Skelleth to the overlord of Ur-Dormulk!"

"Dismount and approach," the voice called. "Leave your sword and axe on the saddle!"

Garth realized that the voice was not coming from above, or at least not from very far above; the speaker was, therefore, not on the battlements at all. The only other place that he could be was in one of the towers, and the overman looked at the runes with new interest, noticing how deeply some of the symbols had been cut. Somewhere in those shadowy tracings were openings into the towers, from which a man could peer out, or shout commands, or perhaps aim a crossbow.

It was a very clever device, he thought; it would be almost impossible to find the actual holes amid the myriad lines and curlicues. He would want to remember this for later, but for the present he had business to attend to. He swung down from the warbeast's back, checked the axe that hung on the saddle, then took the scabbarded sword from his belt—a sword he had borrowed from Galt, since he had not wanted to take time to have a new one forged after shattering his on the Aghadite protective spell, and since human-sized weapons were not suited to his grip—and hooked it through one of the straps that held the saddle in place.

He looked questioningly up at the nearer tower, his hand on the sheathed dagger that remained on his belt; no command or comment came. The knife was apparently not considered a serious threat. He shrugged, lowered his hand, and strode toward the gate, the dagger still in its place.

With a series of rattles and thuds, the bars were removed from the gate, and one side of the great portal swung slowly ajar. A guard in a peculiarly shaped brass helmet and dull green tunic leaned out through the opening.

"You have a letter?" he said. The voice was not the one that had called from the tower.

Garth said nothing, but proffered the folded parchment.

The guardsman took it, looked at the seal, and hesitated. "It looks genuine," he said, not to Garth, but addressing someone out of sight behind the gate.

A hand appeared, and the guardsman surrendered the letter.

A moment later a new voice called, "Let him in."

The guardsman stepped back and motioned for Garth to enter. The overman hesitated. "What of my weapons and my mount?" he asked.

"Your pardon, my lord, but we prefer to be cautious until we have established that you are what you say you are. Your weapons will be brought, if you like, and returned to you when your identity is confirmed."

"I would appreciate that," Garth said. "What about Koros?"

"Your beast? I regret, my lord, that no beasts of burden are welcome in the city, for reasons of sanitation and public safety. We maintain a stable outside the wall to serve visitors such as yourself."

Garth was not happy about that. The indomitable warbeast had served him well in human cities in the past when, on occasion, things had turned nasty. He was, however, on a peaceful errand, one that might well stay peaceful. To the best of his knowledge, even if the people of Ur-Dormulk knew that he meant to take the Book of Silence, they should have no reason to object; he had been told that no one but the Forgotten King could use it and that for anyone else even to handle it might well prove fatal—though his own undesired connection with Bheleu would be sufficient protection to allow him to transport it. Logically, nobody should mind if he were to remove so dangerous an object from the city.

He would just have to hope that nothing went wrong and that no one had any unreasonable objections.

"Do you know anything about handling warbeasts?" he asked the guard, certain of what the answer would be.

"No," the man replied. "I never saw one before."

Garth nodded; he had assumed that to be the case, since the creatures had been invented by the overmen of Kirpa, in the Northern Waste, too late to have been used in any number in the Racial Wars. Even three centuries after the wars ended, they remained rare and valuable and were almost all owned by governments, as being too precious and dangerous to be left in private hands. Garth had one of his own only because he had accepted it in lieu of all further tribute that, under an ancient agreement, the people of Kirpa had owed to him as Prince of Ordunin.

"What sort of animal do you have in the stable ordinarily?" he asked.

The guardsman shrugged. "Horses, I suppose, and oxen; I'm no stableboy. Yackers, too, I think."

Garth glanced at Koros, standing motionless on the highway, triangular ears flattened back slightly, golden eyes half-shut, three-inch fangs gleaming dully in the midday sun. The warbeast would have no objection to being stabled, but it wouldn't mind staying out in the open, either, as long as the good weather that had followed the brief rain held. The other occupants of the stable might not care for its presence; the smell of warbeast was not recognizable to most animals as that of a predator, due to its magical origin, but the sight of one tended to make many beasts understandably nervous.

More importantly, it was possible that Garth might find himself fleeing the city, and in that case he would not want to waste time finding the stable. Having the warbeast waiting right at the gate would be far more convenient.

"I think I'll just leave it where it is," he said.

The guardsman shrugged. "As you please."

The voice that had first answered his hail called out, "Did you say you're leaving that monster where it is?"

Garth called back that yes, he had said as much.

"Would it not be better if you were to move it out of the road?"

Garth realized that Koros might be a serious obstruction to traffic where it was. He bellowed a command, and the warbeast turned and padded off the highway. Once well out of the way, it stopped.

"Is that better?" Garth called.

The voice replied that it was.

"Good. Now, if one of you would fetch my sword and axe, as you suggested, I trust we may proceed. And might I suggest that you feed my beast a goat or a sheep or two; my business may keep me for some time, and I cannot speak for its behavior if it becomes hungry. Water, too, would be appreciated. I will pay the necessary expenses."

The guardsman at the gate nodded. "I'll have someone see to it." He swung the gate open a few feet farther, allowing Garth past him into a small courtyard enclosed by gray stone, its nearer side comprised of the great portal and its farther side occupied by another, identical barrier. Half a dozen men in green uniforms and brass helmets were scattered about the court; one had a golden plume that curled upward from one side of his helmet and was holding Garth's letter of introduction. The overman took him to be the officer in charge of the squad manning the gates.

As one of the others trotted down to fetch Garth's weapons, Garth called a command to the warbeast so that it would not rip the man apart as it would a thief; ordinarily it allowed no one but Garth to touch anything it carried. When the soldier had retrieved both sword and axe while evoking nothing more than a mild growl of displeasure from Koros, he started back, and Garth ventured to ask the officer, "Do you treat all your visitors like this?"

"No, of course not," the officer replied.

"What makes me worthy of such special attention, then?"

The human looked at him uncertainly, as if he suspected that the overman might be slightly insane, or perhaps attempting some sort of bizarre humor.

"We get very few armored overmen arriving unannounced, riding monstrous giant cats and asking to see the overlord," he said.

"Ah." Garth had to agree that the man had a point. "It's a warbeast, only partly a cat, despite its appearance. See the long legs? And I did not ask to see the overlord, but said merely that I carried a letter intended for him."

"Perhaps I misunderstood, then; would you prefer to wait here while I deliver the letter?"

Garth considered very briefly. "No," he said, after only a slight hesitation, "I would like to speak with him, if I may." Dealing with the head of state directly was bound to be more efficient than working with underlings.

"I think he may well wish to speak with you, as well. We see very few overmen here." The officer ventured a small smile.

The soldier bearing Garth's sword and axe had returned to the courtyard, and the other guardsmen were pushing the gate closed. Garth watched with casual interest, noticing from the corner of his eye that the man carrying his weapons was making a concerted effort to stay as far away from the weapons' owner as the small area between the gates allowed.

When the portal was closed and a half a dozen bars and locks were back in place, the inner gates were opened by men on the other side; to Garth's surprise, they opened away from the city, into the court where he waited. That was not the usual custom.

The officer gestured, and Garth found himself neatly surrounded, two soldiers before him, one on either side, and two behind; while the officer led the way and the weapons-bearer brought up the rear, several paces back. Garth had not realized there were as many as eight humans in the group; he wondered if more had joined them from the towers or behind the inner gate, or whether he simply hadn't been paying close attention.

At a command from the officer, the little party marched forward; Garth cooperated, marching with them. His exact status here was unclear, perhaps intentionally; the men marched with hands on their weapons, but swords stayed sheathed, and the lances borne by the pair behind him were shouldered. He was not chained or hobbled, but he was disarmed. If he was a prisoner, then he was being treated with courtesy and a lack of caution; if he was a guest, he was being treated with great suspicion. The escort could be considered either an honor guard or a party of jailers with equal reason.

This uncertainty, he decided, accurately reflected the guards' attitude; he had committed no crime, and claimed to be a person of some significance, but they had seen no proof of his good intentions. They were not eager either to trust him or to offend him beyond what prudence demanded.

He was not particularly troubled by this. The thought did slip into his mind that, had he carried the Sword of Bheleu on this trip, he would have taken umbrage at such treatment and massacred the lot of them.

His first sight of the city of Ur-Dormulk distracted him from questions of protocol or concern over proper behavior. He had expected the inner gate to open onto a street of packed earth or mud, lined with houses of stone, wood, and plaster, such as he had seen in other human habitations; or, if not onto a street, then perhaps into a market square. Skelleth had been built of fieldstone and half-timbered plaster; the buildings of Mormoreth had been faced with white marble; Dûsarra was a jumble of gleaming black stone and more humble structures.

Ur-Dormulk was built of granite, and rather than on a street, he found himself at the top of a long staircase, easily half a hundred steps, whence he looked out at an array of towers and turrets. Crags of bare rock thrust up in the distance, reminding him that he was in the foothills of the western mountains.

He had noticed from without that the ramparts stood atop a ridge, and that the gate was set into the top of that ridge, so he had expected to find the city inside sloping downward from the heights; he had not expected to find the drop so sharp that steps were necessary, or so long that only the higher towers reached above eye level.

He had known that there were stone towers, and had even glimpsed them from a distance; he had known that they were old and weathered and strange, but now he could see that they were more bizarre than he had realized. The towers were not merely pitted and dull, but worn down to near shapelessness; not a single sharp corner remained anywhere in sight. Flat-topped or spired, each of the tall buildings seemed more like a rough mound than anything structured by man—save that they stood as much as a hundred feet above the city streets. Some were almost indistinguishable from the weathered humps of rock with which nature had ornamented the city.

Those outcroppings struck Garth as being slightly eerie, rising up in naked splendor throughout Ur-Dormulk, differing from the towers only because they were larger, windowless, and slightly more irregular. They seemed to form a rough line, beyond which he could see nothing of the city; he wondered if they formed part of its western perimeter and if they had been incorporated into the defenses as the ridge had been used in the east.

A cool, damp breeze brushed his face, and he blinked; then the soldiers were escorting him down the steps, and he was too concerned with his footing to look at the city further. The steps themselves were badly worn, polished by the passage of thousands, perhaps millions, of feet; the central portion had been smoothed down until it was almost a ramp, so that his guards directed him to one side, where the steps, though gleaming smooth and worn far below their original level, still had enough of an edge separating one from the next to make them more readily negotiable than the sheer slope.

When he was reasonably sure that he was not going to slip and tumble down the remaining length of the stair, he lifted his gaze from his own feet to the foot of the steps. They ended in a broad plaza, paved with the same gray stone that seemed to make up the entire city and as level as the plains of Skelleth. He was certain that that level surface was not natural, so close to the steep ridge.

He had at first been certain, also, that the gray stone was granite, a familiar substance in his homeland, but doubts began to creep in. Granite was a very hard stone, difficult to work, heavy and brittle—and it did not erode easily. He glanced at the steps again. There was an old granite wall in Ordunin, not far from his home, that had been erected when he was young, a century before; the edge that ran along its top was still sharp enough to cut an overman's finger. These steps, assuming that they had originally been level all the way across, had worn down a good eight inches in the center. If the stone were in truth granite, and had been eroded only by foot traffic, then its age must be incomprehensible.

The stone, he decided, must be something else, some substance that mocked granite in appearance, but which was far softer. Or perhaps water drained down the steps and had cut them away—though the fact that the wear was so broad argued against that, since water ordinarily cut a single channel, not a wide, uneven swath.

It didn't matter, he told himself.

He reached the bottom and looked around with interest. The plaza at the foot, though paved with this seeming granite, was worn down as well, with paths sunk inches deep into the stone showing where the merchants set up their booths on market day, where the traffic was heaviest, and what were the most popular routes across the square. The streets that led off in various directions were likewise paved and level, and likewise worn. Narrow parallel troughs indicated where carts had passed over the centuries, and broader depressions revealed where pedestrians walked. There were no gutters visible anywhere, save for these signs of wear, and no bare earth, and Garth realized why animal traffic was forbidden. Such streets would need careful cleaning; there was no natural drainage, since none of the streets sloped at all, and what drainage the paths provided would carry sewage directly to those areas that enjoyed the heaviest traffic and, therefore, the deepest wear. It struck him as odd that a city in the foothills should be so flat, save for the single ridge and the distant outcroppings. It was obviously contrived, and probably at great expense. He wondered why the builders had thought it worthwhile.

He wondered also, for perhaps a second, what pulled the wagons that had cut the parallel grooves he had noticed, but that question was answered by the sight of a young man pulling a small, two-wheeled cart, balanced on a single axle for ease in hauling.

The buildings that surrounded the plaza were all of the gray stone, ancient and worn. Most stood three or four stories in height, but were weathered into rounded, moundlike shapes, all corners erased by time. Any surface ornamentation that might once have existed had vanished long ago; only the size and location of doors and windows served to distinguish one from another.

He noticed that here and there gaps were visible, as if some-

thing had fallen away; here a door lintel was sunk back from
the facade, there a few dark holes were arranged above a window. He realized that these must be where substances other
than the gray rock had weathered away completely, and guessed
that iron fittings had succumbed to rust—though if so, then it
must have been a very long time ago, for all trace of rust had
washed away.

The stone walls, he saw, were incredibly thick. They would
have to be, to weather so badly and still stand strong.

The entire city gave the impression of something indescrib-
ably ancient, something that had stood so long that it had been
accepted by the earth as part of itself, rather than being a mortal
creation erected thereon.

The people of Ur-Dormulk gave no such impression; in contrast to their city, they wore gay silks and embroidered velvets
in ornate and fantastical outfits. Garth saw no ordinary homespun anywhere; even the lowliest cart-hauler's garb was brightly
dyed and embellished with colored threads. Red, green, blue,
and purple—the streets were aswirl in color wherever the people of Ur-Dormulk went abroad.

There were no great crowds, but neither were the streets
empty; strollers dawdled along, while others hurried about their
business. Many glanced at the overman curiously, but none
stopped to stare, and no one ventured too near the forbidding
cluster of soldiery.

One figure, wearing a drooping hat and flowing tunic and
cape all the color of dried blood, seemed to look at him for
longer than most, and Garth was reminded very strongly of the
magically protected Aghadite he had fought so futilely in Skelleth. He wondered whether the cult was active in Ur-Dormulk,
whether it was an open, tolerated religion here or a secret
society working underground.

He had not been molested by the sect since the incident in
the market that had cost him his own sword, and his anger had
therefore had a chance to cool slightly, but now it flared up
again. He resolved that he would see that person who stared
at him so insolently gutted by the Sword of Bheleu.

He turned his head to follow the red-garbed human out of
sight and found himself looking at the profile of the soldier to
his left. That reminded him where he was, and he fought down

his ire. The human might not be an Aghadite, he told himself; the color might be coincidence, the gaze simple curiosity.

Or perhaps, his reasonable self had to admit, it was indeed an Aghadite agent, sent to watch him, or to taunt him with his or her presence—he was not certain of the creature's sex beneath the loose robe and overhanging hat. If it were an agent, then Garth had been meant to see him or her; why else would he or she wear the cult's color so ostentatiously?

This assumed, of course, that the cult had known he was coming to Ur-Dormulk, and it was not at all clear how they *could* have known. It would have required either magic or the presence of spies in Skelleth and some way of sending messages faster than Koros traveled.

The cultists did have magic, of course; he knew that well. He knew also that they had not given up their plans of vengeance, however quiet they might have been during his preparations and journey. The figure in red might indeed have been an Aghadite. The overman would need to be very careful, here in a strange city.

His escort was conducting him up the widest and straightest of the streets that led westward from the market, and they were almost at the palace before Garth noticed that no one wore yellow. Every other color was represented, it seemed, but nowhere was there cloth-of-gold or yellow silk, no amber or straw, saffron or chrome. White and beige were in evidence, and he glimpsed copper or orange occasionally, but no hue that could truly be called yellow.

That struck him as very curious indeed. A tradition, he guessed, dating from some ancient respect for the King in Yellow.

The party of soldiers, with the overman in their midst, arrived at the steps of the palace that closed off the end of the avenue and marched without hestitation up them. Great doors sheathed in some metal blackened with age blocked their way; Garth wondered whether the covering might be silver. Flecks of gold clung to the upper portion, forming broken curves, as if a symbol had once been traced there but had worn away, until only these scant traces remained.

The doors opened as they approached, and Garth was led into an ornate tapestried hall. Two men and a woman, wearing vivid red robes, met the party there. As two of the soldiers closed the huge doors, the woman gestured toward a row of stone benches. "Make yourselves comfortable," she said. "We will announce you, and inform you of the prince's pleasure."

The officer nodded to his men; the six who had ringed the overman found themselves places and sat. After a moment's hesitation, Garth joined them, taking a bench to himself, with three soldiers to either side on adjoining benches. The weapons-carrier remained standing, moving to the far side of the room, where he chatted with one of the red-clad men too quietly for Garth to hear.

The officer and the other red-garbed man walked off through the arch at the inner end of the hall, into the interior of the palace. The woman stood off to one side.

After a moment, noticing Garth glancing about impatiently, she remarked, "The wait may be quite long, my lord; would you care for food or drink?"

Garth shook his head and sat there in silence.

CHAPTER NINE

Allowing for the slow passage of time when one was bored, Garth estimated that he waited half an hour in the antechamber before the officer returned, Garth's letter of introduction in his hand and the red-robed man at his heel.

He gave the overman the letter and announced, "Follow me; three guards. Bring the weapons."

Garth rose; after a few seconds of debate over who would go, so did three of the soldiers. They formed a cross, the overman in the center, a soldier on each side for the crosspiece, and the third behind, followed by the swordbearer, while the officer and the red-clad courtier led the way.

From the antechamber, which was gray stone hung with faded tapestries, they entered a long gallery of black and white marble, the floor made up of black and white diamonds of marble, the walls alternating white marble pillars with gold-veined, black marble slabs. Their footsteps echoed from the bare stone. Garth was impressed with the architecture.

An open door gleaming golden at the far end led into the overlord's audience chamber, a vast hall clouded with incense and decorated in gold and red. Lines of soldiery stood to either side, their dull green uniforms and brass helmets identical to those of Garth's escort. Two dozen courtiers stood casually at the foot of the dais; about half wore the brilliant red of the palace staff, while the rest were as variegated in their clothing as the people on the streets—more so, in truth, for one tall, red-haired woman wore a yellow gown beneath a knee-length, sleeveless vest of red velvet. She appeared to be staring at Garth with a strange intensity while she clung to the arm of an elderly man in blue; though it was only natural for the overman to be the center of attention, her gaze seemed unusually fixed.

The overlord himself wore black, glossy black velvet, unadorned save for a circlet of gold set with glittering gems that shone on his brow. He sat upon an immense throne of red plush and gold, raised up on a red-carpeted platform three feet high, at the top of a flight of six golden steps. He was a man in middle age, heavy but not really fat, with pale skin and dark brown hair that flowed down well past his shoulders. He wore a curious ring of carved and cracking wood on the fourth finger of his left hand. His face was broad, his eyes dark.

As Garth approached the dais, the officer stepped off to the right, the courtier to the left; the overman stopped at the foot of the steps and bowed politely.

There was a murmur and a moment of awkward silence; Garth suspected, too late, that some further form of abasement was customary.

A red-clad courtier stepped forward from somewhere and announced, "Behold, O supplicant, Hildarad, seventh of that name, Prince of Alar, Lord Dormulk, Master of the City, Conqueror of Hastur, supreme in Aldebaran and the Hyades! Speak, then, if you dare!"

Garth wondered what Aldebaran and the Hyades might be, and where Alar was, as he replied, "I am Garth, Prince of Ordunin, Lord of the Overmen of the Northern Waste. I come with a letter of introduction from Saram, Baron of Skelleth, to ask a favor of you, O Prince." He had almost addressed the overlord as "overlord," but caught himself at the last moment; the title of prince was more prestigious, and therefore more courteous. He had no idea if the overlord actually had a legitimate claim to it, but he did not care to risk any insult.

The overlord shifted slightly on his throne and said, in a conversational tone, "I have glanced through this letter you bring. My lord of Skelleth asks me to accept you as minister-without-portfolio in his government and to treat you with all respect due himself. If you are in truth Prince of Ordunin—and I do not question it—that might seem little favor, to give you the courtesy due a baron, yet the relationship between my own domain and the Baroney of Skelleth is most exceptionally warm, and I think that is what he had in mind. Therefore, I invite you to ask your favor, knowing that I look upon you as a good friend and ally."

"Thank you, O Prince," Garth replied. "I am seeking a book, an arcane volume known as the Book of Silence. I am told that it lies in or beneath Ur-Dormulk, most probably in what was the royal chapel of an ancient palace."

He had meant to continue with a few meaningless courtesies and then ask for assistance in locating the book, but he was distracted by the expressions on the faces of two of the overlord's courtiers. The woman in the yellow gown had turned pale, her face as bloodless and white as bleached wool; beside her, the blue-clad man's mouth was open, his eyes wide, his broad face flushed.

The overlord, looking at Garth and not to the side, did not notice. He remarked casually, "The Book of Silence? An odd name; is not a book meant to speak to its readers? I have never heard of it; my tax collectors will be grieved to learn that there is something of value within the walls that they had not discovered for me." He smiled at his jest, and Garth smiled in return; some of the courtiers chuckled politely.

The two who obviously *had* heard of the Book of Silence managed to compose themselves while their lord was speaking, Garth noticed, though the woman remained pale and unsteady. He wondered who they were. He was slightly disappointed that the overlord seemed unable to tell him where to find the book, but it looked as if this pair might be of help.

Serious again, the overlord asked, "Is this book some sort of grimoire or book of spells?"

"I don't know," Garth admitted. "I seek it on behalf of a wizard of my acquaintance, who has told me that he requires it to perform certain magics I wish him to perform." That was not quite the truth, but it was close enough to serve.

"And was it this wizard who told you the book was in Ur-Dormulk?"

"Yes," Garth replied. "He told me that it lay in an ancient chapel, or perhaps the ruins of one."

"I know of no such chapel, and this palace is the only one that has stood in this city in all its recorded history."

Garth shrugged. "I have said what I was told."

"This is all strange to me, and I fear I can be of little assistance. Is there any other way in which I might aid you?"

A trace of color was returning to the woman's face, Garth saw, and the man beside her had wholly recovered, pretending that nothing untoward had happened. Those two, Garth decided, were definitely worthy of investigation. He found himself thinking that there was something familiar about them, but dismissed it as overactive imagination.

That could wait, however. He had another concern he wanted to mention to the overlord, and another audience might not be easy to obtain, despite the man's expressed goodwill.

"O Prince," he said, "forgive my ignorance of your city, but is the cult of Aghad active in Ur-Dormulk?"

The overlord appeared momentarily startled. "Aghad? The Dûs god of hatred? There is a temple to him here, certainly, and it has, I suppose, its complement of priests and devotees. We of Ur-Dormulk pride ourselves upon the toleration of all faiths—or at least all save the most repulsive. The dark gods and their followers may be distasteful, but we permit them to remain and worship as they please, so long as they do not disturb the peace. One or two have, in truth, been banished for practicing human sacrifice, but to date, the Aghadites have behaved themselves. Why do you ask?"

"I have a personal interest in the cult of Aghad, O Prince. Its followers murdered my wife."

Garth's tone was flat and dull; the humans probably took it for the emptiness of grief rather than the seething anger it was. A few of the courtiers made vague, sympathetic murmurs.

The overlord was slow in replying. "I am sorry to hear of this," he said at last. "Why do you mention it? What would you have of me?"

"O Prince, I am sworn to destroy those who slew my wife, yet I do not wish to trouble your domain. The Baron of Skelleth, the people of Skelleth, and I would esteem it a very great favor if you were to expel the followers of Aghad from Ur-Dormulk, so that they might be removed from your protection." That seemed the most he could reasonably ask. He would have preferred to demand that the overlord send his soldiers immediately to burn the temple and kill its priests.

"I am reluctant," the overlord admitted. "It goes against the traditions of the city to banish any faith that has not directly harmed my subjects." He paused, then continued. "I will take what you ask for under advisement; I am well aware that it is to our benefit to respect Skelleth's wishes, yet this request is unprecedented. If you could identify any person who had a direct role in your wife's death, I might have him arrested and sent to Skelleth for trial—but to exile the entire sect! You ask much, and I must consider well before making my decision."

Garth bowed in polite acknowledgment. He had both feared and hoped that the overlord would refuse him. He was already planning a venture of his own into the temple. He knew, rationally, that to destroy the temple himself would antagonize both the overlord of Ur-Dormulk and the Baron of Skelleth and would make his life less pleasant all around. Emotionally, however, the prospect of wreaking havoc was very appealing indeed.

"Is there anything else, overman?"

"If I may, O Prince, I would like to consult with some of your advisers regarding the possible location of the Book of Silence, if there are any who might have knowledge of it."

The overlord raised a hand and gestured. "I have here with me two most excellent wizards; if this book is indeed magical, they might be of some assistance." He indicated the woman in yellow and the man in blue. "This is Chalkara of Kholis, Court Wizard to the High King at Kholis, retired recently and come here upon leaving the King's service; and Shandiph the Wanderer, a magician of some note and a native of Ur-Dormulk, returned home to join my court. There is also," he said as he turned and indicated an old woman in somber brown and burgundy velvet, "my court archivist, Silda; she knows more about this city than any other living person. They will accompany you to the Rose Chamber, where you may speak in comfort. Now, if you will forgive me, there is other business I must attend to."

Garth nodded. He had suspected that the pair might be

magicians or seers of some sort and had hoped that the overlord would answer as he had. Only one more point remained to be mentioned before the end of the audience.

"O Prince, I thank you for your consideration; if I might trouble you just a moment longer, however, there is a detail . . ."

"What is it?" The overlord was becoming impatient and trying unsuccessfully to hide it.

"My sword." Garth pointed at the soldier who carried his weapons. "Will it be returned to me?"

"Yes, of course." The overlord waved a hand in dismissal. "When you leave the palace, your weapons will be returned." He gestured at the officer who had escorted Garth. "See to it."

"Thank you, O Prince. May your reign be long and prosperous," Garth said. He bowed, retreated a few steps, and looked about.

A red-clad courtier stood ready to guide him; wary and unsmiling, the three advisers stepped from their places at the dais and joined him.

The party made its way out of the incense-filled audience chamber through a side door, then down a long paneled corridor that seemed chill and empty by contrast, and finally into a small room that opened off to the right.

The walls of this room were lined with rose-colored velvet, and the floor was an elaborate rosewood inlay; chairs of rosewood and velvet were gathered around an ebony table that held a vase of fresh-cut white roses.

This was obviously the Rose Chamber, and Garth settled cautiously into one of the chairs, uncertain at first that it would support his weight. Shandiph took the place opposite the overman, while Chalkara seated herself on Garth's right and Silda on his left, so that each occupied a different side of the table.

The red-clad guide pulled the two superfluous chairs off to one side, out of the way of extended legs or stretching arms, and then vanished discreetly.

For a moment of awkward silence, the four studied one another. Garth noticed that Silda seemed, if anything, slightly bored, but the two magicians were obviously nervous and ill at ease. Chalkara appeared almost desperate, he thought, while Shandiph, fumbling with something small and shiny, was only marginally calmer.

He wondered what had so upset them.

When the silence had dragged on uncomfortably long, Garth said at last, "I saw your faces." He was turned somewhat to the right, leaving the archivist out for the moment. "You two have heard of the Book of Silence."

The two wizards glanced at each other, then back at the overman.

"We have heard of it," Shandiph admitted.

"You seem reluctant to speak of it," the overman remarked.

After a moment's hesitation, Shandiph nodded without answering.

"Why?" Garth asked.

Again the two looked at each other before replying.

"Do you think we should explain?" Chalkara asked.

Shandiph nodded slowly. "I fear we must."

Chalkara turned away and studied the velvet walls. "You do it," she said.

Garth glanced at Silda; she looked very confused and was obviously not a party to whatever conspiracy was afoot.

"To begin with," Shandiph said, "we have met before, Garth of Ordunin, something over two years ago."

Garth gazed with new interest at the wizards' faces; that explained why he had thought they might be familiar. He had encountered various wizards in various ways, but he was fairly sure where he had met these two. They had almost certainly been among the group of fifteen or twenty that had attacked him, appearing out of thin air in the hills north of Skelleth. The Sword of Bheleu had turned back their every assault and retaliated; Garth had seen that several had been killed before the Forgotten King had stepped in and ended the battle by magically transporting the wizards to their respective homes. That was the battle that had driven him to swear his false oath; he was hardly likely to forget it, but in the red haze of the sword's power and the flare and shadow of spell and counterspell, he had not seen clearly the faces of all the wizards.

"I believe I recall the incident," he said.

"I thought you might," Shandiph said. "I hope you bear us no ill will for our attempts to kill you; it seemed at the time to be the only way in which untold destruction might be averted."

"I have wondered, since then, who you might be, why you

chose the time you did to attack me, and why you made no further attempts after your initial defeat," Garth said in a tone of polite curiosity.

Shandiph glanced at Chalkara, then replied, "As for who we were, it doesn't matter any more; our organization was destroyed. The survivors of our conflict with you were scattered, and the wars that followed prevented all attempts to regroup from succeeding. We had attacked you in hopes of halting the onset of the Age of Destruction, which was heralded by your acquisition of the Sword of Bheleu. We made no further attempts after our initial failure because there was no reason to, even had our organization remained intact; you no longer had the sword, and it was obvious that, whatever your part in it might have been, the Age of Destruction had already begun. Eramma was destroyed by civil war."

Garth nodded, though he thought to himself that the destruction hadn't been very complete.

"Chalkara and I fled here, hoping that Ur-Dormulk, which has lasted so long with so little change, would remain safe. We had not expected to see you again. Your arrival was something of a shock—most particularly when you professed to be seeking the Book of Silence."

"And that," Garth said, "brings us back to the original question. What do you know of the Book of Silence?"

"Little enough. What do *you* know of it? Why do you seek it?"

Garth shrugged. "I agreed to fetch it for an acquaintance of mine. I assume it's a book of magic of some sort." He saw no reason to give any unnecessary details, but he could scarcely claim complete ignorance.

Chalkara asked, "Who is this acquaintance?"

"A wizard, of sorts," Garth replied.

"The wizard who took the Sword of Bheleu from you after the battle?" she persisted.

Reluctantly, Garth admitted, "Yes."

The yellow-gowned wizard exchanged glances with her companion.

The archivist broke her long silence and remarked in a slightly querulous tone, "I wish I knew what you three were talking about. What battle was this? Who is this wizard, and what is the Sword of Bheleu?"

Shandiph held up a hand. "Patience, Silda. Let us speak a moment longer, and I will explain it all to you when I can." He paused, and the woman settled back into her silent discontent.

When he was fairly sure that Silda would not make any further protest, Shandiph went on. "Garth, this wizard—the one we saw two and a half years ago. Is he the King in Yellow?"

Silda gasped. "The King in Yellow?" she blurted.

"Silda," Shandiph said. "Please!"

The archivist stifled another outburst. When order was restored, Shandiph repeated, "Is he the King in Yellow, Garth?"

The overman shrugged. "He's an old man who lives in Skelleth. He told me his name once, but I've forgotten it; it was hard to pronounce."

A glance around the table made it plain that both women were now struggling to keep from shouting at him. Shandiph sighed. "I wish you were more cooperative, Garth."

"My apologies, wizard, but I am not here at your convenience, to be interrogated as you see fit. *You* are here to answer *my* questions, are you not? That was the overlord's instruction."

"I know that. I'm sorry. This is very important, though, and very dangerous."

"Why?"

"Because of what the Book of Silence is, damn it!"

"Perhaps if you were to tell me what you believe it to be, we would both gain," Garth replied. This verbal sparring, each side trying to get the most information in exchange for its own, was beginning to annoy him, yet he was not about to end it by telling all he knew. Were he to do so, the wizards would have no reason to reveal their own secrets.

"It's death," Shandiph told him. "It's the end of everything."

One expression that was the same in both species was that of skepticism, and Garth looked openly skeptical.

"It's the totem of death," Shandiph insisted. "You know that the gods each have their unique devices; you must know it. You were the chosen of Bheleu, the one who bore his totem, who was to be his mortal incarnation."

Garth gave a noncommittal nod. "Go on," he said.

"I am no theurgist, no expert on dealing with the gods, but an old friend of mine was; he died in the hills outside Skelleth. He had no protective spells that could defend him against the Sword of Bheleu, though he knew what it was. He explained it to me, and I have studied further since then. Each of the greater gods has a period of ascendancy, an age in which the balance of power is tilted in his favor, and those things that please him are prevalent in our own mortal realm. Each of these ages has its particular herald, someone who wields the totem of the dominant god or goddess. When an age ends, the servants of the waning deity perform a service for the representative of the ruler of the new age, as a symbol of the shift in power. We are now in the Fourteenth Age, the Age of Bheleu, god of destruction, as you know only too well; you are Bheleu's chosen representative, though you have, with the aid of a power I do not pretend to understand, refused that role. I am not aware of the circumstances, but according to theory, a representative of P'hul must have done you a service of some sort, to mark the beginning of this era and the end of the Thirteenth Age, ruled by P'hul, goddess of decay."

Garth nodded. The cult of P'hul had, in fact, spread the White Death in Dûsarra when he had asked, in a fit of madness, for the city's destruction.

"Now, you see, the King in Yellow is the undying priest of The God Whose Name Is Not Spoken. It is a safe assumption that he will be the chosen avatar for the Final God when the Age of Death arrives. That means two things: he must have the totem of the god of death, and a representative of Bheleu must perform a symbolic service for him. Do you not see, then, why we cannot permit you—you in particular—to deliver the Book of Silence to the King in Yellow?"

Garth remained skeptical. "It has been scarcely three years since the Thirteenth Age ended; that is hardly an age."

"No rule is known that limits the length of each god's age, either maximum or minimum. Perhaps your refusal to accept your role, welcome though it is, has cut short the Age of Bheleu."

"Why are you so certain that I wish to take the book to the King in Yellow?"

"I saw that old man who took the sword, Garth, and felt something of his power. Who else could it be?"

Chalkara made a suggestion. "You do not trust us, Garth, but Silda, here, has heard of the King; let her describe him, and we will let you decide whether it is he you serve."

Garth was quite well aware that the Forgotten King was also known as the King in Yellow and that he was exactly what the wizards said he was, but the overman found himself wondering what the archivist knew. He would welcome any new information that might help in his dealings with the old man.

"Speak, then, archivist," he said.

Silda looked at each of the three in turn, then said in a precise voice, "The King in Yellow is a legend in the most ancient histories of Ur-Dormulk. I know of no connection between him and any deity, nor of any connection with a book, or with overmen, or anything else you have spoken of, save only destruction and death. He once ruled an empire from this city, long ago, when it bore another name; one version called it Hastur, another Carcosa. His origins have never been explained; in the very earliest records and even earlier myths, his presence is accepted as an ongoing thing since time immemorial. The legends are all vague as to who or what he was—many seem to assume that any reader will already know—but it is clear that he could not die, and that he was an object of terror throughout the world as these historians knew it. His visage was said to hold death or madness for all who met his gaze.

"Although he was once a king in fact, and a king whom emperors served, he gave up his throne to a successor who founded the ancient Imperial dynasty that the founders of the present Ur-Dormulk overthrew centuries later—yet it was said that in time the King would return and reclaim his rightful place, and when he did, the stars would fall and the earth shatter. He disdained all trappings of royalty and went about the world in scalloped tatters that were a strange shade of yellow—hence the name, the King in Yellow. His servants wore black. This is said to be why the lords of Ur-Dormulk wear black and the people of the city shun all shades of yellow."

Silda paused and shook her head. Chalkara glanced down

at her yellow dress, and Garth was uncomfortably aware of his custom of wearing black armor.

Silda continued. "Such a bare recounting of the facts known to me does not convey the essence of what I have read and heard concerning him. Throughout all the city's recorded history, from times so ancient that we cannot interpret the dates and on until the chaos of the Twelfth Age, the shadow of the King hangs like smoke. In every account of tragedy he is mentioned, and in descriptions of more pleasant times there is always an air of foreboding associated with him. In the wars of the Age of Aghad, the city was sufficiently disrupted so that the continuity was lost and the myths forgotten among the public. But there can be no doubt that, before that age, the tales of the King had persisted, at least among the learned, for more than ten thousand years. This, despite the fact that no historian or storyteller ever dared set down anything but veiled hints as to his true nature. I had thought that no one now alive had ever heard of him, save myself; that only in the ancient books and scrolls was he mentioned—books and scrolls that no one but me has read in three centuries or more. To hear you three speak of him as if he were alive today, as if you had seen him..."

"I *have* seen him," Shandiph said.

"He has been lost for more than a thousand years!"

"You said yourself that he could not die," Chalkara pointed out.

Garth said nothing. He was mulling over what he had heard.

He had thought of the Forgotten King's life span in terms of centuries, not millennia. He could not conceive of anything existing for eleven thousand years. He could not truly conceive of living even *one* thousand years. That would be seven times his own lifetime, roughly; eleven thousand years would be his years seventy-sevenfold. His species itself had not existed for much over a millennium.

For the first time he honestly thought he understood why the King wanted to die. The weight of so many years was surely more than any mind could bear.

He had known that the King had a sinister reputation among any who knew of him at all; Garth had attributed this to his position as the high priest of death, but here there seemed to be something more. Why were the city's histories silent on the exact nature of the King's menace? Why was it said that the heavens would fall if he returned?

Would delivering the Book of Silence truly begin an Age of Death? If so, what would that mean?

That, at least, was a question he might ask. "What would an Age of Death entail?" he inquired.

"Widespread death, obviously," Shandiph replied. "Just as the current age is one of war and chaos and destruction, and the last was a time of stagnation and decay."

"And after it, what?"

Shandiph shrugged. "Who knows? Perhaps nothing will survive the Age of Death, not even the earth or the gods themselves. Perhaps humanity will be destroyed but the rest of the world will go on, and your people will begin a new cycle of their own. Perhaps death will be limited, and many, even whole nations, will survive, and the lesser gods will have their turns as the rulers of the ages. I don't know. I do know that an Age of Death is not something I want to see."

Garth considered these possibilities, particularly the first and most horrific.

What if *nothing* were to survive the Age of Death? The world itself vanished, and the gods dead; would not even time itself cease to be? The end of time would be an actual fact, not just a poetical turn of phrase.

He recalled, with a growing apprehension, that when he had bargained with the King for eternal fame, the King had sworn that Garth's name would be known "as long as there is life upon this earth." When the King had offered him immortality—or so he had understood the offer—the old man had said that Garth might live until "the end of time" if he aided the King's magic. The King had said that his magic would cause many deaths, including those of the entire cult of Aghad. And perhaps most important of all, the priest of The God Whose Name Is Not Spoken in Dûsarra had told Garth that the Forgotten King was bound to live until the end of time. The King sought to perform a feat that would allow him to die.

It appeared very much as if the Forgotten King meant to

bring about the end of time and the death of everything. He had meant to assure that Garth might live and be known until the end of time, not by extending the overman's life, but by destroying the world and time itself.

CHAPTER TEN

After a moment of silence in which Garth absorbed the basic concept that he might be aiding in the utter destruction of the world, he began to consider the possible ramifications and permutations of his situation.

One question came to mind immediately. It seemed reasonable to assume that the world could not end, and the King could not die, until the *end* of the Age of Death. Yet the old man had implied that his death would be immediately achieved by his conjuring. When Garth had believed that the method involved summoning The God Whose Name Is Not Spoken and renouncing his bargain, he had seen no contradiction there. He had thought that the King's offer of eternal life was based on substituting Garth for himself in the Death-God's power, but that no longer seemed reasonable. The offer had not been of eternal life at all.

"How long," he asked, "would the Age of Death last?"

Shandiph shrugged. "I told you," he said, "I am no theurgist, nor am I an astrologer or a seer. I don't know. I have heard philosophers say that the length of an age is subjective and cannot always be predicted or measured. Perhaps it will last a million years, until the sun grows cold and the seas run dry, or perhaps it will be over in an instant, and the world will vanish in a puff of smoke."

That was a very unsatisfactory answer, in Garth's opinion.

"Wizard," he said, "I was told by Bheleu, in a vision he sent while I held the sword and he sought to dominate me, that his reign would last thirty years. Now you speak as if it might be over in just three. How can that be? Could the god have been wrong? That was not part of my understanding of the nature of a god. Might my refusal to serve him have altered that, when the god himself had once said it? I had thought that the ages were fixed in the stars, and that only failures of interpretation caused the uncertainty and disagreement among astrologers."

"I don't know," Shandiph admitted. "Perhaps the stars offer a choice; perhaps the god lied. My friend Miloshir told me that Bheleu's reign would last for either three years or thirty, but could not say which; it may be that his knowledge was lacking, or it may be that it had not yet been determined. Your refusal might in truth have been the crucial event; perhaps you ameliorated the Age of Destruction only to hasten the Age of Death."

Garth remembered the smoking battlefields and charred wastelands he had seen in his journey south through Eramma. If these were the scenes of a *mild* Age of Destruction, what would it have been had he not refused his role? That was a depressing line of thought.

The possibility that by limiting the destruction he had brought the end of the world half a generation earlier—or a full generation for humans—was even more disheartening. It appeared that he had faced a situation in which he would cause disaster, whatever course he might choose.

"You say that my actions might bring the Age of Death; how could that be prevented, if that is to be the next age? Must there be an Age of Death? Need it be the Fifteenth Age, and not the Hundredth?"

"Again, Garth, I cannot say with any certainty. Miloshir spoke as if there were to be fifteen ages to complete the current cycle, the first seven dedicated to the Lords of Eir and the last to the Lords of Dûs, while the Eighth Age was an era when light and darkness were in balance. Whether this scheme of being is truly fixed and immutable I do not know. If it is unalterable, then there will be a Fifteenth Age, a final age, an Age of Death, and it will occur immediately after our current Age of Destruction."

"It seems little to choose, between destruction and death."

Shandiph shrugged. Chalkara, who had been following the conversation closely, said, "I would prefer to live, however terrible the times in which I live, than to perish."

"Do you think that by stopping me from performing my errand you might avert this Fifteenth Age?"

"We feel we must try. It may be that it can be delayed for another twenty-seven years, or perhaps it can be weakened, as Bheleu's reign was, so that some might survive where they otherwise would not."

Garth sat back and thought for a moment. He was not happy about this new information. The possibility that the wizards were making it all up for reasons of their own did not escape him, but that seemed unlikely; it all fitted far too well with what he knew. The blue-clad man had suggested the end of the world as just one of several possibilities, which did not jibe with a lying attempt to frighten anyone; it was Garth's own knowledge of the Forgotten King that convinced him that that was exactly what was fated to occur.

The Fourteenth Age had lasted almost three years thus far; before it, the Age of P'hul had been three centuries, and the Twelfth Age was old when the first overmen were created a millennium ago, as he understood it, so it had lasted at least seven hundred years. The ages appeared to be getting shorter. The Fifteenth might be three days, or three hours. The end of the world, and his own death, might be only a few days in the future.

This assumed, however, that the Fifteenth Age would really begin when the Forgotten King received the Book of Silence. Garth knew of a serious flaw in that theory.

"Would it lessen your concern," he asked, "if I told you that the Book of Silence is not the device of The God Whose Name Is Not Spoken?"

Shandiph considered for a moment, and then said, "Not really. If it is not, then what is? And you, Bheleu's chosen, will still be doing the King in Yellow a service if you bring him the book, even should it be the totem of another god. Miloshir told me that it might be the device of Dagha himself, god of time, the father of all the higher gods. But in that case, what is the totem of Death? He thought it might be the basilisk that dwelt beneath Mormoreth, but that seems unlikely; the creature died, did it not? And bringing the King in Yellow Dagha's totem might easily be as devastating as bringing him his own, whatever it might be."

Garth had to admit the logic in this speech; after all, he had taken the Sword of Bheleu from Bheleu's altar, and not from the followers of P'hul.

"Still," he said, "the Age of Death, as I understand it, cannot begin until *two* conditions are met; I must do the King a service, yes, but more importantly, he must acquire the totem of his god. Is that not correct?"

Shandiph nodded. "I would ask, though, how you know that the Book of Silence is not that totem, when you profess to know nothing about it."

"The King told me," the overman replied; almost immediately, he realized how feeble that sounded. Still, he believed the old man. He knew that the King was a schemer, adept at speaking half-truths and implying falsehoods without actually stating them, yet he had never heard him tell a direct and definite lie. The old man had said, in effect, that the Book of Silence was the totem of Dagha, not of Death. At the time, it had seemed odd that he had wasted so many words, rather than letting Garth believe what he chose, but now it appeared the King had foreseen a moment such as this, when Garth might be reluctant to fetch the book if he believed it to be the device of the Final God.

The Final God—that name suddenly seemed more appropriate, if his age was to end the world.

"You may have reason to accept his word," Shandiph said, "but we do not. Furthermore, how do you know that he does not already possess the symbol of the Unnamed God, whatsoever it may be?"

"He did possess it once, but left it here, in this city, with the Book of Silence."

"He told you this?"

"Yes." Garth remembered that the old man had said also that he was not wholly free of the Pallid Mask even when apart from it, but Garth suppressed the thought. He wanted to bring the Book of Silence to the King so that he might trade it for the Sword of Bheleu and kill Aghadites with the sword.

The thought of killing Aghadites, of watching them bleed and die, was so appealing that he let himself linger over it for a moment, and Chalkara's next question did not register at first.

"I said, what is the totem of Death?" she repeated.

Garth recalled himself and shrugged. "He called it the Pallid Mask."

The two wizards glanced at each other, then at the archivist.

"I never heard of it," Chalkara said.

"Nor I," Shandiph declared.

"I am not sure," Silda said. "It might have been mentioned in the tales of the fallen moons."

"That doesn't matter," Garth said. "I have no intention of bringing anything to the King but the Book of Silence. You have my word."

"I would rather have your word that you would give up this quest entirely," Shandiph said.

"I cannot do that. I need magic for my revenge, a magic that the cult of Aghad cannot counter."

There was a moment of silence. It was Chalkara who said at last, "You want the Book of Silence for *that*?"

"No," Garth replied. "I want the King's aid, which he has promised in exchange for the book." It seemed impolitic to mention that he meant to take up the Sword of Bheleu again; the wizards would surely oppose that as strongly as they opposed the Age of Death. The Fifteenth Age was a theory, but they had seen the sword's power and suffered under it.

"You would risk the lives of every man, woman, and child, every overman and overwoman, every bird and beast in the world, to avenge your wife's murder?" Shandiph asked.

Garth answered simply, "Yes." He did not think it worth pointing out that the cult of Aghad was a menace to all and had threatened further deaths, or that destroying it would be both an act of vengeance and one of prevention. Kyrith's death was reason enough.

Chalkara glanced at each of the others in turn, then whispered to Shandiph, "He's mad!"

She had not allowed for the keen ears of overmen; Garth heard what she said, but ignored it.

"Garth," Shandiph said, "please reconsider. We will aid

your vengeance in every way we can, if you will not bring the King either the book or this mask, or serve him in any manner."

That was a tempting offer, but Garth reluctantly knew he had to refuse it. These wizards had little real power; much of what they had turned against him before, they had lost, either destroyed by the Sword of Bheleu or sealed away by the Forgotten King. They might be a match for an Aghadite magician in a fair contest, one against one, but the cult was clearly widespread and did not trouble itself with fairness; rather, it made a point of being unfair, treacherous, and hateful, in keeping with the nature of its deity. Furthermore, the full party of wizards that had fought him—and surely they had summoned their greatest strength for that combat—could not have exceeded two dozen, and at least one in four had died, perhaps half or more. That meant that far less than a score could have survived, while the cult might well number in the hundreds or even the thousands.

More importantly, he had sworn an oath. For two and a half years, the knowledge that he had made a false vow had eaten away at him, and that pain had finally been alleviated slightly when he undertook this journey. He did not care to let it return. He had regained some trace of honor, tarnished though it might be, and preferred to keep it for as long as he could.

"No," he said. "I am sorry." He rose, before any protest could be made. "I came to this chamber hoping that you might aid me in my search for the Book of Silence, perhaps tell me more of its nature. You have told me much, but it was not what I wished to hear. This conversation has been most enlightening, and I thank you for it, but still, I must pursue my original intention. I do promise you that I do not want to see the Age of Death begin and that I do not intend to aid in bringing it about, if I can avoid it and still meet my sworn obligations. It is plain that none of you would willingly help me in my search for the Book of Silence, and I will not compel you to do so; you act as you see best, as do I. For that reason, I believe there is no point in continuing this discussion." He nodded politely to each, then turned and marched out through the door they had entered by.

The paneled corridor was almost empty, but, half-hidden in

a neighboring doorway, Garth saw a red-clad figure. "Ho, there," he called. "Can you show me the way out?"

In the Rose Chamber, the wizards watched him go and then turned to each other.

"We have to stop him, Shandi," Chalkara said.

"I know that, but what method would you suggest? I have no magic left that can kill from afar, and I see no other way of stopping him. And even if I had some, it might not work; true, he no longer carries the sword, but he is still the chosen of Bheleu."

"Is he really?" Silda asked. "You two and the overman seem to know a great deal more than I do about all this."

"Yes, he is. Everything we have said here is true."

Silda glanced at the door Garth had closed behind himself. "We should tell the overlord," she said.

Chalkara agreed. "She's right, Shandi. Garth hasn't got the Sword of Bheleu; ordinary soldiers should be able to kill him if necessary. At the very least, the overlord might insist that he leave the city; that would make it harder for him to find the Book of Silence, if it really is here."

Shandiph nodded. "I think you're right. If we act quickly, we might be in time to prevent the return of his weapons; even an overman would not be likely to put up too much of an argument at sword point when he's armed with nothing but a dagger."

Chalkara asked, "Who will speak to the overlord?"

"Speed is important, and we must impress upon him how urgent this is. We must all go, at once."

He rose, and Chalkara did the same. Silda got to her feet more hesitantly, then followed the wizards out of the room.

In the corridor, they caught a glimpse of the overman vanishing into a side passage. Chalkara hesitated. "Should we pursue him? One of us, perhaps?"

"No," Shandiph said. "I'm sure that the overlord will have him followed as a precaution, and by someone less recognizable than we are. Let him go for now."

"He'll get his sword and axe back," Silda pointed out.

"He may be delayed, if he chooses to take advantage of the overlord's hospitality by accepting a meal or a drink, and we have no authority to prevent the return of his weapons without the overlord's word. You know that we are all three distrusted here, as wizards always are."

"I'm no wizard," Silda protested.

"You're a scholar, which is close enough for most people. You know things they don't. If we try to interfere without the prince's support, we'll be accused of conspiracy and treason, most likely. Better to risk Garth's arming himself while we talk to the overlord."

"We have no choice now," Chalkara said. "While we've been standing here debating, he's undoubtedly gotten that much farther away."

"True enough," Shandiph replied. "Let us waste no more time, then." He turned and led the way down the corridor toward the audience chamber.

CHAPTER ELEVEN

The overlord did not pay much attention when the archivist and the two wizards re-entered the hall; he assumed that they had finished their discussion with the overman and had come back to the audience chamber in case their prince might require their services. He was rather startled, therefore, when, instead of resuming their accustomed places, they stood before him and made the accepted ritual obeisance.

He had been chatting with his treasurer while the door-keepers selected the next petitioner to be granted a hearing; during the time that the overman had been talking in the Rose Chamber, he had settled a property dispute and refused to hear the appeal of a convicted thief, turning the man back over to the jailer for flogging. The day had been going well, and except for the arrival of the overman from Skelleth and his unorthodox requests, it had been routine.

There was nothing routine, however, in having three of the prince's advisers appear before him, uninvited, while he was holding court. They knew better, he told himself. If they had public business, it could go through the regular channels— though, of course, they would have fewer delays than outsiders would face—and if it was private, it could be handled infor-mally after the day's work was finished.

He paused for a few seconds, letting the trio perceive his

annoyance and grow a bit more nervous, then demanded, "Why have you come here? Speak, if you have any excuse for your action!"

With his head politely bowed, as protocol required in a petitioner, the male wizard said, "O Prince, we beg your forgiveness, but we have urgent business, very urgent indeed, and must speak with you immediately."

The overlord considered for a moment. The formalities and rituals of his life served a definite purpose, in that they made it easier for him to deal with the unending demands made upon him. Each piece of business, whatever its nature, was categorized and run through the appropriate ceremonies, delays, and sortings, so that only a tiny fraction of the whole ever needed to reach him at all; when it did, it was stripped down to the essentials, his choices laid out for him and awaiting a quick decision. Cutting through the rituals was a dangerous precedent; if he permitted the formal structure to weaken, he might be deluged in trivia. Only foreigners, who must be assumed to be ignorant of the usual procedures, were ever allowed to deviate from the pattern, and then only if it seemed a diplomatic necessity—as it had appeared with the overman.

On the other hand, he faced here not a single unknown individual, but three of his most learned counselors. He had not yet had time to become truly familiar with either of the wizards in the months since their arrival, but Chalkara had been the chosen magician of the High King at Kholis, despite her youth—if she was as young as she appeared, which was not something one could be sure of with wizards. She, in turn, deferred to Shandiph, so that he, too, must be considered worthy of respect—unless it was his age that engendered her deference. The vanished Deriam, the overlord's previous wizardly adviser, had spoken well of Shandiph; these two said that Deriam was dead, and the possibility of a magical feud had occurred to the overlord, but that did not detract from the pair's apparent worth. The archivist Silda had lived all her life as a member of the court, under first his father and then himself, but the prince knew less about her than he knew about the wizards; she seemed to care little for his company, or for that of any of his friends or informers. She was given to long historical discussions full of obscure references whenever he

consulted her professionally; he suspected that she hoped to
impress him with her erudition. He was not easily impressed,
but he had to admit that she knew her job well.

These three, he thought, must honestly believe that their
need was urgent, or they would not have interrupted the day's
routine. Despite the unfortunate precedent it set, he decided to
hear them out.

He would not do so publicly, however, whatever the matter
might be. That would be too damaging to his aura of imper-
viousness.

In fact, as he prepared to speak, a way of settling the affair
to his benefit occurred to him, a scheme that would make plain
to all present that the overlord was not to be disturbed without
good reason.

He waved an arm, finger pointing. "Guards! Take these
three to the Black Hall, and summon the executioner! I will
hear their plea, as I must in fairness do, but the penalty for
usurping my attention thus and delaying the work of governance
must be no less than death, if the cause is not sufficient!"

That, he thought, should impress any overeager father wanting reimbursement for his daughter's lost maidenhead, or a
householder demanding that his neighbor's hounds be silenced,
enough to keep them out of his hair. He rose, watching as six
guardsmen snatched the advisers up off the floor, a soldier at
each arm. An officer had gone for the headsman; that was
good. The prince led the way to the black and gold door,
moving in his stately, slow walk, aware that the soldiers were
bringing the three advisers along a few paces behind him.

A footman opened the door into the back corridor, then ran
ahead to the black iron door of the execution chamber. The
overlord entered the room, waited as the wizards and the archivist were brought in, then waved imperiously at the guards
and servant. "Begone," he said.

The seven vanished, and he looked about for somewhere to
sit. The room was empty, save for the black stone platform in
the center and the great block of ebony that stood upon it. The
walls and floor were rough, black stone; the ceiling was black-
veined red marble, arched and vaulted. It was a thoroughly
uncomfortable place, he decided as he settled on the edge of
the platform.

The three counselors stood awkwardly, facing him, unsure whether to prostrate themselves, to bow, or just to stand there.

"Now," the overlord said, "what is it that's so urgent?"

"O Prince," Shandiph replied, "you must prevent Garth from taking the Book of Silence!"

"Garth? The overman?" The overlord was puzzled. "Why?"

"O Prince," Chalkara said, "the Book of Silence is perhaps the most deadly object ever to exist. It is linked with the higher gods, the gods of life and death and even Dagha himself, it seems. Its arcane power is so great that ordinary wizards cannot use it, for to speak a single word from its pages would be instantly fatal." She paused to catch her breath.

The overlord remarked, "That would seem to make it one of the most *useless* of objects."

Shandiph demurred. "I fear not, my lord. As Chalkara has said, no ordinary wizard can use it, but Garth of Ordunin serves one who is not an ordinary wizard. The book was created to be used by a single individual, the immortal high priest of The God Whose Name Is Not Spoken. That is whom Garth intends to deliver it to."

"How do you know this?"

Shandiph asked, "Which part, O Prince?"

"How do you know whom the overman plans to give the book to? He mentioned a wizard, not a priest."

"We know him, Chalkara and I, from a previous encounter. We know that he is associated with the King in Yellow, as the high priest of Death was known of old, and with no other wizards. He admitted as much to us when we spoke with him just now."

"The King in Yellow?" The overlord looked at Silda. "I believe you've mentioned an ancient legend about someone with that description."

"Yes, my prince."

The overlord saw that the archivist had no intention of elaborating, and did not pursue the matter.

"Well, then, what if the overman does take this book to this priest? How will that harm us here in Ur-Dormulk?"

Shandiph answered, "We believe it will bring about the start of the Fifteenth Age, the Age of Death."

"You fear that? Are not the ages preordained and unchangeable?"

Shandiph hesitated, and Chalkara answered for him. "We do not know, O Prince. It may be that they are not."

"We are only in the third year of the Fourteenth Age; it seems to me that any worry about the next age is premature."

"We do not know how long the Fourteenth Age is to be," Chalkara said.

The overlord nodded; he had heard the court astrologer bewailing that uncertainty. "Still," he said, "I cannot believe it will be so brief as that."

"We think that it may be," Chalkara insisted.

The overlord leaned back on his hands and looked at the three scholars. "*I* think," he said, "that you have all managed to frighten one another with old myths and vague suppositions until you have convinced yourselves that we are all in mortal peril, when in truth we are in no more danger from this mad overman than from the Emperor of Yesh." He held up a hand to forestall any protest. "Furthermore, I think you're missing a few essential facts in your worrying."

He shifted, leaned forward again, and held up a finger. "First, the danger you envision may not exist at all. Second, if it does, this overman may have nothing to do with it. Third, whatever else he may be, the overman is a representative of the Baron of Skelleth. You may not realize just how dependent we are upon Skelleth in these unsettled times. You may take seriously my magnificent titles and the splendor of this palace, but I know better; I may call myself a prince and be known throughout Eramma by the title of overlord, but the hard truth is that I'm nothing more than an Eramman baron. Those lesser lords in my court who give me the claim to be an overlord have no power at all; they are worth no more to me than the officers of my guard—probably less, actually.

"Maybe in ancient times Ur-Dormulk was a real nation unto itself and a power to be reckoned with; maybe Alar and Hastur and those other lands I claim really existed; I don't know and I don't care. All I rule is a walled city, a few miles of lakes and mountains, and a good-sized piece of plain that's totally impossible to defend, should one of my neighbors decide to invade. One of those neighbors is the Baron of Skelleth, and right now he's the only one who isn't at war somewhere and the only one conducting any trade at all. We haven't had a caravan in from Therin or Kholis in eighteen months; have you noticed what fresh fruit costs in the markets and shops these days? And what there is, is all our own, at that; I haven't seen a date or an orange in over a year, and if any were available in the city, I'd know it, I promise you.

"That may not mean much to you, but if we lost the trade with Skelleth, you'd know it and you'd feel it. I don't know where the goods are coming from, but we've been getting better furs and wool than we had in times of peace, pickled fish at half what we used to pay, and ivory and gold and a dozen other things—more than a dozen—scores, or hundreds! From Skelleth, which used to sell nothing but ice and hay! It was a gift from the gods that the new Baron began selling to us just about the time the other routes started to be cut, and I don't dare jeopardize that. The Barony of Skelleth covers half our borders, to the north and northeast, and if this Saram can bring us caravans out of nowhere, he might be able to bring armies with equal ease. Now he's sent us a representative, and an overman at that—where in all the world did he find an overman? I thought they were extinct, despite the stories we heard from the traders out of Skelleth. I was wrong. What's more, the gatekeeper tells me that the overman arrived riding a monster twenty feet long with fangs the size of a man's fingers.

"And now you ask me to throw away the goodwill of this overman, and with it the goodwill of the Baron of Skelleth, because of a vague legend. You ask me to risk losing our only remaining trade route, the richest I've ever seen. You ask me to risk an invasion, perhaps led by overmen on monsterback, like those in the tales of the Racial Wars. Why? Because you don't want a magical book no one can read to be taken to a mysterious wizard.

"And that brings me to my fourth, and most important, point. What makes you think that this overman will *find* this Book of Death, or whatever it is? He says that it's in the royal chapel of some palace. What palace? The only palace in Ur-Dormulk is this one, and I promise you all, on my soul and the shades of my ancestors, that there is no royal chapel here containing a mystical book no one can read! If this book exists at all, it must be in the crypts somewhere. Have you ever been in the crypts, any of you?"

The three advisers nodded in unison, like chastised children.

"All of you. Then you should know that you can't find *anything* in the crypts unless you know exactly where it is! They go on forever, in a maze, like a mass of worms tied in knots.

"So do you know what I'm going to do? I'm going to let this overman wander about the city all he likes, and if he wants to get himself lost in the crypts, I'll allow that, too. I'll even give him a guide, if he asks, one who will lead him in nice, large circles through the more familiar corridors. If he persists I'll let him wander all he wants. He can go explore the ruins between the lakes. He can kill a few Aghadite priests, if he does it quietly, and I won't do a thing about it. If he *does* find the book, or anything else of real value, I'll know it, I promise you. If that happens—*if* it happens—then I'll talk to you again, and maybe have it taken away from him if you can convince me it's really that important. *That's* what I'm going to do about this overman, and I hope it satisfies you, because I am *not* going to offend the Baron of Skelleth unless I really have to, for my own safety and for the safety of Ur-Dormulk. Is that clear?"

The three, overwhelmed by this lengthy speech, nodded again.

"Good. So if you want to make yourselves useful, you might apply your magic, you two, to help keep an eye on the overman. All three of you might want to see if you can get some idea where this book is, if it exists, so that we can get to it before he does—if we have to." The overlord waved a hand in dismissal. "So much for that. Now, about the matter of your barging into the audience chamber. As you may have guessed, I am not going to have you executed."

Silda was visibly relieved to hear this; Shandiph and Chalkara, who had never taken the threat seriously, were startled by its mere mention.

"However," the prince continued, "I am not at all pleased that you took it upon yourselves to interrupt my routine; therefore, you are all confined to the north wing of the palace until further notice. I don't want you in the hall with me, I don't want you in my apartments, and I don't want you in the front rooms. Is that understood?"

"O Prince," Shandiph began, "I think you underestimate . . ."

"Silence!" the overlord bellowed.

Shandiph subsided.

"That's better. If you do that again, wizard, you'll be a wanderer once more; I won't execute you, as that would be a stupid waste, but I won't hesitate to banish you from the city if you become more trouble than you're worth to me."

Shandiph bowed his head in acknowledgment.

"Good." The overlord got to his feet and brushed off his velvet robes. "Now let's get back to work." He gestured, and Silda opened the door.

The executioner, hooded and robed in black and yellow, stood outside, his axe in his hands. Behind him, a ring of nervous guards and footmen waited.

The prince spread his arms theatrically. "My thanks, my lord, for heeding my summons. I have decided, however, to be merciful; your services will not be needed."

The headsman bowed low, backed up a pace as soldiers scurried to clear a path, then turned and marched away without speaking.

The overlord spotted an officer among the clustered guardsmen and called, "Captain, if you would escort these three to their quarters, I would appreciate it. They are not prisoners and are not to be confined, but I think they would like to rest. They have been overexcited. See to them; I must return to my own business."

The officer saluted, setting the crimson plume on his helmet bobbing; he pulled two of his men off to one side as the others formed an honor guard around the overlord, then waited as servants, soldiery, and prince marched back into the audience chamber. When the black and gold door had closed behind the last footman, the officer gestured for the first of his two men to accompany Silda and for the other to guard Chalkara, while he himself escorted Shandiph. Thus arranged, he bowed politely and said, "At your service, my lord wizard."

Shandiph was in no mood for pleasantries. "Lead on," he said.

Together the party trooped up the corridor, past the golden door of the Hall of Promotion, and through the ornate gate at the end of the passage. All turned right, but Silda and her guard continued directly down the carpeted corridor, while the wizards and their unwanted companions headed up the gilded staircase. The archivist's apartments were on a lower level, near the archives themselves, which were in an upper part of the crypts. The wizards, in keeping with tradition, were housed on the topmost floor of one of the palace towers. Shandiph, not as young and spry as he once was, sometimes regretted that.

During the long walk along the length of the north wing, ascending each flight of stairs they encountered, neither Chalkara nor Shandiph spoke. Each observed the other, however. Chalkara saw Shandiph's fists clench and unclench, saw him biting back words. Shandiph saw Chalkara's eyes shifting, her face pale, with the look of a hunted animal in her manner.

They reached the spiral stair that led into the tower proper, and Shandiph broke his silence. "You need go no farther," he told the soldiers. "There's no reason to tire yourselves out by climbing all these stairs."

The captain stopped, glanced about, and nodded. "Very well. The prince said you were not under confinement, and at any rate, there is no other exit from the tower."

"Indeed," Shandiph said. "Thank you for your company, captain, and a good evening to you." He bowed slightly.

The officer saluted, but did not depart; instead he stood where he was and watched as the two wizards made their way up the staircase. Glancing back, Shandiph noticed, with some amusement despite his worry over Garth's actions, that the young guardsman who stood at his captain's side was not watching both wizards, but only Chalkara. Unaware that he was observed, the soldier stared at her hips as she climbed the steps. Shandiph was not surprised; Chalkara was worth staring at. He guessed that the youth was wondering whether the tales one heard in every barracks were true, that sorceresses are not like other women.

Shandiph turned away, resisting the urge to comment. The stories were not true; Chalkara was as human as anyone.

The curve of the stair took them out of sight before they

reached the first floor of the tower; their own rooms were in the fifth and highest storey. Shandiph paused, out of breath, at the first landing, but then marched determinedly onward.

"Shandi, we . . ." Chalkara began as they rounded the next curve.

He waved her to silence and trudged upward.

At the third landing he stopped and listened; Chalkara came and stood beside him.

"I don't think they can hear us," he said, keeping his voice low. "Chala, do you like it here?"

"What?"

"Do you like Ur-Dormulk? Do you want to stay here?"

"I don't know. It's comfortable, even if it isn't home, and where else could we go?"

"Sland, perhaps; I understand that it's at peace now, and Karag fled years ago. There might be a place for a wizard or two."

"Shandi, what are you talking about? Why should we leave Ur-Dormulk? If the Fifteenth Age starts, it won't matter where we are."

"It might, but that's not my point. I want to know if you'll go along with me if I disobey the overlord and get us both exiled."

"Oh, Shandi, of course I will! We *have* to do something, whatever he says! The King in Yellow wouldn't have sent Garth here unless he knew the Book of Silence could be found!"

"We'll have to run for our lives, probably. The prince may decide to put us to death if we stay here."

"I don't mind. Maybe we should leave anyway, Shandi, even if he doesn't do anything. I want to see Kholis again; the fighting hasn't reached there yet, not all the way to the castle, and I'm sure the King is over his anger by now. I may not live long enough to go home if we don't stop the overman."

"Don't be so pessimistic, Chala; we'll stop him, at least for now. He's just one overman." Shandiph did not wholly believe that, even as he said it.

Chalkara did not believe it either, but she said nothing to contradict the older wizard. "What are you planning to do?" she asked.

"I'm not sure yet, but I have an idea. Can you make a golem?"

Chalkara considered, then shook her head. "No."

"What about illusions?"

"Oh, I can do those, but they aren't always reliable. What are you thinking of?"

"I'm thinking of ways of killing Garth. I don't have any spells that can do it anymore; do you?"

"No. At least, I don't think so."

"Well, I'm not about to go up and try to kill him in person; he's dangerous. That means we'll have to send someone else to do it."

"Shandi, should we do that? Isn't there any other way to stop him?"

"I doubt it. He's stubborn. I'm sure we can't destroy the King in Yellow or the Book of Silence, but we can probably get Garth killed."

"Should we consult with the rest of the Council?"

"Why bother? The Council is broken, Chala, you know that. We're not bound by its rules anymore. Besides, his death was authorized three years ago, by vote of the quorum."

"You're right. We'll kill him."

"*We* won't; the city guard will. Did you know that Sedrik has always hated overmen? One of his ancestors got butchered in the Racial Wars, I suppose."

"How do you know that?"

"I got him drunk one night; it's always a good idea to learn something about the people who run the place you're living in. I was hoping to find out who was intriguing against whom— there's always some of that in a palace—but instead I got a tirade about murderous inhuman monsters and a lecture about the cowardice of the Eramman nobility in not invading the Northern Waste and wiping the vermin out."

"I see; he'd love an excuse to kill an overman, then, and it's probably one of his men following Garth." Chalkara nodded.

"And if he should receive an order from the overlord himself, I don't think he'd bother to wonder why the prince changed his mind."

"From the overlord?" Chalkara looked puzzled for an instant; then comprehension dawned. "Oh, of course! A golem would be better, but an illusion should work if the light isn't very good."

"I hope so," Shandiph said.

"You start packing, Shandi; the overlord won't like this at all if he finds out. I'll need some things for the illusion, but you can pack up everything else." She hurried up the last two flights; Shandiph, still weary, plodded after her.

Ten minutes later, Sedrik, Commander of the Guard, Marshal of the City, was startled by the appearance of his lord and master in the door of the wardroom. The overlord's voice seemed odd, higher in pitch and not very clear. The corridor was dim and the wardroom's windows did not illuminate the doorway this late in the day, so the prince's black robes seemed insubstantial and almost blended into shadow. There was no sign of the prince's customary entourage. Still, there was no mistaking who it was that spoke to Sedrik, or what his orders were.

Sedrik was absolutely delighted.

CHAPTER TWELVE

Garth acknowledged the return of his sword and axe with a deep bow, then turned and marched down the steps of the palace.

When he reached the stone pavement of the avenue, he paused, unsure where to go. He had two goals to achieve and no clear idea of how to pursue either one. Somewhere in the city was the Book of Silence, and he had sworn to find it and bring it back to Skelleth. Somewhere in the city there was also a temple dedicated to Aghad, and he was determined to destroy it and kill the god's worshippers, regardless of what the overlord might say or do about it.

Finding the book, he decided as he slung the axe on his back, should come first; the overlord had expressed no objection to that, despite the misgivings of his counselors. The wizards might try to change his mind, but so far, at any rate, Garth had a free hand to do as he pleased with regard to the book. The cult of Aghad, on the other hand, was under the overlord's consideration. If Garth were to attack the temple now, the overlord might well take it amiss and try to have Garth killed or driven from the city.

Once he had the book, he would have no objection to leaving Ur-Dormulk. Therefore, the book came first.

That settled, and with his sword on his belt once more, he

looked about, trying to locate the signs and portents the Forgotten King had promised him.

The sun was halfway down the western sky, and the shadow of the overlord's palace stretched over him. To the east, much of the avenue was still brightly lit; citizens were bustling about the gray stone buildings in a flickering river of vivid colors. Streets branched off to either side, in a variety of widths and angles.

As he turned to the southwest, looking toward one corner of the palace facade, a gust of cold, damp wind caught him in the face.

That seemed as good a sign as any; he strolled south and around the corner.

He did not notice the green-clad figure that followed him, nor the two in red—one in the brilliant carmine of the overlord's household staff, the other wearing the color of dried blood—that watched him closely but did not pursue.

He wandered along aimlessly, watching for other signs, yet found none save the occasional wet breezes. He gradually worked his way westward, noticing as he went that the number of people on the streets and the general noise of the city diminished steadily with his increasing distance from the avenue that connected the eastern gate and the overlord's palace. After some time spent thus, he rounded a corner and found himself looking out across a rift. The city appeared to end in a broad stretch of pavement running north and south along the edge of a valley or chasm; from where he stood he could not see what lay in the gap, but he could see the far side, a granite barrier topped with buildings. Something was odd about the view, but mists drifting up from the valley made it hard for him to decide just what he was seeing.

He walked onward, out onto the wide pavement, and noticed to his surprise that there were no people anywhere on it. This promenade was the first completely uninhabited place he had seen since arriving in Ur-Dormulk.

He made his way cautiously up to the edge, wary lest it crumble beneath him—though it looked as solid as any part of the city. When he had gotten as near to the precipice as he cared to, he gazed out beyond it again.

More than fifty yards below lay the smooth, dark surface

of a lake, black and chill; thin clouds rolled across it in bands, like waves upon the ocean, and mist rose in dissipating plumes.

That, Garth told himself, explained where the cold winds came from.

He lifted his gaze, looking out across the lake; the mists blurred his vision, and he could not decide whether the barrier that reared up on the opposite shore was natural or man-made. The buildings atop it, he now saw, were ruins.

It occurred to him immediately that the Book of Silence was quite possibly buried somewhere in those ruins; that would explain why nothing was known of it.

The sun was behind the broken towers, which made it impossible for him to make out much detail, but he guessed that those towers had once been part of a palace or citadel, such as the Forgotten King must have maintained. He stared intently, but the shadows and mist prevented any clear view. The sun itself seemed distorted by the fine spray, broadened to almost twice its natural width.

He turned his eyes away and blinked, then looked at the gray stone pavement for a moment to rest them. As he did, he noticed two things.

First, the pavement here was not worn nearly so much as the city streets. He would have supposed that a lakeside promenade would attract strollers in the hot days of summer, or perhaps fishermen—someone, at any rate—yet there was no one anywhere in sight save himself, and the stone slabs were only lightly marked by the passage of feet.

The second thing he noticed was a sound, a very faint, deep, distant sound; he could not quite make it out.

Neither item seemed of immediate importance; he looked up once more, avoiding the sun for the moment, and scanned quickly around the edges of the lake.

It was long and narrow, with the city on one of its long sides and the ruins on the other. At either end of the promenade on which he stood walls of natural rock thrust up, raising the lakeside cliff to greater heights and cutting off the streets to the east, turning them back from the lake. Garth realized he had seen those stone barriers from the steps at the gate.

Similar outcroppings divided the opposite shore, but beyond and between them lay more ruins. The area directly opposite him was the largest, but there were four clusters of buildings in all on the western shore, each split off from the others by the masses of rock and connected to the rest of the city only by the lake. The ends of the lake, at north and south, were sheer cliffs, with no signs of human habitation upon them. He could not see if there were ruins or other inhabited areas elsewhere on the eastern shore; the outcroppings at either end of the promenade blocked his view.

Once, he guessed, the various enclaves must have kept in touch with one another by boat, so that all were part of a single great city. Now, though, there were no signs of docks or boats, but only the still black water, laced with mist and cloud, far below. He theorized that over the centuries the level of the lake had dropped, making such water travel more difficult, and finally impossible. The lake might be too shallow to navigate—though it looked infinitely deep.

He turned his gaze back to the ruins opposite his present position and noticed for the first time that mists seemed to be rising behind them as well as in front. He was unsure whether this indicated the presence of another lake, or whether it was merely an optical illusion.

With a sudden shock, he spied something very strange that could only be a trick of the mist; the sun had split in two, and twin crimson orbs, like baleful eyes, were sinking behind the towers into the mist of the farther lake—if such a lake was really there.

He blinked, but the illusion persisted, and it was only after a moment of staring that he realized how long he must have been wandering about Ur-Dormulk if the sun—or suns—was setting.

He wondered if this strange vision might be one of the signs he was to follow.

The sound he had noticed before impinged again upon his awareness, and he found himself trying to making out just what it was. It, too, might be a sign, he told himself.

It seemed to be coming across the lake, or up from the ground, rather than from the city behind him. He resolved to follow it if he could.

He still had no idea what it was; it was so low in pitch, so low and drawn-out, that he could barely perceive it at all.

Picking a direction at random, he turned right and strode north along the promenade, then paused and listened.

The sound had grown very slightly louder; he was going in the right direction. He marched on. At the northern end of the lakeside pavement, he stopped and listened once more.

The sound was once again slightly louder; he did not appear to have passed its point of origin. It seemed, more than ever, to be coming from the ground beneath his feet, still barely audible, as much felt as heard, and felt only as slow, crawling uncertainty. A cold wind brought a puff of mist swirling around him, chilling him even through his surcoat and armor.

The sound, or vibration, or whatever it was, was as slow as the turning of the universe, slow as no human-generated sound ever was; a vague foreboding trickled through the back of Garth's mind as he listened to it.

From where he now stood, he could not go west, over the cliff into the lake, nor north, up the sheer stone face of the outcropping; south would take him farther from the sound. That left only east. Two streets led back into the city proper from the northern end of the promenade at diverging angles; Garth took the left-hand, more northerly route, hoping that it would bring him to the source of the mysterious low throbbing. If it did not, he told himself, he would have to find a way across the lake.

The route he had chosen was a narrow, winding street, lined with an assortment of buildings. Garth recognized some as shrines, though they lacked the domes and spires he had come to identify with temples, by the scent of incense and the sound of chanting. He wondered if any were dedicated to Aghad; the thought triggered a rush of anger and adrenaline, and his hand fell to the hilt of his borrowed sword.

He saw none of the dark red robes he had learned to associate with the cult, however, and the name Aghad was not written above any doorways or audible in any of the prayers he heard. He gradually relaxed as he walked on.

Around him, in contrast to the deserted lakeside, large numbers of humans went about their business, going to and from the various shrines and shops. Their bright garments were lighted in fiery shades or lost in lengthening shadows as the sun sank farther in the west and the evening torches were set ablaze. No one interfered with Garth's progress, though several people stared, and almost everyone who saw him gave him at least a second glance. Overmen, he knew, were not seen in Ur-Dormulk.

The street curved to the north, following the contour of the upthrust rock, separated from the bare stone only by the row of buildings that lined the left-hand side. Other alleys and byways led off to the right, but to the left there was nowhere to go.

This road, like all he had seen in Ur-Dormulk, was paved with gray stone; the marks of wear clearly indicated the parallel tracks of carts and the wider pathways of the more common pedestrians. Branches led from this central route to each of the temples and shops and houses. Garth realized that he could judge the relative popularity of the various establishments by the depth of the path that led to each door.

He paused to listen for the sound; he had lost it among the noises of the busy street. As he listened, he noticed that one temple, nestled close up against the rock wall to the west, had no visible path at all. That struck him as curious. He watched for a moment and saw that not only did no one approach the shrine but some people actually veered away to give it a wide berth. The trough in the center of the street swayed to the right in consequence. This avoidance was obviously not of recent development.

His curiosity piqued, Garth approached the shunned building. He could see nothing about it that might inspire dread; it had a low, simple facade, a row of pillars supporting a narrow porch in front of a bare stone wall and a single open door. A central portion of the roof was raised up above the facade. There were no adornments of any kind; no incense drifted from the open portal, and no chanting could be heard. No bells chimed, no draperies rustled; the shrine appeared deserted.

Garth paused for a moment, then heard the dull sound he had been following, just barely perceptible over the pattering feet and flapping sleeves of the passing traffic. He was about to conclude that the temple was completely empty, perhaps a relic of an outlawed death cult, when he realized that the sound itself, that low, slow throbbing, seemed to come from the abandoned fane.

His red eyes fixed on the somber stone, he watched the temple for a long moment. He saw nothing, no sign of life; it was just a building, a row of pillars, a wall, and a roof, jammed in between two other buildings. The sound went on unchanged, and with each moment, each slow beat, Garth became more convinced that it emanated from the building he studied.

With a mental shrug, he took the few remaining steps across the street, up the single step onto the porch, and to the open door.

He paused there as he heard gasps behind him. He turned back for a quick look and saw that several passersby had frozen in their tracks to stare at him. It was obvious that there was something about this temple, about the thought of someone entering it—even an overman—that frightened them.

Superstition, Garth told himself. He turned back to the door and peered through it, into the gloom of the chamber beyond. The sound was louder than ever. He decided that it might not be wise to rush in. He backed down the step and out onto the street.

The people who had stopped to stare remained where they were, still staring. He looked about, picked out a man he judged to be intelligent in appearance, and called, "Ho, there! What is this place?"

The man was reluctant to speak, but those behind him thrust him forward, appointing him their spokesman.

"This is the temple of Dhazh," he replied at last.

"Dhazh? I have never heard of him," Garth said.

"His cult was outlawed for feeding people to the god; it is said that he takes the form of a great monster and still dwells within, asleep."

"What is that sound I hear, that seems to come from this place?"

"What sound?" The man seemed both frightened and genuinely perplexed. "I have never heard any sound here."

"A low, throbbing sound; do you not hear it?"

"I hear no sound from the temple," the man insisted.

"Listen, then; all of you, listen!" The overman held up his hand for silence.

The crowd that had gathered around him listened, and the street grew quiet, though beyond the immediate vicinity people still went about their business, talking and laughing and rattling things.

After a moment, a woman called, "I don't hear anything."

"Nor do I," someone else said, and a volley of agreement sounded.

"None of you? No one hears it?" Garth was surprised; he had heard the sound more clearly than before during the moment of listening.

He was aware that his hearing was somewhat keener than that of mere humans; overmen had several advantages, he knew. But the sound had seemed loud enough for even human ears. Perhaps magic was at work, and he alone was meant to hear the sound, whatever it was. If that was the case, it was almost certainly one of the signs the Forgotten King had meant him to find.

With that in mind, he dismissed the humans from his thoughts and turned back to the temple. There was said to be a monster in there, he reminded himself; he checked his axe, making certain he could get it free quickly if the need arose, then drew his sword and marched back up the step and into the abandoned shrine.

A few moments later, while the little crowd was still largely intact, a cluster of jabbering humanity discussing Garth's presence and actions, Sedrik and a small company of chosen warriors marched up the street.

It had taken Sedrik a quarter hour to find his men; he was not so foolish as to try taking on an overman single-handed, however much it might have suited him to do so. He had been ordered to kill the troublemaker, ordered personally by the overlord himself, and he knew that he would be derelict in his duty if he were to get himself killed in single combat, satisfying as that combat might be. He was responsible for making certain that the overman died, and for that a dozen men were wanted, the very best men he had.

Those he had chosen were now arrayed behind him, armed with sword and spear, four of them carrying crossbows as well, four with heavy shields, and four with maces. Sedrik himself carried an axe in addition to his sword; he hoped to be able to strike off the overman's head with it, as befitted a criminal.

Arming had taken more time, and then he had had to wait until the spies changed shifts and brought back news of the overman's whereabouts. He had marched his men out to the edge of the lake Demhe, only to learn that the overman had left. The commander had sent out the scout he had brought with him, and followed as soon as the fugitive's path had been reported. Now he saw no sign of the overman, but the cluster of people on the street seemed worthy of investigation.

Sedrik gave orders to his men, who formed a quick but effective block across the street, preventing the departure of the gathered citizens. That done, he marched forward and bellowed, "You, there! What is this?" He pointed his sword at the nearest person of responsible appearance. By chance, he had chosen the same man Garth had spoken with.

"My lord," the man said, recognizing the black plume that marked Sedrik as marshal, "an overman has come and entered the temple of Dhazh!"

Startled, Sedrik realized that he was standing before the forbidden shrine. He did not like the temple of Dhazh; to a man born and raised in the weathered streets of Ur-Dormulk, the unworn condition of its step, and indeed of the whole building, sheltered as it was by the great rock barrier, appeared alien and sinister. Furthermore, he was an educated man, as the Marshal of the City had to be, and knew something of the cult itself, outlawed centuries earlier. Dhazh had been a demonic earth-god, and as such did not fit anywhere in the accepted Eramman theology. A destructive male earth deity seemed to contradict several basic tenets of the popular religion. No one had ever visited the shrine but a handful of hereditary priests and their unwilling sacrifices, even in its heyday, and Sedrik considered it a wise decision of an ancient overlord to have outlawed the cult and put its priests to death.

There was also the unpleasant myth of the god's heartbeat, a sound said to be heard by those the god had chosen as servants or sacrifices.

Sedrik's thought was echoed by the crowd's spokesman, who added, "He said he heard something!"

Sedrik glanced at the pillared facade. Perhaps there was some connection between the overman's presence in the temple and the order to kill him. The overlord might be worried that the overman would somehow restore the cult to life.

That was none of Sedrik's business; his duty was to obey orders, not to guess why they had been given. He had been told to kill the overman, and the overman was in the temple of Dhazh. Therefore, it was his duty to enter the temple and seek the criminal out. That such an action might serve to dispel some of the lingering respect accorded the demon-god was an added bonus, really. The more he thought about it, the more he liked the idea of entering and defiling the temple. It should have been torn down long ago, he told himself.

The thought of killing the overman was also pleasant; he found himself looking forward eagerly to the coming battle.

"All right, men," he called. "Follow me, arms at ready!"

With that, he marched up the step and into the temple.

After a moment's hesitation, the twelve soldiers followed him, with varying degrees of reluctance. Each knew that he was one of the city's best, a chosen master in the art of killing, but the dark legends that clung to the temple lingered in each man's mind. The finest warrior was no match for an angry god.

Had one soldier hung back, others might have joined him, but none dared be first to be called coward, and all marched on into the forbidden temple, following their commander.

CHAPTER THIRTEEN

The only light in the temple came from the open doorway; the few clerestory windows were heavily curtained, and the prickets and sconces on walls and pillars held only melted wax, almost invisible beneath dust and cobwebs. There were no torches, no clouds of incense, no chanting priests; there was no sound at all, except for Garth's own footsteps scraping through the dust and the low, dull throbbing he followed. The fane was empty, save for a stone altar on either side of the single great hall that made up most of the building's interior, and dust lay thick everywhere. No carpets covered the stone floors; no tapestries hid the stone walls.

Garth stood still for only a moment as his eyes adjusted to the dimness; then he advanced into the room, sword ready. He saw no sign of a monster, and nothing that might be making the sound he pursued.

He found a large door, black with age, at the rear of the chamber; Garth pushed at it gently, hoping it was not locked, and it fell to dust beneath his hand.

He stepped through immediately, sword held before him, swinging the blade gently from side to side to help him feel his way; though he held his breath and blinked, the dust from the door stung his eyes and nostrils. The inner chamber was even dimmer than the main hall, due to the dust and the greater distance from the main portal, but once Garth had rubbed the grit from his eyes with the back of his free hand, he could see that the room was quite deserted.

The sound, however, was definitely louder here; he listened, trying to ignore the noise that still reached him from the street.

The vibration grew, then dropped, then sounded a long beat like a distant, rolling thunderclap, then began again, with a steady, ponderous rhythm, each cycle taking whole minutes. Hearing it more clearly now, Garth realized what it was, or at least what it seemed to be.

He was listening to a heartbeat, so slow, so deep, that he could only think it to be the pulse of the earth itself; no conceivable leviathan would be a fit possessor of that drawn-out throbbing.

As he listened, his eyes took in the details of the inner sanctum. He was in a small, bare chamber, with a thin trickle of light seeping around the curtain that covered a window high in one corner. There was no furniture, only dust, layered on the floor and drifting in the air around him. On either side of the room were open doors, the areas beyond them utterly in darkness.

At first glance, Garth saw nothing to choose between one door and the other, but a second's careful listening convinced him that the sound was slightly louder to the left. Accordingly, he turned left and stepped through the doorway.

The room beyond was totally black, and Garth found himself groping along cautiously; nonetheless, he almost fell when he reached the top step of a staircase leading down. He had been alert for walls, doorways, or living creatures before him; he had not been paying attention to the floor beneath him.

He caught himself at the brink and paused, hesitant to continue onward in the dark. If there was a monster in the temple, it would have the advantage of him in its lightless lair; he was unfamiliar with his surroundings, but any longtime inhabitant would be at home here.

A slight movement of the air distracted him. The sound was definitely coming up from below, he decided, and that was one attraction beckoning him on, but the faint breeze was strange. It took him a moment to realize what was odd about it.

A slight current could be felt coming from almost any cave

or cellar at times, cool and moist, and he would not have been surprised by such a thing here, particularly since the chill water of the lake might seep in somewhere—but this breeze was *warm*.

That did not seem to make sense. The only places Garth knew of where underground chambers or passages were warm were volcanic, and he had thought that the mountains around Ur-Dormulk were no more prone to volcanic activity than the Yeshitic jungles of the distant south were prone to snow in midsummer. Furthermore, the air that he felt ascending the stairway was damp and slightly fetid, like the air of a swamp.

Fascinated, Garth was determined to investigate further, but the darkness still daunted him. He had flint and steel and tinder in a pouch on his belt, but nothing that would burn well enough to provide a reliable light.

It occurred to him that some of the melted candles in the main hall might still retain enough of their substance to serve him, but he dismissed the thought; he had no idea how far he might want to pursue this venture and he needed something that would last longer than a burned-out candle stub.

Surely, he told himself, the priests who had once used this shrine would have had some way of lighting the stairs. He reached out and felt along first one side of the room, then the other. His hand struck something metallic that rattled, and he heard a faint gurgling as well. He sheathed his sword carefully, reached up, and felt the object he had discovered.

It was an oil lamp, still partly full, hanging from a hook.

Once he had found the lamp, it was a simple matter to light it. The wick was still in place, but cut off from the reservoir by an airtight metal lid that had to be unscrewed; even after he had worked the lid free and dipped the lower end of the wick into the oil, it remained so dry that it ignited almost immediately, only to flare up and burn mostly away before any of the fuel caught.

The oil had thickened with age, and after the first bright flame died away, the light was low and smoky, scarcely reaching above the remaining stub of the wick. Still, it was adequate for his purpose. He marveled that, even sealed, the oil had not all dried up long ago, and wondered whether the temple might not have been completely abandoned for as long as he had first supposed.

With his sword again naked in his right hand and the lamp slung in his left, he began his careful descent.

The staircase was much longer than Garth had first thought, and after about fifteen feet, the steps changed from the solid and unworn ones that he had expected from the condition of the street outside the temple to shorter, narrower treads worn to a slippery polish, sufficiently ancient and used that the center of each step was an inch or more below the ends. They were almost as difficult to negotiate as the steps at the city gate and made for very slow going.

Garth guessed that this change must indicate that he was below the city proper and entering the legendary crypts. When he finally reached the foot of the staircase, he paused to catch his breath and shine the light around; as he did, he thought he heard sounds above him. He dismissed the idea as absurd. He had just come through the temple and seen it to be completely empty; if he was, indeed, hearing anything from above, it could only be street noise, reflected down to him by some freak of acoustics.

He was in a rectangular room, long and relatively narrow, with side walls that sloped inward at the top and curved over to blend smoothly into the ceiling; the corners of the chamber were also curved. The floor was a curious uneven inlay of several different varieties of stone, and the ceiling was low overhead.

The walls and ceiling were gray, and the floor a maze of dull colors half-hidden by dust. The sound of the monstrous heartbeat, if heartbeat it actually was, was louder than ever.

There was a door in the far end; Garth flashed his lamp around, but could see no other entrance or exit, save for the staircase and the single door.

He strode the length of the chamber and pushed at the door, halfway expecting it to crumble to dust as the one in the upper temple had done. It did not; with a high-pitched creak and a flurry of disturbed dust, it swung open, revealing another chamber.

Garth stepped through, lamp held high. This second chamber was identical with the first, save that the walls and ceiling were a dull red instead of gray.

He had now descended at least thirty feet below street level and moved more or less due west, with only the single jog to the left at the top of the stair, since entering the temple. A rough estimate told him that he had come at least a hundred feet from the front pillars—which meant that he was now in or under the great stone outcroppings, since the temple itself had been no more than sixty feet from front to back.

That was very interesting indeed, he thought. He wondered if he might find his way *under* the lake, to the ruins on the far side.

He proceeded through the second chamber and into a third, this one walled and ceiled in dead black, the floor again a dust-covered polychrome. The door at the end of this chamber opened onto another staircase leading down; he followed it without hesitation.

It seemed to run on forever. He had been in crypts before, in the Orûnian city of Mormoreth, but this stair appeared far longer than any he had previously encountered anywhere.

It was also straight, which might have added to its apparent length; the crypt stairs in Mormoreth had wound slightly back and forth, so that he had never been able to see their full length at one time. Here, though, he found it disconcerting to hold up the lamp and see step after step after step, stretching away into the distance both above and below him, both ends lost in the darkness beyond the reach of his feeble lamplight.

Finally, as the lamp swung forward, he glimpsed the lower end; he increased his speed as much as he dared, for the steps were as treacherous as the lower portion of the first set.

The stair ended in a short corridor, and that in turn led to another stair, this one ascending. Garth wondered whether he would find himself in the midst of the ruins beyond the lake.

He did not; the upward-bound steps ran only a tiny fraction of the distance he had just descended. Almost as soon as he reached the first step, he glimpsed the upper end.

A moment later he emerged into another room, away from the confining stone walls of the stairway, and paused to catch his breath again.

Again, he thought he heard noise behind him, but now it

was almost drowned out by the slow beating ahead of him, a sound that had acquired a sinister, menacing note as he drew nearer its source. Something about it made him nervous.

He had not yet given much thought to what the beating might be; he had decided that it was a heartbeat without considering what that might mean. Now, as he stood in a passage that he judged to be several hundred feet below the level of Ur-Dormulk's streets, he wondered what he might find if he went on. *Could* there be a monster with a heart so great? If so, he would stand no more chance against it than a beetle. A mere mechanical dragon had been capable of killing him; how could he think to face a creature whose heartbeat could be heard half a mile away?

On the other hand, why would such a monster even notice him? He need not worry about being devoured; an overman could scarcely begin to feed the appetite of such a thing, and he could easily retreat into places where a behemoth could not reach him.

The idea of such a creature went against all his instincts, and he decided that it was far more likely that the sound was being artificially produced by some lost remnant of the outlawed cult, for reasons of its own. In any case, he was not about to turn back at this point. He held up the lamp.

He was in another long, narrow, low-ceilinged room, longer than the three on the upper level and walled in gray stone. Again there was a single door at the far end, yet this one was not a simple portal in a post-and-lintel frame, but an elaborate carved construction of several different woods, hung in a red stone arch embellished with golden tracery.

Garth approached cautiously; the ornate door, so different from the others, seemed almost threatening. He paused when he had reached it and put a hand to one of the wooden panels. It vibrated beneath his fingers with the slow, slow beating.

For a third time he thought he heard something behind him, the sound only detectable in the interval between beats, and lost thereafter in the throbbing he had followed for so far. He turned and looked back at the stairs, but saw nothing.

This new portal did not yield to a simple push, but the latch handle still moved freely; he lifted it and shoved the door wide.

Beyond lay a chamber unlike the others; although the walls

curved into the ceiling in the same fashion, this room was circular rather than oblong. The walls were black, and the floor here was also black, made up of stones arranged in a spiral leading in toward the room's center.

It was what stood in the center, however, that was most different. A column of horn or ivory projected upward from the floor, yellowed with age but still almost white, tapering from a diameter of eighteen inches or so at the base to about a foot where it was cut off, three feet above the floor, to form a slanting surface. In the center of this tilted top, a single drop of some reddish-black substance was very slowly oozing forth.

A circular trough surrounded this strange column, and Garth saw that there was a trickle of the red-black goo down the side of the column and a shallow pool of it in the trough.

He saw no way in or out of the chamber, save for the single arched door. Garth entered cautiously, lamp and sword both held high.

There was nothing to look at but the column and its curious issue, so he studied that. As he watched, a fat black drop rolled sluggishly from the center of the column's top to the edge, joining the slow trickle. Its separation from the central spot coincided exactly with the end of one of the vast heartbeats, Garth noted idly.

Another drop began to grow as Garth studied the walls, looking for concealed openings. He turned back as a beat ended and saw the new drop follow its predecessor.

That the first drop had happened to fall in time with the sound had struck him as nothing but coincidence, but the second one made it seem more than that. He listened, watched, and soon reached an inescapable conclusion: the sound he had followed came from the base of the mysterious shaft. Furthermore, it was somehow connected with the oozing fluid.

It occurred to him that it might be the vibration that caused the drops to fall in synchronization with the beating, rather than any more direct connection. It did not seem reasonable that so great and ponderous a throbbing should do nothing but pump out a stream of blackish goo. He looked for some secret opening or lever on the column or in the trough surrounding it, being careful to touch nothing, lest he trigger a trap.

His investigation of the small metal pipe that allowed the

excess fluid to drain off when the trough was full ceased abruptly, however, when for the fourth time he heard sounds other than the beating, coming from somewhere outside the arched doorway.

Once, perhaps twice, he could dismiss this as illusion, or the action of overwrought nerves, but now there was no chance at all that noise might be reaching him from outside the crypts. No vermin would be audible over the great throbbing, yet the sound was there once more. It was closer than before, and he did not lose it again after the first hearing. Now that he was no longer moving deeper into the catacomb, whatever made the noise was gaining on him quickly. After listening carefully for a few seconds, he thought that it was the rattle of armor.

He dropped the lamp where he was; it flickered, but stayed lit, as it bounced once and came to rest on the stone floor at a sharp angle, tilted up on the curve of its metal oil reservoir and prevented from rolling by the thick dust.

The circular chamber offered few places of concealment, with no corners, alcoves, or hangings that might hide him. The looming shadow of the central column, stretching up the wall opposite the spot where the lamp had fallen, would provide some cover, but Garth decided against it, preferring the more obvious place behind the only door. Whoever was approaching would probably not realize immediately that he had reached a dead end in the little room. The person would wonder why the lamp was there, certainly, but would probably not think to check behind the door before entering. Putting out the lamp would leave Garth in total darkness, and he did not care for that idea; let his pursuer wonder, then.

Besides, he had no time to think of a better plan.

The sounds were drawing nearer; in the pauses between beats, he could make out footsteps and the rasping breath of human exertion. He pressed up against the wall behind the carven door, sword ready in his right hand, axe swung around within reach, awaiting whoever might come.

CHAPTER FOURTEEN

Sedrik's pursuit of the overman was delayed slightly by the darkness of the temple; he had assumed that he would find his quarry on the streets or in some well-lighted shop and had not bothered to equip his men with lanterns. When it became clear that Garth was not to be found anywhere in the dim precincts of the temple proper, and giving due consideration to the fact that the overman was a newcomer to Ur-Dormulk who could scarcely have known of secret exits, Sedrik had no choice but to conclude that Garth had taken the stair to the crypts. Sedrik had his orders, and his own hatred as well, and was eager to follow—but no glimmer of light indicated the overman's presence: surely he would not have ventured into the depths without a light of some kind! Sedrik had to assume that Garth had either built up a considerable lead, or turned corners, or passed through doorways. To pursue him in total darkness would be reckless to the point of abject stupidity. Therefore, lights were needed, and Sedrik had to wait with half his company at the head of the crypt stairs while the other half returned to the street to fetch torches or lamps from the surrounding shops.

As he waited, the faint, fetid warmth that drifted up from below made his skin crawl.

Finally all his men were together again, torches in hand. No lamps or lanterns had been secured, but a plentiful supply of torches intended for lighting temples and storefronts had been available; the rightful owners had been willing to give them up without payment beyond a promise of government recompense later. The possessors of other means of illumination had not been so obliging, and the soldiers had not cared to argue.

With one man in four carrying a lighted brand, Sedrik and his party descended the steps, following in Garth's wake. Sedrik, in his impatience at the delay and in his eagerness for battle, tried to hurry the soldiers along, but with limited success. The worn steps, the evil reputation of both the temple and the crypts, and the unsteady torchlight all served to keep the pace down.

At the foot of the first flight, some of the men sighed audibly with relief; Sedrik paid them no mind but moved forward more briskly, now that the floor was solid underfoot.

They passed through the gray room, the red, and into the black; here one of the men whispered, "Shh! I think I hear something!"

Sedrik gave the command to halt and held up a hand for silence. His men obeyed, and all listened.

Uncertain, they looked at one another.

"Do you hear it, commander?" one murmured.

Sedrik nodded, reluctantly.

"What is it?" another asked.

Sedrik shrugged.

"'Tis the heartbeat of the god!" someone said.

"Dhazh?"

"That's only a myth!"

Sedrik spoke at last. "This sound is no myth; we all hear it. Perhaps it is what first gave rise to the tales of Dhazh's existence. I suspect it to be an underground waterfall; after all, we must be near Demhe here, and no one knows where its bottom may be, or where its waters come and go."

"I don't hear anything," a soldier at the back confessed.

"Then it's your hearing that's at fault, for the sound is there," one of his comrades retorted.

"Whatever it is, men," Sedrik said, "it is no concern of ours, wherever it comes from. It may well be beyond the walls of the crypts entirely. I doubt that anything could fit into these rooms that we would not be able to handle; certainly the monster-god of the old legends could not squeeze beneath this roof!" He gestured at the low ceiling; someone chuckled, which pleased Sedrik. He saw about an even mix of smiles and worried looks; that was worse than he had hoped, but better than he had expected. Even the best fighters could be discouraged by empty darkness and narrow passages.

"We go on," he said. "We have an overman to catch."

They moved on down the length of the black chamber in formation, six ranks of two, with Sedrik to one side of the second rank. At the door at the inner end, the first rank balked. The foremost torchbearer, in the second rank at Sedrik's elbow, held his light high and forward, its flame spattering on the ceiling, its smoke lost against the black stone, its light spilling down the second stair.

"I cannot see the bottom, commander," the torchbearer reported.

Sedrik stepped forward and peered over the shoulder of one of the first pair. "And *I* cannot see the overman, nor have we seen anywhere he might have turned. We go on." He noticed, but did not mention, that the faint roaring—the god's heartbeat—seemed to be coming up the stairway from somewhere below.

"We don't know what's down there!" another soldier protested.

"The overman is down there!" Sedrik said, repressing the urge to bellow as if on a parade ground; there was no knowing how far an echo might carry, and he had no desire to alert Garth to his presence. "I see no sign of any danger, save that one of you clumsy fools might stumble and crack his skull on the steps." Despite his anger, Sedrik immediately regretted those words; they would only serve to make his men more nervous, which would in turn make their descent still slower and more cautious. "We have orders, from the overlord himself, to hunt down and kill this inhuman foreigner. He's somewhere below, and I intend to find him. Now, come on!" He pushed past the leaders and started down, thinking to himself that he should have taken the lead position right from the first.

Reluctantly, his men followed.

The length of the stair eventually became daunting even to

Sedrik; he heard his men muttering unhappily when the rearmost torchbearer had lost all sight of the top, but he forced himself onward, determined to show no fear in front of his subordinates, and resolved that he could face any dangers that an overman could face. The distant rhythmic rumble became more distinct as they went on; Sedrik had hoped that they would pass its source and lose it, but so far there had been no sign of that happening.

It was fortunate, he thought, that the stair remained barely wide enough to march two abreast; had they been forced into single file, he knew that his men would have been even more anxious.

At last the company reached the short corridor and, with visible relief, continued on, up the ascending steps beyond. They emerged into the long gray room at the top of the final stair, and the beating sound was clearly audible even over the rattle of armor and their heavy footsteps. Sedrik stopped and raised his hand for silence; the men stopped, the first rank just inside the chamber, the rest still arrayed upon the stairs.

He was not absolutely certain, but Sedrik thought he had at last glimpsed a dim light somewhere in the darkness ahead. He pointed to the torch nearest him and made a passing motion; its bearer understood and obeyed, passing it back to the men farthest down the steps, who held it and the two other torches down low so as to disturb the darkness at the far end of the chamber as little as possible.

Sedrik stared into the gloom, shading his eyes against the glare from behind, and made out that there was indeed a light ahead, just beyond a wide doorway.

The light was not moving; whatever the overman had come for, he had presumably found it. Sedrik did not think he had merely paused to rest; the natural place to do that would have been at the foot of the long stair, or the top of the last.

Unless, the commander thought, yet another stair lay beyond the door, and the overman had paused before tackling it.

Still a third possibility occurred to Sedrik. The overman might have brought more than one light and abandoned this one when it burned low. Staring at it, Sedrik observed that it *was* low, far dimmer than any of his own three torches, which had burned almost to stubs.

"Change torches," he whispered, reminded of their state.

Word was passed down the steps, and three new torches were lighted, flaring up brightly; the old were stamped out and cast aside.

The presence of the doorway was not helpful; Sedrik had no way of knowing what lay beyond it. Marching his men in without further investigation would be stupid and reckless. He was tempted to go forward himself and scout it out, but that was not a commander's job, and he knew it. If he were to stick his head through the door and be slain, his men would flee; if another were to do the same, Sedrik knew he could fire up the survivors with a lust for vengeance and lead them to the attack.

Reluctantly, he signaled for one man to step forward.

"Nalba," Sedrik whispered, "I want you to go and see what's beyond the door there." He pointed. "Be careful about it; I don't want you killed. If the overman's in there and you have a chance, jump him and call for help; we'll come. If you don't think you can get him, or if he sees you coming, you come back here and tell me. If he's *not* there, come back and report; don't do anything foolish." Sedrik pointed to the mace on the soldier's back. "Use that if you can; it's harder to parry than a sword, and overmen are strong. You're more likely to keep him busy with that than with your sword, even if you can't kill him. Have you got all that?"

Nalba nodded silently, then crept cautiously past his commander and down the length of the room, unslinging the heavy mace as he went, so that it was ready in his hand when he reached the arch.

He peered through, and saw the lamp flickering on the floor. He glimpsed the tapering column and thought for an instant that it was the overman, crouched to spring. He swung back out of the way; then, when no attack came, he inched forward again.

This time he made out the column's nature more clearly and determined that it was not an immediate threat. He advanced, slowly and carefully, into the room.

Behind the door, Garth watched and waited.

Nalba paused a few paces in, just short of the trough encircling the central pediment, and peered around into the darkness. He saw nothing—no overman and no way out of the room.

A chill ran through him, despite the chamber's muggy warmth, as the notion arose that the overman they pursued had vanished by means of sorcery.

His first thought was to run back and tell the marshal that the overman had disappeared into thin air. He stopped himself, however, and tried to think it through.

It was undeniable that, as far as he could tell, the room was empty of everything but dust, shadows, and the abandoned lamp; but he could not see *all* of the room. Sedrik would be disappointed in him if he were to turn and leave now, and if it were later discovered that the overman was hiding behind some secret panel lost in the gloom.

Besides, he saw no actual danger.

Mace held out before him, Nalba began to make his way around the room, poking his weapon at the wall every so often and peering into the shadows. He came at last to the deep darkness behind the broad door and paused; any concealed opening there would just lead back out into the long chamber, but he knew he should check it for the sake of completeness. Something about it made him nervous; he thought he saw something glinting, or heard something breathing, or perhaps both. He could not be sure of his sight in the unsteady light and clinging darkness, or of his hearing while the dull throbbing pounded on his ears, or of his thoughts in the foul, moist air of the chamber.

If the overman were hiding there behind the door, Nalba told himself, he would have jumped out and cut my throat long ago. The soldier prodded with his mace.

Steel flashed, and the tip of a sword slipped between his chin and the throatpiece of his helmet.

"One word, human, and I sever your head," Garth warned.

Nalba froze, fighting a sudden urge to swallow, his teeth clenched to hold in a scream.

"Put the mace down, slowly and quietly," the overman said.

Nalba tried to obey; he lowered the head, but was unable to handle the weight of the weapon. The metal ball struck the stone paving with an audible thud, and the terrified soldier discovered that he could not reach down any farther to place the handle on the floor. If he dropped it, it would rattle; if he bent down, the sword would be forced into his gullet.

Garth grasped the situation and said, "Drop it." He did not see how it could matter; anything listening would have heard the sound of the mace's head falling.

Relieved, Nalba dropped the mace; the handle rolled down and clicked against the stone.

That done, the two stared at each other, Garth seeing a shadowy backlit figure wearing the green uniform and bronze helmet of Ur-Dormulk's soldiery, while Nalba could see nothing but a great black shape holding a sword at his throat. A few inches of the blade caught a stray glimmer from the fallen lamp, and the soldier thought he could make out something shiny and red where his captor's eyes should have been.

At the head of the stair, Sedrik had been watching Nalba's actions as best he could. He had seen the soldier begin his circuit of the chamber, vanishing to one side, returning to visibility for a brief moment as he crossed back into Sedrik's line of sight to the rear wall, and then disappearing again along the other side.

Nalba seemed to be taking plenty of time to search the second side, Sedrik thought; then he heard the thud, just barely audible over the steady beating sound, of the mace hitting the floor.

Something was wrong, Sedrik was sure. He did not know what, but one possibility was obvious: the overman had been hiding there and had caught Nalba by surprise and cut his throat so quickly that he had no time to cry out. The monster had not managed to catch the mace before it fell, though, and that might prove his undoing.

Sedrik knew there were other explanations available, but he was certain that this was what had happened. He ordered his men, "Weapons at ready!"

Swords slid from scabbards, shields were raised, the thongs of maces were looped around wrists, crossbows were cocked and loaded—all as silently as the dozen men could contrive. Sedrik unslung his war axe, hefted it with his left hand, and drew his sword with his right. The deep throbbing covered much of the noise they made.

Still, Garth heard something other than the beating. He had intended a leisurely questioning of his captive, using long pauses to increase the man's nervousness, but he suddenly realized he might not have time for that.

"Are you alone?" he asked.

Nalba stared, petrified, unable to nod, not wanting to shake his head in a truthful answer, lest it enrage the monster that held the sword.

In the long hall, Sedrik whispered, "Something's gotten Nalba; it must have surprised him somehow. I don't know if it's the overman or not, but it probably is. I don't want him to surprise *us*. If we charge in there at full speed, we may startle him out of attacking; then we'll be able to see where he is and fight him fairly. Understood?"

Most of the men nodded; he ignored those who did not. They would follow along and do well enough, he was sure.

"We want to catch him off guard, so no yelling until we're through the door; then you can bellow your lungs out if you want. We're going to run in there and kill him before he knows what's happening. Right?"

This time almost all of his men nodded.

"Good. On the count of three, then. One . . ."

Garth pressed the point of his sword forward slightly, forcing Nalba's head back. "You're not alone, then. How many of you are there?"

Nalba moved back a step, but the gleaming blade followed, keeping the pressure on his throat. His head was tilted so far back that the base of his helmet was digging into his neck.

"How many?" Garth insisted. "Five? Ten?"

Nalba managed to shake his head.

Sedrik advanced a step, allowing the rest of his men to come up off the stair and into the room. He half-turned toward the door beyond and raised his sword. "Two," he said.

"Twenty?" Garth demanded, his voice slipping into a growl.

"Three!" Sedrik breathed. He charged toward the open door.

Nalba was trying to take another step back, his head forced up by the sword so that he could no longer see the floor, when one of the slow beats ended, allowing both Nalba and Garth to hear the clinking of metal and the pounding of booted feet running toward them. Hoping that the overman—if it was indeed an overman that held the blade to his neck—would be distracted, Nalba groped for the hilt of his sword and tried to twist aside.

Garth was not sufficiently distracted to forget his prisoner; he saw the hand reaching for the belt, though he could not clearly see what weapon hung there. He knew that the man might be of value as a hostage, but he might also be dangerous, since Garth had no time to bind him. The overman could not afford to divide his attention. Unhappily, he rammed his sword forward, through the human's throat; it scraped past the spine and thunked against the back of the bronze helmet.

The soldier died without a sound; Garth pulled the sword out and sank back into his shadowy corner, letting the corpse fall to the floor with a sodden thump. The helmet bounced off and rolled noisily to one side.

An instant later a stream of men burst into the chamber, steel blades flashing in every direction; the first stumbled over the lamp and sent it spinning away toward the far wall.

Startled by the number of foes, despite what Nalba had indicated, Garth did not wait for them all to arrive and surround him; he braced his back against the wall behind him and kicked out with all his strength at the carved door.

It squealed in protest, but slammed with satisfying force into two of the humans; one went sprawling off to the side, within the circular chamber, and the other was knocked back against his advancing companions, gashing himself on an upraised sword.

A second kick closed the door, and Garth braced himself against it, knowing as he did so that a solid blow of an axe from the other side might injure or even kill him.

Not counting the bleeding corpse on the floor, six or perhaps seven men were in the room with him; the shadows made an exact count very difficult. One held a smoldering torch. All carried weapons. One was down for the moment, bowled over by the door; he had dropped a crossbow, but still gripped a sword.

Three held swords and shields, one had a mace and a sword, another bore a mace and the torch while a sword hung on his belt, and the last—there were seven, Garth realized—was coming at the overman with a raised axe.

Garth had no time for finesse; he raised his sword and lunged forward, meeting the axe-wielder's attack with his own. The blade slid between the man's ribs and stood out from his back, gleaming wetly red in the flaring torchlight.

Sedrik had underestimated the overman's reach, and had not been aware of his superhuman speed at all until it was too late. He felt the sword go into him above the belly, and knew he had misjudged. His mouth gaped open, blood from a pierced lung gurgling in his throat, and he made a desperate try with his axe, swinging wildly. His right arm fell aside and went limp; his sword clattered to the floor.

The arc of the axe brought it down across Garth's sword arm, grazing it, but doing little real damage; then Sedrik sagged and fell.

Garth pulled his blade free in time to face the charge of a mace-wielding soldier on his right and a shielded swordsman on his left. He ducked back and to the left, letting the mace slam into the wooden door, hoping the spikes would become caught; splinters flew, but the mace scraped onward.

The swordsman was being cautious, his shield limiting his movement, and missed an opportunity to strike at the overman as Garth slid back off the door and around to the soldier's right. Startled by the overman's speed and fooled by the common human idea that large size meant slow reactions, the swordsman was still turning to face his opponent when Garth gripped the axe in his left hand and brought it around.

The soldier flinched back and the axe missed his right arm, but his sword was knocked from his grasp. The axe continued on and bit into the side of the shield with a loud thunk.

Seizing the opportunity, Garth used the axe to force the shield down and ran his sword into the man's face.

The mace was coming down for another blow as Garth yanked his sword from the shield-bearer's eye; the overman met the descending weapon with his blade.

The parry was successful, but Garth could see that the sword was badly notched—Galt's sword, he remembered, not his own—and he could feel the metal straining as he forced the mace back. He pulled at his axe, using his left knee to knock the shield away. The other two shieldmen were advancing on his left, he saw; he turned, and a crossbow quarrel whirred past his face, then went spinning from the wall beyond. The fallen bowman had recovered his weapon.

Garth did not worry about that; the man would have to reload before he could fire again, and reloading a crossbow was slow work, particularly when lying on the floor. The weapon was designed to be held between the knees and braced against the ground, with the feet holding down the crosspiece.

Someone was banging and calling on the other side of the door; Garth ignored that as well. Three men were down, dead or nearly so, but five were still trying to kill him.

A small part of his mind, unconcerned with the battle, wondered who these men were and why they had come after him and tried to kill him. All wore the uniform of the city guard; that worried him. Temple guards or warrior priests he might have expected, but this party looked official. He hoped that the overlord had not sent them. He had no desire to antagonize Ur-Dormulk's ruler. Perhaps, he thought, it was all a misunderstanding.

The two surviving shieldmen were advancing, confident of their safety behind their heavy protection, and Garth decided that they needed a demonstration of his strength, something that would damage their confidence and thereby diminish the threat they presented. He moved left, away from the mace and its wielder. The shieldmen turned and kept their swords weaving, looking for an opening; the man with the mace stumbled when a swing met no resistance and stepped back to recollect himself.

With him out of the way for a few seconds, Garth held one shieldman back with his sword and brought his axe down on the other in a long overhand smash, like the swing of a sledgehammer, with as much of his strength behind it as he could muster. He had to angle the blow to avoid hitting the low ceiling.

The axe split the man's sword in two, the tip spinning away to the side, the hilt dropping from impact-numbed fingers, and drove on downward, hacking into the riveted steel shield as if it were rotten wood. Had the soldier not had it securely strapped to his arm, he would have dropped that, as well.

Disarmed and terrified, the man fell back, wrenching his shield off the axe and saving Garth the trouble of having to free his embedded weapon. That left the other shieldman's right flank unguarded. Garth sent the axe chopping sideways, behind the shield. It scraped across mail, but did not cut.

Still, the shieldman was disconcerted now. He turned his arm to fend off the axe, and Garth's sword slid into his left armpit, making good use of the overman's superior reach and speed.

Behind Garth, the door started to open again, and he slammed it shut with his foot, throwing himself off balance for a moment, unable to pursue the momentary advantage he had gained. The mace-wielder came at him again; Garth turned, parried the mace with his axe, met sword with sword, and drove both back by sheer strength. When he had forced the soldier's arms up so that the man had to retreat or fall backward, Garth pulled the axe down the shaft of the mace and twisted, yanking the mace from the human's weakened grip.

While he did this, however, his left side presented an open invitation to the two shieldmen; the one who still held his sword gathered enough courage to accept and lunged forward.

Garth dodged, so that the blade scraped across his back, gouging him slightly but not penetrating deeply. He brought his left arm swinging back and caught his attacker on the right shoulder. The man withdrew, wary of losing sword, sword arm, or both.

That permitted the overman to force his way past the guard of his now-maceless opponent and drive his sword into the man's shoulder. The soldier gasped as Garth's blade withdrew and blood spurted; he fell back, dropping his own remaining weapon.

Garth was working himself up into a state of unreasoning fury; in consequence, when he saw the unarmed maceman fall back, he gave no thought to subtlety, but swung around to face the shieldmen—and the other mace-wielder, now advancing to join the attack—head on. "Fools!" he shouted, breaking his silence.

"Inhuman monster!" someone replied.

The crossbowman was still on the floor, apparently just watching; the injured maceman was upright but unarmed and also seemed content to play spectator. The axeman, the first shield-carrier, and the original advance scout were all down for good. That left Garth facing three opponents, one of them twice wounded, with no reinforcements ready to jump to their aid.

That meant he no longer needed to be cautious; no one was going to sneak up on him unexpectedly. He roared wordlessly and brought his axe arcing overhead, barely missing the low ceiling, to smash through a human skull. The man tried to parry the blow with the sundered shield he bore, and his arm met Garth's in mid-air. The soldier's forearm broke under the impact; Garth received a bruise, but the axe continued on and splattered blood and brains across the next man over.

The shieldman dropped, and Garth faced two terrified opponents. The fight had gone out of them; they were retreating, staying out of his reach. To one side, the unarmed soldier was struggling to open the door and escape. The crossbowman had finally gotten to his feet, but showed no interest in anything but flight.

Garth took a step forward, pursuing the enemy. They stepped back; one stumbled over the trough around the central column and dropped the torch. The flame flickered and went out as the burning tip landed, hissing, in the dark fluid. The only remaining light was the faint glow of the oil lamp, still burning where it lay against the far wall.

Garth tried to lift his foot to take another step forward, but something prevented him; something was gripping his ankle. He looked down.

Sedrik was not dead; he supported himself on one elbow, his axe clutched in that hand, while his other clutched at Garth's leg. Blood was seeping from his closed mouth. He was trying to lift himself up and raise the axe to strike, his movements uncoordinated and feeble.

Garth stared at him in surprise for a second, then decided that, mortally wounded as he was, the man was of no consequence. He thrust his foot forward despite the encumbrance upon it.

Sedrik's grip did not loosen; instead he was dragged forward, and Garth turned again to look at him.

The maceman who had dropped the torch saw his opportunity; he danced in and made a desperate, wild, sideways swing. The heavy spiked ball caught Garth's sword where it had been notched, snapping the blade off.

Garth whirled back and roared in anger. That was not his sword! Galt would be annoyed, he knew. He swung his axe and saw it bite deep into the soldier's chest, grating against bone.

It did not come free when he tried to pull it back. He attempted to step forward, the better to brace himself, and found that Sedrik was still clamped onto his ankle. Enraged beyond all thought, he released his axe, letting the dying soldier fall to the ground with the weapon still in him, then flung aside the broken hilt of Galt's sword, reached down with both hands, and yanked Sedrik free.

The man's mouth opened and blood spilled out. "Monster," he tried to say; the word emerged as a croaking gurgle. He struggled to lift and swing his axe.

Garth saw that the man was obviously dying, too weak to be anything but a minor annoyance; infuriated, he flung Sedrik away in the general direction of the surviving soldiers.

At that instant the door burst open and light poured in from the remaining torches, allowing Garth to see clearly what next took place.

Sedrik's body slammed against the central column, his arm flopping, and the blade of the axe bit into the yellowed substance of the thing, the cut penetrating the tubule whence the black fluid oozed. Three great drops spattered forth across the steel head of the weapon, and the beating stopped.

For a moment nothing more happened; the combatants, human and overman, in the inner chamber or the long hall, all froze in astonishment.

"Gods," someone said.

A low rumble sounded, far different from the earlier sound, and the beating returned—but not as the tortuously slow thing it had been before. The new sound was higher in pitch, but still bone-shakingly deep; it was much louder, and faster as well, a single beat now taking no more than a few seconds.

One of the soldiers in the outer room turned and ran; Garth heard others moving uncertainly.

A new sound added itself to the racket, a loud rumble; Garth felt the floor vibrate beneath him. Somewhere, something broke with a sharp cracking. The wounded maceman Garth had disarmed screamed and ran, and others followed him.

More rumblings sounded, and the throbbing grew still louder and faster, as if whatever creature possessed the mighty heartbeat were awakening from sleep. The floor shifted, then seemed to drop a few inches beneath Garth's feet; he saw that the column was sinking downward out of sight.

Then it paused, with only the uppermost foot still showing, and the rumblings subsided for a moment; the heartbeat continued unabated. Garth had a sensation of knowing that something was about to occur without knowing what it would be.

The remaining soldiers who were still capable of fleeing did so during this brief interval, but Garth resolved to stay where he was. He had come to this place seeking a magical device of great power, and it was possible that the shaking of the earth and the mighty rumblings and beating were somehow connected with it.

At his feet lay three corpses; just ahead lay Sedrik, still twitching slightly, his eyes open and staring at the overman. The various movements of the room had left him lying on the floor free of the strange column, his axe still clutched in his hand.

Then the rumbling began again. With an immense crashing, the column thrust upward, splitting the floor of the chamber into scattered shards and sending Garth back against the wall. The wall itself turned and gave, and he fell back into dark emptiness; all around him, he could hear the grinding of stone on stone and the sound of breaking rock. Hot, fetid air rushed past him. He had a final glimpse as he fell of a vast monstrosity rising up before him, its hideous visage twenty feet across. Flat, golden eyes gleamed from sunken black sockets on either side of a great curving nose-horn, its tip broken and oozing dark fluid. Garth recognized that horn; its upper end had been the mysterious column. Here, then, was the beast whose heartbeat he had followed, awakened and unleashed.

A piece of rubble smashed against the back of his head, and he saw nothing more.

CHAPTER FIFTEEN

Garth awoke with sunlight warm on his face, and with no idea of where he was. He lay sprawled across a small heap of rubble, a sharp stone digging into the back of one thigh, his head hanging down off the edge of something, his whole body tipped at an uncomfortable angle.

He lifted his head with effort, closing his eyes against the glare of light, and shifted his leg off the point that gouged it. With a little struggling, he managed to get himself sitting upright, then opened his eyes and looked about.

He was perched on a slab of broken pavement—or perhaps a broken wall—that lay atop a mound of debris, three or four feet high. This pile was one of many, in varying sizes, scattered across a broad stone floor. Most of the wreckage was also stone, but Garth saw metal scraps, shards of tile, bits of wood, fragments of furniture, the remains of various tapestries, drapes, carpets, and hangings, and at least one human body, that of one of the soldiers he had fought, half-buried in a pile near his own. He and the heaps of rubble were all scattered about an immense chamber, but most of the walls were lost in shadow, and he could not guess what the chamber might be, or where. Only one section of the far wall was in full sunlight, a small area centered on an arched doorway. A yellow symbol gleamed brightly on the black door; it seemed familiar, but Garth did not recognize it.

The uneven light and drifting dust made it difficult to judge the size of the place, but Garth estimated that it was a good fifty feet to the far wall.

He turned around to see what lay behind him and discovered that he was only a few feet from the wall. He saw no door, no windows, and wondered where the sunlight was coming from. He looked up.

The room extended upward incredibly far, easily a hundred feet; graceful columns soared out from the walls into elaborate vaulting, the details lost in distance and shadow. Much of that vaulting was in disarray; a large section of the roof was missing, and, Garth realized, a large part of the wall directly behind him was gone as well. He had not noticed it sooner because the wall was intact to a height of twelve or fifteen feet, but from that point up, most of it was gone.

That explained where most of the rubble had come from.

The sunlight was spilling in through the break, and the steep angle indicated the middle part of the day—though Garth could not be certain which day it was. Dust was drifting everywhere, sparkling and blurring in the beams of light; surely, Garth told himself, it would have settled if more than one day, or at most two, had passed since the wall was shattered.

The overman considered his situation. He had no clear idea where he was; he could not even be certain he was still in Ur-Dormulk, but the presence of the dead soldier implied that Garth was still wherever he had fallen when the immense horned monster had burst up from beneath. It seemed reasonable to assume that the break in the wall and roof had been made by the creature. Of the beast itself, however, there was no trace, save a faint, lingering, unpleasant odor; the sound of its heartbeat was gone. The silence, in fact, was nearly total; Garth felt as if he could hear his own breathing, his own heartbeat, and perhaps even the faint hiss of the dust sifting down onto the stones. The air, too, was almost still; no wind could be heard blowing around the broken columns overhead.

That did not necessarily mean that he was safe from the monster; it might be lurking just beyond the walls.

Almost anything might be out there, Garth thought. He had

no way of knowing that there had been only one monster. Even leaving monsters aside, he could reasonably assume that any humans he might find would be hostile. After all, he had been attacked for no reason he knew of, and now any survivors might consider him responsible for awakening the creature— though Garth was sure it had been the blow of the human's axe on the thing's horn that had done that.

He could not in good faith deny *all* responsibility. He had been investigating where he was not welcome, and perhaps he had interfered in things best left alone. He had not, he had to admit, known what he was doing. He had apparently been the indirect cause of more destruction; it seemed that ever since he had first touched the Sword of Bheleu, he brought destruction wherever he went.

That was not of immediate concern, however. He had no desire to sit where he was all day. The sun was reassuringly warm. He was stiff and sore, with several minor wounds, but he was well rested and thirsty. It was time to be up and about.

Garth stretched, hoping that the movement would not reopen any of the cuts he had received in the fighting and his fall, and climbed down off the slab.

He looked himself over carefully; he still wore his mail, which was dented and twisted here and there, with several broken links. The black metal was stained brown in several places, but Garth did not think any of the blood was his own.

His breeches, too, were bloodied but intact, though no one would ever again take them for new. One leg had come untucked from his boot top; he stuffed it back in.

The boots themselves seemed sound, but something had gashed one of them across the instep; Garth doubted it was still watertight.

His sword, axe, and helmet were gone, but his belt was still in place and his dagger still in its sheath; he was not completely unarmed. He recalled that the sword—Galt's sword—had been broken. That was unfortunate.

Nothing remained of his surcoat but tatters; he removed them. His cloak was missing.

He glanced around, seeing nothing but broken stone, scattered debris, drifting dust, and sunlight. There was no sign of life, nothing that could be considered threatening. He decided to take a complete inventory. Slowly, he removed his coat of mail.

The gambeson beneath was filthy, soaked through with sweat and blood, and pierced in several places, though Garth could not remember feeling anything stab through it. He untied it and began to peel it off.

Blood had clotted inside it, and yanked painfully at his fur and flesh as he tore the garment away, but at last he managed to get it off.

He looked himself over, tugging here and there at matted patches of his sparse black fur. He found half a dozen scratches, none of which he could remember receiving. All were healing adequately, though he had reopened at least one when he removed the gambeson. Bruises were more numerous; one arm in particular ached.

He had nothing to clean his wounds with, save his own saliva; he moistened one of the scraps from his surcoat in his mouth and then dabbed at the cuts with it. He had kept medicinal salves in a pouch on his belt, but that was missing; he was not sure what had happened to it. Only his dagger remained on his belt; the pouch and his purse were gone. A wild slash might have cut the pursestrings and the strap that held the pouch, he thought; he had been fortunate that such a blow had not done far worse, if that was what had occurred.

Though the sun had seemed almost hot on his face when he first awoke, he found himself growing chilly with only his fur protecting his chest and back; reluctantly, he donned the stiff, stained gambeson again and pulled the battered mail back on.

That done, he considered his next step.

He had several things he wanted to do. He wanted to find the Book of Silence, do whatever he could to damage the cult of Aghad, and see what had become of the monster, whether it had gone on a rampage or just settled down quietly somewhere. He felt responsible for it and hoped that it had not done too much damage. He had caused more than enough death and destruction already, without the aid of any monsters. He might also want to investigate the attack on him, to find out whether the overlord had sent those soldiers. If he had, retaliation might be called for. Garth had come to Ur-Dormulk on a peaceful errand—relatively peaceful, at any rate, vengeful though it was—and the trouble had begun only when he was attacked without warning or cause.

If the monster was on a rampage, he might want to do something about that, too—but he was not about to try to defeat anything that large without a great deal of help, preferably magical.

All of that could wait, however, because his first priority, as always, was survival. He did not know where he was; he was stranded here without food or water or decent weapons.

Water seemed like the most important concern. He had the dagger and no visible foes, so weapons were not urgent, and if he grew sufficiently desperate for food, there was the corpse of the soldier. He hoped that it would not come to that. He had never eaten human flesh, nor wanted to; no overman had, so far as he knew, despite what some of the nastier human legends suggested. The idea of eating what had once been a fellow sentient being was slightly revolting. Still, if it came to a choice of that or starvation, he did not intend to starve.

Water, then, was what he had to find.

If he was still where he thought he was, in Ur-Dormulk, then water should be available one way or another. He had not forgotten that lake.

He saw no sign of water in the vast chamber about him, however. He would have to find a way out.

He looked up at the broken wall and the missing section of roof. He could, if he had to, leap high enough to pull himself up to the bottom of the opening—but he was not at all sure that he wanted to. He could not be certain that he would be able to go much farther from there. Furthermore, if there were enemies or monsters anywhere about, they would, he thought, probably be in that direction.

The door on the far side of the room looked more promising. He had no idea where it led, but at the very least, it promised a more complete shelter than the great, broken chamber. It was a sign of civilization, and civilization could not exist without water.

It occurred to him that he was far below the level of the city streets—assuming that he had awoken where he had fallen. He had been deep in the crypts beneath and behind the temple and had, he was sure, fallen still farther. This door, then, whatever it was, was also part of the crypts rather than part of the city.

He wondered whether he was below the level of the lake; he had descended a goodly distance, but the lake itself had been sunk down far beneath the city. If he was below the water line, then it would be wiser to turn and head upward; the monster might have damaged the walls enough for water to find its way through the ruins at any time, and he might be trapped and drowned.

Even as he thought of this possibility Garth dismissed it, without knowing exactly why. He intended to investigate the door. He felt himself drawn to it by something more than simple curiosity.

Besides, he told himself, if the chamber did flood, he would be able to swim out through the break in the wall and at least he would not die of thirst.

He began picking his way cautiously across the pavement, dodging the scattered heaps of rubble and watching for any place that looked as if it might crack beneath his weight; the thought that the monster might have damaged the structure of the crypt made him suddenly very suspicious of its stability. He looked up at the vaulting overhead, and around at the walls, trying to learn as much as he could about this place where he found himself.

The hall was square, or nearly so, and about sixty feet on a side, he judged. The walls began curving inward about a hundred feet up, and the peak of the central vault was another twenty or thirty feet above that. The broken side appeared to have been smashed outward all at once—undoubtedly by the horned monster. Garth regretted that; it was one more act of destruction that could be laid to his account.

The architecture was rather odd, in that there was no ornamentation above eye level save the vaulting—if that could be considered ornamentation. It was not needlessly elaborate. There were no galleries, no sign that there had ever been hangings or any other display. The room was bare and coldly functional, which seemed very peculiar in so vast a space. A chamber this size was surely built to be ostentatious, Garth thought, yet it showed no sign of ostentation beyond its size.

As he passed the center of the chamber he noticed that the floor seemed slightly warmer there, and the air fouler, with a vague fetidness about it. That was, he guessed, because the leviathan had stood in this spot while it slept, presumably throughout the city's recorded history.

With that, it seemed plain that this immense hall had existed solely to house the creature; it had been the cage wherein the creature was pent. That would explain its dimensions and architecture; nothing else Garth could think of would do so as well.

Realizing this, Garth grew slightly uneasy. What if, after so long a residence here, the monster considered this its home? How would it deal with any piddling little pest, such as an overman, that it found here upon its return? Most likely, Garth thought, it would stamp him flat, if it had feet in proportion to its head. He felt instinctively for his weapons.

Sword and axe were gone, as he already knew; he had only the dagger on his belt.

It didn't matter, he told himself. The monster would barely notice his best blow with either axe or broadsword. Human enemies he could handle with the dagger or whatever weapons he might find, if there were not too many of them at any one time, and the monster he couldn't handle at all with *any* ordinary weapon. He glanced back at the breached wall, wondering what the creature had done to Ur-Dormulk and what had become of the city's people.

Whatever had happened, there was nothing he could do about it. He stepped forward and studied the door he had come to investigate.

It was not large; he would have to duck to pass through it. It was made of some dull black substance, not ebony, though it appeared to be wood. The yellow symbol, only a single character, was etched upon it in bright metal—not pure gold, Garth was sure, as the hue was more vivid than gold. It was no metal he recognized, and the symbol was also strange—yet somehow familiar. He had an uneasy feeling that he had seen it before and that it had not boded well. He realized he was staring at it and turned his gaze away.

His hand was on the latch, though he did not remember putting it there. It was a very curious latch, made of a metal that gleamed like silver, yet had no trace of tarnish, though surely it had been centuries since any mortal hand had touched it. There was no simple lever to lift, no bolt to draw, but a handle that Garth gripped and squeezed, without having consciously figured out the mechanism.

He felt the latch release and pushed on the door, only belatedly thinking that he was being incautious.

The door gave with a hiss of air, then swung silently back. It did not squeal or creak, but moved as smoothly as if the hinges had just been oiled.

Finally growing wary, Garth hesitated on the doorstep. Something had drawn him here, something beyond his own curiosity. He did not like being compelled; he tried to resist the impulse to step into the room he glimpsed through the open portal.

Perhaps, a part of his mind whispered, this compulsion was one of the signs the King had spoken of; perhaps the power of the Book of Silence, eager to be released, was drawing him to its hiding place. That was what he had come for, and he should follow the urging and seek out its source.

The logic of this swayed him, and he took a step forward into the dim interior. He found himself in a small chamber, about twelve feet wide and twenty feet long; thick, dark carpets, coated with dust and moldering with age, covered the floor, while the tapestries that had draped the walls had fallen to pieces beneath their own weight, leaving only faded tatters on their supports. At the far end, a black stone oval hung on the wall, with the same sign etched in gold upon it as ornamented the door. Below it stood a small altar of finely wrought gold; to either side of the altar stood tall candelabra, holding nothing but low stubs of wax lost in dust and cobwebs. There were no windows, and the only light was what poured in through the door. Garth's shadow lay across much of the floor, and the altar was buried in gloom, but the overman could see something gleaming palely upon the altar's upper surface.

Trying to retain some semblance of caution, yet strongly drawn, Garth made his way slowly toward the altar, pausing after each step, weighing his own wishes and his own will against the force that pulled at him, and allowing himself to yield.

The thing upon the altar, he saw when he had crossed half the length of the room, was a mask, of a size to fit a human face. He tried to see what it was meant to represent, but with each step its aspect changed. At first he had thought it was simply a human face with a peculiarly hostile expression; next it seemed to bear a strange and bitter smile; seconds later, it was not the visage of a living man, but the white, drawn features of a corpse. At his next step it showed the marks of advanced decay, swollen and bloated, with remnants of flesh drawn back from teeth and eyes; then it became the face of a mummy, its dry and wrinkled skin drawn tight over the bone beneath.

Finally, as he stood over the altar and looked down full upon the mask in the shadows of the chamber, it was plainly a representation of a naked skull, distorted so that it might be worn by a human over a living face.

Whatever the thing was, Garth did not like it, yet he found his hand reaching out for it. He drew back, and for an instant the object seemed not a mask at all, but the face of the Forgotten King, its eyes lost in shadow, the wisp of beard trailing from its chin, its skin shriveled but still alive.

Then it was a skull once more.

A vagueness seemed to be invading Garth's thoughts, not totally unlike the sensations he had sometimes felt when holding the Sword of Bheleu, and he guessed that this must be a similar object of power—presumably the Pallid Mask, totem of the god of death.

The aversion that should have accompanied that realization did not come, and it took a ferocious effort of will to draw back his hand and keep from stepping forward and picking up the ghastly thing.

He was not the chosen of The God Whose Name Is Not Spoken; he knew that and asked himself why he should be drawn to the mask. He wondered if he could handle it at all; ordinary people were unable to wield the Sword of Bheleu, and he had seen Galt seriously burn his hands just trying to touch its hilt.

Perhaps, Garth told himself, the Death-God knew that he would be returning to Skelleth in time and seeing the Forgotten King. Perhaps, as the chosen of Bheleu, he could handle the mask without harm, as the King said he could touch the Book of Silence.

Or perhaps the Death-God was hungry and wanted him to pick up the mask and die. The overman was quite sure that its mere touch could be fatal if the god so chose.

A sudden wave of revulsion swept over him; he kicked out at the altar, hoping to smash it and lose the hideous mask in the dust.

The golden framework tilted back, wobbled, rocked forward, and then fell back on its side. The mask slid off into the dust, as Garth had wanted, but he hardly noticed. He was staring at the space where the altar had stood.

The floor beneath the altar was bare stone, made of cut blocks arranged in neat rows, and one block, directly beneath the center of the altar, was missing. In the gap it left lay a book.

The compulsion that had drawn Garth before was as nothing to the force that seized him now; he lunged forward and pulled the thing from its place of concealment totally without thought or volition of his own. As soon as his fingers touched it, he felt an electric tingle run up his arm, and the room seemed alive with eerie colored light. The mask no longer concerned him; he all but forgot its existence as he lifted the Book of Silence.

It was miraculously light, weighing no more in his hands than a single straw. The binding was of some hide that at first glance appeared black, but had a subtle sheen to it in which other colors could be seen as it was moved; it had a faint oiliness to it. Garth stared at the book, running his hands over its surface, and only realized that he had turned and found his way out of the chapel when bright sunlight washed over the cover, sending a wave of iridescence across it.

He forced himself to pause. He had been seeking water, not the Book of Silence, and had found this thing almost against his will. It would seem that the chamber, the mask, and the book were in all probability the royal chapel, the Pallid Mask, and the Book of Silence—but could he be sure that everything was what it seemed? He had been led here by mystical force, yet had no assurance that this was what the Forgotten King had meant by his signs and portents. This was obviously a book of great power, Garth told himself, but could he be so certain that it was the Book of Silence? He took it in one hand and reached out with the other to open it.

A sudden foreboding swept over him, and his hand drew back. He paused again.

The thing was playing with him, manipulating his emotions, making him do whatever it pleased, rather than what he wanted to do. A surge of anger seethed up within him; he reached out and opened the book.

As he lifted the cover, the characters seemed to writhe on the page beneath, and he felt a cold breeze, as if it issued from the book.

The symbols were as stationary as any ordinary writing when he looked directly at them, each lying sedately on the page and forming neat blocks that were words and rows that were sentences. The runes, however, were totally alien, like nothing he had ever seen before, and he could not read a single word or recognize a single letter. The shapes hinted at meanings somehow, sinister and cold meanings, and Garth repressed a shudder.

He was unsure how long he stood staring at the incomprehensible runes, with their subtle suggestions of dark power and evil truths; finally, though, he tore his eyes away.

His gaze came free of the book only after considerable effort; he felt as if there were some physical connection between his eyes and the page, some powerful force keeping his head turned toward the text. When at last he managed to pull away, he suddenly realized that he was walking, not standing still as he had thought. He had moved away from the chapel door, across the chamber toward one of the far corners; furthermore, he saw with a shock that the sun now hung well to the west of where he had last seen it. The patch of sunlight no longer brightened the black door; it had swung over to what he judged to be the northeast corner of the hall, where it illuminated a low-relief carving so worn with age that its subject could not be determined with any certainty.

Garth had apparently walked so as to keep pace with the sun; he still stood in its full light. Frightened, he closed the book without daring to look at it again.

When it was safely shut but still held securely in both hands, he glanced about. Nothing in the great chamber had changed except the light. The scattered piles of debris were undisturbed, and the broach in the wall was just as he remembered it. The door to the chapel was closed again, though he had no recollection of shutting it. He no longer doubted that the room behind him was the Forgotten King's royal chapel and that he held the Book of Silence. The circumstances fitted too well for anything to be otherwise. He remembered the King's mention of posting a guard—for the sake of form—and knew that that guard had been the monster he and his attackers had awakened. This vast chamber had been built around it to hold it.

He wondered for a moment that the leviathan had left as it had, but then realized that its job was done; the old man had sent him to fetch the book and had freed the creature of its charge. The Forgotten King had planned the course of events somehow, Garth was sure. Signs and portents, indeed!

The carved panel in the northeast corner caught his eye; when he had entered the chapel, it had been lost in shadow and effectively invisible. He had thought the walls blank, as most of them were.

He studied the surface, but could not make out what the scene was intended to represent; there were two figures in it, one tall and straight, the other short and stooped, standing against what had once been a detailed background but was now just a maze of broken lines. So blurred were the edges that Garth could not say whether the figures were even meant for humans, let alone their age, sex, or station. He supposed that the carving was much older than most of the chamber, to be so badly worn.

At one edge, however, one detail remained sharp and clear; a circle was incised deeply into the stone, and the hand of one figure was stretched out toward it.

Curious, Garth reached out and felt the knob of stone isolated within the circle; it gave beneath his fingers.

Startled, he drew his hand back, but a moment's thought convinced him that this must be an ancient, secret door and that the knob was the trigger whereby it might be opened. He had no idea why such a door should be here, but it seemed very promising; after all, he had no idea why most of what he had encountered in Ur-Dormulk should be what it was. He did not particularly want to go clambering about the wreckage beyond the broken wall, and he had seen no back door in the chapel; this appeared to be the only other way out of the creature's chamber.

He wondered if the Book of Silence, or the power controlling it, or perhaps the Forgotten King, had led him here intentionally. He guessed that the chamber had been designed in such a way that when the monster broke out, the afternoon sunlight would fall upon this door; he could only imagine what the ancient builders had been capable of in the way of prophecy, planning, and engineering. They might well have foreseen everything that had befallen him since the behemoth awoke.

At any rate, he determined to take advantage of his discovery; he reached out and pressed the stone knob.

Something clicked, and the whole panel swung back beneath the pressure of his hand. He peered through at the tunnel beyond.

CHAPTER SIXTEEN

The need for light, far more than simple caution, was responsible for Garth's decision to gather what supplies he could from the debris in the huge chamber. The passage he had found, unlike the stair down from the abandoned temple, was not conveniently equipped with lamp or torch; he was forced to rummage about in the wreckage for something that would serve. He had an idea that he might recover the battered oil lamp he had had with him in the round chamber, and therefore began his searching in the general vicinity of the dead soldier, on the assumption that the man had not been very far from the lamp when the floor erupted, and that the two might not have become far separated. Only after several minutes of unsuccessful exploration did it occur to Garth to investigate the corpse itself.

The soldier's belt held flint and steel and a small flask of something oily. Garth was not quite sure what the stuff was, but after a broken length of wood was soaked in it and then wrapped in strips of cloth from the overman's surcoat, similarly soaked, it made a thoroughly adequate torch.

Before venturing into the tunnel he also took the opportunity to appropriate the soldier's only remaining weapon, a sword that was ludicrously short for Garth's use, but still better than his dagger. He also gathered up pieces of cloth, scraps of wood, and other items that he thought might prove useful and wrapped them all in a torn tapesty, which he knotted and slung over his shoulder. The Book of Silence he tucked under one arm.

Thus prepared, he marched on into the passageway, his makeshift torch held high.

The tunnel was not straight; it wound sinuously back and forth, but seemed to run generally in one direction, which Garth judged to be east or slightly south of east. Doors lined either side, and side passages occasionally headed off at various angles, but Garth ignored those. He was not eager to get lost in the crypts, and the simplest way to avoid getting lost was to keep his route simple. Furthermore, he theorized that the exit from the monster's chamber had been set up intentionally for the use of someone such as himself, someone who could not be expected to know his way around the crypts. Such an individual would not be expected to make the correct decisions at every crossing or doorway unless those decisions were so obvious as to be unavoidable—and that meant, in Garth's opinion, continuing straight ahead.

Whether his theories were correct, or whether by chance, he eventually came to a set of steps leading upward, just as his improvised torch, which he had moistened and rewrapped until both oil and scraps of fabric had run out, began to burn low. He gazed at the staircase with relief; he had been planning to start tearing strips from his fragment of tapestry, and he was not sure that those would burn well without oil, quite aside from leaving him without his bundle. He started up the steps eagerly.

He had forgotten how far he had descended; his torch flickered and died while he was still out of sight of the top. He made his way on in the darkness, moving entirely by feel. Fortunately, this flight of steps was not worn as badly as the others he had encountered in Ur-Dormulk, and his footing remained secure.

Finally, his outthrust hand struck an obstruction; he stopped and felt it carefully. His hand came across a latch; he lifted the lever and pushed.

It did not yield.

He had a brief moment of uncertainty before it occurred to him that doors could open either way. He pulled at the latch.

The portal swung inward with a dull grinding, and disappointment seeped into Garth's breast as he saw darkness be-

yond. It was not the total, absolute blackness of the tunnel and
stair he had just traversed, but it was obviously not the daylight
he had hoped for, either.

Nonetheless, he saw little choice. He stepped forward through
the door.

To his surprise, he felt a cold, damp breeze on his cheek
and realized that he was, indeed, out of the crypts and on one
of the stone-paved streets of the city. The darkness was the
darkness of night; he had taken longer than he had thought to
find his way through the underground passages. Low-hanging
clouds obscured the moon and stars, but enough diffuse illumination reached him from the surrounding city to let him make
out the immediate area.

He did not recognize the street he was on; there were no
lighted torches or bright windows to help him in making out
details. The area was quiet and seemed utterly deserted. Since
he was unsure of the hour, he could not be sure whether this
atmosphere was natural and ordinary.

It occurred to him that he might have come up into one of
the ruinous districts, but what little he could make out of the
buildings around him displayed no signs of decay or abandon-
ment. Doors were all secure on their hinges and tightly closed,
save for the one he had just emerged from, which was located
near the corner of a large, old house. Looking back at it, Garth
guessed that, when closed, the door would blend in with the
ornate stonework and appear to be just part of the wall. He
stepped out onto the street, away from the shelter of the wall,
and looked about.

An orange glow lit the sky in several places above the
surrounding rooftops; Garth could not decide whether it was
the normal torchlight of the city going about its business, or
something brighter and more sinister. It was the only sign of
life he could see; the street he was on was dark and empty for
as far as he could see—not that that was very far, since, like
most human streets, it curved out of sight in a block or two in
either direction.

Sounds reached him, sounds he could not readily identify;
he heard a distant crashing, and what might have been voices
shouting somewhere, and beneath it all a dull, low-pitched
rumbling.

He turned, listening, and decided that the rumbling and crashing came primarily from what he judged to be the northwest, while the voices were on several sides. Furthermore, the rumbling seemed to be approaching; at any rate, it was growing louder.

He wondered what was going on. Did this eerie situation of deserted streets and strange sounds relate to the freeing of the monster? Might it have something to do with the Book of Silence? It seemed ominous; although he saw no obvious damage to the buildings around him, he suspected that, once again, he had triggered widespread destruction. He hoped that there were Aghadites among the victims.

Now that he was aboveground again, and fairly certain that he could find food and water, he was curious. He suppressed his thirst, tucked the book more tightly under his arm, then turned and headed north, toward the rumbling.

As he did, he realized that he was actually very thirsty indeed, and hungry as well, but he did not turn aside. He might obtain food and water by breaking into one of the buildings, but he was not yet desperate and preferred to obtain them legally. Where there was sound, there was life, as a general rule, so he hoped that he would be able to find someone who could feed him if he headed toward the rumbling.

With that in mind, he quickened his pace, so that it took him a moment to stop when he turned a corner and found himself facing a scene out of a nightmare.

The city was ablaze ahead of him, or as much of it as could burn in a community built primarily of raw granite. Towering over the burning buildings stood the monster from the crypts, upright on two legs, with a wagonload of screaming hogs clutched in its claws, the traces whereby the wagon had been drawn dangling from one side. As Garth watched, the behemoth jammed the animals into its gaping mouth and bit down; the remaining fragments of the wagon fell out of sight with a distant crashing.

The horn on the creature's nose gleamed a sickly reddish yellow in the firelight, a thin line of black trailing down one side where its ichor ran. Its eyes blazed golden and seemed to Garth to be alight with madness. Its hide was wrinkled and black, its body shaped like nothing the overman had ever seen before. It was vaguely humanoid, in that it stood upright and used its forward limbs to grasp, but it had a hunched, ugly shape, its body proportions closer to those of a bull than to those of a man—though no bull had ever stood upon such hind legs, each as thick around as a castle tower, and no bull had such talons, long, agile fingers ending in vicious, curving claws.

The thing stood easily a hundred feet high; in fact, Garth estimated that it must have had to crouch down, badly cramped, to fit into the chamber that had held it for so long. The rumbling sound that had drawn him issued from the creature, though whether from its heart or its belly Garth was unsure.

With the hind legs of a pig still trailing from its jaws, the monster turned and reached down toward something Garth could not see over the intervening buildings. It seemed to struggle, like a man pulling at a stubborn root; then, with a tearing, crumbling roar, it lifted up the complete upper floor of a house.

The stones held together for a brief moment, then crumbled and fell through the creature's claws like sand through the fingers of a child, leaving it holding a pitiful assortment of roofing tiles, bedroom hangings, and broken furniture. It flung them aside and reached down again.

Garth had seen enough. He could do nothing at all against this monster by himself; it would take magic to destroy it.

He was determined, however, that it had to be destroyed. He had not seen it kill anyone since it first burst up through the floor, but it was doing incredible amounts of damage, and he could scarcely doubt that it *had* killed any number of people, perhaps without even meaning to, in making its way through the city. The creature was his responsibility, the overman told himself; he had ventured where he should not have gone, and it had been awakened as a result. He had brought destruction again, as he always did when he agreed to aid the Forgotten King.

He knew what could destroy it, he was sure; nothing could stand against the Sword of Bheleu. That would be fitting, using the tool of the god of destruction to kill such a destroyer. That would not atone for freeing the thing in the first place, but it would put the Sword of Bheleu to constructive use. If for any reason the sword should fail, the Forgotten King might well be able to use the Book of Silence against the monster.

He, Garth, could not use the book; he could not read it. He did not have the sword. The sword and the one who could read the book were both in Skelleth. Any doubts he had about swapping the book for the sword had vanished. He was still concerned about the possibility of the King's bringing on the Fifteenth Age, but that was mere theory, while this rampaging beast was a fact. Furthermore, he was certain that the King required more than the Book of Silence for his final magic.

He had to get to Skelleth without delay. His campaign against the cult of Aghad could wait; this monster was a far more immediate threat to the safety of innocents. The time he had spent in making his way through the crypts, or in his leisurely exploration of the creature's prison, or in the King's little chapel, now seemed to have been horribly wasted; the monster had probably killed dozens or even hundreds of people during that period. Even the time he had lain unconscious now seemed unforgivable.

He wondered how he could have been so thoughtless as to have not given the monster's whereabouts and behavior his immediate attention. Even as he spun and headed eastward on a side street, he berated himself for allowing such destruction.

He did not know the city, nor where in it he had found himself, but he knew that the gate where he had left Koros was near the easternmost extremity; for that reason, he kept heading east whenever possible. Almost immediately, he passed through an area where the creature had obviously already been; many of the buildings were stamped flat, the rubble ground into powder against the granite streets. In places, the streets were indistinguishable from the buildings. Garth marveled that none had collapsed into the crypts which, he knew, honeycombed the entire area beneath the city.

He passed several fires, varying from a few smoldering curtains thrown in an alley to conflagrations consuming entire blocks. Only very rarely did he see any humans, and then it was merely a fleeting glimpse of someone vanishing behind a closing shutter or fleeing around the corner of a building. Nowhere were the streets lighted by the usual torches or lanterns, and the shops and houses were dark.

This both reassured and disturbed him; most of the population had obviously fled from the city, which was probably a very good thing, but why, he wondered, were the few stragglers avoiding him? Did they assume him to have some connection with the monster, or to be a threat in his own right by virtue of his species?

Finally he reached the steep slope that led up to the eastern wall of the city, but he had not managed to arrive at the gate. After some study of the surrounding buildings, the firelit roof-lines and the parapet of the city wall in particular, Garth decided he was north of his intended destination and turned right.

A walk of four blocks south, complicated by dodging around in the tangled web of streets, brought him to the central avenue and the remembered steps. There, however, he stopped, hanging back out of sight around a corner.

The steps were not deserted, as the streets had been. Instead, what looked like the entire city guard was ranged on them, illuminated by hundreds of torches. Perhaps half were just standing and looking watchful, while the other half were coming and going and bustling about. Garth could not decide what they were doing; part of it seemed to be gathering in stragglers and escorting them up to the gate, but that did not account for all the movement.

Crowds of civilians were still in the area; the overman noticed them streaming in and out of one large building, under the gaze of a row of torch-bearing soldiers.

Whatever was happening, there seemed to be a fair measure of order and organization to it; Garth saw no signs of screaming panic and no bodies lying in the streets. That was promising.

It was important that there should be order, because this was the only way he knew that would get him out of the city; he would have to pass through that array of soldiery and do it peacefully. Had it been a desperate mob, that would have been virtually impossible. They might well have panicked at the sight of him.

Having assessed the situation, he saw no reason for further delay. He stepped from concealment and marched purposefully toward the gate.

As he had half expected, several people noticed him immediately, and a cry went up. "An overman! There's an overman here!"

To Garth's dismay, he could also make out shouts of "Kill

the overman! It's another monster!" Other voices muttered and babbled, and he was sure that, despite the outward semblance of calm, this crowd could easily degenerate into a raging mob.

Several of the soldiers had noticed him as well, and one, an officer, was approaching.

"Ho, there!" Garth called. "How goes it?"

"Who in hell are you?" the soldier replied.

"I am Garth of Ordunin; I was a guest of your overlord, but became lost and have only now found my way here."

The man looked uncertain. "What do you want?" he asked.

"To pass through the gate."

The soldier nodded, as if that were what he should have expected. "You'll have to wait your turn," he said.

That was disconcerting. "I think," Garth said carefully, "that it would be wise to let me through immediately." He did not want to seem arrogant, or to take any action that might start trouble, but he also did not want to wait in line; every minute he was delayed from returning to Skelleth meant another minute of the monster's rampage.

"You can wait like anybody else, damn you," the soldier replied.

Garth started to protest, but a call from the dark at the top of the stair interrupted him.

"Have you got an overman down there?" someone yelled.

Startled, the soldier who had stopped Garth turned and looked. The call was repeated.

"We've got an overman here, yes," the officer called back.

"Is it the one who owns this damned animal out here?"

The soldier started to turn back to Garth, who said, "That is my warbeast, yes. I left it there because it was not allowed in the city."

"He says it's his," the soldier bellowed.

"Then get him up here and tell him to get the thing out of the way! It won't move, and it's slowing up the whole evacuation!"

The officer turned back toward Garth with a sour expression. The overman tried to smile ingratiatingly and avoided saying anything that might annoy the soldier.

"Go on up," the man said, waving him on.

Garth obeyed with alacrity, bounding up the worn steps as

fast as he dared. At the top he was waved through, and another officer pointed out the warbeast, standing quietly in exactly the spot where Garth had left it.

The problem was that the entire eastern side of the ridge, from the wall down to the plain, was ablaze with torchlight and jammed with people—except for a wide circle, perhaps thirty feet across, around Koros. That circle happened to take in the only easy path around the south tower, and its north edge skimmed the main highway.

"Can you get it out of here?" someone asked.

Garth nodded.

"Then do it, please."

Garth nodded again, then paused. He was rather overwhelmed by the vast crowd of people; he had never seen so many individuals of any major species gathered together before. He had known, in an intellectual way, that Ur-Dormulk held tens or perhaps hundreds of thousands of people, but that had not prepared him emotionally for seeing most of the population packed together on a hillside at night without shelter or much of anything else but a few personal belongings.

"What are you going to do with them all?" he asked the officer.

"How should I know?" the man replied. "I just follow orders. With any luck we'll be able to start letting them back into the city by daybreak."

"You will?" Garth was startled. "How can that be? What of the monster?"

"The court wizards are trying to drive it into one of the lakes, I understand—probably Demhe, but Hali if they have to. I doubt anything that big can swim."

"How can they do that?"

"How would I know? I'm no sorcerer. They've kept it from chasing the crowds so far; they should be able to handle it."

Garth was far less optimistic, but did not say so. Instead, he asked, "These wizards—do you speak of Chalkara of Kholis and a person called Shandiph?" He had forgotten the cognomen attached to the latter name, if he had ever in fact heard it.

"Those names sound right," the soldier replied. "The two from the prince's court, whoever they are. They were about to flee the city themselves, I hear, when they got ordered to deal

with the thing." He was obviously not interested in such details.
"Now, could you move your animal?"

"Yes, of course," Garth said. He considered telling the man
that he would be returning shortly with the means of dispatching
the monster, but decided against it. This fellow did not appear
to have much authority, and even if he had some, what good
would such a message do? Besides, the possibility of something
going wrong was always present; Garth might be delayed or
might have difficulties with the Sword of Bheleu, or with the
cult of Aghad, that would prevent his return. There was no
point in raising hopes that might go unfulfilled.

He said nothing, but marched down to the side of the waiting
warbeast. The crowd parted reluctantly before him, pressing
back upon itself.

He stowed his possessions, including the Book of Silence,
and made certain they were secure. A moment later he was in
the saddle again; he shouted a warning to the people gathered
before him, then gave Koros the command to advance.

Those immediately in the beast's path moved back as quickly
as they could, eager to stay out of its way, but the resistance
of the mass behind them ensured that Garth's progress remained
slow until the crowd thinned out, a hundred yards farther down
the slope. At that point Koros began picking up speed, and
when rider and mount passed the line of soldiers that marked
the outer perimeter of the clustered refugees, Garth gave the
warbeast the order to run.

Koros obeyed magnificently, hurtling forward so fast that
the overman's eyes stung and watered with the wind of their
passage. He was able to do little but cling desperately to the
harness, casting an occasional glance back to be sure that the
pack behind the saddle that held the Book of Silence remained
secure.

He rode on thus for hours, pausing only at a roadside tavern
for a long-overdue drink and a hearty meal.

It was this scene, of Garth bent over his warbeast's neck,
charging onward at top speed, that Haggat conjured up in his
scrying glass when he found time to check again on the overman's whereabouts. He was startled; he wondered what ur-
gency drove Garth to maintain such a pace. He had not bothered

to follow events in Ur-Dormulk personally, relying instead on reports from the cult's many agents there; half a dozen had been equipped with the communication spells acquired from murdered wizards, which provided almost instant news—a great improvement on the old system of relays and carrier pigeons that they had relied upon before the breaking of the Council of the Most High.

No reports had reached him from Ur-Dormulk, which could mean many things; he told himself that he would have to look into that later.

For the present, Garth was obviously returning to Skelleth with all possible haste, and if the cult were to maintain its image and its hold upon him, then a greeting of some sort would have to be arranged. The overman's homecoming—Haggat thought of Skelleth as Garth's home, even though Garth did not—could not be allowed to go unheralded.

The high priest had already considered this matter in his planning and had devised two possible unpleasant surprises. The better one, unfortunately, was the more difficult and time-consuming, and at the rate Garth was moving, it might not be ready in time; therefore, the other would have to do.

Haggat paused before giving the signal, however, and studied the image in the globe thoughtfully. The warbeast had to be taken into consideration. He was determined that his people would maintain an appearance of total invulnerability, and the warding spells that he had provided his last group of tormentors would not serve against so powerful a creature as a warbeast.

Well, he told himself, he had a device that would. It was one of his most prized possessions, acquired by careful planning and considerable craft from the wizard who had pocketed it in that mysterious vault beneath Ur-Dormulk, whence so much of the cult's pilfered magic was derived. It was truly a shame that the chamber was lost and that all attempts to locate it had failed; if a score of magicians had brought out so much worthwhile magic just by retaining what they had casually picked up in a few hours' stay, what other treasures might still lie there, undiscovered?

One of Haggat's dreams was to find and reopen that vault; another was to obtain and use the Sword of Bheleu. Accomplishing either feat would give him, he was sure, mastery of the entire civilized world. He did not wholly understand why he had made no progress toward either goal. Divinations that were usually infallible came to nothing; spies vanished mysteriously and were never heard from again; healthy agents died of sudden heart failure while climbing the stairs of the King's Inn. It was obvious that some other power was blocking him. He was determined not to be thwarted; once Garth had been dealt with, he would track down and destroy whoever was responsible for the interference.

First, though, he had to deal with Garth, and for that, he wanted to provide the appointed agents with an infallible protection. He had only one, apparently unique in all the world, a simple metal rod that could, if properly used, temporarily render up to half a dozen people immune to all harm. After taking it from Haladar of Mara, he had intended to keep it solely for his own personal use, but this situation was special, and called for special measures. He would, he decided, loan it to the chosen cultists.

That, he was certain, when combined with the other magic at his disposal, would ensure that Garth received the greeting the followers of Aghad thought he deserved.

CHAPTER SEVENTEEN

After further hours of traveling at high speed, with its rider clinging to its neck, Koros slowed as it approached the crumbling walls of Skelleth. Garth rose from his crouch into a more comfortable and dignified posture; thus he was able to see clearly, in the gray light of morning, what awaited him at the gate. He had time, also, to hide his shock and dismay.

Three red-robed figures were slouched comfortably on the broken battlements, gathered around a pole that stood ten or twelve feet high, leaning at a jaunty angle and topped with Kyrith's severed head.

Lying crumpled against the wall below was the dead body of the man assigned to guard the southwestern gate; a long, crooked streak of blood ran from his slit throat down his arm to the ground.

Garth was as much appalled by the pointless murder of the sentry as by the defiling of his wife's corpse. After all, Kyrith had already been dead, insensible to further indignity. Even though she was his own species and his own family, the awful waste of killing the man simply because he was in the way—and Garth was quite sure that was the only reason the Aghadites had slain him, to remove him from the chosen site for their little display—was sickening.

As Garth fought to keep his anger leashed until he knew what he faced, one of the loungers called, "Back again?"

"We've been waiting for you," another said; his accent was Dûsarran. "We didn't want to kill anyone else important while you were off adventuring; that wouldn't be fair. So we've just been playing games." He waved casually at the gory trophy.

Garth growled involuntarily, as much at the calm dismissal of the guard's death as unimportant as at the taunts, and drew the undersized sword he had picked up in Ur-Dormulk.

The Aghadites laughed.

Enraged as he was, Garth remembered what had happened before when he struck at one of his red-clad tormentors. He saw no point in breaking another sword, even so poor a one as he now carried—but he was not sure that the protective spell worked against other weapons. The Forgotten King had called it a warding spell against metal. The overman leaned forward and whispered a word in the warbeast's ear.

Koros roared in reply and plunged forward, fangs bared and claws out. With a bound, it landed atop the three—and slid off, scrabbling for a hold it could not find. It was as if the Aghadites were sheathed in indestructible glass. They obviously had more protection than a ward against metal.

Garth lost his balance and slid from the saddle as the warbeast writhed about, trying to get at its indicated targets; he landed with a heavy thump on a patch of bare dirt, the wind knocked out of him, but not otherwise injured.

When he had regained his breath, he clambered to his feet to find himself facing a truly bizarre tableau. The three humans were sitting where they had been, trying desperately to look unconcerned, while Koros, standing awkwardly upon its hind legs, wrapped its immense forepaws around one man and tried to bite his head off. Garth could hear the grinding of teeth against something impervious.

The warbeast twisted its head for a better grip, but had no more success. The other two Aghadites wore ghastly, contrived smiles; the beast's intended victim was frozen with fear, despite his magical defenses, and his expression was one of sick terror as three-inch fangs skidded across his throat like fingernails on marble.

Garth took a great deal of pleasure in seeing the Aghadites

discomfited, even though he realized that he could do them no real harm. He did nothing to interfere; something else had occurred to him. He stepped forward, sword in hand, climbed atop a pile of rubble, and, leaning over the head of one of the trio, swung the blade against the wooden pole.

As he had hoped, the protective spell had not been extended that far. The wood splintered gratifyingly, and the upper portion toppled over. Before any of the Aghadites could recover, he had stepped over and scooped up his wife's head.

The two not involved with the warbeast called out in protest; Garth ignored them. He watched for another few seconds as Koros continued trying to gnaw off the other's head and wished that it were possible for the beast to succeed. It would have been an appropriate retaliation for the desecration of Kyrith's corpse and the murder of the guard. He regretted leaving the man's corpse where it was, but did not want to burden himself with it and perhaps give rise to unpleasant speculation in Skelleth as to how the guard had died. He doubted that the Aghadites would bother to desecrate the corpse; they were, he suspected, sufficiently ignorant of overman psychology not to realize that Garth would care about the man at all.

Reluctantly, he at last called the warbeast away, afraid that, in its mounting frustration, it might damage its teeth.

The two unmolested Aghadites had gone into a huddle, conferring with each other; they made no move to interfere with Garth as he led Koros onward into the town. The intended victim had fainted; when Koros released him, he tumbled to the ground in a heap.

After the overman had moved on out of sight of the Aghadites, he paused for a moment to wrap the head in his tapestry bundle, dumping unceremoniously the assorted litter that he had gathered and transferring the few items he still thought might be useful to the pack behind the warbeast's saddle. He checked to be sure that the Book of Silence was still secure, then continued on his way.

He ignored the townspeople he encountered on the streets and marched across the marketplace without glancing to either side. At this point he was not concerned with anyone in Skelleth, save for the Forgotten King and the Aghadites. He intended to spare a few minutes, once he had the Sword of

Bheleu, to kill his three tormentors before returning to Ur-Dormulk to deal with the monster. This latest meeting with the cult, he thought, had come out a draw; he intended to be victorious in the next one.

He wondered if Chalkara and Shandiph actually had any chance of getting the awakened creature into one of the lakes and whether that would be enough to kill it. Drowning such a thing would require a very deep lake indeed; he doubted that the one he had seen in Ur-Dormulk would do the job.

The monster might, however, be unable to climb out, given the long drop that surrounded the lake on all sides. If that happened, Garth was sure that the people of Ur-Dormulk would be glad to have it destroyed, rather than have it remain as a perpetual nuisance.

And, of course, if the wizards failed, Garth would have to kill it to prevent wholesale slaughter. Ordinary soldiery, however successful it might be in defending the city against human foes, could do nothing against such a creature.

The thought of soldiery reminded him that the men guarding the eastern gate of the city and serving to control the crowd of refugees had not tried to kill him, nor had hindered him in any way; he wondered again why the party that had pursued him into the crypts had done so. Had they been given orders to slay him, orders that were never spread to the other troops? Or had their commander taken it upon himself to kill the intruding overman?

It was all rather confusing, and Garth decided that none of it really mattered. All that mattered was getting and using the Sword of Bheleu to avenge the wrongs done him by the cult of Aghad and to destroy the monster he had unleashed.

That thought was uppermost in his mind when he reached the door of the King's Inn, but he paused for a moment before entering. He carried the bundle containing Kyrith's head in one hand, intending to keep it with him so that the Aghadites could not recover it once more to taunt him anew. The Book of Silence, however, was in a pack on the warbeast's back. He debated leaving it there; the Forgotten King would not be able to take it from him as readily if he left it outside while he spoke with the old man. On the other hand, thieves might happen along. Koros could easily dispose of most threats and guard anything it carried from them, but if the Aghadites with their protective magic should chance upon it, could the warbeast prevent them from taking the book?

In the interests of at least knowing what became of it, should anything go wrong, he removed the book and tucked it under his arm. Then he ordered Koros to wait by the door and strode into the King's Inn, marching directly for the table in the back corner.

He was halfway across the room before he noticed that though the old man sat in his accustomed place, something new had been added. The Sword of Bheleu lay across the table, the hilt pointing straight at Garth. The immense gem set in its pommel was not the dead black it had been when last he saw it; instead, it was murky and dark, its dull reddish hue seeming to shift as the overman approached, as if something were seething and swirling within it.

The sight of the sword gave him pause; his stride faltered, and his thoughts grew muddy and unclear. He slowed and stopped, still several feet away from the weapon's waiting hilt.

The great jewel seemed to flicker; Garth, staring at it, was now quite sure that something was moving within it. He had an unpleasant feeling that he was being watched by the power that lurked in the sword, and fancied that he could make out the image of a baleful red eye in the strange stone.

The idea of handling the thing was suddenly far less appealing, as he remembered the sick joy and dull thoughtlessness that he felt while wielding it. He started to take a step back, then stopped, angered by his own cowardice. Irritated, he tried to stare back at the stone, to confront directly the hostile power that dwelt therein.

After a second or two of motionless glaring, he realized he must look like a fool, watching an inanimate stone as he would a deadly foe. His annoyance grew.

He knew, vaguely, that he should not let himself be angered so easily, and that only enraged him still further. Confused and furious, he was tempted to step forward and snatch up the sword; that would settle the whole affair. His free hand reached out.

The Forgotten King's hand moved as well, a subtle shifting

of the fleshless fingers, and the gem went black. Garth's anger vanished, and his mind was clear again.

The anger and confusion, he knew, had been caused by the sword. He raised his gaze from the now-dormant gem to the withered face of the old man.

The King had intentionally let the sword affect him, that was obvious. He seemed to be able to damp its power effortlessly whenever he chose and for as long as he saw fit, yet he had let it affect Garth.

Even then, though, he had kept it weak, kept the stone dim; he had not wanted it to seize full control of the overman.

Realizing this, Garth felt a surge of his own authentic, self-generated anger. "Why did you do that?" he demanded, striding up to the table.

"A reminder," the old man replied in his hideous, dry voice.

Garth hesitated. The sound of the Forgotten King's voice was always disconcerting; no matter how often Garth reminded himself that it was horribly unpleasant, it always came as a surprise. Memory and imagination could not live up to the reality.

"A reminder of what?" he said at last, his tone less belligerent.

He did not really need to hear the old man's answer. The King had ways of knowing of events without seeing them; Garth was certain that the human had known he was coming to the King's Inn with the intention of taking the Sword of Bheleu and had staged the brief incident to remind Garth what the sword did to his mind and emotions.

As it happened, the old man did not bother to answer at all; he merely shrugged once, almost imperceptibly.

But why, Garth asked himself, would the King want to remind him of the sword's dangers?

Obviously, the old man did not want Garth to take the sword; that was the only explanation that seemed reasonable.

And why would he want to keep the sword?

Garth thought he knew the answer to that. He recalled that when he had first brought his booty from Dûsarra, the Forgotten King had dismissed most of it as junk, but had been pleased to see the Sword of Bheleu. Later, he had agreed only to *loan* it to Garth in exchange for the Book of Silence, but not to trade it outright. The wizards in Ur-Dormulk, in their theory that the King sought to bring about the Fifteenth Age, the Age of Death, had said that he required a service from the servants of Bheleu. Garth was, as far as he knew, the only servant Bheleu had alive; had events followed their predicted pattern, he would have the Sword of Bheleu.

He believed, therefore, that the old man's final death-magic, the spell that Garth thought would destroy the world, required the sword as well as the Book of Silence—and presumably the Pallid Mask as well. It would do the King little good to acquire one of the tools he needed if he were to give up another in exchange. He was therefore, Garth guessed, trying to coax Garth into giving him the Book of Silence without taking the sword.

Or perhaps it was something subtler than that. Perhaps the old man did not mind giving Garth the sword, but feared that after the overman took it, he would renege on his side of the bargain and keep the book. After all, Garth had admitted that his word was not good. In that case, the King presumably sought to frighten Garth out of taking the sword, so that the only way in which the magically protected Aghadites, or the monster in Ur-Dormulk, could be slain would be by the old man's use of the book.

It might even be that he sought to anger the overman into thoughtless defiance, and then Garth would snatch up the sword immediately. That didn't make very much sense, however, as surely the King could achieve the same result simply by letting Bheleu's power go free, so that it would suck Garth in.

If that last possibility was the truth, Garth decided, the old man might yet have his wish, because Garth was now more determined than ever to take the Sword of Bheleu and use it against the Aghadites and the leviathan. If the Forgotten King wanted to keep the sword, it was almost certainly in the best interests of all mortals for Garth to take it away from him.

As he arrived at that conclusion, Garth reached down toward the hilt of the sword.

The old man's hand shot out with unbelievable speed and grabbed the overman's descending wrist. To Garth's astonishment, he found himself unable to pull free or move the hand either nearer to or farther from the sword. It was as if the bony fingers were solid steel—and a very good grade of steel at that, to resist an overman's full strength without yielding the slightest fraction of an inch. The wrinkled skin even felt cool and dry, like metal.

"Why do you stop me?" Garth was now sure that the old man did not want him to take the sword, but thought it unwise to admit his belief.

"Give me the Book of Silence." Again, even after so brief an interval, the King's voice was shockingly ugly.

Garth struggled to free his wrist; the old man gave no sign he was even aware of the overman's efforts. Finally, after several seconds of useless strain, Garth conceded defeat. "Take the book, then, if you want it," he said.

The Forgotten King rose, the tatters of his yellow mantle rustling. He reached out his free hand, plucked the volume from beneath Garth's arm, and held it before him, but did not loosen his grip on the overman's wrist.

"Release me," Garth said, mustering as much dignity as he could in so awkward and embarrassing a pose. To be held so easily by a mere human, even one as unique and powerful as the Forgotten King, shamed him.

"My reminder, Garth," the King warned. "Bheleu is insidious and powerful and can dominate you with ease, perhaps without letting you know he is doing so. Remember, though, that I can free you of his influence as easily as you can blink an eye. You must serve one of us. The choice of masters is yours. Now, take the sword, if you want it, but remember, I lend it, I do not give it." The bony grip was gone, and Garth watched as the old man, the great black book clutched in both hands, turned away and moved across the room and up the stairs.

When the Forgotten King had vanished into the gloom at the top of the stairs, Garth looked down at the sword.

It lay, untouched, on the table; the gem remained black and lifeless.

Had that, then, been the purpose of the King's actions—to remind Garth that he would never again be free while both the Sword of Bheleu and the King in Yellow existed?

But then, with the Book of Silence in the King's possession, how much longer would he exist? He sought his own destruction and needed the book to accomplish it. Perhaps Garth was wrong about the other elements required, and the old man was even now weaving his final spell, a spell that would destroy the cult of Aghad and perhaps all the world as well.

No, that could not be. The old man had not said it, but he had definitely implied that he would live for some while yet, long enough to require Garth's services. Furthermore, the overman was certain that either the Sword of Bheleu, the Pallid Mask, or both were needed. Other things might also be required; he recalled that the Forgotten King had made him swear, almost three years ago, that not only would he fetch the book but he would also aid in the final magic.

Garth shook his head, dismissing all such considerations as not immediately relevant. He had more important concerns than maybes. He had his wife's murder to avenge, Aghadites to kill, and a monster to dispose of.

He reached down and grasped the sword's hilt; as his fingers closed on the black grip, the gem blazed up a fiery blood-red, washing the overman in crimson light. Savage joy and a blinding fury burst into being within him, and somewhere mocking laughter sounded.

CHAPTER EIGHTEEN

At first the surge of emotion was too powerful to allow any conscious thought or awareness of the external world at all. For three long years Bheleu had been suppressed, held down, his control of his chosen mortal form cut off; now that he was free once more, he reveled in it. The sword crackled with eldritch energy, and the air around the overman's body glowed redly.

Garth's own consciousness was lost for a long moment. He felt himself cut off, drifting in a formless nowhere of red and black, and he struggled desperately to regain his body. He fought to contain the all-consuming bloodlust that possessed him. The initial wave of ecstasy, the emotional overflow from Bheleu's relief, passed away. Anger remained, but as he pushed his way to the surface, he managed to redirect it, to channel it against the usurping presence in his body and mind.

"Bheleu!" he tried to call. "Listen to me!"

He knew, even in his confused state, that the words had not been spoken, that his lips and tongue had not obeyed him; nevertheless, he heard his own voice, made terrible by the god's power, answer him.

"Why do you call me, Garth? You have taken up the sword again, of your own choice, and freed me from all restraint.

201

Now you will serve me in destruction, as you were meant to serve me. What need is there of words?"

"I want to make a bargain," Garth managed to say—or at least to communicate, though he knew he had still not spoken aloud.

The god did not reply in words; instead, Garth felt a wave of contempt sweep over him, felt his consciousness slipping into darkness, and he struggled to retain what feeble control he had.

"No, wait! Bheleu, you are not free yet! There are terms to be set!"

"I am free," Bheleu replied.

"No!" Garth insisted. "You must meet my terms, or the Forgotten King will stop you again as he did before!"

There was a pause that seemed to stretch for hours, a timeless waiting while Garth's awareness drifted in nothingness and Bheleu considered.

"What are your terms?" Bheleu said at last.

Garth did not allow himself to feel relief yet, though he was sure that the god's willingness to listen at all proved that the point had been won, at least for the moment. "I took the sword back for a reason," he said. "I have enemies and I wish to destroy them." He felt a surge of hunger, of desire, as he said that. "They have the means of defying my own strength, so I need the sword and the power that goes with it."

"I am that power," Bheleu said, fury and bloodlust seething.

"I know," Garth answered, struggling against the overwhelming force of the god's driving emotions. "And I'll allow you freedom to destroy my enemies, but no others."

"You would use me, the destroyer god, as a tool for your own vengeance?"

Garth was almost swept down into nonexistence by the god's wrath, but managed to answer, "I would use anything I found necessary. Were you not planning to use me for your own ends against my will?"

"I am a god, Garth; you are nothing."

"I am a nothing who knows how you can be stayed; I am the chosen of a god. Is not the freedom to destroy my foes better than no freedom at all?"

"What do you propose?"

"I propose that you leave me in control of my own body and my own mind; in exchange, I will allow you free rein to work your will upon my enemies. If you refuse, you will surely be restrained again."

There followed another timeless pause; then, abruptly, Garth found himself fully conscious once again, albeit dazed and awash in unreasoning anger. He stood in the King's Inn, the sword clutched in one hand, its blade dripping red fire. The floorboards were scorched beneath his feet, in a circle a yard across, and a line had been burned across the top of the King's table where the sword had rested, obscuring with char the line he had gouged with his broken sword before leaving for Ur-Dormulk.

He could detect no sign of Bheleu's presence save for the heat of the sword, burning without harming him, and the eerie flame that flickered from it. His thoughts seemed slow, but unnaturally clear; a fierce joy suffused him at the realization that he had won his argument, and righteous wrath filled him at the thought of Aghadites lurking somewhere in Skelleth, waiting for him to come and kill them.

No one else was in the tavern; the innkeeper and the handful of other patrons had vanished while he debated with Bheleu. He did not concern himself with their whereabouts; they had, he told himself, undoubtedly fled before his manifest power.

He strode out the door, the sword's fiery aura gradually fading, and mounted his warbeast. With a word, he directed it back the way they had come, out toward the southwestern gate, hoping to find the three Aghadites. The Forgotten King had told him that the red-mist transporting spells were rare and precious; surely, then, the trio would not have wasted one, but would be moving on foot.

By the time Koros reached the south side of the marketplace, the sword appeared to be ordinary steel, though the black grip was hot in Garth's hand.

He found the three robed humans perhaps halfway to the gate, walking toward the center of town. They saw him at almost the same instant that he spotted them; one turned to flee, another hesitated, while the third fumbled with something beneath his ruddy robe.

Garth bellowed, urging Koros into a charge.

The fumbler stopped his actions and stood up straight, defying the warbeast and overman. "Ho, Garth!" he began.

Then the Sword of Bheleu struck his neck; with a roar and a sheet of flame, the blade passed through the protective aura and into the Aghadite's throat. Blood spurted, and the man's severed head rolled forward, tottered grotesquely, and fell to the ground as his body began to crumple. White sparks spattered from the dripping blade, and something hissed fiercely.

The man who had hesitated had no time to react before the sword swung around in a gleaming arc and beheaded him as well, spraying blood and fire across the packed dirt of the street.

Before the second corpse could fall, Garth twisted the sword back and impaled the dead man, holding it upright, the blade thrust through the chest—though the head had fallen to one side, where the overman ignored it. He was not willing to let both these foes escape with so quick and clean a death as simple decapitation.

The third Aghadite was still fleeing; Garth urged the warbeast after him, dragging the headless corpse alongside with the sword.

He gained on the human rapidly, despite the encumbrance of the dead body, but not rapidly enough; he saw wisps of red vapor gathering about the man's head, staying with him as he ran. With a growl, Garth tore the sword from the corpse's chest, letting the body fall aside, and urged Koros to greater speed.

It did no good; the Aghadite vanished before Garth could reach him.

The overman bellowed in rage and frustration. The man had escaped him!

Haggat was standing by the pentagram when the cult's surviving agent reappeared in a cloud of mystic vapor; he had given up trying to follow events in Skelleth. The Sword of Bheleu had the capability of resisting any attempt at scrying spells, should it choose to do so; Aghad's high priest had learned that fact almost three years earlier, at the cost of a good glass. On this occasion he had not bothered to try to observe the overman at all, after the image distorted and vanished at the instant that Garth's hand touched the sword's hilt. Instead he had followed the actions of his three cultists, keeping one of his wizard-acolytes ready with one of his handful of transporting crystals. Even that image had been lost, however, when the overman attacked the threesome, and Haggat's brief resulting confusion had given Garth time to kill the two who had chosen to rely on the protective spell.

It was of interest, Haggat thought, that the spell, which he had believed quite potent, had been unable to resist the Sword of Bheleu for as much as a second. The sword was obviously a weapon well worth having, and a very serious threat in Garth's hands.

He had not thought that the overman would take the sword back from the strange old man in rags. That, it seemed, had been a miscalculation, one that had cost the cult two good men already and that might prove disastrous.

Garth had sworn to return to Dûsarra and wipe out the whole sect; now that he had the sword in his possession once more, there was a chance that he might actually manage it. Haggat considered it essential to distract the overman, to harry him, to do whatever could be done to keep him busy until defenses could be prepared.

With that in mind, Haggat signaled for his advisers and assassins to attend him. Obediently, a dozen red-robed figures clustered around him.

While the Aghadites were gathering about their master, Garth sat astride his warbeast, roaring with anger and swinging the Sword of Bheleu in circles over his head. Streaks of shimmering white fire hung like smoke, emitting waves of intense heat. Thunder rumbled in the distance, drawn by the sword's power.

The human had to be somewhere, Garth told himself. The red mist was merely a transporting spell, nothing more. It did not create people out of thin air, nor snatch them into nothingness. The Aghadite was still alive somewhere, perhaps nearby, perhaps laughing at his escape.

Wherever he was, Garth would find him; he would find him and cut him apart, watch his blood pour out, watch him suffer and die. He promised himself that, ignoring the tiny inner voice that protested this open bloodlust.

Koros had slowed and stopped when its prey vanished; now,

at the urging of its rider, it turned back toward the inhabited portion of Skelleth. As it passed by each of the headless corpses, Garth thrust the sword out casually and set both afire with the weapon's supernatural flame.

That done, he rode on, considering his next move.

His first thought was to return to the marketplace and begin searching for the escaped Aghadite there, but that, he decided, would be a mistake. The man was almost certainly hiding somewhere in the ruins, where no stray villagers would wonder at mysterious colored smoke or strange noises. Garth had lived in Skelleth for almost three years and had not seen anyone wearing the distinctive red robes between the time of his giving up the Sword of Bheleu and his finding of Kyrith's body—yet now these three had turned up suddenly. None of the faces was familiar; he could not recollect having seen any of them in other garb. Therefore, he guessed that they had only recently arrived in Skelleth—and since newcomers, other than caravans, were rare enough to excite a great deal of comment, Garth thought he would have heard of them if they were living openly in the inhabited part of the town.

Therefore, he concluded, they had been living in concealment somewhere in the ruins, and it was in the ruins that he must search for the survivor, and any others who might have taken part in Kyrith's murder.

Somewhere in the back of his mind, he remembered the behemoth destroying Ur-Dormulk, but somehow it seemed far less important than dealing immediately with the cult of Aghad.

Besides, he told himself, surely he couldn't object to destroying ruins, and that would keep the sword busy and Bheleu happy.

That thought troubled him somehow; something seemed wrong with it, and perhaps with his other decisions as well. Something appeared to be clouding his thoughts.

The idea refused to come clear, so he dismissed it. He had an enemy to hunt down and destroy; that was what mattered. He turned Koros off the road leading into the market and set out instead into the ring of ruins that encircled Skelleth's inhabited core.

The town had been built as a border fortress, and its houses were constructed mostly of stone as a result, so that they would not burn readily. After three hundred years of neglect, many houses and buildings had lost roofs and floors, and some walls had fallen, but many still stood, making the streets a maze, with some routes blocked by rubble, others still open, and all divided by crumbling buildings.

Garth, armed with the Sword of Bheleu, did not bother to find his way through this labyrinth; instead, he dismounted and marched in a straight line, Koros trailing behind. Whenever he found his way blocked by a standing wall or a pile of debris, he blasted it apart with the Sword of Bheleu; only open pits were sufficient to turn him aside. When he came across those, he would pause and send a wave of flame down into them, to incinerate any Aghadites who might be lurking therein.

The use of the sword's power, he found, came very easily, almost without any thought or effort at all; the god's long restraint had not affected the increase in power that accompanied the establishment of the Fourteenth Age. Garth discovered quickly that all that vast resource was at his command, ready and eager to be applied.

When he had held the sword before, the Age of Bheleu had been just beginning. The god's power had been erratic, sometimes manifesting itself unbidden, other times appearing only after great mental effort. That was no longer the case. Now, Garth had almost infinite energy literally at his fingertips.

He had been cutting a swath through the ruins for an hour or so, enjoying the exhilaration of battering down the empty houses until he had almost forgotten what he was looking for, when a red-clad figure appeared, perched precariously atop a wall off to his right.

Garth did not notice the human's presence at first; he was basking in the delight of shattering a foot-thick stone pillar with a single blow of his sword and therefore did not see whether the man had arrived magically or had simply climbed up the other side of the wall.

"Ho, Garth!" the human called.

Startled, Garth lowered the Sword of Bheleu and turned toward the source of the voice.

"You'll never find us that way!" the Aghadite said.

With a growl, Garth swung the sword about, pointing it toward the human. After an hour of practicing with the sword's power, he had no intention of wasting time in unnecessary pursuit. He had learned better.

"We've got a surprise for you in town," the man began; then the sword spat flame toward him, blazing across the intervening distance in an instant. Immediately, red mist gathered about him, but Garth listened with satisfaction to the Aghadite's screams as the sword's fire reached him first. The spell would deliver a burned corpse.

It did exactly that; Haggat stared in dismay at the smoldering remains. He had been using up transporting crystals far faster than he liked, and to little effect. He had lost another good agent. He had not expected the overman to react so quickly.

At least, however, Garth was still searching Skelleth and was not on his way to Dûsarra. The cult would have time to devise an effective strategy.

That assumed, of course, that any strategy *could* be effective against the Sword of Bheleu. Haggat was not sure that was the case. He began to wonder whether the cult might have done better to have forgotten permanently about its vengeance against Garth.

It was too late now, though.

Perhaps the overman would think that he had succeeded in killing all his wife's assassins, as in fact he had, and would abandon his retaliation.

Somehow, though, Haggat doubted that, in light of both Garth's oath to destroy the cult's temple and what awaited him in Skelleth's marketplace. The high priest wondered if committing another atrocity might have been a mistake.

He looked down at the blackened, crumbling heap in the pentagram and hoped very much that Garth would be satisfied by the three cultists he had killed.

Garth *was* satisfied, but only for a very brief moment, as he thought of the transporting spell dumping a flaming ruin before Aghadites expecting a living man.

That very thought, however, gave him pause. If he had killed the man, who had completed the spell? Somebody had, apparently, because the red smoke had gathered, thickened, and then vanished, taking the burning Aghadite with it. By the time he disappeared, the man was almost certainly already dead.

Had the human set up the spell in advance so that he would not need to complete it, but only to set it in motion? Garth wished he knew more of the exact mechanism involved.

And whether the man had worked the spell himself or not, could Garth be sure that there were not still more Aghadites lurking in Skelleth? He had, as far as he knew, encountered only the three he had slain, but that did not mean that there were no others.

That corpse had gone somewhere, he was certain of that.

Had he killed all those directly involved in his wife's death, the desecration of her corpse, and the murder of the guard at the gate? Others might still be hidden. For that matter, he could not be sure that these three had actually killed Kyrith at all.

He had every intention of returning to Ur-Dormulk and killing the monster, then proceeding from there to Dûsarra to fulfill his vow to destroy the headquarters of Aghad's cult, but he wanted to be certain first that he had dealt with the sect's outpost in Skelleth and with those who had actually taken part in Kyrith's murder.

He tried to think, to marshal what information he had, in hopes of finding some clue that would tell him what he wanted to know. His thoughts seemed vague and elusive. He wondered if he had been hasty in killing the last of the trio so quickly, rather than taking him alive and interrogating him.

The man's last words had been about a surprise of some kind—"in town," he had said.

That, Garth was sure, meant in the inhabited portion of Skelleth; most likely, he thought, he would find whatever it was right in the marketplace. Perhaps that would provide the clue he needed to lead him to more Aghadites.

He was vaguely aware that the surprise might be unpleasant, but that seemed unimportant. With only the prospect of more enemies to kill in his mind, he turned and headed toward the square. He told himself that he had no time to pick his way through the winding streets and marched straight ahead, continuing to cut through every obstacle with the Sword of Bheleu.

It took a severe conscious effort to restrain himself when he reached the first of the occupied houses, but he managed it; from that point on, he found his way through the streets, forcing down the bloodlust, forcing himself to be calm. Koros followed him placidly, undisturbed by the sword's fiery displays of power and seemingly indifferent to the route it followed.

Garth was still a few short blocks from the market, his anger faded to insignificance under the steady pressure of his will, when he heard the wailing begin.

It was an eerie sound, a wavering, high-pitched note that went on and on interminably. It sounded like a human voice, but not quite natural, somehow; it grated on his nerves and made him feel uneasy, despite the aura of invincibility the sword bestowed upon him.

If it *was* a human voice, Garth told himself, then whoever was wailing had to be in a state of indescribable emotional upset. He had heard men scream and bellow and whimper, but he had never heard a wailing like this. It was not a scream or an ordinary cry; it had no words, no rhythm, no break in the constant stream of sound.

Unsettled, he hurried forward, Koros following at his heels.

He entered the marketplace from the northwest, waving for Koros to stay back out of the way, and found himself at the rear of a silent crowd. The wailing came from somewhere on the far side, near the door of Saram's house.

He glanced back, to be sure that Koros was staying behind; it was, standing in the mouth of the street and glancing about as if the sound made it uneasy, too. Reassured that the warbeast would cause no trouble, Garth peered over the heads of the gathered humans.

Something dark was hanging in the open doorway of the Baron's house; shadows and distance hid the details, but Garth felt a sick certainty that this was the Aghadite surprise. The crowd faced toward the thing in the doorway, but had left an empty semicircle around it, and the wailing seemed to emanate, not from the house, but from somewhere in that semicircle.

Determined to find out what was happening, Garth marched forward and began shoving his way through the crowd; people parted readily when they saw him and almost seemed to be hurrying him onward. He crossed the square as quickly as if it were empty and emerged at last into the little cleared area.

He found there that the wailing was coming from Frima, who knelt facing the door of her home, her head thrown back, her arms limp at her sides, her eyes shut and her mouth open, pouring forth her grief.

Garth would not have guessed that such a sound could come from a lone woman, particularly one as small as Frima; he stared at her in helpless astonishment for several seconds before thinking to look up at the cause of her despair.

The ghastly thing that hung suspended in the doorway by its outstretched arms was all that remained of Saram, Baron of Skelleth. His wrists had been nailed to the doorframe with heavy metal spikes. His eyes were gone, leaving bloody sockets, and more blood spilled from his open, tongueless mouth. The front of his embroidered robe had been cut away and strips had been peeled from his chest, forming four red runes that spelled out AGHAD.

Grief and rage mingled with a feeling of helplessness before such savagery; Garth felt a need to do something, anything, to react to this new abomination, to help the woman who knelt, keening, before him. Fighting down a boiling wave of anger, he suppressed the urge to send forth white-hot flame to destroy everything before him. That would do no good, he told himself; it would only leave Frima still more bereft.

"You," he called, pointing at the nearest man who looked strong enough to be of use, "get him down from there!"

The man hesitated; Garth growled and lifted the Sword of Bheleu. "Help him," Garth ordered, pointing to two more villagers. "You women, prepare a place for him to lie." He spotted Saram's housekeeper in the crowd and called to her, "Find something to dress him in!"

The villagers did not move quickly enough to please him; he struggled against the urge to blast them all. Frima's keening bit through him, adding to his irritation, until he could not tolerate it further. He reached down, grabbed her shoulder roughly, and dragged her to her feet.

She refused to stand on her own; he supported her with one hand as he barked at her, "Listen to me, woman!"

Her wailing died away as the overman shook her; her head fell forward and her eyes opened, but then fixed on her husband's mutilated corpse. She did not speak and would not meet Garth's gaze.

"Listen to me!" Garth insisted. "Your husband is dead; there is nothing that anyone can do about that. It does no good to bewail his death like this. You do yourself only harm by kneeling here and screaming."

Frima hung limply in his grasp, and a sympathetic murmur ran through the crowd. The villagers were all watching intently every second of the drama taking place in their midst.

"Stand on your feet, woman! Do not let the scum who did this see how much they have hurt you!"

Frima met Garth's eyes for an instant, then turned her gaze back to the doorway. The man Garth had chosen was trying to pry out a spike, using a knife someone had handed him. He was making a mess of the wooden frame, but carefully avoiding any contact between the blade and Saram's dead flesh.

The Dûsarran swallowed and twisted her dangling feet about so that she could stand. Garth loosened his grip, and she did not collapse.

"The cult of Aghad has killed your husband and vilely abused his body; stand strong now so that they will not have harmed his dignity as well," Garth muttered in Frima's ear.

She nodded.

"You are the Baroness of Skelleth," Garth reminded her quietly. "You must behave accordingly."

Frima nodded again, then demanded hoarsely, "Where are they?"

Startled, Garth asked, "What?"

"Where are the filth who murdered him?"

"I don't know," Garth admitted. "I killed one of them just a few moments ago, when he came to boast to me of this latest crime, but there must have been others. I have sworn to destroy them all when I find them, and the temples and shrines of their foul god with them."

"I'm coming with you," Frima said.

"There is no need," Garth told her. "Saram's death will be avenged. I swore to destroy the cult for what it did to Kyrith, and this new butchery strengthens my resolve beyond what I can express in words. I will make them all pay for this."

"I am coming with you," Frima insisted. "They killed my man."

Garth thought it best to shift the grounds for argument. "You still live, my lady, and are still the Baroness of Skelleth. You have other concerns."

"They don't matter. Are there any Aghadites in Skelleth, or will you be going to Dûsarra?"

The first spike came free, and the men struggling with it hurried to catch Saram's body as it fell. While two held the corpse, a third began working on the other spike.

"I don't know where they are," Garth replied, "but I will find them."

"*We* will find them."

Garth could not think of any good way to deal with this. He turned from the intense, fixed stare that Frima was giving him and watched as the workers freed Saram's other wrist.

They stood for a moment holding their lord's body, uncertain what to do next.

"Take him inside," Garth said. "The housekeeper will find a place for him."

Two of the men carried the corpse out of sight while the third closed the doors.

Reluctant to meet Frima's gaze again, Garth looked about and realized that the market was still crowded with onlookers. A surge of irrational anger at their gawking boiled up within him.

"Go home, you people!" he called. "There is nothing more to see!"

He was answered with muffled voices and shuffling feet, but the villagers seemed reluctant to depart.

"Go away, I said!" he bellowed, raising the Sword of Bheleu in one hand. The blade glowed white, crackling with chained energy, and the crowd melted away rapidly before the implied threat. In a moment the square was empty of all save the overman, the new widow, and the warbeast that waited at the northwest corner.

Garth glanced about again, trying to decide what to do with Frima; he did not think it would be wise to send her home, into the house where her husband's mangled corpse waited.

He was unsure how humans dealt with the deaths of those they loved.

"Are there any rites you must perform?" he asked.

"No," she replied. "We don't bother with fancy funerals in Dûsarra. When the other cults kill someone, the body usually isn't found; we grieve, but hold no ceremonies. The people of Skelleth can attend to the ceremonies. We have to go avenge him." She looked about the square and noticed Koros, waiting patiently, at ease now that the keening had stopped. Without hesitation, she slipped from under Garth's hand and began walking unsteadily across the marketplace toward the warbeast.

Garth followed. He could easily have stopped her, but was not sure how she would react.

Halfway across the square, she stumbled; he lunged forward and caught her before she fell. They stood for a moment while she regained her balance.

"Garth," someone called, in a hideous dry croak.

The voice was instantly recognizable. Garth turned, astonished, and saw the Forgotten King standing in the doorway of the King's Inn, the Book of Silence tucked under one arm.

"There are no worshippers of Aghad in Skelleth," the old man said. "Their transporting spells are not affected by distance; they have been striking directly from their temple in Dûsarra."

Garth stood dumbfounded by this unexpected speech. He knew that the Forgotten King never volunteered information without a reason.

"Then we have to go to Dûsarra," Frima said calmly.

The Forgotten King nodded, moving his head very slightly beneath the concealing hood of his robe.

"Why are you telling us this?" Garth asked.

"So that you will not waste time."

"Will you swear it to be true, by The God Whose Name Is Not Spoken, at the cost of all oaths I have made to you if you lie?" Garth could think of nothing more binding; he knew that the old man would not be eager to give up the vows Garth had sworn. He was startled by his own cleverness in coming up with such a promise so readily; his thoughts had not been very clear of late.

"I swear it," the King replied.

Garth looked at the shadows that hid the old man's eyes, and at the firm line of his mouth, set in dry, wrinkled skin above the thin white beard that trailed from his chin. He glanced at Frima, who was obviously waiting for him to accompany her in pursuit of revenge, and at Koros, still standing patiently, and finally at the Sword of Bheleu, which dangled from his right hand, its tip almost dragging in the dust of the market, the red gem in its pommel flickering faintly. He still did not know why the Forgotten King should volunteer such information. Perhaps, he thought, the old man was eager to get the sword back, lest it gain too strong a hold upon Garth; he would want the overman to go about his errand as quickly as possible, so that the sword's return would not be delayed. That would be in Garth's own interest as well.

"Very well," he said at last. "Then I will go to Dûsarra and I will destroy the cult of Aghad there. I swore I would and I will honor that oath. But I go alone."

"No!" Frima cried. "I'm coming with you!"

"I do not want to endanger you, Frima, and the journey will be very dangerous. You must stay in Skelleth." His major concern was that the Sword of Bheleu might usurp control of him and cause him to kill any traveling companions, but he did not care to explain that. It would be too much like admitting weakness to say that he feared he would be unable to control his own body.

"I have to avenge Saram! There's nothing I want in Skelleth. Besides, you'll need a guide; you don't know your way around Dûsarra as I do. I grew up there."

"No," Garth began, but before he could continue, Frima interrupted.

"Besides, do you think I'm safe here? You heard what the old man said; the Aghadites can strike anywhere, and they've just heard you say that you don't want me hurt. I'm a target now. If you don't take me with you, I'll follow you on my own."

The overman looked at the human's face and decided that she meant what she said. She had a good point about being in danger in Skelleth, and also about her utility as a guide. She would certainly be safer guarded by Koros and himself than trying to traverse Nekutta on her own.

"Very well," he said. "We will go by way of Ur-Dormulk, however; I have something I must do there." The monster had waited too long already. Garth found himself wondering how he could have delayed so long.

"All right," Frima agreed.

"We'll need supplies," Garth said, his practical instincts coming to the fore.

"We can forage on the way," Frima replied. "I don't want to wait."

"I will provide for your needs," the Forgotten King said.

Startled, Garth turned to look at him. "You will? From here?"

The old man moved his head to one side, then the other, in so brief and smooth a movement that it could hardly be described as shaking his head.

"I will come with you," he said.

CHAPTER NINETEEN

As the little party made its way toward Ur-Dormulk, Garth found himself feeling that he had been rushed into action against his will. He had not intended to dash so precipitously out of Skelleth. Within half an hour of discovering Saram's death, he had ridden out the southwestern gate, Frima perched behind him, the Forgotten King walking alongside.

He told himself that every minute saved meant that much less destruction the monster in Ur-Dormulk could cause, and that he had already wasted far too much time destroying empty ruins. Still, he felt unprepared and harried.

Thinking back, he wondered at his own willingness to delay in order to knock down buildings, compared with the insistent hurry of both his companions. He suspected that the sword had had something to do with his dawdling, and also with his eagerness to come to grips with the Aghadite assassins. Whatever the cause, he had behaved stupidly.

If he had not delayed, the cultists might not have bothered to kill Saram. He was sure that Saram had been alive when he slew the first two assassins. Had he left Skelleth immediately, the Aghadites might not have returned and the Baron might still be alive and well, his wife secure and happy at home, rather than perched on a warbeast seeking revenge. Instead of leaving, though, Garth had gone smashing about the ruins,

wasting time and giving the worshippers of Aghad the chance
to carry out another of their ghastly murders.

Could it be, he asked himself, that Bheleu had diverted him
intentionally, to further the cause of his brother deity? Might
Aghad himself have affected him somehow? Or had it just been
the workings of chance?

Had the Forgotten King been involved? He had certainly
appeared in the doorway at an opportune moment, with exactly
the information that would send Garth and Frima on their way
without hesitation.

The overman glanced to the left, where the yellow-clad
figure strode along as smoothly and silently as the warbeast
itself. The Book of Silence was still held under the old man's
right arm, and Garth reminded himself that the totem was what
enabled the King to travel freely. He would no longer need an
overman to run his errands for him.

What benefit could the old man have gained from Saram's
death? For that matter, what could Aghad or Bheleu gain from
it? Garth would have gone to Dûsarra soon enough without this
added impetus, and the King could have accompanied him or
followed him. Saram's murder had increased his hatred of the
cultists, if that was possible, and had impelled Frima to accompany him, but that was little enough. What good would it
do anyone to have Saram's widow come along? How much
difference could the increase in his fury make?

Garth could see no purpose in it and concluded, reluctantly,
that it had been chance, rather than manipulation, that had led
to the Baron's murder. That meant that his own weakness in
yielding to the whim to search the ruins had been the indirect
cause; he was at fault. Once again he had brought destruction,
this time to an innocent friend.

The cult of Aghad would pay for that, he promised himself,
and if he could ever contrive to accomplish it, the gods themselves, both Aghad and Bheleu, would suffer as well for what
they had done to him.

He rode on, silently mulling this over.

Haggat watched the little group as best he could, trying
desperately to think of some way of diverting them. He could
not focus the scrying glass on Garth while the overman held

the Sword of Bheleu, nor on the old man in yellow at all; he
had to satisfy himself by following the warbeast's pawprints,
or by close scrutiny, just barely possible despite the sword's
influence, of the girl's face and the reflections in her eyes of
the surrounding countryside.

The high priest had thought that Garth would be searching
Skelleth for days, time which the cult could have used to lay
false trails and arrange diversions; instead, he had set out immediately, and there could be little doubt that he was bound
for Dûsarra.

Haggat did not understand what had happened. Something
was interfering with his plans. He suspected that it was the
mysterious old man. The overman had apparently spoken with
him in the market and decided then and there to leave Skelleth
without further delay.

Who, Haggat wondered, *was* the man? He could be glimpsed
only briefly, and even then not clearly, in the glass; most of
what Haggat knew of him came from the reports of spies or
from his occasional reflection in windows and in the eyes of
others. Once before he had become involved in the cult's af-
fairs, when he had put an end to the carefully contrived battle
between Garth and the Council of the Most High, saving the
lives of several councillors and taking the Sword of Bheleu
away from the overman. That had apparently worked to the
cult's benefit in the long run, though its followers had been
slow to take advantage of it, by rendering Garth vulnerable
and by allowing them to track down, rob, and murder several
of the surviving wizards.

Now, though, the old man had given the overman back the
sword and seemed to be leading him in his attack on the sect.

That was not to be borne.

All three of the party would have to be killed. The cult
could neither afford further delays nor waste time on any more
such pleasant preliminaries as the murders of Garth's wife and
the Baron of Skelleth.

Only four of each variety of transporting crystal remained
in the cult's cache of magic; they were not to be squandered.
Furthermore, the Sword of Bheleu was a formidable protection
against any assault, magical or mundane.

Haggat could not afford another failure. He glanced at the

scarred face of his personal acolyte; he was well aware that she would be glad to replace him as high priest, should he allow the cult's prestige to suffer.

He needed to think out exactly what to do. He recalled all too well that, three years earlier, the full power of the Council of the Most High had been unable to do anything against the might of the overman and his damned sword.

Some time did remain, however; the journey from Skelleth to Dûsarra was at least a ten-day ride. Perhaps his best course would be to use every moment of that time to prepare an ambush.

At any rate, although he would want to keep a careful eye on the progress of the approaching party, Haggat decided that he would not waste any of the cult's hoard of magic in tormenting them along the way, nor in abortive attacks that the Sword of Bheleu could easily counter. At least, he would not do so until he had devised something more subtle and effective than a direct assault.

Perhaps the three would lower their guard if left alone, he thought, or would decide that Garth had killed all the cultists involved in the murders after all and turn back.

Haggat wondered again who the old man was and why he had given the sword back to the overman.

As he first came within sight of the walls of Ur-Dormulk, Garth was surprised to see motion along the battlements. The distance was such that he knew he could not be observing any ordinary patrolling sentries, nor even major troop movements.

When the party drew nearer, he realized that he was seeing the head of the monstrous creature, projecting above the ramparts; the movement was its impatient marching back and forth. The wizards had obviously not succeeded in driving it into the lake.

The slope below the walls was still thick with people, though they had spread out considerably from their earlier close-packed arrangement. Tents had been erected, made from robes or overcloaks draped across walking sticks or scraps of wood. The perimeter was still patrolled by brass-helmeted guardsmen; more soldiers were posted along the base of the wall and clustered around the gate, their metal headgear gleaming in the midday sun. The sparse grass of the hillside had vanished into the dirt beneath the tread of so many feet.

The great beast prowled behind the battlements, but the people seemed to pay it little heed; they had already grown accustomed to their situation. Garth wondered at that.

He also wondered why the monster stayed behind the wall when it was obviously eager to leave the city. Surely, he thought, it was capable of breaking through the stone barrier, as it had broken out of its own chamber and had broken apart the buildings of the city.

Then he remembered the long slope on the other side of the wall. The creature might be unable to climb it; the natural barrier could confine it, where the man-made one could not.

There were also the two wizards. Garth saw no sign of them; they had plainly been unable to drive the leviathan into either of the lakes, let alone destroy it, but perhaps they were able to keep it from breaking out of the city.

That assumed that they hadn't been squashed in their attempts to defeat the thing.

The soldiers posted around the ramshackle encampment saw the party approaching while it was still some distance away. That was hardly surprising; the mounted overman, towering far above the tallest of the crops that lined the roadsides, was visible for a thousand yards or more across the flat plain. Had the guards not seen him, they would have been derelict in their duties.

Garth knew he had been seen, but was unconcerned. He had no need for stealth; he had come to perform a vital service this time. He watched as soldiers ran hither and yon, obviously carrying news of his coming up to the gate, and orders back down in response. A party began to form on the road, presumably to greet him and his companions, and to stop them if necessary.

In keeping with his idea of the dignity appropriate to his position, Garth pretended not to notice them, but rode directly forward, head held high, until he came within a dozen yards.

At that point he deigned to react visibly to the presence of an obstruction in his path and spoke a command to the warbeast. Koros could, he knew, have gone straight through the little cluster of men without even slowing down, whether they resisted or not, but that would scarcely have been diplomatic. Instead, at his order, the warbeast stopped dead, and Garth stared balefully at the party before him.

He felt a twinge of familiar bloodlust, an urge to order Koros forward and strike out with the Sword of Bheleu, but he fought it down.

"Greetings," he said.

An officer with a golden plume on his helmet replied, "Greetings, overman."

"May I pass?"

"That depends. As you can see, the situation in Ur-Dormulk is very unsettled at present." The man gestured, taking in the crowded hillside. "A monster," he said with a wave toward the ramparts, "has driven us from our homes. What business brings you here?"

"I have come to rid you of this troublesome creature."

The officer stared up at Garth for a moment, then looked down, turned to one of his men, and muttered, "He's mad."

The soldier nodded agreement. Garth wondered just how poor human hearing was; he had made out the remark without straining.

There was a pause in the conversation; the officer was obviously considering how best to handle an insane overman. He glanced at Garth again, then said, "Forgive me for the delay, overman, but I must confer with my superiors."

"Soldier," said a croaking, hideous voice. Startled, the officer seemed to notice the presence of the Forgotten King, standing beside the warbeast, for the first time.

"Let us pass," the old man said. "What harm can it do if the overman wishes to destroy himself?"

The officer stared for a second, then turned away, uncomfortable with looking at the King. He shrugged. "As you say, old man. Go on, then."

Garth was at least as startled by the old man's intervention as the soldier had been. The Forgotten King was becoming positively chatty, it appeared. He wondered if this was a result of traveling, of leaving his familiar surroundings, or was perhaps some side effect of possessing the Book of Silence. Perhaps the seeming nearness of his long-sought goal had cheered him out of his usual gloomy taciturnity.

If so, he would be disappointed, because Garth had no intention of aiding the old man any further.

The party of soldiers divided in half, allowing the warbeast and its two riders to pass between, and the Forgotten King to follow in the animal's wake. Garth urged Koros forward. Behind him, he could feel Frima shifting uncomfortably.

The officer signaled, and the two groups of soldiers marched alongside, escorting the overman and his party to the city gates.

Once there, they were passed over into the care of another officer and his own command of a dozen green-garbed men, who guided the travelers through the double gates and to the top of the staircase that led down into Ur-Dormulk.

Garth stopped his mount at that point. The soldiers hurriedly departed and closed the gate behind them, leaving the overman and his companions inside the city, face to face with the monster.

The creature was watching the new arrivals with dull interest showing on its immense and ugly face. It stood a hundred yards or so to the north, at the far side of a block of buildings it had trampled flat, and at the foot of the slope below the wall.

Garth looked out over the city and was appalled by what he saw. The monster had torn up or smashed down a significant portion of the buildings, leaving a crisscrossing maze of rubble. Once or twice, Garth saw, it had broken through the streets and cellars into the crypts, leaving great pits partially filled with the remains of the structures that had stood above them. A dozen fires flickered in the daylight, combining with others less visible to draw thirty or forty lines of smoke across the sky.

He was relieved to see no corpses in the streets and no circling carrion birds; the people of Ur-Dormulk had apparently had sufficient time to escape. Nonetheless, the destruction was startling and saddening; less than a week before, he had stood in the same spot and seen an intact and vigorous city where he now saw ruins.

What made it worse was that his own actions had caused this. He had been responsible for freeing the monster.

He turned back to face his foe. It was still standing and studying him; it had not moved.

He paused, unsure just how he was going to deal with the

creature. He was quite certain that the sword had the raw power necessary to kill the thing, but he had not decided how best that power might be applied.

Probably, he thought, it would be wise to approach the monster on foot. He turned away and dismounted, a bit awkwardly due to Frima's presence on the back of the saddle.

Reminded of the Dûsarran's existence, he considered what to do with her and decided to leave her where she was, astride Koros. The warbeast was the best protection she could possibly have, short of Garth himself.

He glanced up at her; she sat motionlessly and stared back, her lips drawn tight. The hurried, high-speed trip from Skelleth had told on her, Garth was sure; she was obviously tired, but still determined. She said nothing.

Garth shrugged and looked about; he realized for the first time that the Forgotten King was not close at hand. Startled, he spotted the old man at the foot of the steps, walking calmly down the avenue and into the shattered heart of the city.

The overman stared after him for a moment, then turned away. The old man could take care of himself; it was not Garth's concern if he went off on his own. Garth reached up and pulled the Sword of Bheleu from where it had been strapped onto the warbeast's harness, along Koros' flank.

Immediately the blade flared up into a bright white glow, and the red gem in the hilt dripped crimson fire; Garth felt a surge of joyous strength, of riotous enthusiasm and vigor. He had not been wholly free of the sword during the journey, but now its power washed over him unhindered. He threw his head back and roared with laughter. The King, Saram's widow, and the warbeast were all forgotten; nothing mattered but the sword, its power, and his intended target.

Frima watched the blazing sword with apprehension; she was exhausted from the ride, still dazed with the shock of her husband's death, and slightly nauseated, but alert enough to recognize the danger the weapon represented. She slid to the front of the saddle and leaned forward, ready to command Koros to carry her to safety, should Garth appear to be running amok.

On the city's ramparts, struggling to maintain the warding spells that kept the monster from climbing up the slope and smashing the wall, Chalkara and Shandiph were suddenly startled by a vivid flash of white light somewhere off to their left. As they glanced at each other in surprise, the sound of inhuman laughter reached them.

"What's that?" Chalkara asked.

"I don't have any idea," Shandiph replied. "I think we had better investigate."

Hesitantly, Chalkara nodded in agreement. The two abandoned the pentangle they had etched in glowing blue on the stone of the battlements and leaned out between the nearest merlons.

Garth, or whatever was using Garth's body, saw them but paid no attention; he was interested only in the monster.

Frima glimpsed a lock of Chalkara's hair as it blew out from the wall for a moment, but mistook it for a military banner accidentally left flying.

The creature itself stood motionless, as if hypnotized, watching the overman with the glowing sword march diagonally down the steps toward it. It seemed unaware of the two wizards who had done so much to thwart it.

When Garth judged that he was close enough, standing on level ground not far from the bottom step and perhaps a dozen yards from the monster's gigantic feet, he raised the sword, gathered his will and the sword's energy, and sent flame ravening forth.

The glare blinded the wizards temporarily; they moved cautiously back, feeling their way, blinking and trying to restore their vision.

Frima, too, blinked and turned her head aside, but could not retreat out of sight so easily. She was farther away and had not been looking directly at the sword; when the initial flare had faded somewhat, she looked back, peering between two close-set fingers, and watched.

The first burst of fire caught the monster full in the chest and splashed upward around its chin; any sound it might have made was lost in the roar of the flames.

Frima, squinting, could see little detail, but it seemed to her that the flame was not so much burning anything as it was washing away the monster's flesh, like a spray of water washing away mud. Swirls of fire spattered in every direction, setting the air shimmering with heat and creating howling, fiery whirl-winds that seemed to pull and tear at the monster's limbs.

The creature clutched at its chest, and the flame swept across its claws, scorching away the talons, melting away their substance and leaving bare bone.

The monster staggered, leaned forward, but did not fall; it was as if the torrent of pale fire pouring from the sword were supporting the leviathan even as it destroyed it.

Its eyes had lost their glowing appearance at the first flash of the sword's power, paling in comparison to the weapon's glare, and now, as Frima watched, the yellow orbs glazed over. The monster was obviously dying, but could not fall.

The flames subsided for an instant, and Frima saw that the creature's lower jaw had been stripped clean of its flesh, leaving gleaming bone that shone white in the sword's bleached, colorless light. No blood or ichor flowed; the heat had cauterized wherever the fire touched.

The girl shuddered at the thought of the pain the thing must be feeling, if it were mortal enough to feel pain at all; her stomach twisted in empathy. Then, as she watched, the behemoth finally fell, not so much forward as into itself, the neck collapsing, the skull sliding down into the cavity where its chest had once been.

She turned away, sickened, while Garth continued to spew forth the sword's destructive fury, stripping meat from bone, wiping the monster out of existence.

Frima closed her eyes against the light and refused to look back. Worn out by the long ride and the ghastly events that had befallen her, she dozed fitfully, leaning forward on the warbeast's neck, her gaze averted and her eyes closed.

On the city ramparts, it was several minutes after the initial flash before the two wizards could see again, and even then they dared not return to their earlier vantage point, for the white glow brightened and dimmed erratically as Garth wielded the sword.

When at last the light died away completely, Chalkara advanced cautiously to the break, motioning for Shandiph to stay where he was.

Although the light was gone, she was almost blinded anew by flying dust; a fine gray powder was being whipped about by a small but powerful whirlwind, forcing her to turn away and wipe her eyes clear with a corner of her sleeve.

She looked at the residue that clung to the fabric; it was white ash.

Wary this time, she again approached the opening and leaned out, squinting to protect her eyes.

She saw no sign of the monster. The whirlwind was dying down, and the swirling cloud of ash that it carried was slowly subsiding. Blinking, her eyes watering painfully, Chalkara looked down to see what remained of the overman and where the monster's trail led.

Garth was still where she had last seen him, but rather than standing with the glowing sword raised, he was kneeling, leaning heavily on the hilt of a sword that Chalkara did not recognize at first as being the same weapon. This sword was black, from the obsidianlike stone in its pommel to the midpoint of its tarnished blade; the remainder of the blade, from midpoint to tip, was buried in a mound of debris that held the weapon upright. The overman's arms were draped across the quillons, his eyes half-closed, his mouth half-open; a perfect portrait of exhaustion.

Where the monster had stood was only the seething ash; Chalkara stared at it, puzzled. As the cloud sank, something white protruded from its heart, and the wizard realized with a shock that it was the end of an immense thighbone.

Fascinated and repulsed, Chalkara watched as the dust cloud sank down to nothing, revealing a pile of dry, white bones, half-buried in ash, that were obviously all that remained of the leviathan that had terrorized the city. The upper portion of the skull stared with empty sockets at the afternoon sky from atop the heap, a few of the longer bones leaning up against it; with the great teeth buried in ash, and the broken-tipped horn lost in a tangle of ribs, it seemed almost pitiable.

"Shandi," she called.

The older wizard joined her and stared down, as fascinated as she.

"I think we should leave," she said.

He didn't answer.

"I think we should get out of Ur-Dormulk and not let anything stop us this time. We should get out of here and keep away from anywhere else Garth is likely to be."

Shandiph nodded, blinking away an errant flake of ash.

"We can visit Kholis, but I think we should keep going— head south, perhaps. Maybe to Yesh. They worship different gods in Yesh. Maybe Bheleu has no power there."

"The gods are the gods, Chala; only their names change."

"How do you know that? It's worth trying, isn't it?"

"Yes, it's worth trying. You're right. It's certainly better than staying here; I've been in one place too long. It's time I wandered again."

"It's time we both wandered. I don't think I care to be Chalkara of Kholis anymore; I don't think it's safe. Chalkara the Wanderer sounds better."

Shandiph nodded again. He did not believe that anywhere was safe, but thought better of saying so.

CHAPTER TWENTY

Garth was not aware of having lost consciousness, but he realized from the altered light that he must have. It had been shortly after noon when he had attacked the monster, with the sun bright overhead, and now the sun was in the west, the shadows as long as the things that cast them. He had been standing, and now he knelt, leaning upon something. The sword had been hot in his hands, and now his hands hung empty, the palms stinging with mild burns. The pain reminded him of the various injuries he had received during his first visit to Ur-Dormulk, and he realized they were gone; he had forgotten until now that the Sword of Bheleu had healing properties as well as destructive ones.

He blinked and leaned back, off whatever had been supporting him. He felt drained, but managed to rise to his feet only through a concerted effort. Once he was upright he looked about, trying to assess his situation.

He had been draped across the hilt of the Sword of Bheleu, which was burned black and thrust two feet or so into a pile of dirt and ash. He stood now in a wide circle that had been blasted flat and carpeted with fine gray ash, extending from the bottommost step of the climb to the wall out across most of a city block. Its even surface was broken by three things: himself, the mound that held the sword, and a great heap of ash and bone that sprawled across the farther side, directly in front of him.

The bones were unbelievably large; had he never seen the monster whence they came, he would have been certain that they were fakes made of stone or plaster. A thighbone that leaned up against the half-buried skull was taller than he, and as thick through as he was in full padded armor.

Whatever else they might be, the bones were clear proof that he had succeeded in the task he had set himself. The monster was destroyed.

Furthermore, he was free of the Sword of Bheleu, and this without the Forgotten King's intervention. Destroying the leaviathan had at last burned out the sword's power—though only temporarily, he was sure. Even now he thought he could see a faint stirring in the black gem, a distant flickering of dull red.

He was not sure whether he wanted to keep the sword or not; he stepped back out of easy reach to consider the matter.

He still intended to take his vengeance upon the cult of Aghad, and it was undeniable that the sword would be useful against the god's followers—but it was also true that the weapon had a continuing influence on his thoughts and behavior, despite Bheleu's acceptance of his terms. He did not know whether the god was attempting to deceive him or was unable to prevent the effects, but he was quite certain that it had been the god of destruction, and not Garth himself, who had wanted to go walking off through the ruins in Skelleth, blasting everything in sight, while the monster trampled Ur-Dormulk. He was convinced that the god had influenced his thinking and his actions, and he did not like that idea.

He stood a few steps away, at the edge of the flattened circle, staring at the sooty sword and trying to decide what he should do. A faint rustling attracted his attention.

Startled, he turned to see the Forgotten King standing three paces away on the worn stone pavement of the nearest street. The old man's tattered yellow mantle flapped in the damp breeze that blew from the lakes, his cowl pulled well forward about his face, a bundle wrapped in black silk beneath his right arm.

The bundle caught the overman's attention immediately.

The Book of Silence had not been wrapped up, and this thing was irregularly shaped and larger than the neat rectangle the book alone would form.

"What's that?" he asked.

The Forgotten King ignored his question and stood watching.

Garth glanced back at the Sword of Bheleu and then at the bundle again.

"What have you got under your arm?" he asked. He had a suspicion that he knew what it was, and a cold knot of dismay formed within him.

"Are you done with my sword?" the old man asked. His awful voice seemed to blend with the wind that stirred in the rubble, but that made it no less horrible.

Without meaning to, Garth replied, "No!" He paused; the King gazed calmly, expectantly, at him out of his shaded and invisible eyes.

Garth looked away, at the heap of bones, at the sword itself, at the devastated cityscape and the high slope that led to the city wall. He saw no cheer anywhere, only destruction or failed protections. The monster's release and its death had both been his responsibility, and he felt sickened by the resulting chaos. He did not want to allow more of the same, but he was unsure how best he might prevent it.

The dangers of taking up the sword again were obvious; he had lived with that before. He had forgotten in his years of freedom what the hold and the power of the sword were like; he knew now that he would never be able to restrain completely Bheleu's personality while he drew upon the god's power, and that he could not carry the sword without wielding it.

On the other hand, he did not want the King to have the sword. He was certain it was necessary to the magic the old man planned, magic that, Garth was sure, would bring on the Fifteenth Age and spread death thoughout the world, even if it did not actually bring time to an end. Garth tended to think that the spell would destroy the world itself. Therefore, as long as Garth kept the sword away from the King, he was preventing such a disaster—but would instead find himself compelled into destructive acts of his own on a lesser scale.

He remembered that he had previously excused himself for

bringing the old man the Book of Silence on the grounds that the King would not have the sword or the Pallid Mask and would therefore be unable to bring about the Age of Death— yet now that bundle was tucked under the King's arm, and Garth was sure of what it held.

That, he was certain, was the Pallid Mask. The chosen of the god of death had reclaimed his master's totem.

To give that person the Sword of Bheleu as well would be to give him all the power and every tool he might need. That was obviously unconscionable. Arriving at that conclusion, Garth started to reach for the sword.

He paused with his arm outstretched. Could he be sure he was doing the right thing? He was acting on a series of assumptions and deductions. He had no objective proof that the Forgotten King intended to destroy the world and needed only these three items to accomplish that goal.

He quickly reviewed what he knew. The King had admitted that his magic would cause many deaths. Further, the old man had expressed interest in the Sword of Bheleu. Garth did not know that the sword was actually a necessary component of the King's great magic, but it seemed almost certain. He knew that the King was the chosen of The God Whose Name Is Not Spoken, of Death incarnate. He knew that the wizards said that the next age, the Fifteenth Age, was to be dominated by the Final God. He knew that it was said that the Forgotten King could die only at the end of time, and that the old man said he wanted to die.

It all added up. Garth still could not *know* that he was right, but he made his decision. A period of such destruction as the Sword of Bheleu might cause, even as much as thirty years of it, could not possibly be worse than the end of time itself and the accompanying extinction of all life. He grasped the hilt of the sword.

The gem flared up redly, and the blade seemed to move of its own volition as it slid from the heap of debris. White light flashed, and the soot that had coated it vanished, leaving the blade gleaming silver, the jewel glowing the color of fresh blood. A wave of heat swept over the overman.

The Forgotten King watched silently, and the initial burst of warmth and bloodlust passed away quickly beneath his cold stare. Garth stared back, the sword in his hands. He knew that Bheleu had again tried to assert himself, but had backed down before the threat of the King's power. Garth realized that he could control the sword only as long as he remained near the King, keeping that threat viable. Were he to become separated from the old man, Bheleu would be able to dominate him easily.

He was, he saw, trapped, worse than he had ever been before. He needed to keep the sword to prevent the King from obtaining it, yet he also needed to remain near the King to prevent the sword from controlling him completely. He could not be sure that he would be able to prevent the King from taking the sword away from him, should the old man ever choose to exert his own considerable power, now augmented by both the Book of Silence and the Pallid Mask.

What was perhaps as disheartening as the situation itself was the knowledge that Garth had brought it on himself. He had chosen to go to Dûsarra and bring back the Sword of Bheleu. He had chosen to go to Ur-Dormulk and fetch the Book of Silence. He had willingly given the King the book, which had made it possible for the old man to move freely and get the Pallid Mask for himself.

Now Garth found himself in a precarious balance between the power of Bheleu and the power of the King, each determined to wreak havoc, with only Garth's refusal to cooperate preventing the unleashing of those powers.

Furthermore, he did not know if he could maintain that balance forever. In fact, he realized that he definitely could not, unless Bheleu, like The God Whose Name Is Not Spoken, bestowed immortality upon his chosen agent.

That was a possibility, as the god did seem to make Garth invincible and invulnerable, but it was not really an appealing prospect. Surely, the longer he held the sword, the greater Bheleu's control would become. The god was insidious.

Garth stared at the blade before him and understood that he was doomed. He could see no way out of his predicament, and if the theology of the humans was correct, insofar as he understood it, then there *was* no way out, no possible solution. His end, and the end of the world, were foreordained and could be no more than delayed—and then only for as long as he was willing to wield the Sword of Bheleu. Even a miracle would

not change the terrible circumstances, for miracles were sent
by the gods, and the most powerful of the gods were those
who had trapped him. Ever since he had first consulted the Wise
Women of Ordunin in his quest for eternal fame, he had been
guided toward this hopeless situation; and furthermore, he realized, the Wise Women had known it. He recalled the reluctance Ao had displayed so long ago, when first she told him
of the Forgotten King. Surely that had been because she had
known what would, in the end, result.

He had not thought this through before, had not considered
the long-term consequences of the events that surrounded and
involved him. Now that he did, anger flared up within him.

He made a brief, desultory attempt to suppress it, knowing
that it was as much Bheleu's doing as his own, but without
success. He found himself furious, eager to lash out at something. The gods had brought him to this—Bheleu, Aghad, the
Final God, and the other Lords of Dûs—but there was no way
he could strike directly at any of them. The Forgotten King,
too, had worked to enmesh him in the workings of destiny, to
drive him and the world to destruction. He lifted the sword
high and strode toward the old man, his anger mounting.

The King stood his ground as the overman approached, and
even through the cloud of rage, Garth remembered his previous
attempt to kill the old man with the Sword of Bheleu. He had
been totally unable to harm him.

Still, as his fury grew, he found it impossible to believe
that a weapon that could reduce so vast a monster to ash and
bone could not kill a scrawny human. He slashed out viciously,
aiming for the old man's throat.

The blade left a trail of sparks. Despite Garth's efforts to
keep it on course, it sheered wildly upward, skimming over
the Forgotten King's head.

Frustrated, Garth spun it back and struck again, this time
slanting downward. Again the sword refused to cooperate,
curving down and to the side, veering away from the old man
without touching him.

Garth growled.

"Stop it, Garth," the old man said. "I am not so easily
destroyed as Dhazh. You cannot do it like that."

The overman fell silent and lowered the sword, his red eyes

flat and dead with rage. He could not kill the King any more than he could strike at the gods.

Perhaps he could strike at one god, though; not directly, of course, but through his followers. He struggled to think, but his mind seemed hazy and slow. He had already slaughtered the cult of Bheleu, when first he took the sword, and The God Whose Name Is Not Spoken had no servants except the King and one or two decrepit priests. But the cult of Aghad still flourished, and more than any other had driven him into his current predicament. He had sworn vengeance upon that god's worshippers, sworn to destroy them. Somewhere in Ur-Dormulk was a temple dedicated to Aghad, he remembered; he looked out across the battered city.

"Where is it?" he muttered, half to himself.

"What?" The Forgotten King's question was calm and indifferent.

"Where is the temple of Aghad?"

"The center of the cult is in Dûsarra."

"They have a temple here, in Ur-Dormulk. Where is it?"

"It is unimportant."

"Where is it?" Garth's tone was flat and dangerous. The King scarcely needed to beware of the overman's anger, but he chose not to argue further.

"I will show you," he replied. He turned and walked down the street.

Garth followed him through the ruins, through sections where buildings stood relatively undamaged, past smoking pits that had once been cellars or crypts, until the pair arrived in front of a low stone structure tucked up against one of the great outcroppings of rock that studded the city.

The King stopped and gestured at the nondescript building.

"This is it?" Garth asked. The temple was nothing like the one he had robbed in Dûsarra. There was no metal gate, no courtyard with poisoned fountain, no names etched in the stone walls, but a simple single storey of weathered granite, with a few narrow windows that peered out, black and empty, upon the deserted streets. The windows flanked a heavy wooden door.

The King said nothing, but nodded once.

Reassured, his anger driving away any lingering doubts,

Garth marched up to the entrance and swung the sword against it.

The heavy wooden door burst outward in a shower of splinters and dust, with a sound like sudden thunder.

Garth stepped through into a small, bare anteroom and looked about in the unlit gloom. Three other doors led further into the depths of the building; he chose one at random and smashed it down with the sword, sending shards rattling against the walls on all sides.

Beyond lay a small room hung in dark red and richly carpeted in soft gray; near the far wall stood a metal altar, and upon the altar lay a woman's corpse, partially disemboweled. Garth stepped closer.

A curtain plummeted down before him; with a growl, Garth hacked it apart in time to see the altar sink into the floor, taking the corpse with it.

This sort of mechanical trickery was similar, indeed almost identical, to what he had encountered in Dûsarra. Any further doubts he might have had were dispelled by his final glimpse of the dead body.

Runes had been carved into the woman's chest, four runes, spelling out AGHAD.

Satisfied that he had found the right place, Garth lashed out with the sword and blasted apart the sliding stone that moved into place to hide the sunken altar and its grisly burden. Without bothering to consider that the victim might deserve better, he then sent a burst of white flame that utterly consumed the corpse, leaving a thin layer of ash. That done, he set about serious destruction, shattering the ceiling and the roof beyond and working his way down the walls.

When at last he was satisfied that the job was done, he stood at the bottom of a great pit, amid a heap of rubble, where no stone larger than a man's body remained and no stone stood intact upon another. He had found and destroyed hundreds of concealed machines and mechanisms, a dozen or so hidden bodies, a handful of dangerous beasts, and a vast armory equipped with everything from siege engines to endless shelves of varied poisons. The single floor aboveground had stood atop three levels of cellars and dungeons that extended out beneath the buildings on both sides and across the street into the house opposite.

Half a dozen doors led from the cellars into the crypts, but he did not bother to investigate those after blowing the doors themselves apart. He knew, even in his rage, that there was no point in destroying the entire system of crypts, and that to do so would mean destroying the entire city he had slain Dhazh to save. He drew the line at the point where the architecture and the texture of the stone changed, revealing the difference between the ancient buried tunnels and the far newer temple built to take advantage of them.

Nowhere in the entire structure were there any living humans.

In Dûsarra, Haggat watched, worried, as the temple in Ur-Dormulk crumbled. He was unable to focus his scrying glass on the overman or the sword and could not watch the destruction directly as a result, but he was able to see the remains. It distressed him to see so powerful an outpost of the cult, second only to its heart in Dûsarra, reduced so quickly to worthless rubble, but he knew he could do nothing to stop the demolition.

He could, however, save the cultists who had used the shrine. The overman's next step, obviously, would be to pick the Aghadites out of the crowd that waited outside the city gates and kill them; Haggat did not want that to happen. He abandoned the scrying glass for the moment, to order his disciples to send a message of warning.

When Garth climbed out of the hole he had made, he found the Forgotten King waiting, motionless, in the street.

"Are there any Aghadites in the city?" the overman demanded.

"No," the old man replied.

Garth was glad of that; he had not relished the thought of hunting them down in their hiding places, one by one. Far easier and more satisfying to blast the lot of them at once! He would divide them out from the crowd as the citizens were readmitted to the city, standing at the gate and stopping them as they passed. He did not consider how he would recognize them; he was sure he would manage it. The old man was apparently in a cooperative mood, having led him to the temple and now having answered his question directly; perhaps he would be willing to point them out.

There would be time for that later. His next step was to return to the gate and arrange with the authorities for permission to dispose of the Aghadites. It seemed a very minor demand to make in exchange for slaying the monster that had done so much damage to their city.

The sun was down, and Garth lighted the way back to the gate with the glow from the Sword of Bheleu. Fires still flickered in the distance, but in a city so largely built of stone, most were rapidly dying out.

Frima and Koros still waited atop the stairs at the gate, just as Garth had left them, save that Koros was now asleep and Frima awake. As a result of her rest, awkward as it had been to sleep in the saddle, she was alert and eager to pursue her vengeance against the worshippers of Aghad.

She had awakened feeling ill shortly before; after she had vomited, she had felt somewhat better and had noticed that Garth was missing. She had not been seriously concerned by his absence; she knew he would return for Koros, if for nothing else, and she had correctly concluded that he had gone in search of their common foe.

"Are there Aghadites in this city?" she asked as Garth and the Forgotten King climbed the last few steps.

"No," the overman replied. "But there are many, I am sure, in the crowd outside the gates. I have just destroyed their temple here; now we must search them out from the other humans."

"No," the old man said unexpectedly. "They have fled."

"What?" Garth demanded. Frima stared silently.

"They are gone."

"They can't be," Garth insisted. "I have to kill them."

"They were warned magically and have fled."

"Are you sure?" Frima asked.

The King nodded.

"They're really gone? You swear it?" she persisted.

The King nodded again.

"Where did they go?" Garth asked.

The old man shrugged.

"To Dûsarra, perhaps?" Garth guessed.

The old man shrugged again.

"To Dûsarra, then," Garth said. Frima nodded agreement.

The conversation had awakened the warbeast; now, at the overman's urging, it turned and followed its master out the city gate and into the torchlit night beyond, where the people of Ur-Dormulk waited to reclaim their city.

CHAPTER TWENTY-ONE

Garth and his companions stayed the night on the hillside by the gate, ignoring a thin drizzle that began around midnight. They kept a careful watch on the line of men, women, and children moving slowly back into the city, while guards stood nearby. A few reports came in of people who had vanished around sunset, wandering off in one direction or another, confirming the Forgotten King's claim that the Aghadites had been warned of their danger. The soldiers had generally not tried to prevent these people from crossing the perimeter; that was not what they had been posted for. Their orders were to keep dangers out, not to keep their own people in, and if a score or perhaps two dozen had chosen to depart for destinations unknown, it was no part of a soldier's duty to stop them. Garth, angry as he was at the escape of the Aghadites, had to admit that that was reasonable.

He and Frima, as well as large numbers of guardsmen, observed the whole re-entry operation, and nowhere did Garth see the dark red robes of the worshippers of Aghad. He knew, of course, that the cultists might well be disguised and that he had no reliable means of spotting them in the horde of muddy, bedraggled citizens who wound their way up the hill and through the gates. Still, he was sure that most, if not all, of those people reported missing had been the god's followers in Ur-Dormulk.

Around dawn, it was noticed that the two wizards could not be found. Garth wondered briefly if they might have been Aghadites, or whether they might have been devoured by the monster the Forgotten King called Dhazh, or whether they were simply lost somewhere. Eventually he decided that the matter did not concern him.

The overlord and his court had gathered in one particular area of the hillside and established themselves in charge of the return to the city, giving orders to the military and generally taking credit for the organization soldiers had imposed. This kept them busy running about, looking very out of place wearing their gaudy robes in the rain and mud. It seemed to Garth that such bright attire would look out of place anywhere other than in a palace—which might well have been exactly what was intended.

Despite the disappearance of the wizards, there were enough witnesses, and enough evidence, to establish to the satisfaction of all concerned that Garth had, indeed, been responsible for the monster's destruction. The overlord's courtiers made at least a pretense of gratitude, confused and wet as they were, and their orders enabled the overman's little party to make a good breakfast from stocks of food brought out of the city by the more foresighted refugees. A fat sheep was found to feed the warbeast, and a few supplies were laid in for their coming journey, all at the city's expense. Someone even managed to dig up a sheath large enough to hold the Sword of Bheleu from an obscure armory in the city wall, and Garth strapped the weapon on his back rather than continuing to carry it naked in his hand.

Finally, at midmorning, when Garth was convinced that it would do no good to watch the remaining population return to the ruined city, he and his party gathered themselves together and departed for Dûsarra.

By then the hillside was almost free of humanity, but had been left a littered expanse of churned mud, where makeshift tents flapped forlornly in the warm breeze.

Garth found himself alternately slipping and sinking in the muck, and rather than struggle on, he climbed astride Koros. The warbeast did not seem to notice the mud at all, and the Forgotten King walked on as smoothly and tirelessly as the beast. Frima had been in the saddle to begin with and stayed there, perched behind the overman.

Garth wondered idly for a moment how soon and how well the people of Ur-Dormulk would rebuild their homes. He doubted that any of them had ever had any experience in building; he had seen no structure in all the city that could have been less than several centuries old.

It occurred to him that it might not matter for long whether they rebuilt or not. If the world were to end, it would make little difference if the citizens of Ur-Dormulk died in the streets or beneath new roofs.

With that thought, his attention returned to his own situation, to the task that lay before him, and the presence and nature of the Forgotten King. He glared at the old man, without effect, and wished that he had never met him.

From Ur-Dormulk their route led southwest along the foothills, then west across a pass in the mountains into the land of Nekutta, across a broad valley, around the southern end of another mountain range, and across another plain to the foothills of a third mountain range, this last one volcanic. There, perched on the side of a volcano, stood the black-walled city of Dûsarra, where the cult of Aghad was centered.

Dûsarra's name meant "gathering place of the dark gods," which was a fair description; each of the seven Lords of Dûs, despised elsewhere for the most part, had a major shrine there, serving as the center of his or her cult. In other lands the Dûs were considered to be wholly evil, and their worship an aberration, at best—though the more decadent and tolerant permitted that worship to continue, as it had in Ur-Dormulk.

In Dûsarra the dark gods were dominant; no other deities were worshipped, as far as Garth had been able to learn during his stay there or in discussions with Frima in the subsequent months, save for a few minor affiliated gods, such as Bheleu's son Koros, god of war, or Tema's servant Mei, goddess of the moon.

Elsewhere, people would have said that since the Lords of Dûs were evil, a society dedicated to them must also be evil and must therefore quickly destroy itself, by the very nature of evil. Yet Dûsarra had survived for centuries, perhaps millennia. Garth was not sure how the Dûsarrans had managed it.

Garth's previous visit had brought fire and plague upon them, and at last report, the city was in a state of chaos; yet the cult of Aghad remained active. Garth was not sure how to explain that, either—but he intended to put a stop to it.

From Ur-Dormulk, however, the journey to Dûsarra would require at least ten days.

It occurred to him that the Aghadites, with their teleporting magic, could cover the distance almost instantly and that the Forgotten King had pronounced their spells to be trivial. Did that mean, then, that the Sword of Bheleu, or the Book of Silence, or the Pallid Mask, or perhaps the King's own personal magic might serve the same purpose?

"King," he demanded without preamble, "can you transport us more quickly?"

The old man did not trouble himself to look up, but merely shook his head negatively.

Garth was not satisfied by that reply. It did not seem reasonable that this party should have such great magical power at their disposal, yet be unable to perform a feat the Aghadites managed with far feebler resources.

He recalled that the King had been confined to Skelleth for centuries and wondered if perhaps the old man wanted to see something of the world before attempting to destroy it and himself. The King was not making any visible effort to study the scenery, marching on steadily without turning his head, but it was a possibility.

Perhaps the powers they carried were too specialized, too strongly dedicated to death and destruction.

Whatever the reason, Garth regretted the delay; it meant that much more time for the cultists to strike against his family and surviving friends. Galt, back in Skelleth, was almost certainly in danger, as well as Myrith and Lurith and Garth's children.

He could think of no way to compel the Forgotten King or anyone else to speed them magically on their way, however, and could merely plot, plan, and worry as Koros strode onward into the mountains.

Behind him, Frima was slowly recovering from the shock of Saram's death. Her initial reaction had been wordless grief, which Garth had transformed into a cold, bitter hatred and a driving need for revenge with the words he had spoken to her in the market. Hatred and anger, however, had to be sustained by something outside oneself in order to dominate one's thoughts over an extended period of time. Had she stayed in Skelleth, Frima would have been reminded repeatedly of Saram's murder by the simple fact of his absence, by the empty side of her bed, by the unused or perhaps usurped baronial seat in the hall, where someone else might be giving orders, or merely by the old familiar places where she had seen him so often and the ordinary objects he had handled so frequently.

Here, though, as she clung to Garth with her arms and to Koros with her legs, riding for days on end through strange country and suffering from a vague illness that came and went, those reminders were lacking.

The sight of Saram's murderers, or any sign of their presence, would have served to sustain her craving for vengeance, but the mountains they crossed, and the plain beyond, were unmarked by any trace of Aghad or his followers. They passed small farms, stone cottages, and other human habitations, but nothing that could stir her dwindling fury. Instead, she found herself distracted by new sights and experiences.

This had begun with the burning of Dhazh. Seeing that had provided a countershock to Saram's death; it had been the first thing she thought about other than death and revenge since she had seen her husband's mutilated corpse.

Now, as she rode behind the overman across the rolling countryside of eastern Nekutta, she was able to think clearly again, her thoughts no longer smothered beneath an unbearable load of grief and rage. For the first time, she began to consider her situation now that Saram was dead.

Was she still the Baroness of Skelleth? She had no idea. She had held the title only by virtue of being Saram's consort, but since both he and his predecessor had died with no other heirs known, that claim might be sufficient to entitle her to rule in her own name. Had the stillborn son she bore almost two years earlier lived, he would have been the new Baron, and she the dowager and probable regent—but he had not lived. Nothing of Saram lived on; he had had no brothers, no sisters, no living family at all. Even his friends had mostly perished in the sacking of Skelleth three years ago.

That thought upset her anew, that there should be nothing left of the man she had loved, and she reaffirmed her vow of vengeance.

It was not fitting, she thought, that so fine a man should die so young and with no offspring—though it occurred to her that she had not known just how old he was. Older than she, certainly. Nor could Frima be certain that he had not sired children; she had not been his first woman, she knew, though she was his only wife.

Still, he had no legitimate heir—and she had no child to ease her loneliness.

She remembered her recurring illness and wondered if she might be wrong about that, but she suppressed the thought as mere wishful thinking. She did not want to fill herself with false hopes, and her bouts of nausea were far more likely to be caused by grief, or the rigors of travel, than by pregnancy.

Perhaps she should have stayed in Skelleth and tried to learn whether Saram had children whom she might claim and raise as her own. She would never have asked so improper a question while Saram lived, of course, but it occurred to her that Garth, who had known Saram before she met him, might know something. She inquired timidly, "Garth?"

The overman did not answer, but glanced back.

"Did Saram have a lover before I met him?"

Garth shrugged. "I don't know," he said. "I never saw any evidence of one." He turned his attention forward again, to the trail ahead, wondering what quirk had brought Frima to be questioning her dead husband's past at this late date. It was an almost-welcome distraction from his own gloomy, repetitious thoughts, which ran over and over again along the same dead-end paths, considering ways out of his predicament that he already knew would not work.

Frima reminded herself that she was not totally alone; she had friends, or at least acquaintances, back in Skelleth, and she was sure that they would not desert her if she returned there. She had Garth, who had agreed to help her in her revenge and who still seemed to feel some obligation toward her from earlier events. She had her father and siblings, perhaps, though she could not be sure that any of them had survived. She had not thought much about them in almost three years, not even long enough to send them a message reporting her own survival and her improved estate as the Baroness of Skelleth, but surely, if they lived, they would welcome her back.

She felt suddenly guilty that she had never told them that she was still alive. They must, she realized, believe that she had died on Sai's altar long ago—unless her father or brother had been in the mob in the marketplace when Garth slew the high priest of Aghad. They would have seen her there and known she still lived, but would have no idea what had become of her after she fled the city.

Of course, if they had been present, they might well have been among the first to contract the White Death, which was invariably fatal. And if the plague had not killed them, the fires she herself had set, and the chaos that ensued, might well have caught them.

Her younger sisters would have been safe at home, she was sure—but the fires and plague and rioting might have found them even there. And if their father and brother had died, how would they have survived? Most probably they, like herself, would have wound up on a sacrificial altar somewhere—but without a strange overman to rescue them.

She was suddenly impatient to see Dûsarra again, to discover how much the stories of its destruction had exaggerated. She wanted to know whether her father, her brother, and her two sisters still lived. What remained of her father's shop? Were any of her old friends still there? Was the cult of Tema still active? She remembered the priestess Shirrayth, who had tried to teach Frima some of the mysteries of the goddess in hopes of recruiting her as an acolyte, and wondered what had become of her. She remembered the magnificent stone idol in the temple's domed chamber, which had awed and comforted her as a child, and longed to see it again. She was certain that it must still be intact; the goddess would protect her own image, Frima was sure of that.

She remembered how she had been consoled by a priest— she had never known his name—after her mother's death and how she had prayed to Tema and sensed her presence in the night sky in response. The knowledge that the goddess watched over her followers had eased Frima's mind many times when she was young, yet during her stay in Skelleth she had neglected her religion completely.

She tried to excuse herself on the grounds that Tema was a Dûsarran deity, not to be found in strange eastern lands, but she knew that for the lie it was. Tema was the goddess of night, and the night came everywhere, not just to Dûsarra.

She had not kept up her childhood faith; she had lived mostly by day, for convenience, since the people of Skelleth, unlike her own, were wholly diurnal. She had relinquished her ties to the night.

That was not right.

Had she remained steadfast, Frima thought, perhaps Tema might have warned her, or protected Saram somehow, or turned away Aghad's followers—or at the very least, eased the pain and grief.

Perhaps the goddess had watched over her family and she would find her father and siblings waiting for her in the tinker's shop, untouched by the catastrophes that had struck the city. They, surely, had remained faithful.

No, she told herself, that was going too far, believing that anyone who worshipped Tema would be preserved against the wrath of the other gods—for it was P'hul and Bheleu who had caused Dûsarra's suffering, at Garth's behest. Tema was the least of the seven Lords of Dûs, unable to stand against any of her six siblings. If P'hul's plague, or Bheleu's flames, or the machinations of Aghad had been directed against Frima's family, then they surely would have died. She could only hope that they had been fortunate.

It would do no good to pray to Tema that they had been spared, for not even the gods could alter the past, except perhaps for the being called Dagha, who had created the gods themselves. If her family still lived, she would find them when she reached Dûsarra; until then, it would do no good to worry about them.

Nonetheless, she worried.

She wanted them to be alive, for there to be someone she could go to, now that Saram was dead. She wanted to return to the comforts of her childhood, to the relative security she had known before her kidnapping.

With that in mind, as the party was coming within sight of

Nekutta's central mountain range, she leaned forward and asked Garth, "Don't you think we should travel by night?"

The overman glanced back at her and asked, "Why?"

"Wouldn't it be safer?"

The overman looked out across the peaceful landscape of green pastures, grazing cattle, and occasional houses or plowed fields scattered along the roadside. Nothing within sight seemed in the least threatening.

Still, he remembered that reports had reached Skelleth describing wars and other disturbances in Nekutta. He had seen no evidence to support the stories—but caution would do no harm.

So far, the party had been spending long days on the road, traveling on well into the evening every day, and rising again before dawn to get an early start. Garth had no intention of slowing the pace, but he saw no reason not to move the sleeping period from nighttime to day. It might, he thought, provide a small decrease in the chance of danger.

"Old man? Do you have any preference?"

The Forgotten King shook his head and walked on, tirelessly, without looking at the overman. He had no trouble in keeping up with the warbeast. An ordinary man would have been left far behind in a single day, or else would have collapsed from exhaustion, but the King marched stolidly and silently onward, his pace always steady and matching the warbeast's own. It was one more little demonstration of his strangeness, but one that pleased Garth because it meant faster travel.

"Very well, then," Garth said. "Tonight we ride until dawn."

Frima smiled; she was returning to the night, where she belonged.

The habits of years were not so easily broken, however, and she dozed off shortly after midnight, only to be awakened half an hour later by the cessation of movement.

Startled, she opened her eyes and saw that Koros had stopped and was standing motionless in the middle of the road. No inn was in sight, and the eastern sky was still black and strewn with stars.

"What's happening?" she asked.

"Silence!" Garth warned in a low voice.

"Why?" she whispered. "What's happening?"

"I see campfires ahead, where none should be," Garth replied.

Frima lifted herself up on her hands and stared over the overman's shoulder. As he had said, several lights were visible on the hillside ahead of them.

"Couldn't it just be a caravan?" she whispered.

"It could be," Garth admitted, "but I think it is not. Look how many fires there are."

Frima peered into the darkness and tried to count the flickering lights; her hand slipped before she had finished, and she bumped down onto the saddle, losing her place.

She didn't need to finish her count, however; Garth's point was obvious.

"I estimate thirty fires," the overman whispered. "At the least. And assuming ten humans to each, that means three hundred people are camped there. I have never heard of so large a caravan. Raiding parties, however, are often such a size."

"Maybe the caravan set extra fires to scare away bandits," Frima suggested.

Garth did not bother to reply to that.

"What are you going to do about it?" Frima asked.

"I have not decided," he replied.

His first impulse had been to make a detour around the encampment, but the thought of going out of his way, even so briefly, annoyed him. He was tempted to ride straight through, as if nothing were out of the ordinary—and if anyone in the camp tried to stop him, well, the Sword of Bheleu could deal with such interference.

In fact, he thought it might be fun to destroy the camp, whether he was bothered directly or not; after all, the fools had settled themselves on the highway, obstructing traffic, and deserved whatever response travelers might be able to make.

He found himself considering with anticipation just how he would go about it. He might burn down the tents first—assuming there were tents—and then hunt down anyone who got out in time. He would pursue them individually, he decided, and skewer each one on the sword, so that he could watch the blood run up the blade and spatter across the ground.

"Garth?" Frima's voice was worried.

He ignored the girl; nothing she could say would be of interest.

"Garth, the jewel is glowing," she said.

He glanced up and realized that she was correct. The red light that had tinged the edge of his vision had been neither his imagination nor the approach of dawn, but the glow of the gem.

An instant's worry vanished. What did it matter, he asked himself, if the stone were to glow? He had made his bargain with Bheleu, and the god would not dare to interfere with his thoughts. The urge to destroy the camp was entirely his own, he told himself.

All the glow did was remind him of the sword's readiness and waiting power. It occurred to him that he might be able to use it to keep his prey from fleeing. A good thunderstorm would douse the fires and drive the people under shelter, making it more difficult for them to escape his anger. He reached up for the hilt projecting above his shoulder.

"Garth!" Frima said, her voice loud and unsteady.

"Silence, woman!" Garth growled in reply. His hand closed on the sword's grip, and he felt a surge of strength.

"Old man!" Frima called. "Stop him!"

Garth bellowed and tried to draw the sword; Frima pressed up against his back, holding the scabbard down so that he could not pull the blade free.

Enraged, Garth tried to twist away while simultaneously reaching up with both hands to lift the blade out of its sheath hand over hand.

"King! Help!" Frima called.

The glow of the gem suddenly died, and the stone turned black, darker than the night sky above.

Garth stopped instantly; his hands fell, and the sword slid back into place. His irrational anger had vanished, and with it all thought of assaulting whoever blocked their way. He felt as if a haze had cleared from his thoughts, a haze that had been present in varying measure ever since he had picked the Sword of Bheleu up off the table in the back of the King's Inn. Even when the sword had been black with soot and unable to hold him directly, he realized, his thoughts had been tainted and muddied by it. Perhaps the most frightening of the sword's effects was that he was not even aware of its influence until it was broken; it made him believe Bheleu's reactions and emotions to be his own.

Now, though, he was free again, at least for the moment.

"Thank you," he said.

"Bheleu is not to be trusted," the old man's hideous voice rasped from the darkness. "He would have delayed us here for no good reason, and I do not wish to be thus delayed. Further, I prefer your company, poor as it is, to his."

"I won't give you the sword," Garth insisted. He was wary, and his thoughts had not had time to reorder themselves fully, so he stated his position directly to avoid confusion, on either the King's part or his own. The old man had made a longer speech than usual, which was, in Garth's experience, often a sign of trouble. The extra words might be part of a subtle scheme, or a result of the old man's excitement—and anything that excited the Forgotten King was likely to be unpleasant for mere mortals.

"As you please," the King replied.

Garth relaxed very slightly. It could be, he told himself, that the old man had spoken the exact truth and that his motives were just as he said—but why had he bothered to explain them?

Frima did not worry herself about that. "Are you all right?" she asked.

"Yes," Garth answered, though he was not yet completely certain himself.

The party had continued onward as these events had taken place; when Garth had reached for the sword, he had urged Koros forward, and the warbeast had obeyed, undisturbed by the actions of its riders. The Forgotten King had marched alongside. Now, Garth realized, they were drawing near to the most easterly of the campfires; furthermore, they had been shouting at one another.

"Wait," he called softly as he signaled the warbeast to stop.

Koros stopped. Garth looked off to the side and saw no sign of the King's yellow mantle. He looked back, in surprise, wondering where the old man had gone.

Something rustled; he whirled to face forward once again, and found himself looking down the shaft of a spear.

CHAPTER TWENTY-TWO

"An overman!" exclaimed an unfamiliar voice very near at hand—the voice, Garth was sure, of an overman, deeper and more resonant than any human's.

"Who are you?" Garth demanded. He looked up from the spear poised at his throat and saw that it was clutched in double-thumbed hands below a noseless, red-eyed face. Two other figures stood nearby, one of overman size, the other smaller; both held their weapons ready.

"Who do you think we are, idiot?" the smaller figure asked in unmistakably human tones.

"More importantly, stranger, who are you?" the overman with the spear inquired.

Garth considered his situation and decided that he did not care to admit his identity yet. "I'm just a traveler heading west! Why does it concern you?"

"You travel at night?"

Garth shrugged. "Why not? It's cooler. I mean you no harm, whoever you are. If you prefer, I will go around your camp, rather than through it. It matters little to me."

"It may be that you won't be going anywhere for some time," the overman who had not previously spoken remarked.

"Why not? Who are you?"

"Who do you think we are?"

"I don't know," Garth said. "I didn't think there were any overmen in Nekutta. Either I was wrong or you have come here from somewhere else—but I have no idea where or why." This was not exactly true, of course; it did not take much intelligence to guess that the camp was a raiding party from Yprian Coast and that these three had been sent out to investigate the noise on the road.

"We didn't think there were overmen native to Nekutta, either, which is why you still live," the second overman said. "You may be a spy, perhaps a loner hired by some village to direct us away from it—but we have not previously encountered such a thing. Why would humans hire an overman, when surely they know we have both species among us? And I might suspect you to be a scout for one of our rivals, save that we had thought ourselves the most easterly party; why, then, would you be approaching from the east? Did you circle around unseen, and then become careless on the way back? It seems unlikely. Therefore, stranger, we are puzzled, and want to hear your explanation of yourself before we do you any permanent harm."

"And I want to know," the human interjected, "what that thing is you're riding, and who that is behind you."

"The animal is a warbeast," Garth replied, unsure how much of the truth it would be wise to admit. "The girl is Dûsarran and has hired me to escort her home." That story seemed as good as any and certainly more acceptable than the truth. He could not know what attitude this group had toward the cult of Aghad.

"Ah," the second overman said. "And who is this Dûsarran? Who are you, that she should trust you enough to hire you?"

"Her name is Frima, Baroness of Skelleth," Garth answered. He hoped that the title would impress his questioners. He did not care to reveal his own name yet; they might have heard it one way or another. "As for why she should trust me, that is her own concern—but I have been known to her for some time, and my word is good." He felt an uncomfortable twinge at that last statement, knowing it to be less than the truth.

"Skelleth?" the spear-carrier and the human exclaimed in unison.

"I think we've got a real prize here," the overman added.

"Think what a hostage she'll be, if she's really the Baroness!" the human said.

Garth had not considered that. He had assumed that these Yprians would not want to interfere with the friendly relationship between Skelleth and their own land.

"That would not be good for trade," he said.

"That, fool, is the whole point!" the human declared.

The second overman held out a hand, gesturing the human to silence. "I think I understand," he said. "You aren't Yprian, are you?"

"You mean he really *is* Nekuttan?" the human asked, surprised.

"No! Silence!" The overman's hand struck the human's helmet with a dull clunk. Turning back to Garth, he asked, "You're from Eramma?"

"No," Garth replied. "I come from Ordunin, in the Northern Waste."

"Ah, yes. That explains everything."

Annoyed, Garth said, "Perhaps it explains everything to you, but it does not to me."

"No, of course not. Come, then, and I'll explain." He sheathed his sword and held out a hand in friendship.

Hesitantly, the human returned his own sword to its scabbard, while the first overman lowered his spear.

At the second overman's urging, Garth dismounted and led Koros, with Frima still astride, into the camp. There was still no sign of the Forgotten King.

Once inside the circle of light from the nearest fire, Garth was able to get a good look at his captors. As he had thought, they were obviously Yprian, wearing the brightly enameled, flaring helmets and gaudy, enameled armor customary on the Coast.

They were not, however, exactly like the Yprians who had traded in Skelleth. The designs and colors on the armor were different, the accents, he realized, subtly altered.

When they had drawn near the fire, Frima was lifted off the warbeast, and both she and it were placed under polite but thorough guard—though Garth was sure that the Yprians were underestimating the warbeast's strength and that Koros could easily leave anytime it chose.

Garth himself was treated solicitously, led to a comfortable folding stool by the fire, and offered a cup of mulled wine. Wary of drugs, he refused the beverage, but seated himself and waited politely while the other overman made himself comfortable.

When both were settled, the other began his explanation. Garth, upon seeing the differences between this group and those who had come to Skelleth, had already guessed part of it.

The Yprian Coast, it seemed, was not a single united region living at peace with itself, but rather a patchwork of squabbling tribes, some human, some overman, most mixed.

For the last century or two, the situation had been relatively stable; each tribe had its area staked out, and borders were only rarely violated. Raids were not unheard-of, by any means, but full-scale wars were a thing of the past. The tribes traded with one another and formed elaborate networks of allies and trading partners, the better to get what they needed. Goods not obtainable on the Coast were bought from the most southwesterly tribe, the Dyn-Hugris, who traded with Dûsarra, and who were consequently the most powerful of the various groups. The Dyn-Hugris, however, were kept in check by an alliance of half a dozen other fairly large and wealthy tribes in the central part of the region. All in all, there had been a stable balance of power and an acceptable division of the available wealth.

Then, almost simultaneously, two things had occurred to disrupt this situation.

Dûsarra had been stricken by plague, its marketplace and warehouses burned and much of the city evacuated. Trade had collapsed. The Dyn-Hugris lost their power base overnight; their control of the trade routes to Dûsarra was suddenly worthless.

In the east, a party of traders had come through the badlands from Eramma and offered to trade with anyone who was interested. The first tribe they encountered had been little more than a small company of bandits, but the second had been the Chuleras, a large and ambitious group previously limited by their poor location and meager resources.

Now, abruptly, the Chuleras had gold, large amounts of it, and were able to hire mercenaries, bribe allies, and generally assert themselves. They had done so with none of the tact the

Dyn-Hugris had developed over the centuries and were in the process of driving the six Alliance tribes out of their central homelands.

Even without the resources of Dûsarra, the Dyn-Hugris were a formidable enemy, so instead of retreating westward, the six tribes had come south, making the hard trek over the mountains, looking for new homes, new lands, and new wealth.

The Dyn-Hugris, not to be outdone, had sent armies south along their now-useless trade routes.

The old alliances had collapsed under the new strains; now the six tribes, and the Dyn-Hugris as well, were all rivals, gobbling up as much of Nekutta as they could. It had been a pleasant surprise to find it all so poorly defended. Usually a company of Yprians could take over as much land as they pleased by simply moving in and declaring themselves the owners. The local inhabitants, mostly farmers, rarely dared protest.

Conquest was so easy, in fact, that the Yprians became nervous, certain that there had to be a catch somewhere, some dire threat that would arise to thwart them. So far, no such thing had appeared—but Garth's arrival had been very suspicious. The camp was the foremost outpost of the army of the Khofros, most easterly of the six tribes, and just recently come around the central mountains hoping to claim the entire eastern region of Nekutta. The presence of an overman to the east of them was an unwelcome surprise.

Garth listened to this explanation silently. He realized that he, virtually single-handed, had managed to disrupt completely the society of the Yprian Coast and had thereby caused the invasion of Nekutta by these semibarbaric tribespeople. Both the destruction of Dûsarra and the rise of the Chuleras had been his doing.

Once again, actions he had thought beneficial had led to mass destruction. He wondered if it was possible for him to do anything significant at all that Bheleu and fate would not twist and pervert.

The Yprian, done with his story, asked, "Is that girl really the Baroness of Skelleth?"

Garth had been waiting for this question. "I wanted to impress you," he replied. "I thought the whole Yprian Coast traded with Skelleth, not just one tribe."

"Is she the Baroness?" the other persisted.

Garth realized that he was not going to be allowed to dodge the question. "Not anymore," he said. "She *was* the Baroness; her husband was recently murdered by his enemies. I doubt that anyone would care much about the widow of a deposed baron. There were no children to claim the title; she was left alone and decided to return to her home in Dûsarra rather than risk her life by staying in Skelleth."

He hoped that the implication that Frima had been exiled by a rival faction would be accepted. If the situation on the Coast had in fact been as the Yprian had described it, such things would probably have been common and familiar.

"Ah," the Yprian said. "A pity, if true."

"It is true." Garth spoke as if offended, his voice flat. As it happened, most of what he said was indeed accurate. It was the way it was said that gave a wrong impression, by implying that the enemies who had murdered Saram had been usurpers in Skelleth, rather than outside foes.

"A shame; she would have been such a good hostage in dealing with the Chuleras."

Garth shrugged. "I am sorry she is of no value to you. She has some worth for me; I am to be paid by her family upon her safe delivery to Dûsarra."

"That seems very odd, you know. Dûsarra is largely deserted now. And how did a Dûsarran ever come to be married to the Baron of Skelleth?"

"I do not know the details; she turned up in Skelleth almost three years ago. The dead Baron was something of an adventurer, you know; he took the title for himself, rather than inheriting it. His predecessor was murdered, as well."

"You still haven't told me your name."

"Thord," Garth said. "Thord of Ordunin, son of Dold and Sherid."

"I am Chorn of the Khofros."

"What do you plan to do with me?"

"I have not decided."

"I would like to point out that I will put up serious resistance if you do not release me very soon. Besides myself, the warbeast is a formidable threat. I do not think it worth your while to keep me here or to kill me. Far better to let me go in peace."

"You have a good point there. I will keep it in mind while I discuss this with our elders." The Yprian rose and signaled with one hand.

Three guards, all overmen, stepped forward and kept Garth under close watch while Chorn strode off and vanished into a large tent. They made no attempt to disarm Garth; he guessed that they judged the great two-handed broadsword too awkward a weapon to be much of a threat in such a situation. Were he to reach for it, he could be killed long before he could get it free of its scabbard—or at any rate, he could have been killed if it were an ordinary weapon rather than the Sword of Bheleu.

Garth was pleased that no one touched the sword; he was unsure how it might react, even when its power was damped by the Forgotten King. He sat waiting patiently for several minutes.

When Chorn finally emerged again he was smiling. Garth did not know how to interpret that until he saw the Yprian gesture for the guards to depart.

They obeyed, vanishing into the darkness beyond the fire's light.

Garth rose as Chorn dismissed the watch on Frima and Koros.

"Our apologies, Thord, for detaining you," he said. "You understand our situation, I'm sure."

Garth nodded.

"You are free to go, and we hope that you will speak well of the Khofros in the future. We bear no malice toward any people in Eramma or the Northern Waste, nor even in Dûsarra, and would welcome peaceful contacts with them. I am sorry that we were not more hospitable, but in war the amenities are neglected."

"Thank you," Garth said, still slightly suspicious.

No one interfered as he mounted the warbeast and helped Frima up behind him; no one attempted to stop them as they rode on westward through the camp and out the far side, past the sentries.

The stay among the Yprians had delayed them for something over an hour, but Garth was not excessively annoyed. He knew that it could have been much worse. He was relieved that the Khofros had apparently decided that they did not need anymore enemies.

He was not sure, however, whether he was pleased or dismayed at the Forgotten King's disappearance; he was still debating the point as he rode out past the final sentry, whereupon it became moot. The old man was walking alongside again as soon as they were out of sight in the darkness, as if he had been there all along—and Garth was not entirely sure he had not been. Invisibility could well be one of his wizardly talents. The overman decided not to mention it, and the old man did not volunteer any information.

Frima, however, was not so reticent. When she noticed the King's reappearance, she demanded, "Where were you?"

The Forgotten King did not reply.

After she had repeated the question three times, each louder than the last, and had finally been hushed by Garth, while the King remained obdurately silent, she gave up. Instead, she asked Garth, "Why didn't they kill us?"

"Why should they?"

"We might have been spies."

"We weren't."

"But we *might* have been."

Garth shrugged.

"*I* think they should have killed us."

"You would prefer to be dead?" Garth inquired politely.

"I didn't mean it that way—though I don't know, really. Maybe when I die I'll see Saram again."

Garth did not like the trend of that thought. "They did not kill us because it was not worth their trouble. Koros and I would have put up a good fight, and they would have lost several warriors before they could kill us—if they could kill Koros at all," he said, hoping to direct Frima away from thoughts of an afterlife. Even though he had come to believe in the existence of gods, or at any rate of supernatural powers, he had not accepted the human superstition of life after death. He did not want to risk saying anything that might tempt Frima to commit suicide or to permit herself to be killed at what might be an inopportune moment.

"I suppose that's true," Frima agreed. There was a brief silence before she asked, "Who were those people?"

"Yprians," Garth replied.

"What were they doing there?"

Garth explained the situation, repeating points every so often, clarifying what Frima did not immediately comprehend, and admitting ignorance when she asked questions he could not answer.

When at last she was satisfied with his explanation and convinced that the whole camp had not been put there by the cult of Aghad, she fell silent.

Garth glanced back and noticed that the sky was beginning to lighten in the east. They would be resting soon.

That, he was sure, would do them all good.

He had been thinking over recent events while answering Frima's questions; one subject was Frima herself. She was talking again, as much as she ever had. Garth took that as a sign that she was getting over the shock of Saram's death and wondered whether she still grieved.

She was certainly more entertaining, if sometimes exasperating, as her normal talkative self than she had been during her long spell of silence. Traveling by night could be boring, with the scenery obscured by darkness, if one's companions refused to speak.

He began looking for somewhere they could take shelter for the day. It would not do to be caught unawares by another party of Khofros, or by any other Yprian tribe.

They found an abandoned, partially burned farmhouse shortly after sunrise, its former owner's skull on a stake by the door. A message was scratched on the wall with charcoal: "This is the fate of our enemies. This land belongs to the Khofros."

Frima was reluctant to enter the ruin, but Garth was insistent, despite the ash and odor. It was shelter, burned or not.

They spent the day sleeping peacefully; no one found them. Garth awoke in midafternoon and found the King sitting, fully awake, on the one intact chair at the unscathed kitchen table. The overman smiled at the familiar pose in the incongruous setting. He said nothing, but roused Frima, and the party set out anew.

Having learned from their first encounter, Garth carefully

avoided all contact with humans or overmen thereafter, circling wide around the camps and outposts they encountered, sleeping in ruins, caves, or other places of concealment, and stealing supplies rather than buying them. They passed several Yprian encampments of varying sizes, and Garth tried to distinguish the various tribes by the differences in their armor and accouterments; he was fairly certain of some identifications, less confident of others. Since they were avoiding contact, they never learned the names of the five tribes between the Khofros and the Dyn-Hugris, but Garth was reasonably sure he saw representatives of at least three of them.

The sword's gem remained black throughout, to Garth's relief. He had no desire to defend Nekutta by destroying the invaders; after all, many of the Yprians were his own species, which the Nekuttans were not.

As well as the invading armies, they came across camps of ragged humans, mostly unarmed, whom Garth guessed to be refugees. Many of the inhabitants of these camps wore the traditional hooded robes of Dûsarra; others wore the homespun tunics of farmers.

Checkpoints had been set up at several places along the road; circling around them became enough of a nuisance that Garth gave serious consideration to Frima's suggestion of abandoning the road altogether, before finally rejecting it. He had traveled this route once before, but he was by no means sure that he would be able to find Dûsarra if he left the highway.

They were, by Garth's estimate, about a day's travel—or rather, a night's—from Dûsarra, with the mountains visible on the western horizon, when their rest was interrupted early one afternoon.

They had taken shelter in an orchard, hidden from view by the thick foliage of the apple trees. Garth did not expect anyone to trouble them unless the owner of the grove should turn up, and a farmer or two was a threat the overman knew he could handle easily.

It was not a farmer, however, who coughed politely to awaken him. He rolled over, reaching automatically for the Sword of Bheleu, and found himself looking up at a man of indeterminate age, muscular in build, and clad in a gray robe and hood.

There was something familiar about him, Garth realized as his hand closed on the hilt of the sword.

"Greetings, Garth of Ordunin," the man said. "I come in peace; you will not need the sword."

The fact that the man recognized him somehow did not surprise Garth; he was certain that they had met before, though he could not recall when or where.

"Greetings, man," he said.

"You don't recognize me?"

"No."

"I am the Seer of Weideth; we met three years ago, on two occasions."

"I recall only one," Garth replied. He had run afoul of illusions sent by the Seer and the village elders of Weideth when first he traveled to Dûsarra. He remembered the incident well and saw that this man was indeed the one who had called himself Seer on that occasion. On the way back to Skelleth he had passed through Weideth without incident, and without meeting the Seer again.

"I was one of the Council that fought you in the hills north of Skelleth," the gray-robed man explained.

"Oh, yes." Garth had not realized that the Seer had been included in that group, along with Shandiph, Chalkara, and a score or so of others whose names he did not know. There had been so many in robes, the traditional garb for a wizard, that he had not noticed the Seer among them. "Why are you here?"

"I have not come to interfere; it's far too late for that. You need not worry. I just wanted to see you and look at the sword that has caused so much destruction and meet the King in Yellow while we both still live."

There was a sadness in the Seer's tone, and something else Garth did not recognize; overmen were not prone to wistfulness, so Garth was not familiar with it. He saw no harm in the man.

"Here I am," he said, "and here is the sword. The King is the old man in rags over there."

"I know." The Seer looked down at the sword Garth held and remarked, "It's hard to believe that that thing can hold so much power."

The overman shrugged.

"And you have the book and the mask, as well. Do you know how long the spell will take?"

"I know nothing about it," Garth replied.

"O King, do you know?"

The old man had been sitting quietly, ignoring their visitor, but he answered, "Three days."

"And you have a day's travel remaining—four days in all. Why, then, can I not foresee my death? Is my gift *that* weak?"

The Forgotten King said nothing.

"You seem certain that the old man will be allowed to work his magic," Garth said, irked. "I am not so eager to see him succeed."

The Seer looked sideways at him. "What can you do?"

"I hold the Sword of Bheleu—and I intend to hold it."

The King stirred, and the gem in the sword's pommel suddenly flared up, vividly red. A wave of unreasoning fury swept over the overman; he propelled himself to his feet, the sword ready, its blade glowing white.

Then the glow died, the stone blackened, and the King muttered, "Do you, Garth?"

"If it is the only way to prevent you from bringing on the Age of Death, yes, no matter what it may cost me." The rage had vanished as quickly as it had come, leaving his head feeling light; his right hand was warm, almost hot, where the sword's grip pressed against it.

"You swore to aid me in my magic."

Garth did not know how to reply to that at first, but finally said, "I did not know then what was involved."

"Do you now?" the Seer asked, openly curious.

"Do you?" Garth countered.

"In part. I have spent much time in study since last we met, learning more of what was to come. My own gift of prophecy is feeble, but it was sufficient to make clear the writings of others."

"Then tell me, Seer, what I am involved in. What is this magic the King pursues? What will it do? What is the Fifteenth Age to be?"

"The Fifteenth Age is the Age of Death; it will last no more than three hours—perhaps less—bringing time to an end. The gods themselves will die, and the Forgotten King with them.

It will be brought about when a ritual from the Book of Silence is performed in the place of Death, a ritual requiring the totems of death and destruction as well as the book itself."

"And the world will be destroyed, as a result?"

"I would think so," the Seer replied. "How can anything exist when the gods are dead and time has ended?"

"The spell requires the Sword of Bheleu?"

"Yes."

Garth turned to the Forgotten King and smiled. "I think that I may stave it off for some time yet," he said. "Can even the King in Yellow, high priest of Death, take the sword from its chosen bearer against his will?"

"You have seen, Garth, how easily I restrain its power," the old man said.

"True, O King, but you have not restrained *me*. I am still an overman, while you are only human."

"Do you think my powers so strained by confining Bheleu that I cannot use them upon you?"

"If that were not the case, O King, then why have you relied upon more mundane methods of bending me to your will these past three years? Why did you not simply compel me to do what you wished me to do? Why did you allow me to return to Ordunin after slaying the basilisk? Why did you not send me directly to Dûsarra? I think that, mighty as you are, you cannot directly force me to act against my own judgment. I don't know why this should be so, but I believe it is. If I am wrong, then I have lost, and the world is doomed, and you have but to command me to give you the sword to prove it."

The King did not answer immediately. At last, he shrugged slightly and said, "I have waited for seven ages; I can endure further."

Elated by what he took as an admission of defeat, Garth grinned. He was still trapped between Bheleu and the King, but he saw now that his position was, perhaps, not absolutely hopeless. He might find some solution if he could hold the King off long enough and remain sufficiently free of Bheleu's influence to think rationally about it.

It did not occur to him to wonder why the King should continue to suppress the god of destruction when Garth had openly announced his intention not to cooperate.

The overman turned back to the Seer and said, "There, you see? Your doom has been delayed."

The Seer nodded, but asked, "For how long?"

Annoyed at this ingratitude, Garth replied, "For as long as I can prevent it."

"And how long will that be? Will you live forever? I cannot foresee your death, any more than I can my own, but my power of foresight is weak, particularly when far from home."

"I expect to live for many years yet, human, and perhaps in that time I will find some other way of forestalling the end."

"I can only wish you well, overman."

Somewhat mollified, Garth relaxed slightly. He stood silently for a moment as the Seer gazed dolefully at him, then at the sword he still held.

Feeling that the silence was becoming uncomfortable, Garth asked, "How is it that you are here, rather than in Weideth? If you came to see us, would you not have done just as well to wait at home? Our route passes through your village."

"Weideth is gone," the Seer replied. "It was taken by a Dûsarran army over a year ago and destroyed a month later by advancing Yprians. Many of us fled, in small groups. I am the only survivor of my company and I have lost contact with the other parties. I've been living alone, a few leagues south of here."

Reminded anew of the chaotic conditions in Nekutta, Garth was uneasy. "I am sorry to hear it," he said.

The Seer said nothing.

"If you wish to join us, you would be safer than while traveling alone."

"Thank you, but no. I couldn't stand it. Sooner or later I would take up the sword, or look at the mask, or touch the book, and I would die, even before the world ends. I prefer to live out whatever time remains to me without facing such dangers."

"As you wish, then," the overman said. He watched as the Seer departed, walking away slowly until he was lost to sight among the close-packed trees.

CHAPTER TWENTY-THREE

Haggat had planned it all carefully. The cult's best assassins and most powerful magicians would be employed systematically, one after another or in small complementary groups, until one or another managed to get through. The overman was to be their primary target; the old man came next, and then the warbeast. The girl was of no importance; she might wind up on a sacrificial altar, as she had once before, but with no rescuer this time.

He was aware of the Sword of Bheleu's power, but he could not believe that it was omnipotent and impregnable. He had gathered all the most potent death-spells the cult could devise or steal, all the most deadly killers, and had laced every water supply between Dûsarra and the plains with the most lethal poisons at his disposal. He had devised stratagems and diversions, methods for separating the overman from his sword, methods of disposing of both simultaneously. He had thought of little else for almost a fortnight. For three days he had not even taken the time to use his scrying glass, save for a quick daily check on the overman's progress each morning. He had forgone the nightly sacrifices and neglected the cult's other business. He had eaten hurriedly, if at all, and had not touched his acolyte — though she remained always close at hand, translating his commands from sign language or writing to spoken words, carrying messages, running errands, and generally attending to his needs. He had not given her presence much thought; he had been too busy to bother himself about her.

Now, though, all was ready. The killers were in place. The overman and his party were in the foothills, advancing along the highway, and Haggat watched his glass avidly. Unable to observe the overman or the old man directly, he had focused upon the road before them.

He was so involved that he neglected one of his customary precautions and allowed his acolyte to remain in the black-draped chamber with him. She stretched up on tiptoe to peer over his shoulder at the glass. Together they watched as the warbeast's forepaws rose and fell, always at one side of the image, moving along the highway toward the crossroads.

Garth remembered the narrow defile that led straight into Weideth; it was a welcome change from the winding of the road through the outer foothills. He judged that they would reach the gates of Dûsarra shortly after dawn; the eastern sky was just beginning to turn pink behind them.

When he had first ridden this road, Weideth had vanished before his eyes almost immediately after he turned the last corner; that had been the doing of the Seer and the village elders, using illusions in hopes of diverting Garth from his path. On this second journey there was no such magical trickery. Nothing disguised the devastation that had befallen the little town.

Where once an inn and a dozen houses had clustered around the crossroads, there were only heaps of ash and jutting, blackened timbers. Stones lay scattered about, strewn across the roads and hillsides. Garth remembered a small stand of trees that had adorned one slope; nothing remained but scorched stumps. Weeds grew thick in what had been tidy little gardens, and here and there white bones showed in pale contrast to the smoky darkness left by the destroying fires, catching the pale predawn light.

It was a depressing sight, and the overman wished that it *would* vanish, leaving his memories of the village untarnished.

The Forgotten King's voice interrupted his thoughts.

"Garth," the old man said, "be ready."

Puzzled, Garth glanced at the King, but saw no sign that would tell him what he should be ready for. The old man was walking along as calmly as ever.

A red glint caught his eye, and he realized that the gem in the pommel of the sword was glowing. With the realization came an uneasiness. He twisted around to look at the jewel, then looked back at the King.

The old man nodded and kept walking.

Confused, but trusting for the moment in the Forgotten King's supernatural knowledge, Garth reached up, leaning forward so the blade would not smack Frima, tipped the scabbard up over his shoulder, and unsheathed the sword.

The hilt felt warm and comforting in his hands.

"What's happening?" Frima asked. "Why are you doing that?"

Garth did not answer; he was too busy enjoying the mounting rush of strength and bloodlust that swept through him as he held the sword. The grip was hot in his hands, the gem glowing brightly, the blade shining faintly in the dim morning light. The sooty ruins of Weideth no longer saddened him; instead, the vista seemed almost inviting, the evidence of destruction somehow satisfying, even though it had been caused by hands other than his own.

There were enemies here, he knew, many of them, hidden away among the heaps of rubble, some concealed by magic, others by natural means.

This, he thought, would be fun.

Something twanged; he whirled the sword about to meet the crossbow bolt that flew toward his head. Sparks trailed from the blade, bright in the half-light, and the quarrel shattered spectacularly against the gleaming metal, sending a shower of splinters to rattle against the rocks beside the roadway. Frima yelped as a stray sliver pierced her arm.

Garth's buoyant energy turned suddenly to rage as he saw the blood trailing down the girl's sleeve; the sword blazed up in a burst of white fire that snatched the pale colors from the landscape around them, stretching sharp-edged bands of light and long black shadows out in all directions.

"*I'a bheluye!*" the overman screamed as he brought the sword sweeping back before him. Flame erupted wherever it pointed, in great rushing waves, and the screams of dying men mingled with the roar of the fires as crouching Aghadite assassins were caught in the blaze.

Something flashed crimson, and Garth laughed horribly as he felt the sword fend off a death-spell. Slung stones whistled past his head or exploded into dust against the sword's edge; arrows of every sort were diverted or destroyed by the blade's coruscating energy. Colored smoke arose from a dozen attempted spells, only to be dispersed and driven away by the force of the supernatural flames. The overman did not bother to locate his attackers, but simply blasted everything in sight, destroying anything that might conceal a foe. The piles of ash were swept away in whirlwinds, the burned timbers powdered by fiery bursts; the ground shook, sending rocks tumbling and bouncing like the spatter of rain on flat stone. The light of dawn was first lost in the more vivid light of the sword and then buried in clouds as Garth gathered a storm about himself. The fire of the sword was joined by flashes of lightning.

Long after the attacks upon him had ceased, Garth drew on the sword's power to keep the earth dancing and to send bolt after bolt of electrical fire onto every available target.

When at last he allowed the fury to subside and the clouds to part, the sun was bright gold above the eastern horizon, but lighted only blackened earth and drifting ash. No trace remained of Weideth or the assassins who had lurked there, save for scattered fragments of bone, shards of scorched metal, and a thin layer of cinders. The surrounding hills themselves had been gouged deeply and reshaped into stark, angular new forms.

Amid this devastation, Garth and Frima sat astride Koros; the Forgotten King stood alongside, untouched by the havoc the sword had wrought. Frima had closed her eyes and kept her head down throughout the conflagration; now she stared about in stunned disbelief, ignoring the blood that trickled from her single wound. Koros growled uneasily and shied away from the heaps of ash that still smoked. Even Garth, who had caused it, seemed impressed by the result of his actions.

The Forgotten King alone remained unperturbed and calm.

In Dûsarra, Haggat stared in disbelief at the final image that filled his glass in shades of gray. He realized, with a sick certainty, that he had done everything he could to destroy the overman and had failed utterly.

That was the last thing he thought; the acolyte who stood at his shoulder throughout had seen the truth as well and knew that Haggat's power was broken. She chose her spot carefully, making certain her thrust slid cleanly between his ribs and into his heart, forgoing the pleasures of a slow death to be sure that the high priest would not live long enough to retaliate.

She smiled as she drove the knife into his back.

CHAPTER TWENTY-FOUR

The gates of Dûsarra were closed and barred; that came as something of a surprise to Garth. It was not, however, much of an obstacle. The gem in the sword's pommel still glowed red, and a single blow sent the splintered remnants of the massive city gate slamming back against the neighboring walls while showering the marketplace that lay just beyond with chips, sawdust, and ash.

Garth had dismounted to wield the sword and remained on foot as he marched into the city. Koros padded along close behind, Frima on its back, and the Forgotten King brought up the rear, the Book of Silence and the Pallid Mask in a bundle beneath one arm.

The overman stopped in the middle of the square, and the others drew up behind him and joined him in looking about.

The market was not as Garth and Frima remembered it. When Garth had first arrived in Dûsarra the square had been lined with merchants' stalls, shaded with canvas and lighted with torches; it had been swarming with people in robes of gray and red and blue, buying and selling and going about the business of the city. Now the sides of the square were bare stone walls, the black stone stained with smoke. Several of the buildings had obviously been gutted by fire; the charred ends of timbers projected, the windows were empty, blackened holes, and the doorways yawned empty. In some cases daylight was visible through the openings, showing plainly that in those buildings the roofs were gone.

The market was totally deserted, and the entire city seemed abandoned; Garth could see nothing alive and could hear nothing stirring, save for his own little group.

"Now what do we do?" Frima asked.

Garth considered that. His ultimate goal, of course, was the temple of Aghad, on the Street of the Temples in the northeastern part of the city. They had, however, been traveling for quite some time, having set out late the previous afternoon and it being now midmorning. For his own part, he was not particularly tired; his use of the Sword of Bheleu had left him feeling more invigorated than drained on this particular occasion. He did not understand why that should be so, yet it was. His companions, however, might not feel up to further activity.

Given that they were to rest, he was unsure where to go. From the appearance of the marketplace, he doubted very much that the Inn of the Seven Stars, where he had stayed before, would be open for business.

"What do you suggest?" he said at last.

Frima gazed about at the desolate market that she herself had set afire so long ago and said, "I want to go home." She was weary and distressed and, at least for the moment, more concerned with her own security than with avenging her murdered husband.

Garth mistook her meaning. "We have come to destroy the cult of Aghad and we are not returning to Skelleth until that has been done. Would you have this whole journey go to waste?"

"I don't mean Skelleth, I mean my *home*, Garth!"

"Oh," the overman said, realizing that he had misunderstood. "Where is it?"

"We lived above my father's shop, on the Street of the Fallen Stars," Frima replied, pointing off to the northwest.

Garth nodded. That seemed as good a course as any; the girl's home would provide lodging and a base from which to work. He would be able to plan his course of action, rather than simply charging in blindly.

Of course, this delay would allow the cultists time to plan

as well, and to lay traps—but they had had ten days and nights already since he left Ur-Dormulk, and the result of all their planning had been the ambush he had destroyed in Weideth. He doubted that they could contrive anything more effective in one day. If they did attempt another, similar surprise, it would most probably give him a chance to kill more of their number.

If they chose to hide, another day could make little difference, since surely they would already have spent considerable time upon their preparations.

Better, he decided, to allow them that time, while he, Frima, and Koros rested and prepared, than to march up to the temple now, in broad daylight, and begin blasting away.

"Lead the way," he said.

Frima leaned forward and spoke a word in the warbeast's ear; she had, by listening, learned most of the commands it was trained to obey.

The beast growled and looked at Garth, who nodded and waved it along.

With a muffled snort, it strode forward, letting the girl direct it by twisting at the guide handle attached to its harness. The overman walked alongside.

The Forgotten King did not; instead, when the warbeast headed for the northwestern corner of the market, he began walking toward the northeast. Garth, glancing back, noticed this divergence.

"Where are you going?" he called.

The King did not answer.

Annoyed, Garth lifted the Sword of Bheleu, which he had not sheathed after breaking in the gate, and set the ground in front of the old man afire.

Without even pausing, the King made a subtle gesture with his free hand. The flames vanished with a rush of air, and the gem in the sword's pommel went black.

Something whistled past the overman's ear.

Startled, he whirled in time to glimpse a human head ducking down below a burned-out window.

"Wait," he ordered Koros. Sword in hand, he ran toward the window. Again something whizzed past his ear; this time he saw it was a dart and realized that it came from a totally different direction. He spun about, but did not see the source.

He was unsure just what was happening, but he found it very inconvenient to have the sword's power repressed at this particular moment. He had come to rely on the weapon.

"I regret, O King," he called, while he kept moving to remain a difficult target, "that I so rashly annoyed you. I beg your forgiveness and ask that you release the sword from your restraint." It had been stupid, he knew, to have tried using the sword against the old man in the first place. His power was able to stifle the sword's greatest fury with ease and had protected the entire King's Inn from destruction during the sacking of Skelleth. It had been foolish for Garth to think that the old man would be hampered by a simple supernatural flame. Furthermore, causing him any offense at this point was probably a mistake. Garth's regret was completely genuine. Most of all, he regretted that he tended to behave stupidly when the sword's gem glowed.

Still walking northeasterly, completely unperturbed, the King waved a hand in dismissal, and the jewel flared red once more.

Awash in power and his mind hazy with rage, Garth promptly turned back and blasted to powder the wall that had concealed his first attacker, revealing nothing but the burned-out shell of a small shop. The assassin had escaped.

Garth could find no trace of whoever had thrown the second dart; he, too, had fled.

Annoyed, but struggling to force his anger down and to maintain careful control of himself, the overman again ordered Koros to wait and then ran after the Forgotten King.

He caught up to the old man half a block away, in a street leading out of the market, and slowed to a walk alongside the King. When he had composed himself somewhat, he said, "Your pardon, O King, for my lack of manners. However, I find it disturbing that you should choose to part ways at this point. I respectfully ask to know where you're going and why you do not accompany us."

"I go to the temple of Death," the old man replied, "to restore the Book of Silence to its proper place, in preparation for my final magic. That was my purpose in coming here. You have your own purposes to pursue. Go pursue them, and leave me to mine."

Garth was unsure how to reply to this; he began to phrase another question, then broke off as he realized that he had stopped walking and that the Forgotten King was moving on ahead of him. He tried to walk, but found that his feet would not obey him. He stood and watched as the old man marched on up the street, around a corner, and out of sight.

A red fury seethed through him, but he knew that there was nothing he could do. He struggled to fight down his irrational anger.

The King could do nothing, either, he told himself. He did not have the Sword of Bheleu, and Garth had not done him the service he had sworn, to aid in the final magic. The Fifteenth Age could not begin while those conditions remained unmet— or perhaps it could begin, since the King had the Pallid Mask and Garth had done him the service of bringing him the Book of Silence, but it could not end, the world could not be destroyed. Let the old man go and make his spells, speak his incantations; they would be nothing without the sword!

That, at any rate, was what Garth told himself, yet even when his anger had subsided, when he had fought down his rage sufficiently to dim the vivid glare of the sword's jewel, he worried. Why should the old fool be so confident, if his magic was useless without the sword? Did he perhaps know something that Garth did not, something that would deliver the sword into his hands?

If that were the case, Garth asked himself, what could he, Garth, do about it? The King's powers had stopped him in his tracks here and could surely do so again. He could only go on, ignoring the old man and dealing with new threats as they arose, relying on the deduced fact that, for some reason, the King seemed unable to take the sword from him without his consent.

With that decision, he sheathed the sword and turned back toward the market. His feet moved normally once more; he had no trouble in retracing his steps and rejoining Frima and Koros.

With Frima pointing the way, they made their way onward into the streets of the city, away from the shattered gate. They were less than a hundred yards from the market when they passed the first skeleton. It lay on one side of the street, partially buried in the dirt; it had obviously been there for some time and had sunk into the mud after a rainstorm. No flesh remained; the skull gazed up from empty sockets.

Frima shuddered and looked away. Koros ignored it completely. Garth gave it a look, then dismissed it as unimportant. It had undoubtedly been a victim of the White Death.

Of course, the presence of an unburied skeleton was a sign that the city was nowhere near recovery. Dûsarra was not wholly dead, since the cult of Aghad still remained alive and active, but any town where the dead were allowed to lie in the streets indefinitely was far from healthy.

They saw more skeletons as they proceeded into the city, but fewer burned buildings; the fire had not spread more than a few blocks to the northwest of the market. Most of the houses and shops were intact, but looked deserted. Some doors stood open; a few had been broken in. Fallen roofing tiles lay in the street here and there, and scraps of rotting cloth could be found in places, as well as scattered bones. There were no people to be seen anywhere; the resulting silence in the center of the city was eerie and unsettling.

Eventually they reached what Frima proclaimed to be the Street of the Fallen Stars and found her father's little shop. The door was closed and the windows intact, but Garth was not very optimistic about finding anyone alive within. The stone doorstep was dusty; no one had gone in or out recently, he was sure. Besides, they had seen no one alive since leaving the marketplace, and Garth thought it very unlikely that, in this dying, abandoned city, they would find the handful of people they sought still living in their old home as if nothing had happened.

Frima did not bother to think logically about such things. She hurried to dismount and ran eagerly up to the door, ignoring the dust on the stoop and windows. She knocked loudly; no one answered. She tried the latch. It clicked, and the door swung open. She stepped in, Garth right behind her.

The shop's interior was dim, and dust lay everywhere; human and overman both left clear footprints. To either side stood wooden display racks, from which hung pots, kettles, ladles, and tin vessels of every description. On shelves behind them were arrayed plates and tankards of pewter, copper bowls, and other implements. The tin and pewter were gray and dusty; the copper was dull and beginning to show flecks of green corrosion.

At the back of the shop stood the tinker's worktable, four feet across and ten feet long, a few tools laid out in a row near one corner, other tools hanging on the wall behind. Scraps of metal lay scattered about.

Sprawled across the center of the table were the bones of a man's arms, his skull grinning between them, his other bones in a heap on the floor behind the table.

Frima was horrified; she froze, stared, and stifled a scream.

Garth waited, ready to lend any help he could, but his assistance was not needed. The girl closed her eyes and fought down her trembling, forcing herself under control.

The overman decided not to ask if she could be sure it was her father. *He* was sure that it was; who but the tinker would be found at the tinker's bench? He saw no point in raising false hopes. Instead, he said, "We should look upstairs."

Frima nodded, took a few steps toward the curtain that closed off the back of the building from the public part of the shop, and then stopped. "You look," she said. "I can't."

Garth nodded. He had lived long enough among humans to understand how strongly they became attached to their homes, and to realize that Frima could not bear the thought of finding more dead in what should have been her sanctuary. He had no idea how large a family she came from; perhaps she was afraid of finding the remains of her mother or stepmother or siblings.

He moved cautiously through the curtain into the back room, and from there up the narrow staircase to the upper floor. Everywhere lay a thick carpet of dust. Cobwebs adorned the corners of each of the three small beds he found upstairs. A metal bowl on a small bedside table, now dry as the dust, had obviously been left full long ago; the bottom had corroded and sprung a leak, and the table had rotted where the water had dripped.

There were no more bones, no corpses, no sign of any other inhabitants.

When he had satisfied himself that no unpleasant surprises

lurked in wardrobes or under the beds, he returned to the shop to find Frima standing over the table, studying her father's skull.

"Are there any others?" she asked.

"No," Garth replied.

"Good."

"Did you have any other family?"

"Two sisters and a brother."

"Perhaps they escaped, then, and are still alive somewhere."

"Do you really think so?"

Garth hesitated, then lied. "Yes, of course."

Frima stared at the skull. "Are you sure this is my father's?"

"No," Garth said. "How could I be sure? I never met him, after all."

"I know, but can't you tell? I've been looking at it, and I can't be sure. It doesn't look like him. There's no hair, no eyes; it could be anybody's."

"I know no more than you," Garth answered. "But who else could it be? Who else would be sitting here at your father's table?"

Frima shuddered and turned away. "Get it out of here," she said.

Garth obeyed, gathering up the skull and several bones and carrying them out into the street.

He returned to find Frima huddled in a corner, weeping. Quietly, he gathered up and removed the remaining bones, placing them in a corner out of the wind, where they were unlikely to be disturbed, between the shop and the house beside it.

When he had finished he went upstairs, cleared away the dust and cobwebs from one of the beds, tested it, and found it marginally usable. Then he returned to the shop, led the girl upstairs, and put her in the bed.

She went willingly and quickly fell asleep.

Garth watched over her briefly, then went downstairs again, found a water pump in the back, and filled one of the larger vessels with water for Koros. That taken care of, he settled himself on the floor of the shop and slept.

Outside, Koros stood guard, dozing occasionally, but always alert enough to warn away with a growl any Dûsarrans who ventured near.

CHAPTER TWENTY-FIVE

Garth was awakened by the roar of a warbeast. Startled, he sprang to his feet and hurried to the door of the shop. There he paused, waiting, the Sword of Bheleu in his hand.

The roar was not repeated; instead, he heard an unfamiliar voice calling his name.

"Garth! Garth of Ordunin! We would speak with you!"

Puzzled, and without opening the door, he bellowed back, "Who are you?"

"I am Uyrim, a priest of Aghad; I have been sent to seek a truce!"

Garth considered that. His immediate suspicion was that it was some kind of trick, an attempt to lure him into a trap, but after further thought he decided that the offer might be genuine. After all, although he had suffered at the hands of the cultists, losing his chief wife and his best human friend, they had suffered worse in return. Perhaps they had had their fill of sending assassins to be fried by the sword; perhaps they did not want to see their temple reduced to ash, as the remnants of Weideth had been.

He lifted the latch and swung the door an inch or so inward, so that conversation would be more convenient, but he did not emerge, nor present any part of his body as a target. "I am listening," he called.

"Haggat, who set assassins upon you, who had your wife killed, who had the Baron of Skelleth slain, who sent the Council of the Most High against you, is dead, and his killer is the new high priestess of our sect. We wish to start anew. We are willing to forgo our rightful vengeance for the killing of Haggat's predecessor if you, in turn, will consider your own vengeance accomplished in the deaths you have already brought upon us. You have slain eighteen trained assassins and our fourteen magicians and cost us almost all our magical arsenal. You have destroyed our temple in Ur-Dormulk and eliminated our influence in Skelleth. Leave those of us who yet survive in peace, and we will, in turn, leave you and yours in peace. Swear that you will accept this offer, and we will swear in return, and you may leave Dûsarra unmolested. Refuse us, and we will strike against you in whatever way we can. We know now that we cannot kill you while you bear the Sword of Bheleu, but we can kill those you care for. For every member of our sect you slay from this moment on, a member of your family in Ordunin will die. Those, O Garth, are our terms."

"They're lying," Frima said close behind him. Garth started; he had been so attentive to the Aghadite's words that he had not heard her approach. The warbeast's roar of warning had awakened her as it had the overman, and she had made her way carefully down the stairs in time to hear most of what the priest had said.

"How can you know that?" Garth asked.

"They *always* lie," she said.

"They lie when it serves their purposes and tell the truth when that would serve better. Perhaps this is such a time," Garth said.

"They aren't going to give up their revenge. Aghad is the god of hatred, remember? And besides," she added, her expression turning hard and fierce and a hand going to the crudely bandaged wound on her arm, "I'm not going to give up *my* revenge."

Garth considered that and quickly agreed that the Aghadites could not be trusted. Still, the offer of peace might be genuine; he had, he knew, cost the cult heavily.

That did not necessarily mean that he should accept the offer. After all, if the cult could thus change direction once, it could do so again, when next its leaders felt they had the upper hand. The fact that they were offering a truce now implied that Garth currently had the advantage—and the essence of tactics was to pursue every advantage. If he were to attack now, he suspected that he could destroy the entire sect; if he accepted their truce and thereby allowed them time to rebuild, they might find some way of attacking him successfully while he was off guard. Quite aside from his desire for revenge, the cult, by its nature, was a menace not just to himself, but to anyone else who encountered it, for so long as it existed.

By the priest's own admission, Garth had destroyed the cult's influence in Skelleth, and he could not believe that they had ever been strong in the Northern Waste—after all, he had seen no Aghadite overmen, save the high priest he had killed in Dûsarra's market three years before, who had almost certainly been Yprian; and had they not had to lure Kyrith south before they could kill her? Therefore, if he were to wipe them out *now*, they would be unable to carry out their threat to destroy his family and friends; whereas if he were to wait, they might well manage some retaliation.

There was no question in his mind as to whether or not they deserved to die; these people were, by their own boast, dedicated to hatred and treachery. They had butchered Kyrith and Saram. They had insulted and reviled him, attacking him repeatedly. They deserved to perish, and he deserved the pleasure of dispatching them.

The thought of spilling Aghadite blood was warm and comforting; a pleasant reddish glow seemed to suffuse his thoughts. He did not notice the literal, physical existence of that glow, emanating from the gem in the sword's pommel.

Frima noticed it but, knowing it to be directed against the followers of Aghad, chose not to point it out.

"Who are you, to offer me terms?" Garth called through the crack in the door. "You are a priest of Aghad, you say, and you speak of a high priestess, and of someone named Haggat. I know nothing of any of you. You say that it was the dead Haggat who sought to harm me; why should I believe that? Your cult has acted against me, not as individuals, but on behalf of your god. I do not defy *you*, or your high priestess, or your dead Haggat, whoever he may have been if he truly existed at all. I defy your god himself. I spit upon your deity. I denounce Aghad as the filth he is. He has defied his brother and superior, Bheleu, god of destruction, and must pay for that affront." An inspiration came to him, and he called to Koros the command that meant, "Attack!"

The warbeast roared in response. An instant later Garth heard the sound of something being crunched, followed by human screams. He swung the door wide and stepped out, the Sword of Bheleu ready in his hand, glowing white and dripping hissing white flame.

The screaming stopped, and he saw Koros standing in the alley across the street, gnawing on the bloody remains of a red-garbed dead man, while another broken corpse lay sprawled nearby. A sling was draped across one limp hand, and half a dozen darts were scattered in the black dust of the street.

Something moved, and Garth swung the sword, spraying flame, only to find that he had roasted a plump rat, drawn by the scent of blood.

It seemed unlikely that the party sent to negotiate a truce had been only two men; Garth looked warily about for more, but saw none. If there had been others, they had slipped away unseen.

Frima emerged from the shop to stand behind the overman; her father's sword, taken from its place behind the curtain, was naked in her hand. Here, in her home city, however changed it might be, she was no longer content merely to watch Garth kill her foes for her. She was determined to kill a few herself, and her father's sword seemed an appropriate weapon. She wished she had thought to bring Saram's blade; that would have been still more fitting.

She knew, however, that she was no swordswoman, and the sling in the corpse's hand caught her eye. She picked it up, gathered up the darts, and tucked them into the pouch she wore on her belt in imitation of Garth and defiance of Dûsarran custom.

That done, she looked about and saw no enemies to attack, only the warbeast devouring its prey and the overman standing warily nearby.

"Now what do we do?" she asked.

"We attack," Garth replied without thinking.

"Attack the temple?"

Garth glanced at her, his red eyes ablaze in the afternoon sun. "Yes," he said.

"Good," Frima said. "Let's go."

Garth turned, looked about, then reluctantly turned back to the girl and asked, "Which way?" He was almost totally unfamiliar with this part of Dûsarra.

Frima suppressed a giggle at the helplessness of the godoverman who needed to ask directions of a tinker's daughter. "This way," she said, pointing.

Garth nodded, signaled Koros to accompany him, and followed as Frima led the way through the maze of the city toward the Street of the Temples and the temple of Aghad.

In a red-draped room beneath the temple, the new high priestess was arguing with some of her congregation, who considered her sudden self-proclaimed elevation and subsequent policy to be faulty. The discussion had been going nowhere; Haggat's former acolyte had an irrefutable claim to her new position by virtue of being the only surviving person who knew all the cult's secrets, and she was utterly unyielding in her determination to abandon any attempt to kill the troublesome overman.

The objectors were equally adamant in their insistence upon following more traditional rules of succession and in pursuing the cult's ancient policy of unrelenting vengeance. There was nothing unorthodox in moving up through assassination, and they agreed that Haggat had deserved removal for his bungling, but the post of high priest was not to be taken by a mere acolyte with no grounding in theology. They argued that the high priestess should immediately begin training a proper priest in the inner mysteries of the cult's workings and return to her own rightful position as first among acolytes—though they were willing to guarantee her accession to the priesthood shortly after that return.

She knew just what such promises from priests of Aghad were worth. After coming into her post as Haggat's acolyte, she had maneuvered for three years to obtain power and was not about to relinquish it now to please a bunch of doddering traditionalists. She was saying as much, thickly laced with invective, when a messenger arrived, gasping from his long run.

"Your pardon, O priestess, chosen of Aghad, blessed of the darkness, mistress of treachery, but I bear urgent news," he said.

"Speak, then," she commanded.

"Garth refused the offer of truce and sent his warbeast against us. Uyrim and Hezren were slain; the rest of us escaped."

"Aghad devour you!" the priestess shouted. "Why? What went wrong?"

"I don't know, O mistress. Uyrim spoke well, I thought, yet the overman refused to parley. He said that his quarrel was not with Haggat, but with Aghad himself."

"That's idiocy! It was not Aghad who slew his wife, it was men, men acting on Haggat's orders. Haggat was a fool, attacking the overman openly; the essence of Aghad's power is deceit and coercion, not magic or brute force."

"Yes, mistress," the messenger agreed; the gathered priests remained silent, but many wore expressions approving the priestess' words.

"Did Uyrim warn him of reprisals?"

"Yes, mistress."

"He must know how weak we are in the east, that he does not fear such a threat. We'll have to show him that we are not so weak as he believes. He has two more wives; I want them brought here as quickly as possible, alive and intact." She turned to the closest thing the cult still had to a wizard, an apprentice who had been given charge of the few remaining magical devices. "Do we have any means of teleporting them?"

"No, mistress," the girl replied. "The last were used in Weideth."

"Oh, gods, may Haggat's soul be Sai's plaything forever! Do we know where more such magic may be found?"

"No, mistress—at least, I do not."

"Then we must do it the hard way and hope that we can hold out until the overwomen are brought here. That could be a month." The high priestess had a tendency to think out loud, now that she was free of her master. Haggat had been unable to speak, having had his tongue cut out in punishment for killing his own master long ago, before he had joined the cult, and in consequence had been resentful of those who spoke freely around him. His acolyte, who had always been near him, had learned quickly to keep her mouth shut. Since killing him, she had taken much pleasure in being able to speak as often as she wanted and for as long as she chose.

She turned back to the messenger. "Does the overman still have the Baroness of Skelleth with him?"

"Yes, mistress."

"He treats her well?"

"Uh . . . I am not certain, mistress."

"He seems to care for her, doesn't he? And she's not protected by the magic sword. And the strange old man is no longer with them to protect her. We'll have to make use of what we have. She won't be as good a hostage as Garth's wives would be, but she may serve, at least for a time." She paused and was about to speak again when another messenger entered the room and prostrated himself before her.

"Your pardon, O priestess, chosen of Aghad . . ." he began.

"Speak, messenger," she ordered impatiently.

"The overman is on his way to the temple, with his sword blazing and the warbeast beside him."

"You're certain?"

"Oh, yes, mistress."

"P'hul!" the high priestess spat. "Tell everyone. We can't face him yet."

"What?" one of the older priests protested. "You can't mean to abandon the temple?"

"You are free to stay here and die if you choose, Sherrend, but I, and anyone else with any wits, will be hiding in the tunnels. Nothing can stand against that sword of his. I saw in the scrying glass what it did, and our surviving scouts have told all of you. You heard what it did to our temple in Ur-Dormulk. Only a fool would stay here to face it." She ignored the priest's sputtering objections as she climbed down from her cathedra and announced, "Gather everything of value and make sure everyone is armed; we leave immediately. And I still want people sent after those overwomen, and after that woman he has with him."

The messengers and the wizard's apprentice bowed obediently; the priests squabbled among themselves, some bowing and hastening to obey, others staying to voice protests that the priestess ignored.

Even the stodgiest, however, had some sense of self-preservation, and within minutes the room was empty as the Aghadites prepared to evacuate their stronghold.

Garth was completely unaware of this activity. He reached the Street of the Temples as the sun was sinking behind the western mountains, washing the shrines in shadow. The topmost edge of the silvery gate of Aghad's fane caught a stray beam and glinted brightly as the overman drew near.

Garth smiled, and the Sword of Bheleu blazed up whitely, chasing away the shadows and drenching the metal gate in its own sickly glow.

The valves of the gate were worked into ten-foot-high runes, two to each panel, spelling out AGHAD; the top of the GH rune was still dented where Garth had struck at it three years before. The walls of the temple were built of blocks of stone, each block carved into those same four runes, a myriad reminders of his enemy's name.

When last he had been here, he reminded himself, he had been unable to deal with the trickery of the Aghadites. His sword had broken against these gates. Now, though, he carried the Sword of Bheleu. He swung the blade up and brought it crashing down against the top of the gleaming metal valves.

The blade sheared through the metal as if it were paper; it could just as easily, Garth knew, have exploded the gates into shards. That was not what he wanted; he wanted to destroy this place slowly, at his leisure, and enjoy each step of the process.

He slashed again, cutting away a triangular slice of the second A rune. Another blow removed the top of the GH, and another cut apart the D.

Half a dozen blows reduced the gleaming gates to scrap, and Garth stepped through into the courtyard beyond, leaving Koros and Frima waiting in the street.

The colonnade that ran around three sides of the court was dark, the torches mounted on its columns unlit; the fading sunlight did not penetrate its gloom. The fountain in the courtyard's center gurgled, but Garth could not see the spray; it was hidden behind a barrier of rotting severed heads, stacked up like bricks around the fountain's rim, five deep. None were of recent origin, that was obvious; the bottommost tier was comprised mostly of almost-bare skulls, and those in the top rows were sufficiently decayed for the worst of the stink to have passed.

Although the majority were human, of both sexes, the skull that faced him most directly on the lowest level was that of an overman.

Revolted, Garth swung the sword up and sent a bolt of crimson flame at the grisly pile. The heads scorched, blackened, and crumbled to ash, revealing the bubbling spout of the fountain.

When Garth had first visited this place the fountain had pumped clear, clean water, liberally laced with poison; now, the fluid that pumped forth was thick and red. He did not care to investigate further, but simply reinforced the sword's power and reduced the stone and metal of the fountain to powder, boiling away whatever liquid it had held.

He paused and considered his next step. It occurred to him that no one had, as yet, opposed him; no voice had addressed him from the shadows. In fact, there was no sign that anyone was in the temple at all. That worried him; was it possible that the Aghadites had seen him coming and had fled, giving up their sanctuary?

Wasting no more time, he began blasting away at the temple itself, slicing the columns that supported its porches, breaking down the walls beyond. Masonry fell roaring, and the temple crumbled about him. He marched forward into the rubble, continuing to blast at the walls that still stood.

In the street that fronted the shrine, Koros and Frima waited, alert for an attack. Frima was eager to spot and kill any Aghadite who might flee from the destruction; Koros, as always, was not concerned with the reasons for its master's orders, but was ready to obey them and slaughter anyone who came near.

No one came. Walls tottered and fell, sections of roof caved in spectacularly, stones shattered, but no one emerged from the temple of Aghad.

Garth's rage grew steadily as he broke into chamber after chamber without finding a living foe. Clouds gathered in the sky above him, lightning flashed, and the earth shook beneath his feet, breaking open the extensive temple basements.

He continued to wreak destruction, working his way down beneath street level into the catacombs under the shrine. He found corpses, some of them fresh, some ancient, but none wearing the dark red robes of the cult, none that were still warm. He found animals—bats, serpents, great cats, and others—and slew them, but he found no humans. He saw machinery and smashed it, but saw no one operating it.

At last, as he had done in Ur-Dormulk, he found himself standing in a great pit where the temple had been, a pit that was as empty and lifeless as the one in Ur-Dormulk. His foes had escaped him. He had destroyed their stronghold, but they had escaped.

He bellowed with rage, the sword swinging in circles above his head; thunder rumbled, and lightning flickered through the clouds, as if reflecting the streak of fire the blade left hanging in the air.

He lashed out in frustration, blackening the smoking rubble and cutting a groove in the stone that surrounded him. The ground trembled below him.

A pile of debris tumbled aside, revealing an opening into the black, volcanic bedrock; the flame from the sword sliced through a stone slab, uncovering another. Alerted, Garth hacked away at the walls of the pit and found several such openings, thirteen in all, ranging from broad passageways skillfully concealed behind camouflaged stone doors to narrow crawlways, too small for an overman to enter, that had been hidden by the heaped rubble.

Here, then, were the means by which his enemies had fled. He could pursue them, overtake them, destroy them; he needed only to learn which of the passages they had taken.

He growled in frustration; there was no way he could know which routes they had chosen. He pointed the sword at the nearest and sent a gout of flame into it, illuminating the dark stone with an orange glare, but he could see no sign that would tell him whether the tunnel had been used or not. No dust lay on its floor; no footprints showed.

Enraged, he sent the flame winding on into the depths, out of his own sight, a writhing serpent of living fire.

A moment later he heard an immense explosion, and shards of stone and wood spattered across the rubble from somewhere well beyond the edge of the pit, hidden from his view. Gobbets of flame flickered across the night sky, and he knew that his fiery messenger had reached the end of the tunnel.

He also knew that it had not found any Aghadites.

"Garth?" Frima's voice called from the edge of the pit, at the spot where the silvery gates had once stood.

He growled a wordless response.

"What happened? A house up the street burst apart; did you do that?"

"Yes," he said. He struggled to think, to plan; the raging fury in his head made it difficult to do so. "Did you see anyone leave that house?" he called.

"I don't know; I might have," Frima answered. "There were some people on the street just after we got here."

Garth growled. "Those were Aghadites," he said. "I'm sure of it. They had a dozen escape routes here. They could be anywhere in the city by now." He realized, as he spoke, that they might even have left the city. A party might well be on its way to Ordunin, to carry out the god's vengeance against Garth's family. Quite aside from his desire for revenge, the cultists were an ongoing threat to innocent people everywhere, and Garth was more determined than ever to destroy them all.

"Oh," Frima said.

"We will hunt them down, wherever they hide," the overman said as he turned the sword's flame against one side of the pit to carve himself a way out.

CHAPTER TWENTY-SIX

The logical place for someone to hide, Garth and Frima agreed, would be in one of the temples. Each one had its secret entrances and hidden chambers, or so the legends said, and each was suitable for fortification.

They resolved to explore the nearest first; that was the temple of Sai, goddess of pain, Aghad's twin sister.

Garth blasted open the spike-steel gate with the Sword of Bheleu and, remembering what had happened to his boots when last he had entered this shrine, he melted smooth the jagged, broken obsidian courtyard. That done, he marched on into the temple, Frima at his heels, Koros waiting outside.

They found no one in the sanctuary. Garth was ready to give up and go, but Frima, recalling her own uncompleted sacrifice, pointed out the secret doorway through which she had been brought up from the vaults below.

Garth agreed that the vaults were worth exploring—a decision he found himself regretting a few hours later, when an extensive search had turned up no Aghadites, but an impressive array of dungeons and torture devices, as well as a handful of half-starved, desperate worshippers of Sai who had taken shelter there when the plague began, three years earlier. Despite a surge of bloodlust, Garth did not kill these people, but instead drove them out into the streets. They promptly headed toward the market, obviously intent on leaving the city.

By the time he and Frima had investigated all the corridors and rooms beneath the temple of Sai and radiating out from it under the surrounding buildings, it was almost dawn, and Garth was tired. He had used up a great deal of the sword's energy in blasting the temple of Aghad, and the expenditure was telling upon him.

Neither Garth nor Frima saw any point in returning to Frima's old home; instead, they broke in the door of a convenient house and made themselves comfortable there. Frima found a store of preserves in the kitchen, and dried salt beef that had not yet spoiled; the wine cupboard included several bottles that had not yet turned to vinegar, though Garth was not impressed with any that he sampled.

At last, when they had both eaten their fill, the girl and the overman found beds and went to sleep.

Garth did not sleep very well; the bed was far too small for him. Around noon he gave up and moved to the floor, which served him better.

He awoke again well after dark to find Frima hacking off strips of beef for their breakfast.

They debated what should be done next. Garth suggested the temple of P'hul as their next target; Frima objected that no Aghadite would venture into that disease-ridden pesthole. That, after all, was where the White Death had come from in the first place.

Garth had to concede the truth of her argument.

He then considered the temple of Bheleu, but dismissed that immediately; it was a ruin, with no roof and an earthen floor. Where could anyone hide in there?

The last temple on the Street of the Temples was the temple of Death. That, Frima insisted, would be the very surest place. Any Dûsarran would consider himself safe from pursuit there, as no one would dare to enter it looking for him.

Garth doubted this hypothesis. Would not the Aghadites, he asked, be at least as frightened by The God Whose Name Is Not Spoken as by their pursuers? After all, the cultists knew that Garth had entered the temple once before and emerged alive, the first person not a devotee of the Final God to do so.

Frima agreed with this reasoning finally. That left the two temples located in other parts of the city—those dedicated to Tema and to Andhur Regvos. Accordingly, the little party headed for the temple of Andhur Regvos, god of darkness.

Here Garth did not waste time in exploring every nook and cranny; instead, he simply used the Sword of Bheleu to blast the domed pyramid into rubble, as he had done to the temple of Aghad.

As with the temple of Aghad, however, he found no trace of any Aghadites in the wreckage. The sanctuary held the desiccated remains of a dozen people, all dead for quite some time; Garth guessed them to be the blind priests of the god, slain by the plague three years before. Nowhere else in the maze of chambers and tunnels did he find anything that might have been alive recently.

That left the temple of Tema. Garth proposed to treat it much as he had the shrines of Aghad and Andhur Regvos, but Frima protested violently. After some argument, the overman gave in. The followers of Tema had not done him any real harm, unlike the Aghadites.

He did not like the delay, which would allow the surviving Aghadites that much more time to devise new schemes and for their emissaries to travel toward Ordunin, but he decided that he could live with it.

It was well after midnight when he and Koros, with Frima on the warbeast's back, reached the steps leading to the temple's entrance. He helped the girl off the beast and then led the way to the door, up between the serpent-carved balustrades.

To his surprise, the door swung open as he approached.

He entered the antechamber and stopped. Frima proceeded on past him toward the concealed inner door, but before she reached it, a voice said, "Please wait, girl."

Startled, Frima stopped.

A blue-robed, white-haired priest emerged from the darkness into the sword's light, blinking in the vivid glare. "Your pardon, but we have grown cautious in these unhappy days. We cannot admit you to the sanctuary until you give an account of yourselves, and swear that you do not carry the White Death."

"We do not carry the plague," Garth said, "and I will swear

that however you like. We have come seeking the Aghadites who fled the destruction of their temple."

"There are no Aghadites here," the priest said patiently. "This is the temple of Tema, goddess of night."

"You will forgive me if I insist upon investigating for myself," Garth replied.

The priest hesitated, and the overman held up the glowing sword; it dripped streamers of white flame. "You will, I think, see that I have the means of enforcing my wishes. I intend to search this temple without delay, and if you or anyone else should oppose me, I am afraid that I will feel it necessary not only to kill you, but also to destroy this entire building, lest my enemies escape me."

The priest stepped back and said reluctantly, "As you wish." The inner door swung open, and Garth stepped through it into the great domed sanctuary.

This chamber was the first place he had seen since returning to Dûsarra that could be called crowded; fifty or sixty ragged people had made themselves at home here, sleeping or sitting on beds made of bunched rags, each with a few meager possessions clustered about. Many of them glanced up at the new arrivals, then stared at the strange, fiery sword the overman carried.

Garth looked at the motley collection of humans and demanded, "How long have these people been here? Did any arrive within the last two days?"

The priest at Garth's elbow shook his head. "Oh, no," he said. "You are the first newcomers in half a year."

The overman swung the sword around and held it at the man's throat. "Will you swear to that, by your goddess and all the other gods?"

"Oh, yes, my lord," the man said, not nodding for fear of cutting or burning his throat on the sword's point if he moved his head. "I swear it, by Tema and by all the gods! These people have been here for months."

Garth decided that he could trust the human. He lowered the sword, ignoring Frima's loud protests regarding his treatment of a holy man.

Again he looked over the great hall, noticing that in the sword's light the stone idol was rather less impressive than he recalled. It stood against the far side of the chamber, the goddess' cloak stretching up to cover most of the dome. It was still a fine piece of sculpture, beautiful and comforting, but he could see the marks of the carvers upon it, which he had not seen in the dark; its ethereal quality was gone.

He spotted dark stains on the wall near the door, but did not inquire after their origin. He was afraid that they might be from his own previous visit, when he had killed a priest very near to the spot where he now stood.

Escorted by the priest, with Frima trailing along behind, Garth made his way around the room, investigating every place that looked as if it might conceal a doorway or niche. From the sanctuary he moved on into the vestry, and from there to the refectory and the dormitory, and finally into the crypts below.

Nowhere did he find anyone in a red robe, or anyone out of place. All those who wore the blue robes of the priests of Tema also had the red eyes and white hair required of her servants, and he could imagine no way in which the Aghadites could have disguised themselves to pass as such, unless they possessed some magic of a sort he was totally unfamiliar with.

He passed the remainder of the night searching the temple, and on into the morning, until at last, around midmorning, he was satisfied that no Aghadites lurked anywhere in the great edifice.

He apologized, more or less, to several of the priests and took his leave, Frima still trailing after him.

Koros was waiting at the foot of the steps, and together they found themselves a new resting place where they might spend the day. Tired as they were, they did not bother about searching for food.

Garth awoke around sunset, ravenously hungry, and discovered that the house they had chosen to sleep in had nothing edible left in it. He began smashing in back doors and investigating the neighboring homes, and eventually came across a wheel of cheese that was still good, and a keg of ale that had almost gone flat but was still more or less potable. He brought these finds back, and found Frima awake and hungry.

When both had eaten, he asked whether the girl had any

suggestions, since none of the temples they had explored had yielded anything.

Frima suggested returning to the Street of the Temples and looking into the remains of the temple of Aghad again, in hopes of finding a clue that might lead them to the vanished cultists.

Having no better suggestion to offer, Garth agreed, and by the time the last trace of twilight had faded in the west the two were standing at the rim of the pit, Koros close behind.

They found nothing of any conceivable use. Garth had been thorough in destroying the shrine, and no papers or documents of any sort remained, nothing that might provide any information except for the tunnels themselves. Garth explored a few of those, but all came to the surface relatively near at hand, and none showed any sign of continued habitation.

The overman stood, at last, at the edge of the hole, looking up the Street of the Temples toward the shadowy blankness at its northern end that hid the entrance to the temple of Death. He found himself doubting his own logic in dismissing the underground temple as a possible hiding place. The Aghadites were the disciples of hate, and the high priest he had slain had said that self-hatred was the most basic of all the things that an Aghadite must possess. Such people might well be willing to hide in a place where no sane Dûsarran would go. Furthermore, they might follow his own earlier line of reasoning through to its conclusion and decide that, because they would be expected to be more frightened of it than Garth would be, the temple of Death would be the one place where the overman would never bother to look.

This convoluted thinking seemed exactly the sort of thing he had come to expect from the followers of Aghad, and the temple entrance was only a short stroll away. It was certainly worthy of investigation, he decided; he led a rather startled Frima northward, up the Street of the Temples.

Along the way, however, he found himself distracted by the ruins of the temple of Bheleu. The skeleton of the ancient dome was gone, but the jagged fragments of the wall that had supported it still remained. A wide gap indicated where the door had once been, and a heap of ash in the center was the last trace of the burning altar whence Garth had drawn the sword.

It occurred to Garth that there was something unnatural about that pile of ash. Surely, after three years, it should have been buried or scattered by the wind.

He had taken the sword from that spot; he had come full circle in the three years since that moment.

It had been three years almost exactly, he realized. He tried to calculate the interval, but could not do so; his memory was not sufficiently precise. He was not even absolutely certain of the present date, let alone when he had taken the sword. Still, within a margin of three days or so, it had been exactly three years since he first touched the Sword of Bheleu.

He wondered whether he might be able to leave the sword here, replacing it whence it came. It seemed worth attempting. Furthermore, an Aghadite or two might have decided to take shelter here—what shelter there was. He stopped at the entrance, startling Frima anew.

"What is it?" she asked. "What are you doing?"

"I want to look in here," Garth said.

Frima peered into the darkness within the stone circle. "Why?" she asked.

"It is a temple, is it not? You thought that the Aghadites might take shelter in the temples."

"Not *this* one!" she protested, obviously having forgotten her earlier suggestion.

The overman did not bother to argue further, but simply marched into the temple, the sword lighting his way. Frima and Koros followed, Frima reluctantly, Koros with its usual calm.

Garth strode unhesitatingly across the earthen floor, directly to the little gray mound in the center, where he stopped. He looked down at the heap, then reached out with the sword to stir the ash.

A sudden warmth surged up through the hilt, through his arm, and into his mind, and he was no longer in the eerie gloom of the broken temple, but floating in a crimson void flooded with ruddy light.

He froze, waiting for whatever would happen next.

"*Garth,*" said the voice so like his own, the voice he recognized as the thing that called itself Bheleu. "*Why have you come here?*"

Garth could not answer that; he was unsure of his own reasons. He had entered the temple on a sudden impulse, thinking two contradictory thoughts—that he might find Aghadites here and slay them with the sword, or that he might be able to free himself of the sword here without the Forgotten King's intervention. He was not sure which was his true desire. He had been carrying out his revenge against the cult of Aghad, but it was, so far, unsatisfying. There was no pleasure, no recompense, in the sight of a dead cultist or a blasted temple. The only pleasure came in the instant of destruction, and that was a fleeting and unhealthy passion that he did not believe was truly his own. He still felt driven to destroy the cult, but he no longer found any real value in that destruction, nor any easing of his own mind.

He wanted to be free of the sword, he knew. Despite his bargain with the god, he knew that his thoughts were tainted, that he had become an unclean, irrational thing, and that he would remain such as long as he wielded the sword. Yet he wanted the sword's power, the ability to strike down whatever affronted him, and he feared what might happen if the weapon should fall into the hands of the only other earthly being who had demonstrated the capacity to handle it safely: the Forgotten King.

He did not know how to answer the god's question.

"Garth, my time is drawing to an end, and you have denied me my freedom throughout what should have been my reign over the mortal realm. You have cut my age to a tenth of its anticipated length. There is nothing left to me but the last destruction, the end of myself and my fellow gods. If you wish, I will free you of the sword and relinquish all claim to you; you need but thrust the blade into the ash and leave it there, and there will be no more little destructions by your hand, but only the final cataclysm, when the time for it has come. Decide now; I will not allow you another chance. Take the sword and go on as my emissary, or leave it and be free."

Garth struggled to think, to weigh his decision logically. He wanted to leave the sword, to leave behind all his involvement in supernatural events; if he still planned further acts to avenge Kyrith and Saram, he could carry them out with his own abilities. He had done well enough for over a century without any divine assistance. He released his hold on the weapon, and it seemed to float motionlessly in the void before him.

On the other hand, Bheleu's mention of a final cataclysm frightened him. He tried to convince himself that a god would see time differently and that this last destruction might still be millennia away, but he could not bring himself to believe it. He knew that somewhere in the city the Forgotten King was preparing magic that was meant to destroy the world, and he was absolutely sure that if he were to leave the sword in the temple of Bheleu, it would find its way to the old man and the final spell would be completed.

He could not allow that to happen. "I will keep the sword," he said. His hand closed on the hilt.

He had expected the god's mocking laughter, but there was only silence; the red light faded, and he was in the ruined temple again.

Frima had watched with concern as her overman companion had walked up to the pile of ash, poked the sword into it, and then frozen. "What is it? What's happening?" she called, but Garth did not answer; he stood staring off into space. She came nearer, waved her hand before his face, but got no response. Worried, she fished the sling she had appropriated from the dead Aghadite out of her pouch.

Garth released the Sword of Bheleu suddenly; it wobbled, but remained upright, held by the mound of ash. Its glow died away, from a vivid white light to a pale yellow flickering, but Garth did not move or speak. He still stared ahead blindly.

Something appeared off to one side; Frima whirled, a dart in the sling, and let fly.

Not one dart but two rattled off stone; her own had struck the broken wall near where she had glimpsed the movement, and another had whizzed past Garth's head and hit the far side of the chamber. "Koros!" Frima called. "Kill them!"

The warbeast looked at her, as if debating with itself whether or not to obey someone other than its master. Another dart flew, ricocheting from Garth's armor with a sharp ringing, and Koros decided; with a roar, it leaped toward the hidden attacker.

Garth remained unmoving. Frima had another dart in her

sling and was crouched, ready and waiting, glancing warily about.

Someone screamed, the cry mingling with the warbeast's growl and ending in an unpleasant bubbling. Frima could not see what was taking place in the darkness, but it was obvious that Koros had found its prey.

Again something moved, and she turned to see a dark shape approaching with sword held high. She flung the dart in her sling, and the figure staggered and dropped.

Light flared up; Garth held the Sword of Bheleu once more, the blade burning brightly with its unnatural white flame. The overman was moving as well, turning away from the ashen remains of the altar. He and Frima gazed with almost equal surprise at the red-robed man who lay, his fallen sword nearby, midway between the Dûsarran girl and the temple's entrance.

The man was not dead, but only stunned. Garth picked him up with one hand, the sword blazing in the other, and demanded, "Where are the rest of you?"

Koros emerged from the shadows, its jaw smeared with blood. The Aghadite stared in terror, first at the warbeast, then at the flaming sword, and finally at the grim overman.

"I don't know!" he cried.

"Yours is the god of treachery, filth; betray your comrades!" Garth demanded.

"I can't," the man insisted. "I would, I swear to you by Aghad, but I can't!"

"You swear it, by all the gods?"

"Yes!" The man was nodding and weeping. "Yes, yes, I swear it!"

Disgusted and enraged, Garth flung the human aside; his head hit the stone wall with a sharp cracking sound, and he slumped in a heap at the base.

Garth had not intended to kill the man, but he did not doubt that he had done so and he did not regret it. "There may be more," he said.

"Koros got one," Frima told him. "I haven't seen any others."

"We'll search," the overman said.

They did search, going over the entire temple area carefully. Frima stopped and became ill when she saw what Koros had left of the sling-wielder. They found no more Aghadites, though, nor any evidence that others had been there.

When Garth was satisfied, he led the way back out onto the street and onward toward the temple of death. Frima followed reluctantly, Koros beside her. Garth did not look back, but he did find himself wondering whether he had done the right thing in keeping the sword.

That might, he realized, have been his last chance to get rid of it; still, he resisted the urge to run back and try to bargain with Bheleu. If he released the sword, the Forgotten King would get it, he was certain. He could not allow that, now or ever. He marched up the street, sword held up before him to light the way.

The city seemed deserted; nothing moved on the Street of the Temples save himself and his two companions. He wondered if anything still lived in Dûsarra other than the Aghadites, the huddled people in the temple of Tema, and his own little group.

At the end of the avenue, the glow of the sword revealed black volcanic rock forming a narrow defile that led into a cave; the sword's light did not penetrate the shadows of the cave's entrance, visible as a deeper blackness amid the surrounding stones.

A human corpse lay sprawled half in, half out of the shadows. That was hardly surprising in this city of death, where Garth had found himself almost tripping over bare bones at every turn. This body, however, was still fresh; it had not yet begun to rot. Garth could detect only the faintest scent of incipient corruption and judged that it had been dead no more than three days at the most.

The remains were those of a very old man; Garth paused to study them, and recognized who the man had been.

He was clad in a robe of so pure a black that the sword's light, or almost any other light, was not reflected at all, making the corpse seem almost a heap of tangible shadow. It was small and frail, with one leg twisted and shrunken, one hand missing, half the face hidden beneath a purplish growth, one eye long gone and the other buried beneath white cataracts.

This pitiful thing had been the caretaker of the temple of Death.

The overman glanced around warily, but saw no sign of anything that might have killed the ancient priest. It was entirely possible that age had caught up with him at last. Even the priests of Death died eventually—with one exception.

It was very near this spot that the overman high priest of Aghad, whom Garth had later slain, had once taunted him from concealment. One of the tunnels leading from the temple of Aghad might, Garth guessed, come up in this vicinity. He peered at the surrounding rock, but could see no sign of human presence.

"What happened to him?" Frima asked, staring at the corpse.

"He died," Garth said. After a pause, he added, "Probably of old age."

"Oh," Frima replied, suppressing a shudder. She found so fresh a corpse, dead so mysteriously, to be far more unsettling than the less recognizable remains of the plague's many victims.

Garth was no longer interested in the body and felt reasonably certain that no assassins lurked in the immediate area. "Come on," he said.

"That's the temple of Death," Frima said, not moving.

"Yes," Garth agreed, "it is."

"I don't want to go in there," she said.

"Why not? You suggested before that Aghadites might hide here; are you frightened of them? Have you decided to abandon your vengeance?"

"No, that's not it!" she cried. "I'm frightened of Death!"

"I am here to protect you," Garth replied. "I have been here before and emerged alive. I have the power of Bheleu to defend us. However, if you prefer, you may wait here while I investigate the temple."

Frima hesitated, but finally said, "All right. I'll stay here if you leave Koros with me."

Garth had no objection to that; he had not intended to take the warbeast into the temple in any case. He was not sure the huge creature would fit through the entry passage.

He ordered the beast to guard the girl and then strode onward into the cave.

CHAPTER TWENTY-SEVEN

The floor sloped gently downward; there was no gate or door, but the corridor narrowed slightly at one point. Thereafter it gradually widened, opening at last into a large chamber, the heart of the temple. Although the passageway was entirely natural, this main room had been artificially enlarged, the floor smoothed and leveled, the walls carved into elaborate friezes separated by columns, and the ceiling around the sides ribbed with carved vaulting. The central portion of the ceiling remained rough, natural stone, and beneath this stood the altar, cut from a large stalagmite and carved in the form of a lectern, with a strange horned skull riveted to its upper edge.

The glare of the sword was not the only light here; a sullen red glow came from the tunnel that led down and away from the far side of the chamber. The carvings and the altar cast strange double shadows in this eerie illumination.

Garth paid no attention to any of this. He had expected the temple to be deserted; he had completely forgotten, in the press of other concerns, that the Forgotten King had announced his intention of coming here and beginning his magic. The overman had dismissed that, convincing himself that the King could do nothing without the Sword of Bheleu, and had somehow assumed that the old man was lurking somewhere in the city, waiting for Garth to relinquish the sword to him.

He had been wrong. The Forgotten King stood before the altar, his back to Garth, chanting something unintelligible. The Book of Silence lay upon the altar, open, and it was evident that the old man was reading from it.

The sound seemed to reverberate from the stone walls, turning the Forgotten King's already-hideous voice into an unspeakable cacophony. Garth could not recognize the language of the spell, save that it bore no resemblance to his own tongue. The words were harsh and sibilant, with unpleasant combinations of vowels, and consonants that seemed to be all either hissing or guttural. Words and phrases ended in the wrong places, and the rhythm was broken and hard to follow, but the King appeared not to notice; he chanted on, the words spilling forth in a constant stream.

Garth watched for a long moment, unsure what to do. He knew that he did not want the King to complete his spell, but he did not know whether it would be safe to interrupt it.

The chant ended abruptly with a high-pitched grating sound, and without hesitation or pause the King said, "Greetings, Garth." He did not turn.

"Greetings, O King."

There was a moment of growing silence as the last echoes rebounded, faded, and died.

"What are you doing?" Garth asked at last.

"I prepare the final magic," the King replied.

The overman stepped forward, circling wide to the left so that the old man would not be able to reach out and snatch the sword away from him. "How can you do that," he asked, "without the Sword of Bheleu?"

"The sword is required only in the final stage, at the end of the three days, a point that will arrive shortly. I can prepare the magic, but I cannot complete it without both the sword and your assistance."

This answer troubled Garth, not so much because of what was said as because it was given so freely and seemed so cooperative a response—totally out of character for the old man. Something about him had changed; Garth guessed that having begun his spell, after so long a wait, had affected him.

The overman took another few steps and looked at the old man's face.

For a moment he did not realize what he was seeing, but only that something was wrong. The King's face seemed to shimmer and alter as the overman watched, distorting itself, and after several seconds Garth realized that the old man was wearing the Pallid Mask. The mask had fitted itself to the contours of the King's face, but remained smooth and pale and metallic, retaining its unsettling ability to shift its appearance inexplicably. The old man's long wisp of beard was caught up inside the mask's chin, out of sight, and the eye sockets were less sunken than his own—though his eyes remained invisible, hidden now, not by the shadows of his cowl, but by the mask.

"You will not receive my aid," Garth said. "It may be that you will somehow get the sword from me, but I swear I will never help you to destroy all the world just so that you may die."

"No, perhaps you will not—but might you not destroy all the world so that your enemies, the followers of Aghad, will perish with it?"

"No."

"Do not speak so quickly, Garth. Think first. You seek to slay them all; you have sworn to destroy them. How else can you do this? With the Sword of Bheleu you can destroy the entire city of Dûsarra, it is true—but to do so will take time, and in that time many will be able to escape, to flee elsewhere. Some may already have done so. Will you hunt them down throughout the world, one by one? Do you expect to live forever, then? Are you ready to devote centuries to this pursuit? It will take centuries to find and kill them all, Garth. You cannot destroy each of them that way. Nor can you use the Sword of Bheleu to destroy every place that they might hide; the sword's power is not great enough to destroy all the world. Together, though, we might send them all to their deaths with a single simple spell, this same spell that I have almost fully prepared."

"And in so doing, consign the rest of the world, as well, to destruction, myself along with it."

"Would that really be so unbearable? A moment, and it would all be over. Is your life so pleasant, then, that you must cling to it so tenaciously? Would it not be a comfort simply to let go, to let yourself fall into the nothingness of death? I have sought for that peace for long centuries now; can you find it so repulsive?"

"My life is my own, old man, and none of your concern. I do not want to die, nor to be responsible for the deaths of millions of innocent people."

"Innocent? Who, Garth, is innocent? The overmen of Ordunin, who exiled you for aiding them and refused even to consider your pardon? Your family, who refused to leave a frozen wasteland to join you? The Yprians, perhaps, who squabble among themselves and have invaded, without cause, the lands of their neighbors? The Erammans, who have turned the richest empire in this decadent world into a chaos of civil war, who drove your people into the wilderness to die? The Orûnians, who tried to take advantage of their neighbors' internal strife? The people of Skelleth, who despise you even after three years, despite all you have done for them? The people of Ur-Dormulk, what few remain, who sent soldiers to kill you? Who among these is worthy of your consideration? Where are the people who deserve to live so much that you would give up your just vengeance and go on living a life that has become a burden to you, merely so that they might survive a few years longer amid war, plague, and famine?"

"You distort the truth with words, old man," Garth said, resisting an urge to give in, to admit that the Forgotten King was right. He was uncertain whether this impulse came from himself or from Bheleu or from some magic wrought by the King, the book, or the mask. Whatever it was, it was powerful, almost hypnotic; his gaze was fixed on the Pallid Mask, white and gleaming, and he found it hard to think of resistance. "What of Frima?" he asked, grasping at the first memory he could dredge up. "She has done nothing to deserve death. Surely there are millions more like her."

The old man did not answer; instead, he leaned his head forward and began chanting again.

Garth remembered suddenly why he had come to this place and demanded loudly, "Old man, are there any Aghadites here?" He doubted that there were. The Forgotten King would not care to be disturbed by their presence, and Garth knew that the King was capable of enforcing his whims.

The chanting broke, and the King said, "We are alone here, Garth, alone with our gods."

The overman, refusing to trust the old man, tried to figure out some way in which this pronouncement could be interpreted that would allow for the presence of cultists. He could think of none; after a moment's hesitation he nodded and turned to go.

The King was chanting again, but his voice was suddenly drowned out by another sound, distorted by the echoes of the passageway and by the distance, but still, unmistakably, the roar of a warbeast.

Startled, Garth froze, staring into the shadows of the entry passage; then, with the glowing sword held out before him, he broke into a run.

Chapter Twenty-eight

Blood spattered across his face as he emerged from the cave. Garth blinked and raised his free hand to shield his eyes. His ears were filled with human screaming and the roaring of the warbeast.

His first impulse was to strike out with the Sword of Bheleu, blasting whatever stood before him, but he restrained himself. Koros and Frima were around somewhere, and he did not want to harm them. The sword's power was not selective enough to leave them unscathed in a blind attack.

After the first shower of blood across his face, nothing more struck him, although Garth did not yet realize what had actually hit him. He lowered his hand and opened his eyes.

Koros stood before him, fangs bared and dripping blood, several mangled corpses beneath its massive paws, others flung up against either side of the defile, weapons scattered on all sides. Its roar had died to a sullen growling.

Garth wiped at the liquid on his face, looked at the residue on his hand, and then understood that blood had been flung upon him by the warbeast's attack on the last of the Aghadites. It was, he was sure, human blood.

The warbeast was not uninjured, however. Three crossbow quarrels protruded from one shoulder, and a fourth from one of its forepaws. Something had gashed it across the face, narrowly missing one of its great golden eyes.

No further threat remained. There could be no doubt that every human in sight was dead.

With that thought, Garth became aware that Frima was not there. He looked over the bloody bodies, but saw none that might have been his Dûsarran companion.

The sound of screaming was still continuing, he noticed, coming from somewhere beyond the rocks to his right. Koros was looking in that direction, apparently trying to locate the sound's source. It was only then that Garth realized he was hearing, not the wordless yelling of dying men, but a human female calling, "Koros! Koros!"

It was Frima's voice, but no sooner had Garth recognized it than it fell silent.

"Frima!" the overman bellowed.

There was no answer; his cry echoed from the surrounding rock and was followed only by silence.

"Frima!" Garth called again. Koros growled; there was no other response.

It was obvious that the Aghadites had gotten her, separating her from the warbeast somehow, and then killing her. Garth felt his anger mount. He saw the glow of the sword deepen to red and brighten to a ferocious glare. The Aghadites would pay for this, he promised himself. They would all die, every one of them, no matter where they might hide. They had destroyed an innocent girl and they would regret it—if they lived long enough to know what happened.

He remembered the Forgotten King's words, and his own reply. Frima was gone now, and with her, his concern for the world's inhabitants. The world might be full of innocent victims, he told himself, but if he didn't destroy them, someone else would.

"*I'a bheluye!*" he cried. "Aghad, I will destroy you!" He turned and strode back into the temple of Death.

Watching from their concealed vantage point at the mouth of a tunnel in the surrounding stone, the high priestess of Aghad and two of her companions saw the overman's magic sword blaze up a baleful red, and heard him proclaim his anger.

"I think," the high priestess said, "that we should wait until he's had some time to calm down. If we try to bargain with him now, he's liable to fry us all before we can speak a dozen words; he's too mad to worry about the girl. When he's had more time to think, we should be able to make a deal."

Her companions made noises of agreement, peering warily out. Farther down the tunnel, a loud thump sounded, followed by muffled cursing.

"Be careful with her!" the high priestess warned. "She may be the only thing that keeps us all alive!"

"I beg your forgiveness, mistress," someone answered. "But she fights like a mad creature. She chewed through the gag already, and we had to drop her to prepare another."

The priestess turned away from the tunnel opening and stared down at the struggling form of their captive, barely visible in the light of the single shuttered lantern allowed so near the entrance. "You can hurt her if you need to," she said, "just as long as you don't kill her or cripple her."

Frima thrashed harder and tried to scream; one of the Aghadites jammed another wadded cloth into her mouth, stifling the sound.

Garth did not hear Frima's struggles, and would not have paid enough attention to recognize them for what they were if he had. He was convinced that she was dead. Whenever someone else had fallen into the hands of the Aghadites, he or she had died. Kyrith had died and Saram had died; Garth saw no reason to think that Frima had fared any better. He expected to be confronted with her mutilated corpse when next he emerged from the temple of Death—if he ever did emerge.

He strode down the passageway with the sword blazing before him, the glow feeding on his anger and stoking it as well. His rage, or the combination of his own despair and rage with the malign influence of Bheleu, had driven all conscious thought from his mind, save the necessity of destroying the cult of Aghad, regardless of the means or the cost. He stormed into the inner chamber of the temple just as the Forgotten King's chanting paused.

"What must I do, old man?" Garth demanded.

"You will know when the time comes," the Forgotten King replied. He began to chant again.

Garth was in no mood to wait, but he forced himself to stand behind the King, awaiting the instructions he was sure would come. The old man would give him a sign, some way of knowing what was expected of him, and he would act; the spell would be completed, and the world would end.

His enemies would be destroyed—the cult of Aghad would be wiped out to the last stinking, treacherous member. The city of Dûsarra, which had so blighted his life, would vanish. The gods themselves, the foul Aghad and Garth's own unwanted master Bheleu among them, would die. The Forgotten King would perish, and his Unnamed God with him.

Garth himself would die, but what of it? He had little enough left in the world. His people had scorned him, Kyrith and Saram and Frima had been murdered, and his world had sunk into an era of chaos and destruction.

The old man would have his wish; his life, which had lasted so impossibly long, would be over.

Everything would end.

Everything.

Koros would die—both the warbeast and the god it was named for. It was hard to imagine the animal dying. The sun would go out, or so he assumed; there would be nothing left for it to shine upon. The green fields of summer would never be again; sun above and earth below would both be gone. The farmers in the fields would be gone, human and overman alike.

There would be an end to war and hatred and death, Garth told himself.

Yes, and an end to love and life as well. The destruction would swallow up the good with the bad, and there would be no more world, no more time, no chance to make anything right. He would never again feel the wind in his face or the sun on his back, not only because he would be dead and beyond all feeling, but because there would be no more wind, no more sun, ever again. Fish would no longer swim in the sea, for the sea would be no more, and birds would not fly. No new year would ever follow this one, no autumn would supplant this final summer—all because he, Garth of Ordunin, had defied the gods and lost. He had been defeated by Aghad, Bheleu, and Death; he had lost himself in the anger and despair that the dark gods sent. He was allowing the gods to manipulate him.

This must not be.

The Forgotten King's harsh voice cut through to him, raised suddenly to a new pitch and volume, wrapped around the massed consonants of the chant, and Garth felt magical power seething around him.

He wanted to stop, to retreat, to reverse his decision. He did not want the world to end, did not want to aid in its destruction, but he could not move. He felt a fierce compulsion to give in, to do what the old man wanted, to serve the gods who had shaped the world in this one final act, and he fought desperately against it.

The chanting stopped, and the old man turned to face him, the mask gleaming dully in the red light of the sword, as if washed in blood.

In desperation, struggling to destroy the compulsion that he felt overtaking him, Garth lashed out with the Sword of Bheleu, striking at the old man, hoping to disrupt the spell before his part in it was needed. He thrust the glowing blade against the King's chest, expecting it to be turned aside and to receive a backlash of magical force, a resistance that would break the web of power that held him.

The blade sank easily through the old man's frail body with a sound like a soft sigh, emerging a foot or more from his back and scraping against the stone of the altar. Thick, dark blood oozed slowly forth onto the shining metal.

The Forgotten King smiled, the Pallid Mask twisting to fit his face, and Garth realized, even before the first rumbling began, what his part in the final ritual had been. He had been destined, all along, to plunge the Sword of Bheleu into the heart of the King in Yellow.

He stared in horror at the mask. Something was happening to the King; his blood was evaporating from the sword, and his body was fading, thinning away to nothing. The mask was melting into the flesh of his face, blending with it, reshaping itself; it sank back against the bone of the old man's skull, pulling itself tight.

The King's yellow mantle fell open, and Garth tried to

scream at the sight of what lay beneath, but something had happened to the flow of time; he was unable to move normally. An eternity wound itself past him and through him as his mouth came open.

The King in Yellow turned insubstantial and seemed simultaneously to grow and shrink, departing from Garth's presence in some impossible direction. He was no longer more than a vague caricature of a human being. His head was a fleshless, grinning skull, the mask indissolubly joined; his fingers were gleaming bone, his whole being somehow smoky and indistinct.

Then he was gone, and Garth remained frozen in an instant of distorted time, waiting for his own death.

The Sword of Bheleu was still held out before him, impaling the space where the King had been; and now, as Garth watched, his mouth still opening in his need to scream, the blade puffed away in glittering, luminous powder, and the gem in the pommel burst into a shower of crystal, light, and blood. The grip crumbled away, and his hands were empty.

He became aware of a deep rumbling all around him.

He felt himself standing in the temple, suddenly conscious of every instant, of every action of his body. He felt his heart pumping blood, an age passing between each beat, felt his muscles contracting, and waited for it all to stop, waited to die.

It did not stop. Time dragged on, horribly elongated. He felt eldritch energy whirling about him, filling the air.

Then, abruptly, it was over—but he was not dead.

He stood in the cave that had been the temple of Death, his mouth open as if to scream, but the need to cry out had passed. His mind was clear and calm. The air was still, and the forces that had filled it with tension were gone. The sword of the thing that had called itself the god of destruction was gone. The old man who had called himself the Forgotten King was gone. The strange pale mask was gone, and the old book on the altar as well. Nothing remained but a hollowed-out cave, its walls carved into ugly friezes. A dull rumbling still persisted.

Behind him, a voice said, "So it's finally over."

Chapter Twenty-nine

Garth whirled, reaching automatically for the dagger on his belt.

An old woman stood in the entryway; she wore heavy robes, their color indistinguishable in the dim red glow that lit the cave—a glow that seemed brighter than Garth remembered it. He attributed that to the distorting effects of whatever he had just gone through.

The woman smiled cheerfully at him, looking utterly harmless despite the eerie light, but Garth was not comforted by her expression. He noticed, rather, that he was unable to focus clearly upon her face. Her features appeared to shift subtly as he watched.

"Who are you?" he demanded.

"I am Weida, goddess of wisdom and learning," the old woman replied, crossing her arms over her chest—or perhaps they had already been crossed, Garth could not be certain. He wondered if something was wrong with his vision, or if the weird events of the last few moments had addled his brain. Nothing else was affected; the walls were as solid as ever. It was only the old woman whose appearance was uncertain.

Even so, he relaxed somewhat. She might be a wizard of some sort, but she was obviously mad, and probably harmless. He guessed that she was a survivor of the plague who had wandered into the temple by accident. The absurdity of her presence was such a relief after the terrifying experience he had just undergone that he smiled broadly.

"I really am Weida," the woman insisted. "Observe."

She vanished.

Garth's smile vanished as well.

She reappeared again, seeming to coalesce from motes of dust. "I know," she said. "It's a trick any good magician could probably have managed a few days ago, but honestly, I really am Weida, and I am one of the Arkhein, what you would consider a minor goddess."

"If you are a goddess," Garth asked slowly, though he was still not ready to accept the idea, "then why are you still alive? Did not Bheleu and all the others perish? What else could it mean, when the Sword of Bheleu crumbled and the Book of Silence vanished?"

Before the woman could speak, he added, "For that matter, why am *I* still alive?"

"Why shouldn't we be alive?" She smiled, her face shimmering as she did, and for an instant Garth thought he saw the image of Ao, one of the Wise Women of Ordunin. Before the overman could protest, she went on. "No, never mind. I know what you're thinking—that's my province, after all. You thought that all the world would end, all the gods would die, when the King in Yellow completed the ritual. The King thought so, too. It may be that he convinced himself that would be the case, back when he first realized he would prefer death to unending life; he couldn't stand the thought of anything living on after him."

That sounded plausible, but Garth objected. "What about all the prophecies? Everyone agreed that the Forgotten King would live until the end of time! That was the bargain he made with the gods!"

"It was the bargain that deceived the oracles and prophets. The bargain was fulfilled, in a way, and the Forgotten King did live until the end of time. The problem lies in the exact meaning of that phrase. You must understand it, not in mortal terms, but in the way the gods meant it. It is not 'the end of time,' where 'time' is a common noun, but 'the end of Time,' where 'Time' is a proper noun, the name of a god. The King could not die so long as the gods that had given him immortality still lived—all three of those gods. He was not given eternal life by the Death-God alone, nor even by Death and Life in partnership, but by Death, Life, and Time—the god you knew as Dagha. It was Dagha-Time that created the Lords of Eir and Dûs, who in turn created the world and everything in it— myself included, and much less directly, you as well. And it was Dagha that ended when the King completed his spell."

Garth grappled with this explanation for a moment, then asked, "But how can the world exist if time is no more? How can I move? How can we speak?"

"*Time* still exists; it is *Dagha* who is no more. Dagha created time, but does that mean that the two must perish together? When a house-carpenter dies, do all his houses fall in? We are more than the dreams of the gods; though they created the world, it has an existence of its own. Dagha, itself, misunderstood this; it was incapable of conceiving of our world continuing after the fourteen gods who had created it ceased to be."

"The fourteen gods are truly gone, then?"

"Oh, yes; they had no real independent existence of their own. They were not so much Dagha's dreams, perhaps, as parts of itself—concepts that Dagha split off from itself. They couldn't exist beyond Dagha; each merged with his or her opposite and returned to the nothingness that brought them forth."

Garth considered this. "But then why," he asked, "do you still exist, if you're a goddess?" He was beginning to believe the woman's claim to divinity; her knowledge of the King's passing, and the calm rationality of her explanations, did not accord with his theory of a mad wizard.

"Dagha didn't create *me* from nothingness, Garth; Leuk and Pria did. Dagha, self-obsessed and self-contained, could not create anything directly that could have an independent life of its own, but the fragments it broke off and gave names to were not so restricted, being already incomplete and out of balance themselves. Dagha didn't create the world, either, nor living beings such as yourself; it was the fourteen beings Dagha had created who, in their turn, did that. We were all started by the Lords of Eir, and Dagha thought that, in balance, we'd all be finished off by the Lords of Dûs—but Dagha got that one wrong. Its playing at creation threw the balance out. I wasn't sure, though, to be truthful, how much of our little world would come through intact."

A sudden cold uncertainty soaked into Garth's thoughts.

"How much *did* come through?" He had visions of finding nothing but space outside the temple cave; perhaps nothing remained alive anywhere save for himself and this peculiar self-proclaimed goddess.

"Oh, almost everything; you need not worry, Garth. A few stars may be missing, a few things may be changed in how the world works, but in general, Garth, everything remains as you knew it."

"You're sure?"

"Oh, yes. I'm a goddess, Garth, and the goddess of knowledge, at that. I know a very great deal. We are not alone. The world remains much as it was; most people are probably unaware of any change, save a brief spell of dizziness."

"And you knew that the world would survive?"

"Well, as I said, even I was not certain until right at the end."

"How could you know what the other, greater gods did not?"

"Because I am what I am, Garth, the goddess of wisdom. I saw through the deceits and partial truths that Dagha used to fool itself and its constituent deities. I knew from the start that it had done more than it knew in creating our world, creating something so removed from itself." She smiled wryly, and for a moment her face seemed solid and normal. "I must confess, however, that I had my doubts. I saw the pattern of time that Dagha had set up, and saw how neatly the world followed along its set path, and feared that it might all end as Dagha had planned. It was not until you refused the service of Bheleu, three years ago, and thereby cut short the Age of Destruction, that I could be certain the pattern was broken. That act, more than any other in all the fifteen ages, threw the world aside from its predestined course and assured it of continued existence when its creators had gone. You disrupted the whole cosmic balance, Garth, by favoring life over death."

Garth was falling behind in following the explanations.

"But why are you different from the other gods? Did all the lesser gods survive, whatever they're called?"

"We are called the Arkhein, Garth, and I am not yet certain whether we have all survived. Some of us were closely tied to our creators; others, like myself, were more independent. I am not bound up in the time that Dagha controlled. The Eir and the Dûs were all predestined, with no say in their own existence; each took his turn for an age, tied to the scheme that Dagha had set up. The order of the ages was established from the beginning and the nature of each predetermined. Each had its rules, symbols, totems, and intended duration, all part of the pretty pattern that Dagha had designed for its little creations to dance through. When the pattern was finished, so were they. The Arkhein, however, were not part of that grand pattern. We were free to do as we pleased, pretty much—or at least most of us were. Dagha hadn't made us, didn't control us, and had no place for us in its designs. It hadn't made the world and it didn't control that; surely you knew enough theology to know that nobody bothered praying to Dagha, since it never did any good."

"Yes, I knew that," Garth admitted.

"Garth, if it confuses you so, don't worry about reasons and explanations. Just accept the situation as it is. The fifteen higher gods are gone, but the world continues. We're all free now, coasting on, as it were. There are no more predetermined ages— you survived the Fifteenth Age in the three minutes it took the higher gods to die. Nothing is set anymore; there is no more predestination. You are no longer the chosen of Bheleu, but merely an overman. There is no more Bheleu."

Garth thought that over, watching Weida's shifting features. The rumbling grew louder, and the floor trembled beneath his feet. The red glow appeared to brighten.

"What is that sound?" he asked. "It seemed to start during the King's spell."

"That's the volcano. Dûsarra was built on an active volcano, you know, and the priests of the seven dark gods worked a great spell to restrain it. Now that the gods are dead, the magic they powered won't work anymore. Major theurgy is a dead art—and nobody ever called on us Arkhein very much. Most magic drew on the higher gods, either Eir or Dûs; and when they died, all their magic went with them. Their totems. all burned out during the Fifteenth Age; the dying gasp of the fifteen gods, I suppose you might call it. You saw three of them go yourself. And because the magic is gone, the volcano is free; it's been pent up since the city was founded back in the Eighth Age, so I suppose it will erupt any minute now. This cave is one of its old exhaust vents; it will probably fill up with lava quite quickly."

Garth turned around and stared apprehensively at the brightening red glow. "Wouldn't that kill us both?" he asked.

"Oh, I suppose it will kill you, but it will take more than a volcano to harm a goddess."

The overman turned back, enraged—and relieved to realize that it was wholly his own anger, untainted by Bheleu's malign influence. It was a clean and simple feeling, very unlike the seething, perverse fury the god's power had engendered so often. "Why didn't you warn me sooner?" he demanded.

"Why should I? What does it matter to me if an overman dies?"

"If you don't care what happens to me, why are you here? Why have you manifested yourself and spoken with me?"

"Ah, you've seen through me. I do care, Garth, at least somewhat. I wanted to watch the fireworks, to see the end of our old order. I wanted to speak with the mortal involved, and to congratulate you on the part you've played in everything. Most of all, I was curious; it goes with wisdom. Only the curious ever learn much. That's why I alone am here, of all the Arkhein. But that's all done now, and it's not the place of a goddess to become too attached to a mortal. You must die eventually, after all—and have I not now warned you?"

Garth heard the rumbling grow louder, and the stone floor shook from a sudden shock far below. He glanced back at the red glow, which now seemed dimmer.

"You have a few minutes yet, Garth," the goddess said.

"A moment," Garth said. "If the god of death is gone, can I still die?" He wondered if the goddess, if she was in fact what she claimed to be, might be amusing herself at his expense. Could it be that he had inadvertently obtained immortality, not just for himself, but for all the world?

"The old god of death is gone, The God Whose Name Was

Not Spoken, who was a Lord of Dûs and a part of Dagha, but there is still death. There must always be death. We have a new god of death now, one that you helped to create."

"What?"

"Certainly. You didn't see the King in Yellow die, did you? You were watching; he changed, and moved out of your realm of perception, but he did not die. He merged with the Pallid Mask, assuming the power it signified, and became Death himself. You saw it happen."

Garth remembered what he had seen beneath the King in Yellow's mantle and knew that Weida—if it was Weida— spoke the truth. A perverse amusement twitched his mouth into a smile. "Then after all that, he didn't die? His great spell was for nothing?"

"Hardly for nothing, Garth. The human part of him perished utterly, and Yhtill of Hastur is no more. The King in Yellow no longer has any material existence, but he still goes on, the embodiment of the power and concept of Death."

Half a dozen other questions came to mind while Garth puzzled this over, but the rumbling changed again, with a deep, slow, grinding sound, and the overman decided that any further inquiries were inessential. He ran toward the entrance.

Weida might or might not have stepped aside to let him pass; he was not sure whether she did, or whether he passed through her, or some impossible combination of both. Disconcerted, he stumbled against the wall of the passage and glanced back.

The woman was gone—or the image, or goddess, or whatever it had been.

The voice, however, lingered, calling, "I think you had better hurry, overman."

Garth righted himself and hurried on. While moving, he asked aloud, "How is it that you materialized here before me in this cave? None of the other gods I was involved with ever did that, not Aghad, nor Bheleu, nor any of them. Bheleu could only speak to me in visions."

"They were Dûs, Garth, and not tied to this world as we Arkhein are," the voice said quietly, speaking from the air near his right ear.

"All right, then, if the Arkhein can manifest themselves

where the Eir and Dûs could not, why have I never heard of it happening before?"

"The rules are different now," the voice replied. "We were restrained by Dagha's rules, confined by the power of the higher gods even while we drew much of our own power from them. Now, things have changed. Everything has changed. Even I don't know all the differences yet; I have never been so free before and have not yet had time to learn what this freedom means."

A brutal shaking distracted Garth from the conversation; he staggered up the dark passageway, grateful that there were no branches where he might make a wrong turning. Ahead, he glimpsed a pale gray glimmering; he moved onward and saw that it was the first faint light of dawn.

CHAPTER THIRTY

Frima had been blindfolded as well as bound and gagged, and did not see what happened to her captors. She heard a rumbling, then a crashing, and then the deafening roar of an angry warbeast, mixed with human screams. The hands that had held her fell away, and she tumbled heavily to the floor, bruising her elbows on the stone. She tried to call out, but the gag stopped her voice. She struggled with her bonds in an attempt to work the loops of rope and fabric down over her hands.

She heard thrashing sounds and the scraping of stone on stone in those brief instants between the warbeast's growls and roars; the screaming of its victims was almost constant. At least once she heard a crunching she knew to be the splintering of bones. Something warm and wet sprayed across her legs where they protruded from her disarrayed robe.

Finally, when the roaring seemed to be almost upon her, the screaming faded and died.

The roaring, too, died in its turn, and she heard a harsh, inhuman breathing. Something viscous and unpleasant dripped onto her face.

She managed to work one hand free, thanking Tema and the other gods for giving her such small, delicate hands. Saram had complimented her on them more than once. She reached up and pulled away the blindfold, both hopeful and afraid.

Koros looked back at her, its golden eyes gleaming strangely in the faint dawning light that filtered into the Aghadite tunnel. She saw, behind the beast, that a large part of one wall of the tunnel had been broken away; Koros had obviously managed to track her down and come to her rescue, letting nothing bar its way.

That moment of realization seemed to stretch on forever; time distorted and slowed, and she felt herself drawn out across an eternity, staring into the warbeast's eyes for endless eons.

This was more frightening than anything the Aghadites could have done to her; the three-minute piece of warped and broken time was utterly beyond her experience or conjecture, and she was certain, while it was occurring, that the universe had come to an end for her, that she was dead or dying. She could think of nothing but death that might be so unlike life as she had known it.

Then, abruptly, time returned to normal. She wrenched the gag from her mouth and called, "Koros!"

The warbeast growled a greeting in reply, and she noticed for the first time that it was standing astride a disemboweled corpse, and that the substance dripping upon her face was blood from the creature's jaw.

"Get me out of here!" she cried, still unsure what was happening, but eager to be away from the dead and mangled Aghadite, away from the place where she had felt reality coming apart around her.

Koros seemed to understand; it backed up into the opening it had smashed through the stone wall of the hiding place, ignoring the ruined corpses it trod underfoot as it moved.

Frima reached down and struggled with the ropes that bound her ankles, getting them free after a few moments of tugging. She staggered to her feet, pulling at the bindings that still remained, and tottered after the warbeast, out onto the Street of the Temples and into the light of dawn.

She realized for the first time that the rumbling she had heard was still continuing, even growing. She had thought it to be caused by some Aghadite machine, but now discovered that it was coming from the earth beneath her feet, and that the ground was beginning to shake. She didn't like it.

She was unsure what to do; she did not know where Garth

had gone, whether he was still in the temple of Death, whether it would be safe to enter the temple. She stood for a long moment, glancing about indecisively, trying to decide upon a course of action.

Finally, as she was about to try to coax Koros into hunting down its master for her, Garth emerged from the shadows of the temple cave, running unsteadily. She let out a glad cry at the sight of him, happy to see him still alive, and then noticed that the Sword of Bheleu was gone. She started to say something about it, concerned lest it fall into the wrong hands.

Garth ignored that; he stopped, stared in surprise at the sight of Frima alive, saw Koros, and called, "Mount up! Quickly!"

Confused, Frima obeyed; she had learned not to argue with Garth when he gave her direct orders so urgently. She clambered awkwardly onto the warbeast's back.

An instant later the overman leaped up behind her and called a word to the beast. Koros growled in response, then bounded forward and set out at full speed for the city gate. It seemed unhindered by its recent injuries, or by the two crossbow quarrels that still protruded from its shoulder. One had come free from the shoulder, and Koros had worked out the one in its paw, leaving an oozing wound.

For a long moment Frima had no time to do anything but hang on, as Koros moved at incredible speed through the city's deserted streets.

The rumbling sound grew and deepened, and she could feel the ground shaking whenever the warbeast's paws touched it for more than an instant. The air had turned very hot and dry and was full of sound and vibration; black dust was rising from the ground and vibrating off the buildings on either side. Something terrible was obviously happening, or perhaps was about to happen, but she did not know what it was.

The street in front of them cracked open, and a stone house at one side fell inward with a roar; undaunted, the warbeast leaped the crack and bounded onward. It seemed untroubled by the trembling of the earth. When it reached the open ground of the market, it charged across at a speed that forced Frima to close her eyes and gasp for air.

Then they were out of the city, past the broken gate, and still Koros ran, headlong down the slope of ancient black lava.

Finally, when they had left the stone surface behind and reached the end—or the beginning—of the highway that led eastward through the site of Weideth, Garth leaned down and signaled to the beast with a blow on its flank. It slowed to a limping walk, its head low. Even its huge supply of energy was not inexhaustible. Frima struggled up into a sitting position, releasing her armhold around its neck, and peered back under Garth's arm.

A column of thick black smoke was pouring up from Dûsarra, from every part of the city, as if the black walls were the rim of a vast chimney; an orange glow lighted the sky. More smoke and more of the orange light streamed from the crater above the city. As Frima watched, she saw one of the temple towers sway and then collapse. The rumbling was now a steady roar, but comfortably distant.

Nobody emerged from the gate. She watched, expecting a fleeing multitude, but no one appeared; instead, the walls on either side of the ruined gate abruptly tottered and fell inward. Something red and glowing poured forth where they had stood, and she realized at last that the volcano had awakened and was consuming Dûsarra.

Garth glanced back at the crumbling black city and the lava that was devouring it. "So much, then, for the cult of Aghad," he said.

"Do you think they're all in there?" Frima asked.

Garth shrugged. "Enough of them are. Their god is dead and their temples destroyed; I won't trouble myself about any who may have survived." Without the Sword of Bheleu driving him on, he was no longer obsessed with the cult's destruction to the last man. He had his revenge.

Frima looked up at the overman's leathery, noseless face, then back at her vanishing birthplace. She did not understand what Garth meant about the god; gods did not die, she told herself.

Still, she, too, felt that she had had her fill of vengeance. She was ready to begin finding herself a new life. She suspected, as well, that she might be carrying more than her own life; she was beginning to notice other indications, in addition to her bouts of nausea, that she might be pregnant. The prospect delighted her. She turned away from Dûsarra and looked eastward toward the rising sun.

About the Author

LAWRENCE WATT-EVANS was born and raised in eastern Massachusetts, the fourth of six children. Both parents were longtime science fiction readers, so from an early age he read and enjoyed a variety of speculative fiction. He also tried writing it, starting at age seven, but with little immediate success.

After getting through twelve years of public schooling in Bedford, Massachusetts, he tried to keep up family tradition by attending Princeton University, as had his father and grandfather. He was less successful than his ancestors and, after two attempts, left college without a degree.

In between the two portions of his academic career, he lived in Pittsburgh, a city he considers one of the most underrated in the country. It was at this time that he began seriously trying to write for money, as it seemed easier than finding a real job (he had previously worked in a ladder factory, as a feature writer for a small-town newspaper, as a sandwich salesman on campus, in a supermarket, and at other trivial tasks). He sold one page of fiction in a year and a half.

In 1977, after leaving Princeton for the second and final time, he married his longtime girlfriend and settled in Lexington, Kentucky, where his wife had a job that would support them both while he again tried to write. He was more successful this time, producing a fantasy novel that sold readily, beginning his full-time career as a writer.